THE
SWAGGER
SWORD

Templars, Columbus and
the Vatican Cover-up

A novel by

DAVID S. BRODY

Eyes That See Publishing

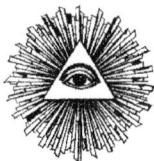

The Swagger Sword
Templars, Columbus and the Vatican Cover-up

Eyes That See Publishing
Westford, Massachusetts

ISBN 978-0-9907413-4-3
1st edition

Cover by Kimberly Scott and Renee Brody
Book Interior and E-book design by Soumi Goswami

Printed in USA

Praise for Books in this Series

"Brody does a terrific job of wrapping his research in a fast-paced thrill ride."
—PUBLISHERS WEEKLY

"Rich in scope and vividly engrossing."
—MIDWEST BOOK REVIEW

"A comparison to *The Da Vinci Code* and *National Treasure* is inevitable….The story rips the reader into a fast-paced adventure."
—FRESH FICTION

"A treat to read….If you are a fan of Templar history you will find this book very pleasing."
—KNIGHT TEMPLAR MAGAZINE

"An excellent historical conspiracy thriller. It builds on its most famous predecessor, *The Da Vinci Code*, and takes it one step farther—and across the Atlantic."
—MYSTERY BOOK NEWS

"A rousing adventure. Highly recommended to all Dan Brown and Michael Crichton fans."
—READERS' FAVORITE BOOK REVIEW

"The year is early, but this book will be hard to beat; it's already on my 'Best of' list."
—BARYON REVIEW

In Memory of Zena Halpern

You paved the way for a
whole generation of researchers.
Best of all, at the age of 88,
you were still looking under rocks,
trying to find the truth.

Rest in peace, dear friend.

About the Author

David S. Brody is a *Boston Globe* bestselling fiction writer named Boston's Best Local Author by the *Boston Phoenix* newspaper. His children call him a "rock nerd" because of the time he spends studying ancient stone structures which he believes evidence exploration of America prior to Columbus. A graduate of Tufts University and Georgetown Law School, he has appeared as a guest expert on documentaries on History Channel, Travel Channel, PBS and Discovery Channel, as well as the *Coast to Coast AM* radio program. He lives in Westford, MA with his wife, sculptor Kimberly Scott.

The seven prior books in his *Templars in America* Series have been Amazon Kindle Top 10 Bestsellers in their category, with three titles reaching #1.

The Swagger Sword is his eleventh novel.

**For more information,
please visit DavidBrodyBooks.com**

Also by the Author

Unlawful Deeds

Blood of the Tribe

The Wrong Abraham

The "Templars in America" Series

Cabal of the Westford Knight: Templars at the Newport Tower (Book 1)

Thief on the Cross: Templar Secrets in America (Book 2)

Powdered Gold: Templars and the American Ark of the Covenant (Book 3)

The Oath of Nimrod: Giants, MK-Ultra and the Smithsonian Coverup (Book 4)

The Isaac Question: Templars and the Secret of the Old Testament (Book 5)

Echoes of Atlantis: Crones, Templars and the Lost Continent (Book 6)

The Cult of Venus: Templars and the Ancient Goddess (Book 7)

Note to Readers

1. **Though this story is fiction, the artifacts, sites and works of art pictured are real. See Author's Note at end of book for more detailed information.**

2. **This is a stand-alone story. Readers who have not read the first seven books in the series should feel free to jump right in. The summary below provides some basic background for new readers:**

Cameron Thorne, age 43, is an attorney/historian whose passion is researching sites and artifacts that indicate the presence in America of European explorers prior to Columbus. His wife, Amanda Spencer-Gunn, is a former museum curator who moved to the U.S. from England while in her mid-twenties; she has a particular expertise in the history of the medieval Knights Templar. They reside in Westford, Massachusetts, a suburb northwest of Boston. Newly married, they have recently adopted a thirteen-year-old girl named Astarte, who is of Native American descent.

Chapter 1

Newport, Rhode Island
December, Present Day

Cameron Thorne squinted into the morning sun, relieved that the thin clouds on the horizon had dissipated. He exhaled, his breath rising in the still winter air, and strode across the snow-covered park. "Hello, beautiful," he said, looking up at the round stone tower standing imperially in front of him. "Looks like you're going to have quite a few admirers today."

Once a virtually unknown phenomenon, the winter solstice illumination at the Newport Tower had in recent years attracted an increasingly large crowd. And an eclectic one. As Cam approached the Tower along a shoveled pathway, he noticed Freemasons sporting aprons and sashes, white-robed Wiccans carrying wooden staffs in the fashion of the ancient Druids, Native Americans attired in fringed buckskin vests … and a hulking man wearing bright green pants carrying a short-bladed sword.

Cam blinked. The man, who stood alone off to the side of the arched tower, seemed to spot Cam just as Cam eyed the weapon in his hand. Nodding curtly, the sun at his back, the burly man slashed the sword once through the air and marched to intercept Cam. Cam angled his head. There was something familiar about the way he moved, but Cam was more focused on his stern expression than on his gait. And of course on the sword itself, which the man held out in front like a knight wielding his lance.

Cam hesitated. His controversial research on the medieval Knights Templar sometimes angered those with traditional religious beliefs. He had no interest in settling the debate with a joust.

The man continued his march, chin up and sword raised, now only twenty feet away. Cam took a deep breath. If it came to fight or flight, there really was no choice. He cleared his throat and half-turned, ready to run. "Please stop right there."

The man paused for half a stride before guffawing and lowering the blade a few inches. "Really?" He raised his voice into a whine,

1

mimicking Cam. "*Please stop right there.*" He grinned and resumed his march. "What a fucking wimp you've turned into."

Cam shielded his eyes with his hand. Something about the voice. "Do I know you?" Ten feet now, not much time.

"*Know* me?" He stopped suddenly. "Christ, Cameron." Holding the sword in his right hand, he grasped the blade with his left and squeezed. Releasing the blade, he held a bloody palm out to Cam. "When we were kids, we were blood brothers." A pair of hard grey eyes held Cam's. "And as far as I'm concerned, we still are."

✠

It took Cam a few seconds to wrench his eyes away from the man's bloody hand and focus on his jowly face. "Brian," he said as he took a step back. "Brian Heenan."

Brian nodded. "What it's been? Twenty-five years?"

Cam looked away. Not long enough. They had been neighbors and best friends from kindergarten through middle school in Westford, Massachusetts, drawn together by their passion for sports and treasure-hunting. At one point, Cam now recalled, they had pricked each other's fingers, pushed them together, and sworn a blood allegiance. But when they reached high school Brian discovered pot and later cocaine, and the two drifted apart. Their lives intersected again during Cam's fresh-man year of college, when a drug-addled Brian robbed Cam's parents' house, using the spare key he had known about since grade school. Scumbag. Stealing from a family that fed him when his own mother was too busy playing pool and keno at the local dive bar to give a damn. From the capillaries visible on Brian's nose and cheeks, the absence of most of his bottom teeth, and the gray pallor of his skin, it looked like Brian still didn't have his shit together. "So what do you want?"

Brian swallowed. "I'm dying." He blinked but otherwise held Cam's eyes. "Doc says I have a few months, at best. Pancreatic cancer."

"Oh. Um, sorry to hear that." Cam looked down at his feet. Hopefully there were no children being left fatherless. He motioned with his chin toward the Tower. "But why come here? And what's with the sword?" Not to mention the melodrama with the blood.

"Monsignor Marcotte told me I could find you here." He had balled up his hand, but blood continued to drip down his wrist.

Cam nodded again. Marcotte, a priest in Westford, sometimes helped Cam with his research. Cam was not Catholic, which had allowed them to build a friendship outside the religious tent—Cam didn't need his soul saved, and Marcotte appreciated being off-duty once in a while. Which is not to say the cleric had not provided valuable spiritual advice. A particular insight resonated when Cam first heard it, and it popped into his head again today: *You don't have a soul. You are a soul. You have a body.* The soulless person standing in front of him, Cam sensed, might test that model.

"That's right, your aunt is a nun at Saint Catherine's," Cam said. That explained how Brian knew Marcotte. "And the sword?"

"A peace offering."

"Peace offering?"

"Or maybe a bribe."

Cam studied the sword for the first time. A steel blade with a dark wooden handle. No cross-guard or fancy pommel. Just a broomstick-shaped handle with a two-foot blade, probably designed to slide into a narrow swagger stick case. Cam had seen them before, used as hidden weapons by military officers in old war movies. "What's so special about it?"

Brian flicked his wrist and turned the sword, revealing a series of engravings on the blade. Wavy parallel lines that looked like a river with markings inside it, a rock with a table atop it, a letter that looked like a 'P' superimposed over the number 9…

"Wait a second." Cam's eyes widened as his heart thumped. He leaned closer, the blade reflecting the sun into his eyes. *It couldn't be.* "Where'd you get this?"

Brian grinned. "I thought you might recognize it."

Cam reached for the swagger stick blade to study it more closely, surprised that Brian would release it to him.

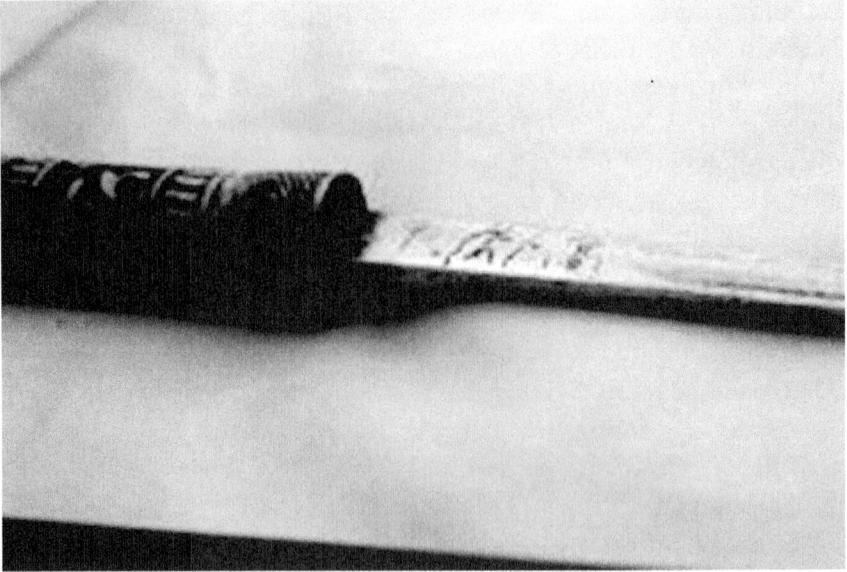

Swagger Stick Blade

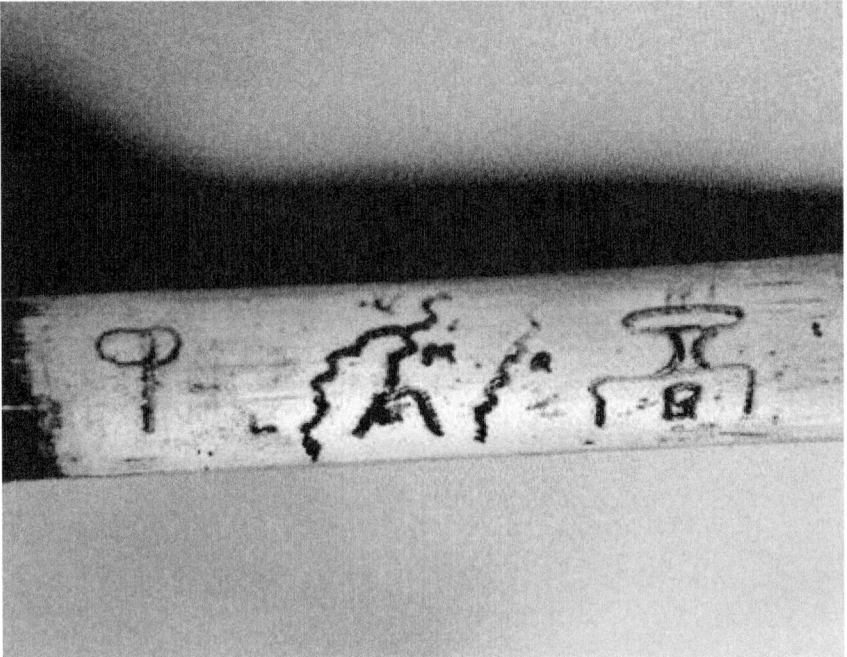

Markings on Swagger Stick Blade

"Where'd you get this?" he repeated. The markings were identical to those Cam had seen on a 12th century Templar map showing the location of buried artifacts in New York's Catskill Mountains. And he had read about the existence of swagger stick blades, also called swagger swords, with mysterious ties to the Vatican. But he had never seen a sword himself. Until now.

Brian took the sword back. "Like I said, it's a bribe. You can have it, but only if you give me what I want." He flicked his wrist, turning the sword over, teasing Cam by momentarily revealing another set of markings—Cam saw a cross and an X with a dotted line joining them—on the back side of the blade.

Cam blinked. There was always an angle with Brian. "And what is it that you want?" Brian still hadn't told him where he got the sword.

"I'm going to Ireland. I've never been, and it's really the only thing on my bucket list." He lifted a leg, as if his Irish heritage explained both the green pants and his desire to visit his ancestral homeland. "But I don't want to travel alone. I want you to come with me."

Cam hadn't seen that one coming. "Me? Why?"

Brian opened his hand to show again his bloody palm. "Because we're blood brothers." He lowered his voice and let out a long sigh. "Or at least we used to be. And because, well, I really don't have anyone else I can ask."

✠

Amanda Spencer-Gunn circled the block, slowing as she approached the cluster of young children waiting for the neighborhood school bus at the end of a cul-de-sac. This had become her daily routine: Drop Astarte off at the high school, grab a cup of coffee, and wallow among the grade-schoolers. Watch them run, laugh, hug their parents. A little boy with a low-hanging backpack built a snowman and rushed to push a stick in its face to make a nose as the bus approached. A girl bent to kiss her dog goodbye. Another tiny girl, probably a kindergartner, bravely pulled herself up the steep stairs of the yellow bus. And Amanda's tears came, mingling with her coffee, as she imagined what might have been. Imagined a life with the child, a life *for* the child, who had not lived.

She rubbed her nose as the bus pulled away. She almost wished someone would report her to the police just to break the routine.

Her therapist told her it was normal, part of the grieving process. Step four, depression. After this would come acceptance and hope. But step four had lasted almost three months now. She might someday get to acceptance. But never hope: Her doctor had put an end to that when she explained that the miscarriage was not just bad fortune but rather as a result of Amanda's overactive immune system, which perceived the fetus as some kind of invader. Amanda's body rejected pregnancy the same way some people rejected organ transplants.

She loved Astarte with all her heart, but she and Cam had not adopted the girl until she was eight years old. They had skipped her first word and learning to walk and *Goodnight Moon* and gone straight to soccer and Girl Scouts. Amanda sniffled. All the bus stop parents had departed and she was still idling at the stop sign.

From deep inside her cocoon of misery a smile somehow bubbled to the surface as she recalled reading about the 'Wandering Uterus.' During the Classical era, it was believed that a woman's uterus, when not weighed down with a fetus, floated around the body like an untethered balloon. This wandering organ was blamed for all sorts of female ailments, both physical (such as shortness of breath) and emotional. In fact, the word *hysteria* derived from the word *uterus*, doctors believing that the floating uterus caused a woman's emotional outbursts and instability. Had she lived in Greek or Roman times, her post-pregnancy depression would have been treated by eating garlic and perfuming her vagina, the belief being that the uterus could be repelled from the head and lured back toward the pelvis by appealing to its olfactory sense.

She took a deep breath. She should have perfumed her vagina and gone with Cam to the Tower. But she had been such a drag the past few months that Cam was probably happy to be free of her and her wandering uterus. She checked her watch. Only six hours until it was time to pick up Astarte from school. Plenty of time to go home and chew on some garlic.

✠

Cam's legal training had taught him to compartmentalize his thoughts and emotions. But even he was having trouble focusing on the

Tower illumination unfolding in front of him. Was this really one of the Vatican swagger swords? And if so, where had Brian obtained it? More to the point, why had a dying Brian dropped into Cam's life after a quarter-century of no contact?

He shook his head clear. The solstice illumination only occurred once a year, and even that was dependent on weather conditions. He'd worry about Brian later. And there were more than fifty people standing around, including a lifestyle reporter from the *Providence Journal*, waiting for him to explain the phenomenon.

He led the group down a path to the western side of the park, the morning sun temporarily blocked by the Tower. Together they waited, watching as the sun slowly bore its way through one of the structure's windows, emerging on the dark side of the Tower in a sudden starburst pattern of sunlight.

Newport Tower Winter Solstice Starburst

Cam cleared his throat, turning so the reporter—bundled against the cold with a pair of thick earmuffs—would not miss his words. They had spoken on the phone yesterday for an hour; she had impressed him with her preparation, though he sensed she was skeptical the Tower was anything other than a Colonial gristmill. "This only happens on the winter solstice." He shrugged. "But it could just be a coincidence." He began to walk back toward the structure. He understood the importance of not overstating his case; sometimes a starburst was just a starburst.

They returned to the sunny side of the Tower. "But what happens in about a half-hour is definitely not a coincidence." He pointed up. "Take a look at that window on the south side."

Newport Tower Winter Solstice Window

He explained that the Tower featured a handful of seemingly randomly-placed and oddly-shaped windows which had long mystified historians. Why would a gristmill need windows? "The first time I saw this window, I was instantly struck by the sloppiness of the masonry work. Just look at the shape of the blue sky framed by the window. I mean, what kind of self-respecting stonemason would craft such a poorly-shaped window?"

"A drunk one?" a man wearing a Masonic apron offered with a grin.

Cam laughed. A Mason answering a question about masonry. "I think even a drunk mason could do better work than that. I think something else is going on." He paused. "Back in the 1990s an astronomy professor named William Penhallow concluded the windows were built to mark celestial and astronomical events." He smiled. "Which is why we're here today. The most dazzling alignment is the winter solstice illumination."

He turned and squinted into the sun. As he did so he spotted Brian, hanging toward the back but listening intently. At least he was no longer waving the sword. Brian had always been fascinated with buried treasure, mostly because he was allergic to hard work. Was his newfound interest in the Tower related to the Templar treasure? Pushing thoughts of his childhood friend aside, Cam checked his watch. "In fact, we can see the alignment beginning now. The sun passes through that window—we'll call it the 'drunk mason window'—and forms a light box on the interior wall of the Tower. As the sun ascends and moves southward, that light box creeps along, descending and changing shape as it moves."

He allowed the crowd to study the structure. "The other thing I want you to focus on is the arch directly opposite us, on the western side." There were eight identical arches in the Tower, which was built in the Romanesque style. "If you notice, of the eight arches, only one has an actual keystone. And that keystone is egg-shaped. In fact, that is practically the only round or ovular-shaped stone in the entire Tower. Everything else is flat and horizontal. Plus, it's a different color than the other stones." He smiled. "All of which tells us it must be important." He stepped back. "Now's a good time to snap a picture, with the light box approaching."

Newport Tower Keystone with Light Box Approaching from Left

Cam continued. "This is my ninth consecutive year visiting the Tower." The first year, there had been only a handful of people. He looked around. The crowd had grown to over a hundred. "In just under fifteen minutes, as many of you know, you are going to see something amazing. That light box is going to perfectly frame the egg-shaped keystone. It only happens once a year, on the winter solstice."

One of the Native American elders cleared his throat. "I notice that the keystone is not exactly in the center of the arch."

Cam nodded. He was glad to see representatives of many of the New England tribes in attendance. Most Native Americans, for good reason, did not feel inclined to focus on the painful history of the European takeover of their lands. But over the years Cam had forged friendships with a few of the tribal leaders, and they had told him that their oral history confirmed what he had long believed: The Tower was built in the late 14th century by remnants of the outlawed Knights Templar, who had formed an alliance with the local Native Americans.

"Good point," Cam said in response to the question about the keystone. "It's like the drunk Mason window. I think it took them a few tries to get the alignment to be spot on. They had to reverse-engineer the window, reshaping it to make the light box fit the egg perfectly. And, from the looks of things, they had to move the key-stone over a bit to make the alignment work."

They had about ten minutes before the light box reached the egg. The crowd had grown by another couple of dozen while Cam spoke. "I'm not going to spend too much time on the reasons we think the Tower is *not* a Colonial gristmill, as mainstream historians insist," Cam said, hoping to sway the reporter. "But I'll give you a few while we wait." He moved a quarter-way around the structure and pointed to a recess in the interior of the structure above one of the archways. "That's a fireplace. Which itself is uncharacteristic for a gristmill, given the danger of the grain dust conflagrating. But even more tell-ing is that the flue for the fireplace is a double flue, shaped like devil's horns. That kind of design feature is unique to 14th century Scotland." He paused, allowing the reporter to jot some notes. "And, speaking of Scotland, the unit of measurement used to build this is the old Scottish ell, used during medieval times. The Colonists, of course, would have used English inches and feet." He continued, explaining how the Tower had many other architectural similarities to Templar-related structures built in Europe during medieval times.

"Finally, the Colonial gristmill theory dates construction to the 1675 through 1677 period." He lifted his chin toward the Native Ameri-cans clustered together. "As my Native American friends can tell you, those dates coincide with King Philip's, or Metacomet's, uprising.

The Colonists were fortunate to survive—many settlements were completely destroyed. If the Colonists were going to build any kind of stone structure during those years, it would have been a fort, not a windmill."

They edged back around to the east to watch the light box continue its march. At precisely 8:43, the light box kissed the egg. Cam explained, "This is not just a random time. At this longitude, 8:43 is exactly three hours before solar noon. That's how medieval monks determined the times for prayer. So, 8:43 would have been the time for prayer called *Terce*." He smiled. "The sun kisses the egg, and prayers begin. Now watch what happens next."

The light box continued to move across the Tower's back wall. The group watched, cameras clicking, as fifteen minutes later the light box framed the egg completely. "This only happens once a year," Cam said. "On the winter solstice."

Newport Tower Winter Solstice Alignment

Cam allowed the moment to sink in. "What's happening here? I think the allegory is clear. On the darkest, shortest day of the year, the sun—which historically has been associated with the male deity—appears and symbolically fertilizes the egg lodged on the inner wall of the womb-like Tower. Rebirth. Life is renewed. The sun is reborn." He spread his arms. "The days begin to lengthen again. So what do the people do? They plan a big celebration, of course." Cam smiled again. "Usually held on December 25. Today we know it as a celebration to mark the birth of the *son*. But in its original form, it marked the rebirth of the *sun*."

☩

Cam appreciated that Brian had the decency to keep himself—and his sword and bloody hand—at the periphery while the reporter asked a few more questions. But his childhood friend pounced as soon as the journalist left.

"I should have asked earlier. How's your mom?" Cam had forgotten how Brian had a habit of flicking his tongue around behind his teeth. As if at any moment it might need to snap out and snatch an insect.

"Good, thanks."

"She still pissed at me? Not that I blame her."

"Honestly, Brian, I don't think she's given you a thought in twenty years."

Brian bit his bottom lip, showing yellowed teeth and receding gums. Girls used to find him attractive in a thick, roguish sort of way, but now he just looked, well, sloppy and decayed. "Yeah, I could see that."

Cam shuffled, wondering how to end the encounter.

"How about your dad? I thought he was going to kill Father Samuelson that day."

Cam nodded. "He's good." Their friend, Marty, had been molested by Father Samuelson on a church getaway, a camping trip, up in Maine. Marty was a shy, sweet kid who had lived down the street. His father had been one of the last to die in Vietnam, and Cam's dad had always tried to serve as a surrogate father figure. But Father Samuelson, as God's servant, had the inside track.

Cam didn't like to talk about this stuff, but Brian plowed ahead. "I wish he would've. I still remember him smashing that scumbag's head against the curbstone in the parking lot with Father Marcotte trying to pull him off. It took, like, four guys to finally get him to stop."

They stood in silence for a few seconds. A couple of months later, Marty had hung himself by his belt in his bedroom. It wasn't until then that Cam understood what had happened, understood why his father had attacked the priest. "What were we, eleven, twelve?" Brian asked. "That really fucked me up for a while."

For the first time, Cam wondered if the priest had molested Brian as well. Cam hadn't known about Marty at the time, so why would he have known about Brian? And Brian had been on that same camping trip. It had simply never occurred to Cam, but something in Brian's voice resonated. It might explain why the kind-hearted Brian of Cam's youth had grown into such a nasty piece of work as an adult.

They stared at the trees, each with their private thoughts. Brian sighed. "You driving back to Westford? Can I catch a lift? I took the bus down early this morning."

Cam faked a cough to cover his lie. "Sorry, I'm staying down here to do some research." He felt bad for the fib, but he really had no interest in letting this particular childhood friend back into his adult life. With Brian, things like sharing a sad memory were just as likely ploys to manipulate. "I can drop you off at the bus station." He turned to walk to his car. "Just don't get blood on my seats."

"That reporter going to give you a good story?"

"I think so. It's hard to see the illumination and still believe this was built by the Colonists in the 1670s. I mean, that was the time-frame of the Puritans—"

"Scarlet letters and hanging witches," Brian interjected, smiling, his flicking tongue visible behind a missing tooth. "I did pay attention in school once in a while."

"Right. Even though the settlers here in Rhode Island were not as religiously zealous as in Massachusetts, they were still pretty strict. The sun and the egg and the womb symbolism would have been considered heresy."

Cam reached into his Pathfinder, grabbed a bunch of napkins, and handed them to Brian. "You might need stitches for that."

They climbed in. "Nah. It'll scab."

Brian had always been tough. Cam recalled the time he took a groundball to the chin, rubbed some dirt on it, and finished the game. Turned out to be a broken jaw. "So, why Ireland?" Not that Cam had any intention of going with him.

"Heenan. As in shortened version of Henihan. My grandfather came over after World War I. Like I said, it's on my bucket list."

Cam sensed there was more to it than that. There usually was with Brian. "Where'd you get the sword?"

"Pulled it out of a boulder, like Arthur and Excalibur."

"Look, Brian." He spoke with an edge. "You want my help, stop being such a smartass."

Brian angled his head. "Far as I recall, you haven't agreed to help yet."

"Yup, you're right, I haven't." Cam pulled away from the curb, curious as to where Brian got the sword but also content to be at loggerheads with his old friend. They drove in silence for a few minutes.

Brian broke it. "Mind if I ask you some questions about the Templars?"

Cam shrugged. "Sure."

"Reason is, I think the two might be related. Ireland and the Templars, that is. Which is the other reason I want you to come with me."

Here it was, the angle. "Okay, shoot."

"I read that the Templars brought treasure with them when they came over. That true?"

"Probably. But it depends on what you mean by treasure."

Brian wrinkled his face. "You know, treasure. Gold and silver."

"Maybe. When the king of France raided the Templar treasury in Paris in 1307, it was empty. Nobody knows where their treasure went. But they may have had other stuff, even more valuable than gold and silver."

"Like what?" Brian sniffed.

Cam twisted his way through the narrow streets that rose up from the harbor. "Like religious artifacts. The Ark of Covenant. The Holy Grail. That stuff would be worth more than gold."

Brian grunted. "Yeah, I see that."

"And I'll give you another possibility: Ancient documents or scrolls. Maybe writings from Jesus or the apostles. Maybe documents about early Christianity." He angled his head. "Maybe a marriage contract—a *ketubah*—between Jesus and Mary Magdalene. The bottom line is that the Templars spent a decade digging and searching under the Temple of Solomon when they first went to Jerusalem. Who knows what they found?"

"Reason I ask is I read about that stuff up in the Catskills. And I know the markings on the sword are some kind of map. But I figure I need someone like you to put it all together for me."

Cam nodded as he pulled to a stop in front of the bus station. "I get that. But, again, what does Ireland have to do with all this?"

Brian shook his head. "Honestly, I'm not sure yet. But the person who gave me the sword told me that's where I needed to go." He grinned as he opened the car door. "And if nothing else, we can drown ourselves in Irish whiskey."

"I didn't agree to go, Brian." But Brian had slammed the door before Cam could get the words out.

Chapter 2

Astarte walked the halls of Westford Academy, still conscious of being the youngest student at the entire high school. Not that it bothered her. She was easily able to keep up academically, she had made the JV soccer team, and she had a core group of theater friends she hung out with. The only time it really mattered was times like this. At thirteen, she knew she probably shouldn't consider dating a sophomore. But he sure was cute, with his shy smile and dark eyes and polite formality. Plus his cheeks flushed every time he saw her. Like now. Which made her feel a bit tingly inside.

"Astarte!" he said, weaving around other students toward her.

It had taken him a few tries to get the pronunciation right, with the accent on the middle syllable rather than the first. "Aha," he had finally proclaimed. "The accent is on *star*." He had smiled and bowed in mock formality. "I should have known!"

"Hi Raja."

"Please wait." He paused a few feet away. "How are you?"

She swallowed. "Um, good." *That's the best you can do? Good? Ugh.* She slid against a row of lockers to give them room to talk. He stood a bit closer to her than most of her friends did, but not enough to make her feel pinned. They each had minor roles in the fall musical and had been paired together as dance partners. The familiar smell of his body spray wafted over her, bringing back memories of his arms around her waist and his breath on the side of her neck.

"So, um, do you want to go with me to the basketball game tonight?"

"I still haven't had a chance to ask my parents. But I think they'll say yes."

"I can pick you up. I'll call an Uber."

She kicked at the floor. A real date. Her hands felt sweaty. "Um, they might want to drive me themselves."

He nodded. "That's okay." The bell rang. "I'll text you." He held her eyes for a second and grinned. "Bye."

She ducked into her study hall, glad to have a few minutes to think. Originally she had planned to go with her dad to view the Newport Tower alignment this morning, but a snow day earlier in the week had pushed her math test back to today. Opening her math notes, she reviewed for the exam. But her mind kept drifting to Raja. He wasn't like the other boys, acting all goofy and tough around the girls. And he liked sports as well as theater, so they had a lot in common. Not to mention there was that whole tingly feeling she got when she was around him. But her parents would not like that he was more than two years older than her.

She sighed. Originally she had wanted to go to an all-girls high school, similar to the one she had visited last spring up in Vermont. If she was going to be some kind of feminine spiritual leader, as the Native American prophecies foretold and as had been drummed into her head for as long as she could remember, she thought it would be best to focus on her female side. But her parents had argued that any leader—feminine or masculine—should be exposed to the widest possible variety of stimuli. Mum had pointed out, "That's the biggest problem with the Catholic Church. They have priests trying to counsel people on marital issues and raising children and situations involving tight finances, but their priests never have to deal with those issues themselves. It's like asking a fish for advice how to fly." Astarte smiled at that. And Mum was right. Part of growing up was being around boys, understanding what all that tingling meant.

In fact, that's exactly the argument she'd make when her parents hesitated about letting her go out with Raja: *I'm supposedly destined to be some kind of spiritual leader. I need to go through all this, be a normal teenager. I can't be the fish telling people how to fly. Besides, what kind of leader will I make if I can't even handle a teenage boy?*

✠

After texting Amanda that he was on his way home, Cam dialed Monsignor Marcotte's number as he cruised north away from Newport. Why had the cleric told Brian where to find Cam? Getting voicemail, he left a message. "Two words: *Brian Heenan.* Call me back."

He shifted in his seat. Amanda should have been with him today. They could have spent the day in Newport, maybe toured a mansion and had lunch on the waterfront. But he sensed it was best not to push her, that she needed time to work through her grief in her own way. And an allegory centered on fertility and rebirth probably wasn't the best way to take her mind off the miscarriage.

The two-hour drive gave his own mind a chance to wander, rewinding six weeks back to a November drive he had made to Long Island and which now seemingly took on added importance in light of Brian's sword...

Cam parked in front of a modest ranch-style home in a subdivision a few miles off the Long Island Expressway. Approaching the door, he smiled in appreciation at the whimsical Halloween decorations—a "wrong-way" witch, her face plastered against a tree; a skeleton wearing a Boston Red Sox cap holding an "RIP" sign in a lawn chair; a vampire hanging upside down from a tree, a Red Cross blood drive poster clenched in one hand. The adornments perfectly reflected the playful, quirky, clever personality of the home owner, his friend Ruthie Sanders.

A few stray leaves tumbled around his feet as he approached the front door, which opened even before he could ring the doorbell. A wide smile and a wider hug greeted him. "Cameron," Ruthie sang.

"Hi Ruthie. It's great to see you." He stepped back. Her eyes danced, and the features that had once made her a beautiful woman were still evident. "You look great."

"And you are a big fat liar," she grinned, "though a well-raised one. I'm eighty-four. A good day for me is when my shower fogs up the mirror."

"Nonsense. You look like Sophia Loren."

She touched his cheek gently with her fingertips. "So sweet. You tell Amanda that if I were forty years younger, I'd try to steal you away." Laughing, she lowered her hand to grasp his, her grip firm despite her slight stature. "Come. I know you are a busy man."

He had left Boston at nine o'clock, shooting for a mid-afternoon arrival so she wouldn't feel the pressure to serve him lunch. "I can stay as long as you have energy to regale me with your stories."

She led him to a round Formica kitchen table. A bowl of matzo ball soup, a light steam rising up from it, sat waiting. So much for no pressure. She smiled. "And some marzipan cookies for dessert."

He shook his head. "Both my favorites. How did you remember?"

She tapped at a worn three-ring binder on the kitchen counter. "My mother, may she rest in peace, taught me to record every meal I ever served, so I never serve the same thing twice."

He angled his head. "But this is what you served me last time."

She smiled playfully. "I'm not my mother, may her memory be a blessing."

They had met at a conference a decade ago and become instant friends, bonding over their shared research of artifacts indicating exploration of America before Columbus. In some ways Cam was the son she never had.

He sat and took a bite of matzo ball. He closed his eyes. "Perfect. Just like last time. Not too dense, not too soft." He leaned forward. "I love my grandmother, but her matzo balls are like paperweights."

"The secret is to use seltzer water, not baking soda. Matzo balls are meant to float, not sink." She said the words as if they were written in the Old Testament itself. "Anyway, it's the least I could do. A small thank you for all the help you gave Zena on her book."

The recent book by Ruthie's friend, Zena Halpern, The Templar Mission to Oak Island and Beyond, *describing a secret Templar mission to New York's Catskill Mountains, had become a must-read for Templar historians. And the journal and maps upon which it was based had become integral to the search for Templar treasure on the History Channel show,* The Curse of Oak Island. *"The book is doing well?"*

"Very," she said, knocking on a wooden chair.

They made small talk for a few minutes, then Cam pushed his bowl away. "So, you said you have a favor to ask."

"Do you want your cookies first?"

"Work first, treats later."

"That's a good rule in life, Cameron. Just make sure you don't work so hard you never get to the treats." She leaned back and reached for a manila envelope on the counter. "You found some very important artifacts on Hunter Mountain. And I did as well. But there are things hidden still, things we haven't found. Things I didn't share even with Zena."

Cam raised an eyebrow. The revelation that the Templars had been in America centuries before Columbus was a history-altering discovery. But almost as fascinating was the insight into Templar religious beliefs which the artifacts and journal offered. Central to these beliefs was the understanding that early Christianity recognized the importance of the feminine—whether in the form of the Virgin Mary as a representation of the Earth Mother, or Mary Magdalene as an embodiment of a strong wife. It was this belief that caused the Templars to seek a safe haven in the New World in 1178 and which also later caused the Church to turn on them in 1307. Was it possible there were secrets hidden in the Catskills, and kept by Ruthie, even more explosive than this? "What kind of things are still up there?" Cam asked.

She swallowed. "I don't know for certain. And they may have been moved and hidden elsewhere. Maybe treasure. Maybe ancient religious teachings and documents. Maybe both. I just know we haven't found everything yet." She took his hand. "And I'm too old to look." He waited for her to continue. She stared out the window. "Like I said, there were things I didn't share with Zena, things I've never shared with anyone, things I thought I would take to the grave with me. A map, documents to help explain it…"

"Why?" he asked quietly.

"Because I feared the world wasn't ready for them." She fixed her eyes on his. "You know, I am a child of the Holocaust. I lost my entire family. I've seen how religion and dogma can tear people apart, can cause people to do monstrous things. I'm worried, Cameron. I'm worried the things that were hidden may be … destabilizing. Dangerous." She squeezed his hand. "But at night, before I fall asleep, I feel so guilty. What if I don't wake up, what if the secrets die with me?" Her eyes clouded. "Do I have the right to make that decision? The right to deny humankind its history?" Exhaling, she shook her head. "I can't do it. I need to pass it along. And I trust you, Cameron. I trust you to do the right thing."

"And what is that?"

"I don't know. Honestly, I don't know." She took a deep breath and handed him a slip of paper. "This is my Dropbox account. Please keep it someplace safe. I scanned all the documents."

She had always been technologically savvy. "Okay."

She smiled. "I made the password something you'll remember: 'matzo ball soup.' Three words, all lower case."

It was Cam's turn to smile.

She continued. "But don't log on until I'm gone, until I'm dead. Promise?"

"Of course. Then what?"

"Then," she shrugged, "just do what you think is right." She stood, clearing his bowl and ending the conversation. "I feel better already." She stood tall. "Now, it's time for those cookies…"

Cam's phone rang, interrupting his musings. Marcotte.

"So did you really tell Brian where to find me?" Cam regretted the edge in his voice. In his late sixties, tall and cultured, Marcotte reminded Cam of a European diplomat. And apparently he needed those diplomatic skills—his progressive positions on things like reproductive rights, gay marriage and social justice often put him in conflict with Vatican doctrine. Recently he had campaigned for the ordination of female priests and for the rights of male priests to marry, arguing that the policy of a celibate male priesthood was both archaic and unproductive, leading to a dysfunctional and oftentimes predatory group of clergymen. Not that he had made much headway—the newly elected Pope Francis seemed receptive to reforms, even radical ones, but only if they rested on a sound doctrinal foundation.

"He needs you, Cameron." He had a way of speaking that always made Cam think of sipping an expensive glass of wine. "He has nobody else. Give him a chance. You may find he's a reformed man."

Cam shifted lanes. Marcotte liked to simplify things, but of course life was more complicated than that. Maybe Brian had nobody because he had spent his life screwing people over. "You know I'm already going to Ireland next week with Amanda and Astarte during Christmas break." It was going to be a surprise for Amanda, a way to try to get her out of her funk.

"Exactly. It makes things nice and neat."

Nice and neat? "Wait, you think I'm going to let Brian come with us?"

"Not *with* necessarily. But if you're there at the same time, maybe take a day or two and spend it with him. Amanda and Astarte can do tourist things on their own." He paused. "Besides, where else can he wear those pants and not get laughed at? You should know, he wears them every day. I think he has more than one pair. Likes to show off his Irish pride."

Cam squeezed the bridge of his nose with a free hand. He could think of nobody with whom he'd less like to travel.

As if sensing his hesitancy, the priest continued, "He doesn't have much time, you know. Maybe only a month or two. Pancreatic cancer moves quickly."

It was hard to say no to Marcotte, mostly because the things he asked for were always for other people. But Cam had no interest in

Brian poisoning his family vacation. He shifted the conversation. "What's up with the sword?"

"All I know is that he thinks the markings on it are some kind of map."

"How about this: Brian said something about a Templar treasure being connected to Ireland."

"I know the Templars spent some time in Ireland. But I never heard they brought their treasures there."

Another dead end. Brian, as usual, was playing his cards close to his vest. "Okay, one more question. Any idea why a guy who is dying would want to spend his last days looking for a treasure? I mean, he can't take it with him."

"Hmm. Good question. I remember as a boy looking for buried treasure. As I recall, the allure of it, the thrill of it, was in the chase, in the adventure. I don't think I ever thought about what I would do with it once I found it. It's like those brothers hunting for treasure up on Oak Island—they don't care so much about the money as the adventure. Perhaps that's the case with Brian. Perhaps he just wants one final adventure before he dies." The priest paused. "With his childhood best friend."

Cam shook his head. "Damn it, Marcotte," he said beneath his breath. It was hard sometimes to live up to his friend's standards.

"I heard that, Cameron." Marcotte chuckled. "But I don't take it personally. You're a good man. You'll do the right thing."

✠

Cam had swung by his Westford law office on the way home from Newport, then made a stop at the grocery store mid-afternoon. He texted Amanda from the parking lot as he was leaving. *Happy Solstice. Missed you at Tower. I'm making dinner tonight. Surprise to follow.*

She had replied immediately. *Ice cream?*

Smiling, he turned the ignition off and jumped from the car, glad to see she was in a playful mood. He should know better than to plan an event without ice cream; it was one of the few foods that Amanda, now almost ten years in the States, conceded the Americans did better than the Brits. He texted as he returned to the store for the desert. *Make that two surprises.*

Twenty minutes later, Venus greeted him at the door, the tawny Lab licking his nose as he bent to her. Normally he would have brought her with him to Newport, but he wanted Amanda to have some company with Astarte at school. He tossed a tennis ball and watched the lab scurry after it down the basement stairs, then began to unload the groceries. He was still unsure how to handle the Brian situation. But how he handled it was largely predicated on how Amanda reacted to the idea of a family vacation to Ireland, and that wouldn't be determined until after dinner.

Ten minutes later Amanda and Astarte returned, announcing their arrival by stomping the snow off their boots on the front porch. Venus bounded up the basement stairs to greet them, Cam close behind.

"How are my girls?" Cam asked, trying to judge Amanda's mood with a glance.

"Good," Astarte answered. "I think I did good on my math test."

Cam angled his head. "Lucky it wasn't a grammar test." Winking at Amanda, he kissed her, her cold nose contrasting with her warm mouth. It had been a tough few months for them. When she was pregnant and fighting morning sickness, he had felt there was little he could do to share the burden. Now there was little he could do to assuage her grief. Not to mention her guilt. Which was why he thought getting away—away from the half-painted baby room and the stack of Christmas cards with glowing children and all the reminders of the past few months—might be a good thing.

He kept the mood light, putting Astarte to work slicing vegetables and filling Amanda in on his day at the Tower, leaving out the Ireland trip detail.

"Where in the world did he get the swagger sword?" she asked, sitting on a bar stool opposite the counter where Cam and Astarte were preparing food. She pulled her flowing blond hair into a ponytail as he prepared the food. Amanda was part of the Gunn clan of Scotland, which was what had first brought her to Westford a decade earlier (Sir James Gunn being the knight memorialized on the Westford Knight carving). The Gunn clan claimed an even more famous ancestor than Sir James—Queen Guinevere of King Arthur fame, Guinevere meaning 'daughter of Gunn.' Guinevere and Amanda were similar types, fair-skinned, green-eyed beauties. Cam recalled that Brian had made an Excalibur quip; did that mean he saw himself as a modern-day Arthur? Would he make a play for Amanda, believing her to be his Guinevere?

Cam wouldn't put it past his ex-friend, not that Amanda would have any interest in a lout like him.

Cam shook the thought away, finished a cut, and looked up. "Brian wouldn't say where he got the sword. But I'm pretty sure it's authentic. It has the same markings as that map we used when we climbed Hunter Mountain." He smiled wryly. "At least from what I remember."

"Which probably isn't much," Amanda replied. They had been searching for artifacts described in the 12th century Templar journals written about by Zena Halpern. Cam had taken a bad fall on their climb and suffered a concussion. He had been barely functional for the rest of the day and was lucky not to have experienced any permanent ill effects.

"I do remember a table rock, like the drawing on the sword. It looked like a pedestal sink, except the sink was flat like a table. From there we paced to another boulder."

"Where Astarte found the bird carving," Amanda replied.

"The bird's peak was like an arrow, pointing to the cave," Astarte said.

Amanda continued, "Where you found the ancient artifact inside."

"At first you wouldn't let me go in the cave." Astarte chopped down angrily on a head of broccoli. They had made her stay outside and be the lookout. But the opening for the alcove inside the cave was low, tucked underneath, and Cam and Amanda missed it. Only when the four-foot tall Astarte later entered the cave did they find the hidden nook.

Amanda's voice dropped. "You were so young then, Astarte." She reached across and squeezed Astarte's arm. "Only eight. We had just met you."

The girl nodded. "I was pretty scared. But I remember thinking that hunting for that treasure with you guys was pretty cool."

Cam replied. "Yeah, well, it may be that we end up going back up there, based on this sword. It looks like there might be some things we didn't find. I didn't get a good look at it, but there were some markings on the back side of the blade I've never seen before. A cross and an X and some dots connecting them. Maybe another map."

"Did you keep the sword?" Amanda asked. "Let's have a look."

Cam shook his head. "No. With Brian, there's always a catch. For now, I don't want to owe him anything."

☩

"Happy Winter Solstice," Cam announced as he marched in off the deck with a platter of steaming food, pleased that the evening was going well. He had surprised Amanda by not only making dinner, but grilling salmon and vegetables outside on the grill, which was how she liked it best.

After dinner they poured hot chocolate over strawberry ice cream, then took Venus for a walk on the frozen lake as a light snow fell. At 7:30, as they kicked the snow off their boots at the back door, Astarte reminded them she was going to the basketball game. Amanda looked at her watch. "Didn't it already start?"

"Yes, but I told Raja I only wanted to go to the second half." She smiled. "Didn't want to miss the ice cream."

"Wait," Cam interjected, "who's Raja?" Astarte was almond-skinned with long dark hair and cobalt blue eyes. Not to mention fit and funny. It was only a matter of time before the high school boys came sniffing around.

"Just a friend," Astarte said nonchalantly.

"Sorry, Cam," Amanda said, "I forgot to mention it. Astarte asked me earlier if it was okay."

Cam shrugged. "Okay." He put his jacket back on. "I'll drive you."

"Actually, Raja is going to pick me up. He called an Uber. He'll be here in fifteen minutes."

Cam tried to keep his voice even. At least an Uber was better than the boy driving. "We'd like to meet him. And you can go to the game, but then straight back home, no other stops. Okay?"

✠

Amanda watched Raja and Astarte drive away, remembering what a monster she had been at that age. The lies she told, the risks she took, the stupid decisions she made.

Cam mulled apple cider, added a cinnamon stick and some spiced rum, and invited Amanda to join him in an oversized chair in front of the fireplace.

"So it starts," he said. "The teenage years."

"If she's anything like I was, we're in trouble." She sighed. "At least he seems like a nice boy."

"A nice boy two years older than her."

She curled into the nook of his arm. "Well, it's good to have some alone time." She kissed him lightly. "Dinner was a sweet surprise. Wonderful, actually. Thanks."

He grinned. "That wasn't actually the surprise. That was just the prelude." He reached under the chair cushion and pulled out a manila envelope. "For the third time, Happy Solstice."

"What's this?"

"Open it."

She stared at the flyer Cam had made, comprised of scenic images of Ireland—the Cliffs of Moher, Newgrange, the Giant's Causeway, the Hill of Tara. And the dates December 26 through January 2. "Next week?" she stammered.

"Yup. Six days, back the day before Astarte's winter break ends. My cousin will take Venus. You told me once you went as a girl and loved it."

"Yes. I did. It was the only family holiday I ever remember taking." She lowered her head. "It's just … I'm not sure I'll be such good company."

"Of course you will be. Getting away will do you a world of good."

"No, Cam, I don't think it will. There's such a heaviness in my chest all the time." She repeated, "I'll be terrible company."

He turned and took her hand, looking deeply into her eyes. "Amanda. Sweetheart." He paused for effect and lowered his voice. She felt her eyes begin to pool. He had been so patient, so kind. "We're not bringing you for your company," he said, the hint of a smile on his face. "We're bringing you because you're the only one who knows how to drive on the wrong side of the road."

✝

Amanda hesitated, as Cam knew she would, but eventually he made some headway, arguing the change of routine would jar her out of her funk. He tossed a log on the fire and sat on the hearth, facing her, and played his trump card. "You know, this is important for Astarte as well." He took her hand. "We promised to do all we could to teach her how to fulfill her prophecy, how to be a messenger of the Goddess." When she had first come to live with them at the age of eight, after her uncle died suddenly, they decided the best way to deal with the odd prophecy was to accept it matter-of-factly, expose the girl to as many spiritual experiences as they could, and let the prophecy play out as it may. "The ancient sites in Ireland are a huge part of the old Earth Mother worship rituals. Newgrange, Carrowmore, Knowth, Tara. She needs to see these sites, to really *feel* them for herself."

Amanda bit her lip. "I suppose you're right."

"And one more thing." He chose his words carefully. "I'm worried Astarte might be taking your … somber mood … personally."

"How so?"

"Well, maybe she's wondering if she's not enough for us. You know, the whole adopted child versus biological child thing."

Amanda closed her eyes. "Oh, God, you're right." She pounded her thigh with a fist. "I hadn't even thought about that. The poor girl. She's resilient, but she's also at that age. Of course those doubts have crossed her mind." She exhaled. "That decides it, then. We're going." She shifted; Cam stayed silent, letting her talk it out and hopefully convince herself. "And it would be nice to visit those sites myself. Maybe they'll help give me some perspective." She stared into the fire. "After all, places like Newgrange really are all about the cycles of life. Birth, life, death, rebirth. They're fertility shrines. Women have been giving birth, or not giving birth, for millions of years." She lowered her voice and offered a sad but brave smile. "I'm not the first who had a miscarriage."

Cam took her hand and kissed it, then looked her in the eye. "Wonderful. Thanks, honey." He'd bring up the Brian stuff tomorrow. "And if you're not having fun, we can take an earlier flight home."

She rolled her eyes. "Not bloody likely. My guess is you saved the whiskey distillery for the last day to make sure I don't bolt."

✝

Raja seemed to know everyone in the school, but Astarte appreciated that he made a point of leading her to a section of the gym where a cluster of her theater friends were sitting. Luckily they walked in during halftime rather than sauntering in together like a pair of Hollywood A-listers while everyone else was already seated.

The bleachers were crowded, and Astarte couldn't tell whether his leg rested against hers because of the crush of humanity or because, well, he had a crush on her. She made no effort to edge away.

Normally she would have followed the action on the court. But for some reason tonight she was more interested in breathing in Raja's body spray and feeling the heat of his thigh against hers and laughing a little too loud and long at his jokes.

She was surprised when the horn blew, signaling the end of the game. Had an hour really passed? He stood and smiled. "I promised your parents I would bring you straight home." He swallowed as she nodded. "And since I plan to ask you out again, it is in my best interests to keep that promise."

She met his smile and held his dark eyes. "Good." She offered him her arm. "I might even say yes."

✠

Cam was preparing documents for a real estate closing on his laptop in front of the fire while Astarte showered after her date and Amanda did yoga on the floor of the living room next to him. He was glad to see Amanda in her yoga pants; normally a health nut, she had rarely exercised since losing the baby.

"Who gains ten pounds *after* a miscarriage?" she hissed. "At this rate you'll have to buy me a bloody second seat on the plane."

Cam smiled and reached over to pat her ass. "Everything looks fine to me."

"Yeah, well, that's because you haven't had a very good look lately." She arched an eyebrow. "Might I suggest it's time to remedy that?"

He had been patient, waiting for her to come back to him, not sure what the protocol for intimacy was after a miscarriage. "You might," he laughed.

She finished her bend and exhaled. "I'll shower when I'm finished."

"And I'll try to wait patiently."

Whenever they traveled abroad, Cam made a point of doing research to see if there were any Templar sites or history worth investigating. It was as good a way as any to kill time waiting for Amanda. He closed the real estate file and did a quick Google search.

He surfed for ten minutes, surprised to learn that Ireland had such a rich Templar history. Apparently in the late twelfth century, when the Irish submitted to English rule, a number of Templars were given estates and land holdings in Ireland after returning from the Crusades, both as a reward and as a way for the English king to police his Irish subjects. Cam jotted some notes and was about to end the search when something caught his eye: Christopher Columbus had visited Galway, on the west coast of Ireland, in 1477, apparently to learn more about the legendary journeys of Brendan the Navigator, the Irish monk believed to have crossed the North Atlantic in the sixth century. While in Galway, Columbus visited a church with known ties to the Templars.

Cam sat back and thought about Columbus. His ships sported sails adorned with massive Templar crosses. He married the daughter of a nobleman with close ties to the Knights of Christ, the Portuguese successor order to the Templars. His signature incorporated the Hooked X symbol, believed to be the secret calling card of Templars who explored America in the 14th century. And just where did he get his maps to the New World? Cam stared at the fire. Was it possible Columbus was doing more in Galway than just listening to old seafaring legends?

✠

Astarte's parents had come up to say goodnight while she read in bed. Forty-five minutes later she heard their bedroom door close; Venus trotted in and jumped on her pillow. That usually meant they were fooling around. Which, come to think of it, hadn't happened in a long time as far as she knew. Hopefully it meant her mom was feeling better. Astarte didn't like to think about what her parents did in their bedroom too much. It was too personal, too intimate. Like being in the bathroom while someone else was on the toilet. But tonight, with the taste of Raja's lips still on hers, her mind wandered.

He had kissed her after pulling into the driveway and before walking her to the door, moving in slowly and lingering briefly before recoiling as if her mouth had shocked his. She hoped it wasn't her breath, hoped it was just his awkwardness or shyness. Or concern she might turn away. *As if.* She sighed. Either way, it was her first real kiss. Somehow the placement of his lips on hers had sent a warm, tingling feeling through her whole body, including between her legs. It was such a weird thing if you really thought about it, the whole kissing thing. Aliens visiting earth would probably laugh, the way humans laughed at dogs sniffing each other's butts. And why should it affect her private parts in any way?

Venus' ears perked as the bed creaked down the hall. Astarte heard a faint moan. Some kind of mysterious magic. And, apparently, it all started with a kiss.

✝

Brian Heenan paced the cold, low-ceilinged room above the garage of his aunt's ranch home in Westford. She hadn't been thrilled to see him back in town, and he couldn't stand her sanctimonious piety, so the secluded room with worn industrial carpet and a pair or fluorescent lights worked well for both of them. The only problem was the single bathroom. Apparently her shit didn't smell, because she pointedly left him a candle and a book of matches with a note— *Light candle after doing business*—the first night he had stayed with her, even though she didn't extend him the same courtesy. Did she really believe her piety made her odor-free? He had been tempted to take the candle and set her pink furry toilet seat cover on fire instead.

Actually, there was a second problem as well—no cable TV. Who in the 21ˢᵗ century didn't have cable? His viewing options were limited to a few local channels, and even then only when the electric space heater wasn't running. It was barely sixty degrees in the poorly-insulated room, so he threw on another sweater and a thick pair of socks before snapping the heating dial to the off position; frostbite or not, he'd go crazy without something to help him kill time. At least today he had been able to do something, to get out of this room and set their plan in motion. He flicked his tongue against his teeth. Now it all depended on Thorne…

The cell phone he had been given chimed in the pocket of his green pants. One of the reasons he so liked the pants was because of the oversized pockets. But mostly he wore them because he wanted to let people know he didn't give a damn what anyone thought. He reached to remove the phone from his left pocket, cursed as the bandage on his hand caught, then finally wrestled it free with his right hand. He jabbed at the buttons, trying to figure out how to take the call. "Damn it, answer." It had taken him more than a decade to find someone who took his sword seriously. Now, all his hard work, his planning, would be lost because he couldn't make the phone work? He finally poked the green phone icon. "Hello, hello?"

"Mr. Heenan." A male voice, the words spoken slowly, as if trying to hide a foreign accent.

"Yes." He sighed. All this cloak and dagger shit, taking orders from people he never actually got to see. "I'm here. Hello."

"I am calling for a report."

"I made contact with Thorne." Brian described the encounter.

"And when will Mr. Thorne get back to you with his answer?"

"I'm guessing tomorrow."

"We are running short on time, as you know."

"Look, I'm planning on going to Ireland no matter what Thorne says. If I have to bump into him while I'm there, so be it."

"But it would be better if he agrees to your company."

"Yeah, well, it's been a long time since someone willingly agreed to my company. But fuck 'em. Sometimes they're stuck with me, like it or not."

✛

Cam startled awake in the middle of the night, a scream caught in his throat. He gasped, blinked away the images of his nightmare, and fought to control his breathing. *Just a dream.* He kicked the sheets away and rubbed his eyes, but the images remained burned into his pupils: An oversized bloody palm, pushing into his face and covering his nose and mouth, choking off the air as metallic-tasting blood seeped into his mouth and down his throat. Out of the corner of his eye he could see Amanda, but she either didn't hear his struggles or didn't care, as she calmly sliced vegetables with the swagger sword…

He rubbed his hand over his face. *Not too hard to figure out the meaning of that dream.*

Amanda turned and reached for him, sensing his unease. "You okay?" she murmured.

"Yeah. Just a bad dream." But not random. Obviously his subconscious was struggling with the whole Brian thing.

She moved closer. "Tell me your dream and I'll tell you what it means."

He grinned at the familiar line. Astarte had played Golda in *Fiddler on the Roof* this past summer at theater camp. Even with a British brogue, Amanda's Yiddish accent was pretty good. He sat up against the headboard. "Okay." He did his best Tevya. "But don't be *frightened.*"

Cam recounted how he and Brian had been best friends, how they had grown apart, how Brian had broken into his home. Then he described the nightmare. "But now Brian's dying. And it sounds like he's not exactly surrounded by people who care for him."

She looked at him with wide green eyes, her blond hair splayed across the pillow. In the dim light, he could see the flush in her cheeks from their lovemaking. Or maybe that was just his imagination. She said, "Can't understand why not. Doesn't everyone like it when their friends steal from them?"

"It turns out Brian knows Monsignor Marcotte. His aunt is a nun at Saint Catherine's. And it also turns out Brian is hell-bent on seeing Ireland before he dies. Marcotte knows about our trip, and wants me to spend some time with Brian while we're there. Obviously, I was feeling guilty about not telling you about all this earlier tonight."

She took his hand. "Not just guilty. Sounds like you're a bit frightened of him as well."

He nodded. "My sense is he's lived a tough life. He's been a bouncer, a bounty hunter, who knows what else? As a kid he was always the one looking for a fight. Sometimes it seemed like he didn't even care if he won. So who knows what he's capable of."

"But on the other hand, he's dying. And you want to do the right thing."

"Exactly. Marcotte is like the good angel on my shoulder, telling me to carve out a few hours for him."

"And who's the devil on your other shoulder?"

"I guess that would be you." He shifted. "I sort of expect you to say you don't want him in Ireland with us."

"I don't. At least not in our hotel or touring with us or at dinner. But if you want to spend half a day with him while Astarte and I do something else, that's fine. I mean, the guy's dying."

"That's not very devilish of you."

She slid closer and reached her hand beneath the sheets. Smiling, she drummed her fingers up his thigh. "I try to pick my spots."

Chapter 3

Bleary-eyed, Cam, Amanda and Astarte landed in Dublin on the morning after Christmas, Cam remaining hopeful that the European adventure would jar Amanda out of her malaise. They took a taxi to their hotel, where he had arranged for an early check-in.

Astarte wheeled her suitcase into the room and peered out the hotel window. "Hey, there's a castle next door."

Amanda replied in an animated tone. "Welcome to Europe. We've got castles like the States has strip malls." She pushed the curtain aside. "That's Dublin Castle. The tower dates to the 13th century, but the rest of it was rebuilt in the late 1600s after a fire." She shrugged. "We'll see many more impressive structures than this."

"I think the Irish Templars were imprisoned in the castle after the Pope outlawed them in 1307," Cam said. "Maybe in that very tower." He checked his watch. Almost ten. He knew the best way to deal with the red-eye flight was to power through it rather than trying to catch up on missed sleep. "Let's wash up and grab a quick breakfast. Then go explore."

They spent the early part of the day walking the city, beginning with a tour of the castle and then ducking in and out of shops in the Temple Bar area. Cam and Amanda were more interested in the ancient Druid sites, but they couldn't very well go to Ireland and skip Dublin.

They crossed the iconic Ha'penny Bridge and ate a quick lunch. They then waited for Brian in front of the Two Irish Ladies statue, which depicted a pair of middle-aged women with shopping bags on a bench. Cam and Brian planned to take in a soccer match at Aviva Stadium. Which, for Brian, no doubt would mean an excuse to start drinking early.

Brian and his green pants seemed to appear out of the shadows, his face suddenly a few feet in front of Cam's. "I see you found The Hags with Bags." Unshaven and wearing a tweed Irish flat cap, he grinned and motioned at the statue. "That's what the locals call it."

Cam could smell beer on his breath. He was glad they hadn't chosen to meet at the Irish Spire, a 400-foot needle near the Liffey

River which the locals had nicknamed The Stiffy by the Liffey. No doubt Brian would have had plenty to say about that.

"This must be your beautiful family," Brian continued. He offered an exaggerated bow before handing a semi-wilted red rose to Amanda and another to Astarte. He studied Amanda, nodded in approval, and turned to Astarte. "And how old are you, my dear? Sixteen? Seventeen?"

"Thirteen," she said, smiling, apparently not put off by his clumsy attempt at charm. "Nice to meet you." Cam shook his head. How was it possible she wasn't repulsed by him?

"Yes." Brian leaned closer. "You as well."

"Well, we should head over," Brian said to Cam, his eyes lingering on Astarte. "The match begins in a half-hour." He offered his arm to her. "Young lady, do you like football?" He leaned in again. "That's what they call soccer here in Europe."

Cam stepped between his daughter and his childhood friend. "They won't be joining us," he said, now relieved that Amanda had begged off. "You know, shopping calls."

"Oh." Brian's shoulders dropped. "Okay then."

Cam said his goodbyes and, a short train ride on the DART later, they arrived at the modern stadium's front gate. Brian handed Cam a ticket, his left hand still bandaged. Cam pulled out his wallet.

"Forget it. I got it."

"Thanks. But where you getting all the money for this trip?" Brian had told Cam he was broke.

Brian offered a crooked grin consisting of a half dozen stained upper teeth. "Credit cards. I've got, like, six of them. By the time they get around to chasing me, I'll be dead in the ground. Fuck 'em. Greedy bastards."

Brian surprised Cam by being a knowledgeable fan of the game. "I used to live in Salt Lake City. They had a pro team. No shit, there's nothing to do in that city. So I started going to games." He flashed what passed for another smile. "Got friendly with some of the players and made a few bucks betting on the games." He shook his head and laughed ruefully. "One time I slipped a laxative into our keeper's breakfast shake, then bet on the other team. He never made it out of the locker room. I won five hundred bucks."

Brian bought a couple of beers and changed the subject. "So, I found out my family is from County Limerick, on the west coast. I'm taking a bus out there tomorrow. Then heading up to Galway."

Cam nodded. They were planning to be in Galway also in a few days.

They watched the match in silence for a few minutes. "You know," Brian said, "as much as dying sucks, it's sort of liberating. I want a beer for breakfast, why not? Or a Snickers bar for lunch. Or maybe I want to drop a grand on a hooker." He shook his head. "But it also makes you think about shit you don't usually think about. I mean, I've got no kids ... at least that I know about. And nobody really gives a shit if I live or die." He sighed. "So what's it all about? The only time I really remember being happy is when we were kids, running around in the woods, playing ball, going sledding, whatever." He shook his head. "But since then, nothing. Just a wasted fucking life."

Cam wasn't sure what to say. "You're right, we had a lot of fun as kids. Those were carefree days."

"Yeah, but you've made a life for yourself. A wife, a kid, a career, all that research of yours." He angled his head. "You know, I read your book. Do you really think the Templars were here ... I mean in America ... before Columbus?"

"I do. At first it was just a theory, but all the evidence points to it. Every time we find another artifact or old map or old journal, it confirms our theory." He paused to organize his thoughts. Explaining it aloud, to someone who had not lived it the way he and Amanda had, helped keep things clear and simple in his mind. "So here's what we know." He summarized the evidence, counting the points off on his fingers, describing a dozen artifacts and sites supporting his theory over the next five minutes.

Finishing, Cam glanced at Brian to make sure he was still listening. He actually preferred to keep the conversation on his research, rather than on Brian's sickness or what Brian might really want from Cam. "It's a lot to just pass off as coincidence. I think what happened was that the Templars, because of their exposure to ancient documents while in the Middle East, came to question many of the Church teachings. I think they learned that early Christianity, true Christianity, understood the importance of women to a healthy society and that Christianity was not meant to be this all-male, patriarchal, suppressive movement that it had become during the Middle Ages.

That was their heresy. When the Church turned on them, the Templars fled to America as a safe haven. They probably had maps they had obtained in the Middle East, likely drawn by the ancient seafaring Phoenicians. The Native Americans welcomed them because the Templars respected the Native American culture and religion and values; they had learned how to deal with different cultures in the Middle East. No way could a group just come over here and force their way in. They weren't trying to colonize or do missionary work. But as friends, allies, trading partners, they were welcome."

"What do you mean, *no way*? The Pilgrims forced their way in."

"They had guns. Game changer."

"Yeah. All right."

Cam continued. "And when the Templars came, they brought their treasures with them. Over time, they reconstituted themselves as the Freemasons, eventually becoming the Founding Fathers of the United States. And they set up a government guaranteeing individual liberty as a way to protect citizens from the powerful Church." He shrugged again. "Like I said, the pieces all fit together. We may have some of the details wrong, but I think the big picture is correct."

"One thing I'm not buying is the Templars being, like, feminists. Shit, they were soldiers. They weren't even allowed to take a friggin' bath."

Cam nodded. "I get that. But did you know the Templar order was dedicated to the Virgin Mary? And when I'm talking about their belief set, I'm talking about the leadership, not the common foot soldier. The monk who wrote the Templar charter and was largely responsible for their formation, Bernard de Clairvaux, bore the personal title, 'Knight of the Virgin,' because of his veneration for the Virgin Mary. In fact…"

Cam pulled out his phone and found an image. "Bernard, later Saint Bernard, was famous for a dream he had, in which he drank breast milk from the Virgin Mary. There are dozens of medieval paintings showing it." He turned the phone toward Brian.

Saint Bernard de Clairvaux and the Virgin Mary

"Hard to miss the symbolism," Cam said.

"Can't blame the old dude. She's actually sort of hot."

Cam rolled his eyes. "Anyway, hope that answers your question."

"Yeah. They didn't teach that shit in school. But I've always been interested in the Templars."

"You mean in the Templar treasure."

He chuckled. "Okay. The treasure." The laugh morphed into a sigh. "Not that I would have time to spend much of it even if I found it."

"I assume you left the sword at home."

Brian tilted his head back and laughed. "At home? Why would I do that? I put the fucking thing in its case, stuck it in my golf bag, and checked it through. It's the only thing I own that's worth a damn. And who knows, maybe it'll come in handy over here."

So he had it with him. Which indicated to Cam that Brian thought the sword was authentic; otherwise, why bother bringing it? Cam had wondered if it was a fake. Still might be, but this tilted the scales a bit.

"You promised to give it to me if I came to Ireland."

Brian nodded. "That's why I brought it." He grinned. "But you gotta figure a way to get it back on the plane."

Classic Brian, always looking for an angle. "Just give it to me when we get home. And you never told me where you got it."

"That's right, I didn't."

Cam waited. "So?"

"Let's just say a friend gave it to me."

Cam knew better than to push it. But he also knew Brian didn't have any friends.

☩

Amanda and Astarte stood on a street corner, the traffic of Dublin zipping by. "Remember, look to the right before stepping off the curb, not to the left," Amanda warned, glad to be free of the leering Brian.

"Got it, Mom." Astarte grinned. "Barney taught us to look *both* ways."

"Well, never ignore advice from purple dinosaurs." Amanda's spirits had, as Cam hoped, lifted. It was good to be out of Westford, away from the things that reminded her of the past few months. But also good to be back on this side of the pond. America was home now, but she would always be a Brit.

Astarte moved frenetically through Dublin's downtown, wide-eyed, curious about the people and the food and the city's history. She was always an upbeat kid, but especially so over the past few days. Amanda guessed it was because of Raja. Amanda had walked in on them Skyping over the weekend. Amanda smiled at the memory; she had never seen Astarte blush before. Her daughter's excitement for the trip and joy for life further buoyed Amanda's mood. She allowed Astarte to lead, to simply wander and follow her curiosity.

"The cars are all so small," Astarte said. "No SUVs."

"That's what it used to be like in the States also, apparently."

"And is it usually so warm this time of year?" It was in the high forties, almost thirty degrees warmer than when they left Boston. "I looked at a map, and we're further north than Calgary."

Amanda knew better than to question the girl's facts. "The Gulf Stream keeps it warm here. But you'll notice it gets dark at around four o'clock." She looked at her watch. That gave them a couple of hours of daylight. "You fancy a visit to Saint Patrick's Cathedral?"

"What's so special about it?"

"It's the largest church in all of Ireland."

The girl shrugged. "I don't think so. Churches are just buildings. I want to see things that help me understand the people."

Amanda considered the request. "Well, there's an old expression that one can judge a society by how it treats its criminals." She waved down a taxi. "So come on."

"Where we going?"

"Kilmainham Jail." As they rode she gave a quick overview of the history of Ireland. "For centuries Ireland was ruled by the English. Whenever there were attempts for independence, the leaders were thrown into jail, usually at Kilmainham. Then, during World War I, there was another uprising, and this one eventually led to independence. But, again, a lot of the revolutionaries were imprisoned—and executed—at Kilmainham. That's why it's considered a monument to the Irish independence movement."

Ten minutes later the taxi dropped them off in front of a massive cream-colored stone building surrounded by a wrought iron fence. They entered through an arched doorway. Astarte pointed up at the decorations on the arch. "Look. Snakes."

Amanda nodded. "Those are the five deadly sins represented by five snakes. Not the sins from the Bible, but the ones that could get you hanged—murder, treason, rape, arson and larceny. The snakes are all chained by the neck to represent control."

"I get it. People get sent to jail to control their impulse to sin."

The jail was empty, but ghosts of its past occupants, and their sins, haunted its cells. During the tour Astarte's eyes grew wide as she learned of the horrors within. Seven-year-old children imprisoned for theft. A special room just for hangings. Each cell limited to a single candle for both light and heat. Women forced to share cells with men. Male prisoners shipped to Australia.

Halfway through, Amanda pulled her aside. "That's enough, I think." Perhaps this had been a bad idea. "You get the picture."

Astarte swallowed. "How far away is that Saint Patrick's Cathedral?" For some reason her mind went back to the church she hadn't wanted to see.

"Not far. You can see the spire from here."

The girl shook her head, her eyes pooling. "I don't understand how the priests and the nuns could have been so close by and not done anything about all this suffering."

Amanda took her hand. "I know, honey, I know."

Amanda wished she could protect Astarte from the ugliness of the world. But she also knew that was not possible, especially as the girl—fast becoming a young lady—seemed intent on fulfilling what she believed to be her destiny. Most kids wanted to be a doctor or teacher or professional athlete. Astarte aspired to unite the Western world in a revamped version of Judeo-Christianity that recognized the importance, and even primacy, of the Sacred Feminine in the godhead. A world returned to the ancient ways, when the Earth Mother reigned supreme. It would be a monumental shift, yet Astarte viewed the transformation matter-of-factly. "It really has nothing to do with me," she had said recently. "It's just my destiny."

Replying to Astarte's comment about the priests and nuns not doing anything to relieve the suffering, Amanda said, "You know Dad's friend Monsignor Marcotte. He's been pushing for allowing women to become priests, and for allowing all priests to marry as they do in the Eastern Orthodox Church. He believes that being in a marriage, and being a parent, are crucial parts of the human experience. How can we expect our religious leaders to be effective when they have no experience in so much of what it means to be human?"

The girl nodded. "Plus, like, don't you want the priests to have big families? In the LDS we do." She had been raised by her uncle in the Mormon Church. "The priests are the smartest people, so it's better if they have children."

"It's the same in the Jewish religion. Rabbis are expected to have large families." They walked toward the curb. "And it used to be that way in Catholicism. But the priests were leaving all their money and land to their children when they died. The Church figured, why not figure a way to keep all that money for itself?"

Astarte had already turned the experience at the jail into a learning moment, her spirits rebounding. "That's the problem with organized religion," she said as Amanda flagged a cab. "It all gets corrupted." She looked back a final time at the prison. "People care about their pretty churches and fancy clothes and beautiful choirs and not about the poor and the sick."

Amanda carefully chose her response. "So, one of the reasons we wanted to bring you here was for you to get a better understanding of Europe. Especially the old ways, the old religions. What many people call paganism. Before religion became, as you said, organized. In the States, we don't really have that. There are some Wiccans who still worship in the old manner, but most people are what we would call modern Christians or Jews or Muslims."

"I know all that, Mum," Astarte said with a sigh as they stepped into the taxi.

"Oh. Yes, yes of course you do." Amanda had been so self-absorbed the past few months that her brain seemed sluggish, like a computer running slow because too many background programs were open. She gave the cabbie the name of their hotel. "Anyway, your dad and I believe the Templars actually adopted many of the old ways. During their travels they learned about the importance of respecting the earth, and the importance of male and female balance for a healthy society, and the importance of, like you said, taking care of the poor and sick and not just being concerned about how fancy the churches were. These beliefs were the main reasons we think the Templars butted heads with the Church. But this was also why the Native Americans were so willing to accept them as friends and allies."

Astarte looked out the window and yawned. Amanda, too, was lulled by the movement of the cab. They had been awake for more than twenty-four hours. They would have an early dinner with Cam, then crash and hopefully be refreshed in the morning. "So," Astarte replied, "I know the Templars weren't traditional Christians. But you think they were, like, pagans?"

"That's probably not the word they would have used, but in many ways they seemed to be. Like I said, they learned a lot from traveling. And they also probably learned a lot from studying the old megalithic sites here in Europe. Stonehenge. The ancient Druid sites. The burial mounds, like the ones we're going to visit tomorrow. They believed in Christ, but believed he was part of a larger tapestry that included the ancient worship of the sun and earth and stars as well. Because of that, they didn't always agree with the teaching of the Vatican. They understood that religion was more than just about stained glass and fancy robes."

Amanda reached over and squeezed Astarte's knee, waiting for the girl to meet her gaze. "Anyway, I'm very proud of how you are handling the pressures of your prophecy. It's no small thing to be expected to change the way the world thinks about God." She smiled as she felt her eyes mist. "And for what it's worth, I think the Templars would have felt very much at home in this church you want to build."

✞

Cam raised his glass of Irish whiskey to Amanda, his hand on her knee, as they sat at the hotel bar. "Cheers."

"*Sláinte,*" Amanda replied, clinking his glass. "It means, 'To your health.' And the reason we clink glasses is to scare the demons away."

Cam smiled, holding her eyes. It was good to have her back.

Astarte had gone up to the hotel room to Skype with some friends, it being early afternoon in Boston. "Think she's Skyping with Raja?" Cam asked.

"It's a good wager," Amanda smiled. "She was positively giddy at the idea of having some privacy in the room."

"Sounds like she was bothered by the jail," Cam said.

"Very much so. She has an incredible amount of empathy, which also means she experiences an incredible amount of pain when she sees suffering." Amanda lowered her drink, the glass clanking loudly against the mahogany bar. "It's a tough way to go through life."

"Well, the stuff we're seeing tomorrow should be less disturbing."

"Yes. Just an uplifting day examining mounds full of dead bodies."

Cam smiled. "Point taken." He sipped his drink. "But no stories of suffering. Ancient people lived happy lives, then they died and were buried."

"Speaking of people dying, how was your day with Brian?" She held up a hand. "Sorry, that came out wrong."

"That's okay." He shrugged. "It was fine. But I feel a weird sort of pressure when I'm with him, trying to make sure he gets the most out of the last few days of his life."

She nodded. "Like being on a first date, trying to be constantly witty and interesting."

Cam lifted his drink to her and smiled. "Glad you remember our first date the same way I do."

She rolled her eyes. "I'm sure Brian found you as irresistible as I did. As long as he didn't try to get fresh."

"No. He was the perfect gentleman." Cam paused and angled his head. "Actually, that's the wrong way to describe him. As you could probably tell, he's sort of a pig."

"Sort of? He practically took a bite out of Astarte."

"Yeah, he was always the guy making inappropriate comments to the girls."

"Well, Astarte can take care of herself. And she actually seemed to like him, which is weird. But I'm worried we're in for a rough stretch. Those cobalt eyes, that bright smile. She's going to be a beauty."

"And Brian's definitely a beast."

"Yuck." Amanda washed the thought away with a sip of whiskey. "I'm hoping we're done with him."

"Me too. But he knows we're going out to Newgrange tomorrow. Wouldn't surprise me if he showed up on some tour bus."

"Ancient burial mounds don't really sound like his style."

"No. But he's obsessed with the Templar treasure." Cam shrugged again. "And he's convinced somehow I can help him find it."

Chapter 4

Cam awoke at six the next morning. He still felt lethargic from the flight and wanted to get a morning run in, hoping the adrenaline would recharge his system. "I'll be back in time for breakfast," he whispered to a sleeping Amanda after dressing. Astarte rested peacefully on a cot near the window; at the inn they would be staying at tonight, she would have her own bedroom.

The inn had been recommended by Monsignor Marcotte. "I stayed there myself in September," Marcotte had said. "It's very close to Newgrange and some of the other burial mounds. The owner gives private tours. And the food is excellent, all farm fresh."

Cam cut through the downtown area to the river, dodging a few taxis and street-sweepers as the sun began to rise and the city came to life. He ran along the river to the Famine Memorial, a haunting collection of metal sculptures depicting gaunt sufferers of the potato famine that killed over a million people in the 1840s. Slowing, he studied the emaciated figures. In addition to the million who died, another million emigrated, many to the United States, dramatically changing the history of both countries. Incredibly, the population of Ireland today remained below 1840s levels.

He re-crossed the river and snaked his way to the Trinity College campus, where tourists were beginning to line up to view the Book of Kells, an extravagantly-illustrated 9th century manuscript containing the four gospels of the New Testament which somehow survived Viking-era plundering raids. The book, and the fact that it was considered a national treasure, was a reminder of how prominent a role Christianity played in Ireland. Christianity came late to the remote island, which had a long history of Druidic influence, but once it arrived it established deep roots.

The potato famine and Christianity. Cam had read that these two influences (including in the latter's case the Catholic-Protestant conflicts) had together largely shaped Irish society. But it was the pre-Christian culture that most interested him. Especially the Druids and their pagan worship customs. Cam turned a corner and began to sprint the last quarter-mile. Today they would be visiting the ancient burial

mound of Newgrange, dating back 5,000 years, to the time of Stonehenge. The American patriot and historian Thomas Paine had written
that the Freemasons, and the Templars before them, were spiritual
descendants of the ancient Druids, who worshiped at the mounds.
Cam sensed that the ancient sites like Newgrange would teach him
much about the Templars.

✠

Only a couple hundred yards from their hotel, his lungs beginning to burn and his legs feeling heavy, Cam fought to maintain his
pace as he ascended a final incline. He had ventured further than
he thought—his smart watch said just over five miles—and he was
beginning to fear that his curiosity had outpaced his stamina.

A steel-blue minivan with flowers painted on its side rumbled
toward him, Cam still not accustomed to vehicles using the left side
of the road. Both the driver and his companion in the passenger seat
were smoking, but as they approached they flicked their butts out
the window, as if in response to spotting him. Cam tensed as the van
slowed. Both men eyed him.

Cam glanced around. No other vehicles, no other pedestrians.
His hotel beckoned like an oasis in the distance. The sidewalk narrowed ahead, funneling due to some building construction. *What the
hell do they want with me?* He thought about reversing course, but
did not want to turn his back on his possible assailants. Instead he
upped his pace.

The driver responded immediately, swerving toward Cam, the
vehicle's front wheels jumping the curb, the van ominously blocking Cam's path. The incongruity of the cheery floral decorations and
the looming danger presented by the van was not lost on Cam. The
passenger leapt out even before the van stopped, a burly man in a
hooded sweatshirt carrying a black club. He silently closed on Cam
before Cam could retreat, swinging the club more like a gladiator than
a florist. Cam raised his left arm to block it, the blow crashing against
his forearm and sending bullets of pain up his arm. What the hell was
going on? Acting instinctively, Cam dropped to the ground in a crab
position and whipped out his right foot, catching the thug behind the
ankle and upending him. Before the driver could join the fray, Cam

jumped to his feet, pivoted, and ducked under some scaffolding into the ground floor of the nearby building under construction.

His eyes darted as he tried to quiet his breathing. Drop cloths covered the floor, and sawhorses and ladders filled the space, which looked to be the lobby of an office building. The burly assailant, now joined by the driver, stumbled in after him. Cam, his left arm numb, did not wait for round two. He ran toward the back of the darkened building, grabbing a two-by-four propped against a wall. He rubbed a hand across his face. Perhaps entering a dark, secluded space was not the best decision.

Squinting, he moved parallel to the street. Hopefully there would be another egress back to the sidewalk up ahead. But as his eyes adjusted he realized he was leaving footprints in the sawdust. Faint, but visible. A flashlight snapped on, its beam crisscrossing the construction area. His assailants must have stumbled upon the light. Or perhaps they had come well-equipped. Either way, maybe Cam could use his footprints and their newfound light against them.

Running now, he found what he was looking for. A stairway along the back wall of the lobby, heading down. He glanced back. His pursuers were moving methodically, the beam along the ground, apparently following his tracks. They must have figured, as Cam had now done, that there was likely only one entrance into an office lobby. They had him trapped. Bypassing the stairwell, he ran ahead another ten steps and stopped in front of a closed door. Rather than pushing through it, he lowered a ladder that had been leaning against the back wall to the ground and walked its length back toward the stairs. At the end of the ladder he grabbed a paint can, placed it a few feet beyond the ladder, and jumped. Using a combination of saw horses and construction debris, he hopscotched along, managing to retrace his steps back to the stairwell—without leaving any footprints.

The light beam approached. As silently as he could, Cam rolled over the stairwell half-wall, caught himself atop the bannister, and slid down feet first into the darkness below.

He waited a few seconds, listening. "Here," a voice said, the Irish brogue unmistakable. "More footprints." And less audibly. "They stop at this door."

"Open it."

"It's locked."

"Well, knock the fucking thing down then. Obviously that's where the bloke went." A pause. "We need answers about that sword."

Sword? Did I hear that correctly?

A crash echoed a few seconds later, followed by the sound of footsteps. Cam didn't wait for them to discover they'd been duped. He ran up the stairs, back through the lobby, and out onto the sidewalk. The van sat, two wheels on the street and two on the sidewalk, still running.

Cam reached in and took the keys, tossing them down a storm grate. "Assholes," he cursed as he sprinted the final block to his hotel, his left arm limp by his side, wondering how they knew about the sword and why it was so important to them.

✠

After showering and taking a couple of Advil, Cam pulled Amanda aside while Astarte got dressed in the bathroom. Downplaying the incident, he described the encounter. "So I slipped into a building under construction and lost them. Lucky for me there was a second exit." He showed her the welt on his forearm. "But I banged my arm on some scaffolding." He couldn't not tell Amanda, yet he did not want to unnecessarily alarm her.

Her green eyes flashed in anger. "What did they bloody want?"

He shook his head. "I don't know. I didn't stick around long enough for them to ask. But I think I heard them mention wanting to find answers about the sword."

"Brian's swagger sword?"

"I assume so. What else could it be? Maybe someone was following him and saw him get in my car in Newport. Maybe they think I have it."

"And they followed you to Ireland?" She shook her head. "That doesn't make any sense."

"Could be they followed him, and saw me with him at the soccer match yesterday."

She nodded. "Perhaps."

He shrugged. "Look, I could have heard wrong. The guys had thick accents. Maybe it was just a random mugging attempt. Maybe it had nothing to do with the sword."

She rolled her eyes. "And maybe tomorrow we'll be invited for tea with the queen of England."

✛

They ate a quick breakfast at the hotel, packed their bags, and were in the hotel lobby by eight. At Amanda's insistence, Cam had reported the incident to security, who in turn called the local police. Her instincts told her this had not been a random attack.

A female officer, about Amanda's age with brown hair pulled back in a ponytail, met them in the lobby. Cam described the encounter. "I'm pretty sure it was just wrong place, wrong time," he said. Amanda knew he didn't want to mention the swagger sword. And she sensed he had downplayed the severity of the incident when describing it to her and, now, to the policewoman. "You know, tourist running around aimlessly, probably with cash in his pockets."

Big-boned but not fat, the officer studied him closely. "Do joggers in the States normally carry cash?" She glanced at Amanda, as if the two of them together needed to treat Cam like a child. "Because here in Ireland, they don't generally stop to shop."

Cam shrugged, flushing as Amanda grinned, appreciative of the sarcasm. "No. I guess not."

"Are you sure there's nothing you're not telling me?" She didn't seem angry, just bemused.

He shrugged again. "Not that I can think of."

"Okay, let's do this." She smiled, again directed at Amanda. "We both know you're pretending to tell me the truth. So I, in turn, will pretend to do a full investigation. And I'll also pretend to call ahead to the other cities you're traveling to, to ask for local police to keep an eye on you and your family."

"Okay." Cam exhaled. "There is actually one other detail that may be important."

She titled her head. "Is that so?"

Cam explained, as succinctly as he could, the possibility that the secret to finding a medieval treasure might be imbedded in the carvings on a sword blade smuggled over to Ireland by his childhood friend. It was Cam's turn to tilt his head. "See why I left that part out?"

"I do." The officer sucked air through her teeth, making a whistling noise. "You think that's what our boys were after?"

"I heard them mention something about finding answers about the sword."

"Well, I guess that explains motive." She explained to them that fellow officers had found the van on the curb as Cam had left it; it had been stolen the night before from a florist who had left it running while making a delivery. "So not much to go on. But now that I understand what this is all about, I'll dig a little deeper."

"I appreciate that," Cam said. "And if you could keep the sword stuff quiet, I'd appreciate that also."

"I understand." She handed him her card, then took it back and wrote something on the back. "I assume you're heading to Galway at some point?"

Cam nodded.

"My brother's a Guard there." Amanda knew that's what the Irish called their national police force, the *Garda*. "I just wrote down his name. Give him a ring if you need anything." She smiled. "We both fancy a good mystery. Especially one with a treasure."

Amanda smiled at her and offered her hand. "Thanks for your time. And your patience."

Hotel security had arranged for the rental car to be brought to the parking garage under the hotel, just in case the thugs from the van were still about. Their departure, with Amanda driving, went without incident.

Even so, it wasn't until they put several miles between themselves and the hotel that Amanda began to relax. Danger always seemed to follow them. Or, more accurately, they attracted it—their research into the Templars and their legends acted like a magnet, luring rogues and conspiracy theorists and other shadowy types. This Brian bloke was a perfect example. She wished Cam would have simply refused his overtures. But she knew better. Cam always seemed to look for the good in people, always wanted to do the generous thing, especially with Monsignor Marcotte prodding him along. No matter how many times it seemed to burn him. But, of course, that was the man she had fallen in love with.

She sighed, pushing her introspection away. On the city streets, moving slowly, she had no trouble staying in her lane. But as they picked up the pace, she had to concentrate on driving on the left. "Wow," she said, fighting her instincts, "I've never felt more like a bloody American."

"When you finally get used to it, it'll be time to go back home and mess you up all over again," Cam chuckled. For the first twenty minutes, Amanda noticed he had been focused on his side view mirror, concerned they might be followed. Now he, too, had relaxed.

The city of Dublin quickly gave way to farmland. Even in late December the landscape remained the lush green hue that Ireland was famous for. Unlike in America and most of the rest of Europe, little of the land surrounding Irish cities had been converted to residential use. Without a growing population, there simply was no need for suburbs. Or, for that matter, superhighways. The roads were winding, rutted and narrow, and Amanda often had to slow and edge toward the thin shoulder to allow a large vehicle coming at them to squeeze by.

"It's actually fortunate that so many of these farms have been preserved," Amanda said, eyeing goats only feet away from the road, "because by preserving them the burial mounds have also been preserved. Elsewhere in the British Isles many of the mounds have been plowed over."

Astarte sat in the back, behind Cam. "I read the Irish are also, like, wicked superstitious and don't like to disturb the dead," she said.

Amanda smiled. She wasn't surprised the girl had done some research on the mounds. "What else did you learn?" Amanda asked.

"Well, Newgrange and other burial mounds are older than the Pyramids. Some of them are more than five thousand years old."

"The only manmade site I can think of older than that is Gobekli Tepe in Turkey," Cam said. "And that's off the charts, built over eleven thousand years ago."

An hour later, after a few wrong turns and reversals of course, with Cam navigating, they finally honed in on their destination. Amanda teased, "You certain you don't want to circle around again? I think we passed that little market three times already."

"I'm doing it on purpose." Cam smiled. "To make sure nobody's following us."

Astarte rolled her eyes. "I don't think *anyone* could follow what we just did. Good thing I don't get carsick."

"There," Cam declared victoriously. He pointed to a sign reading 'Milano Farm and Inn,' and Amanda turned onto a dirt drive in a gap between farm plots. A few trees dotted the landscape but for the most part the land had been cleared for crops and grazing. A fieldstone structure, L-shaped with each span featuring a bright red door at its center, sat at the end of the winding drive. A mud-covered black pickup sat parked in front. A woman wearing a cloak and bonnet balanced on a tree swing at the far end of the L, swaying slowly. She watched them but did not greet them or otherwise acknowledge their arrival as they came to a stop.

"Odd," Amanda commented as she opened her door.

As if she could hear Amanda's comment, the woman slid off the swing and half-ran, her arms held stiffly at her side, toward the back of the farm, disappearing behind it.

"No way could she have heard you," Cam said.

"Well, I don't reckon I've made a new friend."

They stood by the side of the car, uncertain how to proceed. "Maybe she went to get someone," Astarte said after a few seconds.

Cam eyed the structure. "I think that's a slate roof. They don't make them like that anymore."

"And look at those windows," Amanda said.

Cam explained to Astarte, "The older the structure, the smaller the windows usually. So this must be 1600s, maybe earlier."

Astarte made a face. "Do they have, like, internet?"

Cam winked at Amanda. "I don't think they even have electricity." He pointed to a small shed. "And I think that's the outhouse."

"Actually," an olive-skinned, middle-aged man said, ambling down the drive from the street side of the farm, "that's a woodshed. We make all our guests chop wood before breakfast." He grinned at his own joke. "I'm Roberto. Roberto Fulcani," he said, his accent clearly Italian. He held his grin. "Irish to my core. You must be Cameron." He shook Cam's hand and turned. "And you must be Amanda." This time he cupped her hand in both of his, his dark eyes kind and playful. "And our woodcutter here must be Astarte." He smiled at her. "Welcome to Milano Farm."

Amanda met his smile. "Well, that explains the name."

"Actually," he said, "I am a huge fan of the Mint Milano cookies, made by Pepperidge Farm. I visited America once and ate three boxes." He patted his stomach and eyed Astarte. "I have not been the same since. But I do love the Girl Scout Thin Mints cookies also. Perhaps you brought some with you?"

"Sorry, no," Astarte laughed. "So you named your farm after a cookie?"

He held his palms up to the sky. "My family is originally from the city of Milan. It seemed appropriate." He turned toward their rental car. "Come. Let's get your bags and I will show you to your rooms." He angled his chin at the farmhouse. "The back part of the L is where I live with my family. Three of us. The guest rooms are here in the front."

Amanda probed. "We saw a woman, in the swing?"

"Yes." He nodded. "That is Emmy. My sister." He shrugged. "She hit her head as a child and has never been the same."

"So how did you end up in Ireland?" Amanda asked, taking the cue from their host that he seemed comfortable discussing his family life.

He flashed an easy smile. "How does any man end up so far from home? I followed my heart." A thin, austere woman in a flannel shirt and blue work pants opened the front door to them. "And there she is," he bellowed. "My Kaitlyn."

She sighed and glanced their way. "Welcome," she said unsmilingly in a thick brogue. She could have been pretty once, Amanda thought, with a stylish dress, her hair down, and a smile on her face. "Roberto will show you your rooms. Dinner is at seven, and breakfast tomorrow at eight. Both in the front room here." She gestured behind her. "Otherwise you may come and go as you please."

As they followed Roberto, Amanda wondered at the family. Running an inn, letting strangers into your life on a regular basis, was not for everyone. Or even for most people. Typically one partner pushed for it and the other went along. In this case it wasn't hard to guess which was which. And then, on top of that, add a sibling with a mental disability of some kind. And apparently no children of their own, Amanda concluded with a pang. Probably not the life Kaitlyn dreamed of. And probably not the bonnie lass Roberto left Italy for, either.

Chapter 5

Their suite of rooms, despite the farmhouse's age, was modern and tastefully decorated. It even had internet. Cam glanced at his watch. Not yet eleven. "Roberto apparently is an expert on Newgrange," he said to Amanda and Astarte. "He's going to take us over. And then to some other burial mounds also." He grabbed his fleece jacket, carefully easing his injured arm into the sleeve. "Wear shoes for walking."

In the driveway, Roberto leaned against the pickup truck in the late morning sun. Emmy stood behind him, hunched, her head down, wearing a brown wool hooded poncho that hung just past her knees. "Cameron, Amanda, Astarte, this is my sister, Emmy. She's going to join us today. Emmy, please say hello."

From deep inside her hood the woman whispered a greeting. "It's a short drive on a back road," Roberto announced cheerfully. "We can all fit in the truck." Astarte and Emmy climbed into the bed of the truck and sat on the wheel wells while Cam and Amanda squished into the front seat with Roberto. Roberto followed a rutted path around to the back of the farm, where he merged onto a dirt road that climbed over yellowish-green farmland toward the horizon.

"Our farm backs into the Newgrange land," Roberto explained. Cattle and sheep grazed leisurely on both sides. "This is easier than going out and around on the main road."

"It's still so green," Cam said, scanning the land.

"It'll start to die off in January, but we haven't even had a frost yet this year." A large section of the farmland had been mowed and tended. Roberto explained, "I love to golf, so I made myself a six-hole course. Many of our guests enjoy the privacy as well."

Cam smiled. "The way I play, the fewer people watching, the better."

As they crested a rise, Roberto pointed. "There it is. Newgrange. Atop that next ridge."

Cam leaned his head out the window to shout to Astarte. "Look. Over there."

She turned and stared. "It looks like a giant moss-covered flying saucer."

Cam laughed as he snapped a picture. "That's a good description."

Newgrange Burial Mound

The mound sat atop the next ridge like a nipple atop a breast. It was much larger than Cam expected; the chambers in New England were the size of a baseball dugout. This was more like the size of an entire stadium. "How big is it," he asked Roberto.

"Eighty-five meters in diameter. About the size of a soccer pitch. And it rises up as high as a four-story building."

"It's massive," Amanda said.

"We call it a burial mound," Robert replied, "but that really is not an accurate description. Ancient temple would be more fitting. This mound, and others like it, had astrological, spiritual, religious and ceremonial importance. Yes, important people were buried in them, much in the same way dignitaries and royalty are buried in religious cathedrals in modern times. But burial was only an ancillary use."

Roberto stopped the truck at the edge of his farm, a couple hundred yards away from the mound. He helped Astarte and Emmy from the back. "I like people to walk around the site for maybe a half hour before going inside. Just to get a feel for it." The five of them climbed an incline to join a few dozen other visitors, most of them with cameras out, milling around the massive mound. "In the summer, you'd see perhaps a few hundred tourists. But this is the offseason."

Emmy seemed to have taken a liking to Astarte, and she hung on Astarte's hip, a step behind like some kind of maidservant, as the group crossed the open field and circled to the front of the mound. Cam focused on the woman. Though olive-skinned like her brother, there was not much family resemblance. Where he boasted a round face with wide nose and mouth, her features were more classical—high cheekbones, strong chin, slightly upturned nose. But the most striking thing about her was that her eyes were different colors—one a deep blue, the other a dark brown. Not that she looked up often to allow them to be seen. Cam had seen her offer a shy smile to Astarte while they walked. He guessed she was about his own age, mid-forties. Most would describe her as pretty, or perhaps even beautiful, though her social awkwardness and disheveled look made it the kind of beauty that men would not likely find attractive. And some might be scared off by the mismatched eyes.

Cam drew his attention back to the ancient wonder. "What are those stones that make up the front wall?" he asked Roberto.

"The façade is controversial, rebuilt in the 1970s. Nobody is sure what the exterior really looked like."

A dozen or so standing stones, many taller than Cam, ringed the mound. Amanda asked about them.

"Originally there were more, perhaps three dozen." Roberto shrugged. "Probably used to mark various astronomical events." He smiled. "But, of course, the mound is most famous for marking the winter solstice. Come."

Roberto led them toward the entryway, a doorway-sized gap in the facade. In front of the gap rested a massive horizontal boulder with a series of carved spirals covering its face. "The spiral," Roberto explained, "is an ancient symbol of the Goddess. These decorations tell us this was likely a shrine to her, the Earth Mother."

At this, Cam and Amanda both glanced over at Astarte. She had dropped to a knee and was tracing one of the spirals lightly with her forefinger. Emmy watched her for a few seconds before crouching next to her to do the same. "In ancient times," Astarte explained to her new friend, "all people worshiped the Earth Mother. The female was the giver of life."

Emmy nodded. Her hood had fallen back, but a dark blue bonnet covered her head. Astarte took her hand and together they stood.

"Notice the opening above the entryway," Roberto said as Cam snapped another picture and studied the opening. It looked like a transom window above an old office door.

Newgrange Entryway

Robert continued. "That aperture turns out to be the most important architectural feature in the entire mound. Come. I will explain." He rested a hand kindly on his sister's shoulder. "It's okay, I promise."

Roberto led them inside, through a narrow passageway toward the center of the mound. The passage walls were formed by five-foot high stone slabs, standing upright, most of them decorated with carved shapes—chevrons and lozenges and arcs in addition to more spirals. They moved slowly, the air dank and thick. After about sixty feet the passageway opened into an igloo-like domed chamber.

"Look. Corbelled," Amanda said as Cam snapped another picture.

Newgrange Chamber Corbelled Roof

Cam nodded. They had seen this identical style of construction—in which the stones overlapped each other as they climbed, finally meeting in the center at the dome's peak with a single capstone—in stone chambers in New England. "If I put you in the Upton Chamber, you wouldn't be able to tell the difference," Cam said, referring to a stone chamber near Boston which had been conclusively dated to predate Colonial settlement and which Cam and Amanda believed to have been built by Irish explorers visiting centuries before Columbus.

"Last week," Roberto explained, "on the winter solstice, the rising sun entered through the light box above the front door. The sun beam ran down the path of the passageway and illuminated this chamber." He turned to Astarte. "I bet you know what this signifies."

She swallowed and stood taller. "Traditionally the sun was considered a male deity. And the earth was the female. On the winter solstice, when the world was getting darker and everything was dying off, the ancient people needed a way for life to be reborn. That's what this is. The sun is the man. The passageway is the birth canal. And this chamber is the womb. The sun is fertilizing the womb."

"*Bellissimo*," Roberto clapped his hands once and beamed. "Life is reborn. I could not have said it better myself."

"Is the time exact?" Amanda asked.

"No." He shook his head. "The light enters four minutes after sunrise."

Cam nodded. "The wobble of the earth." He and other researchers had documented similar imperfections in the alignments at America's Stonehenge, an ancient calendar in stone in southern New Hampshire believed to date back approximately 3,500 years, to the time of the Pharaohs and the Exodus from Egypt. The earth wobbled in its rotation, like a child's top, causing these ancient alignments to become slightly askew.

"Precisely," Roberto responded. "Computer calculations show that five thousand years ago, when the chamber was built, the light would have entered the chamber exactly at sunrise."

"Are there other alignments, like for the summer solstice?" Amanda asked. Other sites like Stonehenge focused on the summer solstice rather than the winter, celebrating the sun at its most powerful.

Roberto held up a finger. "Yes, but not here at Newgrange. We are in an area called the Boyne Valley. This small area, only about three square miles, has dozens of mounds, including two other massive ones like Newgrange. Plus standing stones and chambers and other enclosures. The two other large mounds, called Knowth and Dowth, are oriented to mark other astronomical events. Before they collapsed, Dowth marked the winter solstice sunset, and Knowth the equinoxes. My guess is that at one time there were mounds and stone circles all around this valley marking the key occurrences of the year—sunrise and sunset on the solstices and on both equinoxes. Perhaps also the cross-quarter days." He paused to make sure they understood that the cross-quarter days marked the halfway point between solstices and equinoxes. Cam nodded for him to continue. "The people would simply move from sacred site to sacred site, depending on the time of year."

Astarte responded. "So it's like instead of having one church, they had a different church for every holiday."

Roberto beamed. "Yes." Clearly he was passionate about these sites and appreciated a captivated audience. He led them back down the passageway toward the entrance. "Now I will give you time to look at the art on the base stones, called kerbstones." He turned to Cam. "But, before I do so, I will offer you one more piece of knowledge."

He waited for Cam to ask for it, a self-satisfied smile on his face. "And what is that?" Cam complied.

"From our correspondence, you told me you were interested in the Knights Templar. And specifically how they might have been influenced by these ancient megalithic sites."

"That's right," Cam said. "We are all interested in that."

They emerged out of the mound, to the light of day.

Roberto took a deep breath. "I know that the Templars were closely affiliated with the Cistercian monks, yes?"

"Yes," Cam said. "They were sister orders. Bernard de Clairvaux, who later became Saint Bernard, founded the Cistercians and wrote the charter for the Templars. They were essentially two sides of the same coin—the Cistercians prayed and farmed, while the Templars fought and traded."

"You said the Cistercians farmed. What if I told you they farmed *here*, in the Boyne Valley? *Here*, amidst these burial mounds?"

Cam blinked. "Really?"

"The Cistercians owned all this land, all these mounds, for hundreds of years, beginning in the twelfth century. This was where they built their first abbey in all of Ireland."

Amanda made the obvious connection. "They would have known about the alignments, about the ancient religions. Cam, that could be where the Templars came up with the idea for the Newport Tower winter solstice alignment. On the shortest day of the year, the sun—at around nine o'clock, just like here—rises and passes through an aperture to allegorically fertilize an object in the womb, marking the rebirth of the sun." Her green eyes fired in the sunlight. "It's the same thing. One's a tower and one's a mound, but the allegory is identical. Fertilization. Rebirth. The male and female together giving life." She exhaled. "It really is quite extraordinary."

"And I think it gets even better," Cam said quietly, trying to hide his excitement. Something in the recesses of his brain called to him. Could it really be? The back of his neck burned. "Roberto, what was the name of the abbey? The one here in the Boyne Valley?"

"Mellifont. Mellifont Abbey."

Amanda gasped. She understood as well. "What?" Astarte asked.

Cam replied, "I've been corresponding with an architect who believes that the Mellifont Abbey lavabo is the architectural model for the Newport Tower. It's in ruins now, but it matches almost perfectly.

Stone construction featuring eight Romanesque arches. Technically it's an octagon rather than a circle, but the similarities are striking." He found an image on his phone.

Mellifont Abbey Lavabo

They stared at the image. Amanda broke the silence. "Cam, that would explain so much. We've always thought the Tower inspiration came from Scotland. But perhaps it came from here. From Mellifont Abbey. The Cistercians would have accompanied the Templars on any journey to North America—they would have served as scribes and farmers."

Cam smiled. The Tower's architecture and its winter solstice alignment both could be traced back to Mellifont Abbey. "And, it turns out, maybe the Cistercians served as architects also."

✝

Roberto's wife Kaitlyn had packed them a picnic lunch. Astarte watched as Emmy, her head down, helped her brother spread a blanket in the sun not far from the Newgrange entrance. Acting as if he owned the place, he unpacked sandwiches, chips, fruit and drinks. When he finished handing out the food, Emmy lowered herself slowly to the ground next to Astarte, her poncho billowing around her.

As impressed as Astarte was by the ancient burial mound, which her mom had explained was at its core a shrine to Mother Earth and the cycles of the seasons, she was equally fascinated by the woman-girl with the different colored eyes. She had once read a book about a six-year-old girl turned into a vampire—her body never grew beyond its childhood size, yet her mind continued to mature, trapping a woman inside a girl's body. The opposite was true of Emmy. Though fully grown, she viewed the world through a child's eyes. When Emmy saw a handsome man or a movie with people kissing, did she feel the same things Astarte felt now when Raja's thigh rubbed against hers? Astarte shuddered. It was hard enough to figure all this out as a teenager. But with the mind of an eight-year-old? No wonder she had run away when they first drove up. And no wonder she always seemed to hide inside the hood of her cloak.

Emmy's sandwich had the crusts cut off, and she picked at it the way a child did when she knew she had to finish it to get to dessert. After finishing two-thirds, she looked up at her brother, who sighed and nodded. He handed her a pair of lollipops, one red and one purple. She in turn offered them to Astarte, who chose the red one. Emmy quickly went to work on hers, turning her face away from the others to show Astarte her purple tongue. It was actually pretty gross, sort of like a cow's, but Astarte swallowed and played along and flashed a red tongue back at her new friend.

Roberto interrupted their game. "After lunch I will bring you to another burial mound. One that only I know about. This one is oriented toward the winter solstice sunset. We are only a week past the solstice, so the alignment is still mostly, well, in line. Yes?"

"Sounds wonderful," Amanda replied.

They finished lunch, walked back to Roberto's truck, and bounced their way across his land to the farmhouse, Astarte and Emmy in the back again. Astarte used the time to learn more.

"So how long have you lived here?"

Emmy had a habit of looking down whenever she spoke. Perhaps shyness, perhaps embarrassment about her eyes. Either way, combined with the hood, it made it almost impossible to make eye contact.

"When I was a little girl we lived in Italy. In Rome. And before that Roberto says we lived in Milan, but I don't remember Milan."

"Do you remember Rome?"

"Yes. My father was a counter for the Vatican. And Roberto was his assistant."

Astarte leaned lower to look up into her face. "Counter? Do you mean accountant?"

She blinked and nodded. "Yes. Sorry. Accountant."

"Don't worry. You speak very good English."

"My brother does not like it when I speak Italian. He says it is not fair to Aunt Kaitlyn." She swallowed. "Anyway, when my parents died, Roberto and I came to Ireland."

It was weird that she called her sister-in-law her aunt. But that was probably a fairer description of their relationship. "Did they die together?"

"Yes. In a car crash."

Astarte decided to show respect and not ask for more details. "How long have you been here?"

"Since I was twelve. I'm forty-six now."

Over thirty years of a little girl not having birthday parties, not going to school, not even having playmates. Growing older but not growing up. Astarte shuddered again. Imprisoned. That's what she was. "When you moved here, was that after your accident?"

Emmy nodded again. "Yes. I think I was nine when I hit my head. I fell off the swings at school." She shifted uncomfortably on the wheel well. "But I don't remember that."

"Well," Astarte said cheerfully, "I think you're lucky to live on a farm like this. Do you like the animals?"

Emmy brightened. "Yes. Especially the sheep. I get to help shear them in the spring. That's when we do it, so they don't get too hot in the summer."

They pulled to a stop in front of the Milano Farm.

"This time we travel on the main roads," announced Roberto, helping them down, "so we will need to take both cars."

✛

Amanda drove the rental car, content to listen as Astarte and Emmy chatted in the back while Cam rode in the pickup with Roberto.

Out of the blue, Emmy dropped a bombshell. "Are you friends with the man with the sword? He's from America also."

Amanda's eyes widened in the front seat, but she swallowed her reaction as Astarte caught her eye. Astarte replied, her voice even, "What man with the sword?"

"He came yesterday. Last night. It looked like an umbrella, but it was really a sword. He showed my brother some designs on the metal part."

"That sounds neat. My father does have a friend with a sword like that. Do you know why he came to your house?"

Emmy shrugged. "He said something about a treasure. I was in the kitchen listening. But then Aunt Kaitlyn told me it wasn't polite to bees-drop when people are talking."

Amanda swallowed a giggle, but Astarte remained poker-faced. "I love searching for treasure." She leaned closer conspiratorially. "Does your brother know where some is buried?"

"I don't know. Maybe. But since he used to work in the Vatican, he knows a lot of secrets. I heard them talking about Archbishop Marcinkus." She pronounced the name wrong, adding a few extra vowels to make it sound Italian, but Amanda understood what she meant. "I remember him. He was my father's boss." Emmy turned and looked out the window. "But I didn't like him. He was mean to my father. He called him 'Mr. Spaghetti Arms.' And he used to make him stay at work late."

"Why Mr. Spaghetti Arms?"

"I think because he wasn't very strong. Not like Archbishop Marcinkus. They called him the Gorilla. They say he saved the pope once from an angry mob all by himself."

That seemed to end the conversation, though Amanda's mind raced as she followed the black pickup truck through the Irish countryside. Archbishop Paul Marcinkus was an American, from Chicago. More importantly, Cam had mentioned him as being linked to the Catskills artifacts and the Templar treasure. It could not be a coincidence that Brian was asking about him.

☩

Cam sensed Amanda had something important to tell him. She pulled him aside as soon as they had parked on the shoulder of the road next to some pasture land, apparently the location of Roberto's secret burial mound. "So Brian was here. Yesterday. With the sword." She recounted everything Emmy had said, including the part about Archbishop Marcinkus. "Hard to believe it's just a coincidence."

Cam chewed on his lip, studying the horizon as Roberto led them up a rise past yet more grazing sheep. Brian knew Monsignor Marcotte, and it was Marcotte who recommended Roberto's inn. This was possibly all innocent, with Marcotte suggesting Brian ask Roberto about Archbishop Marcinkus. But he was more inclined to side with Amanda on this. "I don't believe in coincidences," he said as they dropped back a bit to talk in private.

"So what's going on?"

"Clearly Brian thinks the sword—that is, the symbols on the blade—lead to a Templar treasure. He must have heard the same rumors I did, that Marcinkus knew about it also and was hot on its trail."

"Wasn't Marcinkus part of the Vatican Banking Scandal?"

"Not just part of. At the center. So much at the center that some people believe Marcinkus actually assassinated Pope John Paul I as a way to cover up the scandal and save his job."

"Really? That's a serious charge."

"I know. It was in all the Italian papers. Anyway, despite Marcinkus' efforts to cover everything up, eventually it blew up in his face. This was in the early 1980s."

"Emmy said her father was an accountant working for Marcinkus. I wonder what he knew." Amanda paused. "And if Marcinkus murdered the pope, would he hesitate to kill an accountant who knew too much?"

The question hung in the late afternoon darkness, Cam wondering whether Brian knew more than he was letting on about a possible Templar treasure in the Catskill Mountains. When Amanda and he had searched there five years ago, following maps and clues given to them by Astarte's now-dead uncle, they had been focused on locating ancient artifacts described in a Templar travel log recounting a secret journey across the Atlantic in 1178. The travel log had been discovered by an American black ops team in war-torn Italy after World War II, the manuscript apparently having originally been the property of the Vatican but somehow lost during the chaos of the war. The team brought the manuscript back to America and, with the help of experts such as Astarte's uncle, followed the maps and clues left in the travel log to find artifacts proving the authenticity of the history-altering excursion to the Catskill's Hunter Mountain. Though they were successful in locating many artifacts (and later Cam and Amanda located others), pieces of the puzzle—including a purported Templar treasure—remained lost to history. Or not.

In 2017, historian Zena Halpern, with the help of Cam's friend Ruthie, gave new life to the mystery by describing the Templar journey in great detail. Her book had refocused attention on the possibility of a lost treasure, and amateur treasure hunters like Brian had descended upon the trails of Hunter Mountain to follow the clues contained in Ms. Halpern's narrative. Clues which, based on Brian's visit to Roberto, apparently led here to Ireland.

Cam glanced at Amanda and Astarte. This trip was supposed to be about Amanda healing and Astarte experiencing the ancient pagan worship sites. Plus some quality family time. But apparently the fates had other plans.

His mind turned back to the 1178 travel journal. One of the fascinating things about it, and the thing that in Cam's mind conclusively proved its authenticity, was the fact that it was purchased by top Vatican officials in the mid 1990s from the then-elderly remaining member of the black ops team. Actually, 'purchased' was probably not the correct word. The Vatican official conducting the negotiation made a generous offer, and also made it clear that it was an offer that should not be refused. The identity of this official? Archbishop Paul Marcinkus. Marcinkus had returned to the U.S. from Rome after being disgraced, but otherwise not punished, in the Vatican Banking Scandal of the late 1980s; the scandal saw the Vatican Bank charged with laundering money for organized crime and be forced to pay $240 million in penalties. As Cam and Amanda had discussed, a 1984 book accused Marcinkus of assassinating Pope John Paul I to save his job and, more importantly, avoid jail time. Another book accused him of ordering the assassination of Soviet leader Yuri Andropov. Still another tied him to the deaths of fellow Vatican bankers involved in the scandal—one dying of cyanide poisoning and the other found hanging from London's Blackfriars Bridge. Cam shook his head. No wonder the surviving member of the black ops team had not refused Marcinkus' offer to purchase the journal.

From what Cam had read, Marcinkus had long been tracking the Templar's Catskills treasure. He turned his full attention to it upon his return to the United States in 1990 with the purchase of the Templar travel journal. But poor health apparently prevented him from completing his pursuit of the treasure. Now, a generation later, the mystery of the Templar treasure seemed to be bubbling to the surface again.

All of this passed through Cam's mind as Roberto led them toward a large oak tree atop a gentle rise. Did Roberto know anything about this mystery? According to what Amanda had heard, Roberto's father worked for Marcinkus as an accountant at the Vatican Bank and had died suddenly. Another curious coincidence.

Cam pulled Amanda back as the group marched. "Am I remembering this correctly? In Zena Halpern's book, doesn't she mention the swagger sword and say it was connected to the Vatican?"

"Yes."

"Did she say Marcinkus ended up with it?"

"I can't be certain, but that rings a bell."

But the timing was off. "So that would mean Marcinkus bought the journals *after* he already had the swagger sword with the symbols carved on it."

She nodded. "I don't see a problem with that. He probably needed the journals to understand what the symbols meant."

"Then who carved the symbols onto the sword in the first place?"

"The book said the swagger sword dated back to the 1930s. Maybe whoever knew what the symbols meant died in the war. Somehow Marcinkus found the sword, but didn't know how to interpret it."

"Okay. Makes sense. But that would indicate someone back in the thirties knew about the treasure. What if they already found it?"

"Then why bother carving the clues onto the blade of a sword?"

He shrugged. "Good point. We're just going in circles."

She took his arm. "Enough of this." She gestured toward where Roberto stood between the tree and a standing stone wedged against the side of the hill. On one knee, he pawed away a pile of grass, leaves, acorns and small stones. Turning sideways, he grinned and ducked into what apparently was the entry to the secret mound. Amanda tugged Cam. "Come on. Let's appreciate what we're about to see. It could be magical."

First Emmy, then Astarte and Amanda, and finally Cam—careful not to put too much weight on his injured arm—followed Roberto through the car window–sized opening in the side of the hill. Once inside, they slid down a dirt incline for a few feet to a narrow passageway lined with massive stone slabs. Roberto shone his light on the walls and ceiling. "Imagine. This was built over 5,000 years ago." Crouching, they waddled down the passage. Twenty feet in, the channel opened into a round, domed chamber similar to the beehive chamber in Newgrange. Its walls were, like the passageway, comprised of stone slabs, with the domed roof built in the overlapping corbelled fashion. Roberto shone his light, this time on an egg-shaped slab of clear quartz, about the size of a loaf of bread, set in the wall at the far end of the chamber. Near the center of the wall, but not exactly so. Just like at the Newport Tower.

"Note this is the only quartz stone in the entire chamber," Roberto said.

Amanda nodded. "That's where the sunbeam will fall. They probably set the quartz in last, after they saw exactly where the sunbeam hit."

"Correct." Roberto stood aside. "Today, the old oak serves a useful purpose in keeping this chamber hidden. But its branches can also block the illumination." He smiled. "I think the Earth Mother will forgive me that I removed a few branches. Gently, of course."

Astarte asked, "What's this chamber called?"

"It has no name," Roberto replied. "I found it myself, and I only bring special guests to see it."

"Can we name it?"

"Why don't you and Emmy decide together on a name?" He checked his watch. "We have about fifteen minutes before the light comes in."

Cam and Amanda shared a smile, watching as Astarte pulled Emmy to the far side of the chamber to confer in private. The trip was serving its purpose—Amanda was almost back to her usual merry self. After a few minutes, Astarte cleared her throat. "We think *Quartzbarrow* is a good name." She explained, "A barrow is another name for a burial mound. And, well, the quartz is obvious."

"Excellent." Roberto brought his hands together. "*Quartzbarrow* it is." He pulled a blanket from the rucksack he had been carrying and spread it on the dirt floor. "Now, let us wait and watch. Remember, we are a few days past the solstice so the illumination will be slightly off."

Ten minutes later, the light from the setting sun began to shine through the barrow opening and illuminate the floor of the passageway. Roberto snapped off his flashlight. The light beam crept along, inching its way toward the domed chamber interior like an incoming tide.

Suddenly the slow creep became a sweeping onslaught as the setting sun plunged to the horizon. Within seconds the sun cast a light beam onto the quartz stone. The quartz glowed to life, illuminating the chamber in a soft radiance.

"Amazing," Amanda breathed. She took Cam's hand, squeezed it, and leaned her head onto his shoulder. "This is just what I needed."

✝

They returned to Milano Farm just after five o'clock on Tuesday. Emmy tugged on Astarte's sleeve. "Usually I have to help Aunt Kaitlyn make dinner. But tonight she said I can play with you instead."

"Okay." It was the least she could do for the girl-woman.

In the twilight Emmy led her to a red wooden barn. She pushed open a wide door and flicked on a light. The barn had been converted to a garage, with a concrete floor and a number of pieces of farm equipment and tools scattered about. Emmy led them to a cleared out rectangular area in the back corner of the barn, its borders outlined by tall metal shelves. "Roberto lets me use this as my play area." She pointed to the floor. "Hopscotch is my favorite. Want to play?"

On the floor, in chalk, she had drawn a hopscotch board. But rather than the usual numbering, with one closest to the start line and ten at the far end, Emmy had numbered the board in a seemingly random fashion. "I'll go first," she said, pulling back her hood, her hair still secured by a dark bonnet. She flipped a beanbag onto the first square and called out its number. "Two!" She proceeded along, skipping some squares in a haphazard fashion. She moved stiffly, befitting her forty-six-year-old body, but with the exuberance of youth. It reminded Astarte of the way some adults moved when they were drunk. "One! Seven!" When she reached the last square, she yelled, "Three!" Then she repeated the sequence. "Two, one, seven, three," and concluded by lifting her arms in the air and declaring, "Emmy!"

She returned to the start line and handed the bag to Astarte. "Is that how you want me to do it? The same order you did?"

Emmy nodded. "Yes. Please."

Astarte followed the girl-woman's path. It was more challenging than normal hopscotch, because by skipping squares, many of the jumps were longer. Perhaps Emmy changed the rules to challenge her adult body. When she finished, Astarte called out the numbers and her name, "Two, one, seven, three, Astarte!"

Emmy stomped her foot. Her mismatched eyes narrowed. "No. That's not how you play."

Astarte wasn't sure what she had done wrong. "Am I supposed to call out your name then?"

"Yes. Do it again."

Astarte rolled her eyes but held her tongue. "Okay." Apparently doing this the right way was really important to Emmy. Astarte repeated the course. "Two, one, seven, three, Emmy!"

Emmy clapped, her face aglow. "Yes. That was perfect. Let's play again."

They spent a half hour playing, always the same pattern, always calling out the same victory chant when they succeeded in not stumbling or landing on a line: "Two, one, seven, three, Emmy!"

Finally Amanda appeared. She watched for a few minutes as Astarte and Emmy each reached the final square and called out the victory chant. "Come wash up for dinner," she said. "Did you have fun?"

Emmy took Astarte's hand as they walked through the barn. As if in answer, she called out, "Two, one, seven, three, Emmy!"

Astarte sighed. That chant would echo in her head for weeks.

✛

Roberto excused his family immediately after dinner, explaining that farm life began early. "The sun does not rise until almost nine, but the animals are not so lazy." Astarte said goodnight to Emmy, opting out of trying to hug the woman-child and settling instead for a wave and smile. She joined Cam and Amanda in the guest wing of the house where they did a jigsaw puzzle and watched the news in the common room between their two bedrooms.

"I asked Kaitlyn if I could go with her to the farm stand tomorrow before breakfast," Amanda said at around nine. "I'm going to call it a night."

Astarte read in bed for a while and then tried to sleep, but every time she closed her eyes the hopscotch chant sounded in her head. When she finally drifted off, the hopscotch game turned into a nightmare: Astarte sat in a swing, arching higher and higher until she soared so high that she turned upside down. She tried to hold on, but her fingers slipped and she spilled out, headfirst, the ground rushing at her from below. As she fell, a group of girls playing hopscotch nearby looked up and grinned, chanting, "Two, one, seven, three, Emmy!" Astarte startled awake just before crashing into the ground, only to fall back asleep and have the dream repeat itself. Finally, in the middle of the night, she kicked the covers off and went in search of a glass of water.

A doorway from their common room led to the main part of the house. Astarte quickly found the kitchen and filled a glass, gulping greedily. When she turned the faucet off, she heard a bed creaking and some low moaning. It sounded similar to Cam and Amanda when they made the floorboards squeak, but was coming from the innkeeper's side of the house. Probably Roberto and Kaitlyn. For some reason her mind turned to Raja. Would she want him atop her like she had seen in the movies? The thought made her shudder. The idea of someone on top of her, controlling her, scared her. But if she were on top, kissing Raja, maybe that would be okay…

A sound down the hall, in the living room, startled her. Was Emmy awake? Astarte peered out in the dim light. A woman sat in a chair, backlit by the moon filtering through a window, working something in her hands. Her head turned, perhaps sensing Astarte. Kaitlyn. Holding what looked to be prayer beads. But if Kaitlyn were in the living room, what was the noise Astarte heard? She ducked into the shadows. She didn't like Kaitlyn, and for some reason now felt guilty intruding into their living area. She tiptoed back to her room. Whatever sound she had heard before had stopped. Maybe it had been her imagination.

But she knew she would not sleep. She dreaded the idea of the dream haunting her again. And the thought of Raja, beneath her on a bed, had washed away any desire for sleep.

Chapter 6

Amanda's phone alarm woke her at six. After doing some stretching and calisthenics in the common room of the inn, she took a shower, grabbed an energy bar, and said goodbye to Cam. She let Astarte sleep.

"When it gets lighter, I'm going for a run," Cam said.

It was seven, but still almost pitch-black. "Okay. I think breakfast is eight-thirty. I'm going to the market with Kaitlyn. I was surprised she agreed to take me. She's not exactly Miss Hospitality."

"No. Clearly this inn is Roberto's baby, not hers. She never looks very happy." Cam smiled. "Maybe she wants your bright personality to cheer her up."

"More likely she needs me to help carry groceries."

Kaitlyn was waiting for Amanda in the kitchen. "I think your daughter came in here last night to get some water." She looked as if she hadn't slept much. But more than that she looked unhappy.

"Um. Okay."

"I put glasses in the Jacks for you."

"The Jacks?"

"The toilet."

Right. The Irish didn't call it a loo or bathroom. "At home we only drink the tap water from our kitchen faucet, where we have a filter. Astarte probably came to the kitchen out of habit." Amanda wasn't sure why she had to defend this.

Kaitlyn sighed, as if this were just another of many crosses she had to bear in life, flicked on an outside light, and led Amanda to the driveway. They climbed into the pickup truck and drove the ten miles into town in silence. Just as Amanda was beginning to wish she had stayed home, Kaitlyn raised her chin and spoke. "The muppets at the market are horrible gossips. Pay no heed to what they say about us."

"Okay."

Kaitlyn parked on the side of the road in front of a large blue tent containing a few dozen stalls displaying fresh produce, baked goods and dairy products. Only a third of the tent was full—Amanda guessed that in the summer it would be more crammed. "Fresh bread, two loaves," Kaitlyn instructed.

Amanda wandered off on her task, content to be free to immerse herself in the local culture. She followed her nose.

A heavy-set older woman, her grayish-brown hair pulled back and tied with a yellow ribbon, offered a wide smile. A pair of eyeglasses hung from a cord at her chest, the stems framing a large but simple silver cross she wore atop her floral smock. "Tastes even better than it smells," she said with a thick, sing-song accent.

"Are they all soda breads?"

"Aye, of course. Baked them myself." She pointed. "I recommend the spotted dog."

Amanda thought she had heard wrong, but then noticed the raisins in the brown bread. She also noticed the cross shape lightly carved into the top of the loaf.

The baker read her thoughts. "Is tradition to cut a cross into the bread, to let the devil out."

Amanda smiled. "I'll take two loaves, thanks. And, as you said, please hold the devil."

The woman winked and leaned forward. "Speaking of which, I see you're with Mrs. Fulcani. Are you boarding at her farm?"

"Yes."

The woman crossed herself. "Careful of that one. She's a local lass, but not well-liked around here. She's too good for us now that she married herself a foreigner."

"How so?"

The vendor explained how Kaitlyn went to Dublin every Sunday, to Saint Patrick's, for mass. "As if our little church is not good enough for her." She arched an eye. "Or maybe her sins are too weighty. I hear the bishop himself takes her confession."

What could Kaitlyn possibly have to confess to? Amanda didn't like to gossip, but the words poured out of her mouth before she could stop them. "She seems unhappy."

"Aye. Cursed, I think." The baker reached for a glass shaker on the counter and tossed salt over her shoulder.

The conversation continued. They had to go back and forth a few times because of the woman's accent, but apparently Kaitlyn's parents died when she was a teenager. She was supposed to join a convent, until Roberto arrived. "Next thing you know, they're getting married."

She sniffed. "And not even with child. Never seen such a long-faced bride." The baker leaned forward and whispered, "The sister has the mark of the devil, you know."

"You mean her eyes?"

"One blue, one brown." She crossed herself again. "Sharing a house with her, I suppose I'd have the bishop hear my confession too."

Enough of this superstition. Amanda paid for the bread. "Thank you."

The vendor patted Amanda's hand as she took the loaves. "Like I said, be careful around that one."

✠

Cam leaned back, riding shotgun again while Amanda drove the rental car. Astarte sat behind him. They had eaten a big breakfast at the Milano Farm and thanked their hosts, Emmy stooping to engulf Astarte in an awkward but heartfelt hug. "Will you be my Facebook friend?" she asked shyly.

"Of course." Astarte flashed a big smile. "You'll be my first friend from outside America. What's your Facebook name?"

Emmy looked to the ground and chewed her lip. "You could probably guess. It's *2173Emmy*."

Astarte took her hand and squeezed. "Perfect. I won't forget that." She arched an eyebrow toward Cam and Amanda. "Ever."

With the memory of a cloaked, hooded, sad-faced Emmy standing in the driveway waving goodbye still fresh in their minds, they headed west. "How long before we get to Galway?" Astarte asked. Not as sunny as yesterday, it remained temperate, already pushing fifty degrees. And no traffic to speak of, though it should have been midweek morning rush hour.

Cam glanced at his guide book. His arm boasted a yellow and purple welt, and it throbbed at times, but he seemed to have escaped serious injury. "It's less than three hours, but I thought we could go leisurely and make stops along the way."

Amanda teased him. "That's very generous of you. I know you're dying to get to Galway."

He was. The west coast of Ireland, of which Galway was the major city, seemed tied to almost every journey, both real and legendary, across the Atlantic. Many people were familiar with the legend of

Brendan the Navigator, the monk purported to have crossed the Atlantic in an animal-skin boat in the sixth century. Cam and Amanda had studied many stone structures in New England—most particularly chambers that looked remarkably like burial mounds such as Newgrange, but on a smaller scale—which could have been built by Brendan or other Celtic visitors. But fewer people knew of the writings of Plutarch. Cam wondered if Amanda did.

"I've heard of Plutarch, I think. Roman, right?"

"Yes. He wrote about ancient voyages to the New World. He lived around 100 AD." Cam pulled his Kindle out of his pack. "Barry Fell gives a good summary of Plutarch's writings in *Saga America*." Fell was a Harvard professor whose 1976 book about ancient Celts voyaging to America, *America BC,* had been a bestseller.

"Okay, I'm listening."

"This is Fell quoting Plutarch," Cam read: "*Sail westward from Britain and you will pass three Island groups on a northwest bearing, where the sun sets in mid-summer. These are equidistant from one another, and also from an island called Ogygia, which lies in the arms of the ocean five days' sailing from Britain.*"

Amanda, who prided herself on her knowledge of the geography of the British Isles, jumped in. "So the three island groups are the Orkneys, Shetlands and Faeroes. And Ogygia is Iceland."

"Right. The description fits, and Iceland is about five days sail from Britain, assuming an ancient ship would sail around 100 miles per day." He read more. "*If you continue to sail westward for another 5000 stades, you will reach the northern coast of a continent that rims the great ocean.*"

"Ten stades is about one mile," Amanda said. "So another 500 miles."

"Yes."

"That puts us in southern Greenland."

"Agreed. Plutarch continued: *Then if you sail along this coast in a southward direction, you will pass a frozen sea.*"

"That's the southern part of the Davis Strait, between Labrador and Greenland. It's an impassable mass of floating ice in the winter."

"With you so far," Cam said. "Now things get a little confusing. Plutarch says you cross the frozen sea and come to *a land where Greeks have settled and intermarried with the native barbarians.* And he says this land is the same latitude as the Caspian Sea. The Caspian is roughly at between forty and forty-five degrees."

"So you're essentially talking the coast of New England."

"Right."

Astarte said, "But what about the Greeks?"

Cam smiled. "Fell figured it out. Plutarch says that the original source describing the journey is a Carthaginian sailor, and that the journey began in Carthage." He explained to Astarte that Carthage was one of the key Phoenicians trading ports, along the coast of northern Africa. "Most of the Phoenician ports were Greek-speaking, since Greek was the most popular language back then. So when Plutarch says Greeks, it's likely he is really talking about Greek-speaking Phoenicians. Carthaginians, from Carthage."

Amanda nodded. "This is big, Cam. This supports the theory that America's Stonehenge was built by the Phoenicians. I mean, Plutarch puts the Phoenicians in New England almost a thousand years before Christ."

They were getting off-topic, but it was a long drive, perfect for ferreting around in dusty corners of history.

"You know the counter-argument," Cam replied. "If the Phoenicians were in America, why is there no archeological evidence?"

Amanda slapped the steering wheel. "That argument is such a crock. First of all, when's the last time anyone did a dig? No matter how much evidence we show them, we can't get any of the university eggheads to get off their backsides. Last I checked, you can only find something in the ground by digging. And second, we're talking almost three thousand years ago. This isn't the desert—bones and wood decay. And third, who says there's no evidence? Go to America's Stonehenge. It's full of evidence—alignments, carvings, structures. And when we do find something, like a Roman coin, the so-called experts explain it away as an intrusion." She exhaled. "Remember that archeologist who said a seagull probably carried that Roman coin across the Atlantic and dropped it on the beach? Screw them. I'm sick of listening to fools."

Cam grinned. "Glad you're feeling better." It was the most worked up he'd seen her in months. And anger was definitely preferable to disinterest.

"I mean, at what point do people take their heads out of their … out of the sand?"

Astarte grinned. "You were going to say out of their asses, right?"

Amanda laughed. "No. I was not."

"Yes, you were."

"Don't argue with me, Astarte, or I'll make you walk to Galway."

Cam smiled. It was nice to have the feisty Amanda back. "You make a good point. In law school they taught us that, once we build the theory of our case, when new evidence comes in, it better fit that theory. If not, we need to rethink things. The theory has to account for all of the evidence, not just most of it. What's happening with our research is that pretty much every new piece of evidence we find fits right in. Like this Plutarch stuff. We're here in Ireland, thousands of miles away from both America and the Phoenician home-world, and we find evidence to help prove the ancient Phoenicians came to America, just like we thought." He smiled. "In my experience, that only happens when you're on the right track."

Chapter 7

Cam, Amanda and Astarte arrived in Galway late Wednesday afternoon and checked into the Meyrick Hotel, a 19th century Victorian landmark overlooking Eyre Square in the city center. Cam, figuring it was only for a few nights, had splurged for the executive suite on the fifth floor, with 12-foot ceilings, crystal chandeliers, and panoramic views of the city. According to the desk clerk, both John Wayne and Bing Crosby had slept in their room, though presumably neither was researching cross-Atlantic historical voyages.

Cam stepped back and watched Amanda take in the opulent furnishings. "Cam, this must be costing us a fortune."

"It's not. It's off-season, and the dollar's strong."

She flopped onto the four-poster bed. "Then let's never leave."

After cleaning up, they crossed Eyre Square to wander the city center, a labyrinth of narrow streets—most closed to vehicle traffic—crammed with shops, restaurants and pubs, with some structures dating back to medieval times. Cam said, "The reason I brought up Plutarch back in the car is because of Columbus. Columbus was trying to figure out how to cross the Atlantic, and what was on the other side, so he was studying the ancient writings, including Plutarch. Columbus came to Galway in the 1470s. From here he sailed to Iceland, and maybe beyond, following Plutarch's directions. I think that's why, later on, in 1492, he took a more southern route—he knew the northern route led to land that was not Asia."

Amanda bit her lip. "Didn't Columbus' sails have Templar crosses?"

"Nobody's ever been able to figure out why. But I think there may be some clues here in Galway."

They stopped for Amanda to take a picture sitting on the lap of a statue of Irish playwright Oscar Wilde. She kissed his bronze cheek, Cam pleased to see her fun-loving self reappearing. "You know what Wilde famously wrote?" she asked. "He wrote: 'Many people discovered America before Columbus, but most of them had the good sense to keep quiet about it.' Spot on, I'd venture to say."

81

Cam nodded. "Like I said, there seems to be a history here, especially on the west coast, of travelers crossing the Atlantic."

Astarte dragged Amanda into a souvenir shop while Cam, after making plans to meet them back at the hotel, continued toward the waterfront. He wanted to see the church in which Columbus supposedly prayed while visiting Galway in 1477. Cam didn't expect to learn much, but it struck him as odd that the explorer, not known for being particularly religious until much later in life, had been remembered by historians as spending time in prayer.

"Heading to St. Nicholas Church?"

Cam instinctively recoiled, quickly recovering and turning to see Brian loping along at his side. For a big guy who always seemed to lurch through life like a bear crashing through the forest, he had a rare ability to appear out of the blue, even with his signature green pants. "Yes, as a matter of fact. How did you know?"

"I beat you to it. Not much to see." Brian turned away. "I thought you were going to call me when you got here."

"What is this, middle school?" Cam shook his head. "We just arrived an hour ago."

"Well, an hour is a good chunk of the time I got left, you know?"

Cam sighed. Fair point. "How you feeling?"

"Shitty. I'm exhausted but I can't sleep because my guts feel like they're being eaten away by a million fire ants."

Cam glanced sideways at his childhood friend. Cancer sucked, and pancreatic cancer was one of the most deadly kinds. Cam's grandfather had died of it, spending his last few weeks living in their home when Cam was in high school. Brian looked as bad as he apparently felt, his skin alternating blotches of dull yellow and purplish pink, as if his face had served as a punching bag. And it didn't help that he hadn't shaved; random long gray whiskers protruded from his face like weeds on an unkempt lawn. Brian's face spoke volumes: If they were going to discover this treasure, it would have to be soon. "So did you find anything at the church?" Cam asked.

"Like I said, no. Columbus was here, he prayed, he left." Brian shrugged. "But you're better at this history shit than I am."

They angled off the main thoroughfare and stopped in front of a dark stone church. "Here it is," Brian said. "St. Nicholas."

Cam stopped twenty feet away to study the structure. After years of studying churches, he had developed a keen eye. "Look." He pointed above an archway to the right of the main entrance, oddly located at the side of the church rather than its end. "A skull and crossbones."

Skull and Crossbones, St. Nicholas Church, Galway

Brian grunted. "Like the pirates have on their flags? What's it called, a Jolly Roger?"

"The pirates stole it from the Templars. The Templars flew it on the flags of their ships. Then, when they got outlawed in 1307, some of them turned to piracy."

"So where'd the Templars get it from?"

"Most people think it was a reminder of their mortality, to keep them humble." Cam paused. "I also read it was because they never left a fallen comrade on the battle field and always brought at least his head and thigh bones back for burial. And it could be because they worshiped a skull, called Baphomet, which some people think is the head of John the Baptist. But nobody knows for sure."

Brian stared up at it. "Well, it seems strange to see it on a church."

Cam motioned toward the archway. "Looks like at one time this was the entrance. Then when they put an addition on they must have moved it. Let's go in. I wonder what's on the other side of that arch."

Cam paid the admission fee for both of them, too curious about the mysterious church to bother calling Brian on it. They wandered up the nave of the church toward the closed-off archway. "Hey, look at that tomb," Brian called. He pointed to a jail cell-sized alcove tucked into a wall where the nave transitioned into the chancel of the church. A stone tomb rested on the floor in the center of the alcove. "I think the skull-and-crossbones are on the other side of that wall."

Cam glanced at the informational sheet he had been given when paying the admission. The back of his neck tingled as he read. "It says here that's a Crusader's Tomb. The inscription is in French. The cross is stylized so that its arms form fleurs-de-lis, those three-sided lily flowers. It dates back to 1320." *1320? Really?* Just after the Templars fell. He snapped a picture.

Crusader's Tomb, St. Nicholas Church, Galway

Cam read further from the sheet. "Apparently this section of the church is the original structure." He pointed to the left wall of the alcove, only a few feet from the Crusader's Tomb. "In fact, that wall is angled slightly off, different than the main nave of the church."

"Then was this originally a Templar church?"

"Just this section. Probably built in 1320. That would be just after they were outlawed. Lots of them left France and fled to the other parts of Europe."

"Well, that explains the French writing."

Cam's mind turned to Columbus and his Templar ties. Not only did Columbus' sails bear Templar crosses, but his father-in-law was himself an explorer and member of the Knights of Christ, the Portuguese branch of the Templars. Furthermore, Columbus lived on the island of Madeira for a number of years along with the grandson of Scottish Prince Henry Sinclair. They both married into the Perestrello family. Cam explained this all to Brian. "Sinclair came from a long line of Templars himself. He's the guy who came to Westford in 1399 and carved the Westford Knight. Many historians think that Columbus got Sinclair's maps from Sinclair's grandson. And that he got other Templar maps and charts from his father-in-law as part of the dowry."

Brian took two steps away from the Crusader's Tomb, examined the floor, and said, "Maybe there are other clues."

"Let's look around."

Brian kicked at the floor. "Cam, listen to me. Don't look around. Look *down*."

He was standing on a stone slab, set into the floor, one of perhaps a dozen grave slabs built into the floor in this section of the church. This slab, however, was decorated with Templar crosses. Excitedly, Cam dropped to a knee and ran his fingers along one of them. "No doubt, these are Templar." He glanced around, tried to imagine how this section of the church—the original, Templar section of 1320— would have looked before the massive additions. And also tried to imagine Christopher Columbus, kneeling and examining the crosses just as he was doing now.

Brian had wandered off. As Cam stood he noticed the six massive columns, three on each side of the nave, supporting the arcades above. He blinked. Five of them were circular and plain. But the sixth, closest to the Crusader's Tomb and not far from the Templar crosses, was markedly different. The pillar had been divided into four quadrants, each quadrant grooved out so that, viewed in cross-section, the column formed a Templar cross. Cam smiled and shook his head. "Look at that." He studied the pillar, then had a thought. He glanced at his information sheet to get his bearings: The Templar pillar was at the southeast corner of the six-column arrangement, closest to Jerusalem. It was exactly the type of architectural symbolism the Templars would have employed. In fact, it was similar in concept to the Apprentice Pillar that Prince Henry Sinclair's grandson, William, built into Roslyn Chapel in the 1450s—in the southeast corner of the chapel, in fact.

Cam took a deep breath. He wished Amanda, and her sharp eye, were here; he would return with her later. A skull-and-crossbones, a Crusader's tomb, Templar crosses on the floor, a Roslyn Chapel-like pillar. And they had only been inside for twenty minutes. Who knew what other secrets St. Nicholas Church held?

✝

Amanda allowed Cam to lead her and Astarte along the crowded streets of Galway, dodging street musicians and jugglers. She loved Cam's passion and his energy, and it was never more apparent that when he was on a research quest. Home, and the smothering sadness she felt there, seemed blissfully far away.

"Where are we going?"

He grinned. "To church."

Astarte rolled her eyes. "As if."

"No. Seriously. There's something you guys have to see. Then we can go to dinner."

Cam had ditched Brian, keeping his promise not to allow him to ruin their family vacation. But Amanda guessed they had not seen the last of him. Practically jogging, Cam led Amanda and Astarte to the Crusader's tomb, then showed them the Templar crosses on the floor and imbedded into the pillar. "I think this corner of the church was originally a Templar church built in 1320," he said breathlessly. "And on the outside wall there's a skull-and-crossbones."

Amanda wasn't sure why he was so excited. "Okay. But we already knew the Templars spread all over Europe after being outlawed. Maybe not the western coast of Ireland, but..." She shrugged, leaving the thought hanging.

Cam took a deep breath. "Sorry, I'm not being clear. The point isn't that the Templars were here, in Galway. The point is that this is where Columbus came to, quote-unquote, pray." Cam swept the space with his arm. "Was he praying, or did he come to get information? Maybe maps, charts?"

Now she understood. "Didn't you say earlier that he continued on, to Iceland?"

"Yes, that was in 1477. But maybe he went beyond Iceland. Somewhere down near the harbor is a sculpture of a seabird given by the city of Genoa to Galway, dedicated to Columbus." Cam looked at his phone to a page he had saved. "It reads, *On these shores around 1477 the Genoese sailor Christoforo Colombo found sure signs of land beyond the Atlantic.*"

"Sure signs of land beyond the Atlantic, huh?" Amanda repeated.

Cam nodded. "I thought he was following Plutarch's directions. But maybe he was following the Templars, or more accurately, Prince Henry Sinclair. Not just to Iceland, but beyond. Like the plaque says."

"Seems logical."

"Before I met you guys," Cam said, "I did some quick research. In his diary Columbus writes about seeing fifty-foot tides after leaving Iceland. Some historians think he went all the way to Nova Scotia."

"That would be the continent beyond the Atlantic," Amanda said. "But if he knew about North America, why then did he think he found Asia in 1492?"

Cam shook his head. "That's a mystery. Maybe he thought if he skirted south he would bypass the continent up north. Either way, I need to look into this more. It seems like Columbus was thinking about an Atlantic crossing way back in 1477."

Astarte had been quiet during their conversation. She weighed in. "What about the people from Cathay? That might be why Columbus thought he could sail to India."

Amanda and Cam both turned. "People from Cathay?" Amanda repeated.

"Yes. Cathay is what they used to call China." She held up her phone. "While you guys were talking, I Googled Columbus and Galway. I found this article. Columbus made notes in a book about his time in Galway. Here's what he wrote: *People from Cathay come towards the west. We saw many remarkable things and particularly in*

Galway in Ireland a man and a woman on two pieces of driftwood of the most extraordinary appearance."

"So Columbus saw Chinese bodies washing ashore here in Galway?" Amanda asked.

"Could be Inuit," Cam replied. "They look Asian."

Astarte had the final word. "I think that's why Columbus thought he could sail to China. Because of the bodies on the driftwood."

✝

Cam had wandered off to explore the north side of the nave of St. Nicholas Church, where more grave slabs were imbedded into the church floor, while Amanda and Astarte climbed the stairs to view the gallery. He spotted the thugs from the Dublin florist truck as soon as they entered the church. *Shit.* Before he could hide himself, they in turn spotted him.

Cam made a split-second decision: He pushed through the side exit into a narrow alley and ran, hoping to lure the men away from Amanda and Astarte.

His mind raced. Both men had been smoking in the florist van. How much stamina would they have for a long run? And the burly guy with the club hardly looked like a distance runner. Cam sprinted along the church wall onto a main street running along the River Corrib, roiling with rapids. To his left, the city bustled. Crowds, traffic, congestion. He cut right instead, onto a wooden pedestrian walkway on the near bank of the river. The Riverside path. He had planned to run along it in the morning, in fact. Heavy footsteps thundered behind him. Apparently he was going to get his workout in tonight instead.

He paused for a second, straining to hear. Clap, clap, thud, thud. *Good.* Two pair of footsteps rather than one. At least Amanda and Astarte were safe. He tore ahead, searching for an escape route or weapon or some kind of plan. Though it was not yet six o'clock, the well-lit path was largely abandoned in the winter twilight.

After a few hundred yards, the pathway turned to dirt. At least he would not be announcing his location with every footstep. A number of private homes lined the Riverside walkway, and Cam briefly considered exiting the walkway down some narrow alley and losing himself in the labyrinth of the city streets. But many of the exits from the walkway were blocked by locked gates, and he couldn't risk running into a dead end. He glanced back. The driver was keeping pace at a hundred yards. Perhaps gaining a bit, his wide shoulders straining at his shirt as he ran. His burly cohort was nowhere to be seen. Better odds, at least.

Cam considered the situation. From what he remembered of the tourist map, the Riverside walkway ended abruptly ahead, at a peninsula extending into the river where the waterway widened and pooled. Would Cam then be trapped, his pursuer on one side and water on the other? Cam had been in a few tussles over the years, but he didn't like his chances one-on-one with the broad-shouldered ruffian. Cam needed something to even the odds. Like the element of surprise.

He angled around a bend and spotted a large bush ahead, hanging partway over the path. Using the bend to stay out of sight, Cam darted behind the shrub and crouched, fighting to quiet his breathing. A few yards away a lifesaving ring hung on a yellow pole near some river rapids. A sign on the pole read, *A Stolen Ringbuoy—A Stolen Life*. Cam snared the ring, lifted his arms, and dropped it over his head. He might end up in the teeming river, and that life not stolen might be his.

A few more seconds passed, and his pursuer appeared twenty yards away, his stride strong and confident, his powerful arms pumping in rhythm with his legs. Cam didn't like the idea of those arms squeezing the life from his body. The thug was now only a few strides away. Staying low, Cam exploded from the brush. He drove forward, his shoulder aimed at the runner's midsection like a football tackler. The man saw Cam too late to turn away. The two combatants hit the ground and rolled, locked in an embrace. Immediately Cam noticed the man's strength and sensed his confidence, apparently pleased that the engagement had careened from pursuit to conflict. As they rolled, Cam made a split-second decision.

Grasping his assailant tight to him, Cam flipped his hips and continued their roll, this final rotation plunging them over the edge of the walkway and down a steep embankment into the roiling river. Cam opened his mouth to fill his lungs just before their bodies crashed into the frigid river. Bracing for the cold, Cam clenched his mouth closed so as not to gasp and inhale water. Limbs still intertwined, they began to sink, until suddenly the life ring propelled them upward. They surfaced together, their faces inches apart, the river washing them back toward the old city. The thug sputtered even as his strong hands closed on Cam's throat, collapsing his windpipe like a soft tomato. Cam thrashed, clawing, poking at eyes, trying to free himself from the vice-like grip. But the thug buried his face against Cam's shoulder, his massive thumbs pressed at Cam's jugular as the life ring kept them both afloat. Was the man actually trying to kill him? Until now Cam figured they were just trying to scare him off, or get information about the swagger sword and treasure. Perhaps choke him into unconsciousness and drag him somewhere for questioning. But maybe he had misread things. The grip on his neck showed no signs of loosening. He felt his world darken, his body begin to slump. *No.* Not like this. There was too much left undone, too much life still to live.

With a desperate surge of energy, Cam grabbed a handful of hair, yanked the man's head back, and swung his elbow into the thug's face, catching him flush on the nose. Blood spurted. The ruffian coughed, water entering his lungs as he sucked for air in the churning river. His dark eyes narrowed in anger and he brought his own right arm back to return the blow. It was just what Cam hoped for. Cam turned his chin and bit down on the man's left hand, which remained grasped around Cam's throat. The hand withdrew reflexively, and the thug, now disengaged from Cam's buoyancy, began to sink. Panicking and still gasping, he lowered both arms into a dog paddle in an effort to stay afloat. Cam took the opportunity to kick at his assailant, thrusting himself further away. The whirling river did the rest, twisting Cam in one direction and his pursuer in another.

Cam gasped for air, his legs working to angle himself toward the riverbank. The ruffian had turned onto his stomach and, with a strong crawl, began to make for the far shore. After a few strokes he stopped, turned, and eyed Cam, apparently considering reinitiating his pursuit. But the angry rapids between them made it a futile venture. Instead he lifted a middle finger to Cam. "This isn't over," he shouted.

Cam didn't doubt it. Nor did he doubt the man had been after the sword. Someone wanted it, or at least the secrets it revealed. He swam hard for the near bank and found a boat ramp to drag himself up to land. Amanda would be panicked, knowing he wasn't the type just to disappear like that, especially in light of the Dublin attack. And Brian was probably in danger also. Cam fished his phone out of his pocket. Dead. He allowed himself a couple of deep breaths before rolling to his feet. Sloshing along, he began to jog, his neck throbbing, the neon lights of a drug store on the next block serving as his beacon.

☩

Cam slogged along, the drug store outside the old city walls beckoning half a block away. Fortunately he had not lost his wallet. The temperature was near fifty, but the river water felt at least ten degrees colder. Cam shivered. He needed dry clothes and a new cell phone. And a plan.

He froze as a figure rounded the corner. The burly thug from the florist van. Cam ducked into a conveniently-located doorway just before the man turned. *Close call.* Cam had read once that heroes were never lucky, only good. Well, he was no hero, and he was happy for some good fortune on what was turning out to be a bad day.

He peered out, his neck barking in pain as he whipped it around too quickly. A dark pickup truck idled at the corner, facing away from Cam. Had the burly man climbed into the passenger seat? Cam couldn't see, nor could he see the face of the driver. But before he could edge closer, the truck drove off.

Inside the drug store he found a rack with souvenir sweatshirts, t-shirts and hats. And also a few kilts—apparently the Irish wore kilts similar to their Scottish neighbors. Nearby, some rubber rain galoshes were stacked in a bin. A few aisles away he found a burner cell phone. Sheepishly he approached the counter. "I stumbled into the river, I'm afraid," his voice little more than a rasp. He dropped his credit card onto the counter along with a twenty Euro note. "Any chance you have a place I could change?"

Five minutes later, looking ridiculous in a lime-green sweatshirt, red-and-blue plaid kilt and black galoshes, he exited the store and phoned Amanda. Quickly he explained what had happened. "So I jumped into the river to get away. Call hotel security and ask them to guard the room. And of course lock your door." He paused. "And pack up."

"To go where?"

"I don't know. But they seem to have tracked us. I'll be there in ten minutes. I think we need to keep moving. Oh, and give me Brian's number. I got away, but he may not have been so lucky."

Three cabs slowed but passed him by, probably figuring he was drunk. But the fourth stopped when he jumped in front of it. He held up his hand. "I know I look like a fool. But this is an emergency."

He gave the name of their hotel and slid into the back. He phoned Brian, who answered on the third ring. "You okay?" Cam asked.

"What, I can barely hear you?"

Cam spoke directly into the microphone. "I said, you okay?"

"Yeah. Other than, you know, dying. Why?"

Cam told him about the chase. "Nobody came looking for the sword?"

"No. I just checked it an hour ago. It's still in my golf bag."

Odd. They must know about it, and about Brian. So why continue to focus on Cam? "Okay. I have to go." He didn't want to give specific information over the phone. And he wasn't sure he wanted to give *any* information to Brian—Cam had learned twenty-five years ago not to trust him. But he wanted to keep the lines of communication open, at least until he had a chance to study the symbols on the back side of the sword. "I'll call you tomorrow." He hung up before Brian could ask for more details.

Too impatient to wait for the hotel elevator, Cam kicked off the galoshes and took the stairs two at a time. At every switchback of the stairs, he slowed and peered around the corner, half-expecting to see the pair of ruffians. But the hotel seemed secure. He jogged down the hall to their room. "Amanda, it's me. Open up."

She greeted him with a tight embrace and whispered in his ear. "Thank goodness you're okay. I told Astarte we're leaving because the heating system broke. And she thinks you were off chasing a pickpocket."

"Good thinking. Things quiet here?"

"Yes." She stepped back into the room and smirked. "Astarte, did you lend Dad a skirt?"

"Very funny." For Astarte's benefit, he said, "I saw someone grab a woman's purse in the church. I chased him, but I slipped and ended up in the canal. Drank some skanky water, which caused me to lose my voice." He did a little pirouette as Amanda locked the door behind him. "These were the only dry clothes I could find."

Astarte rolled her eyes. "Nice look."

Cam wasn't sure she was buying their lies. But she went along. For now. "If you're nice to me, I'll let you borrow the kilt."

"Only you have the legs for it, Dad." She ducked into the bathroom.

"I've already checked out by phone," Amanda said. Their packed bags were stacked by the door. "And they're bringing the car around for us. But where to?"

"Good question." He lowered his voice. "For now, I think we just need to move."

"I looked for flights. Nothing back to Boston until the morning."

Cam nodded as he threw on a pair of jeans and his boots. "But we could fly to, say, London. Just to get out of Ireland."

"And whoever is tracking us could have new operatives waiting for us when we land." She shrugged. "At least you recognize these Irish blokes."

"Okay. First things first. Let's get out of here."

"And I think we need to tell Astarte ... something. She's not an idiot. And she needs to know to be on guard."

"Agreed. When we get in the car, we'll tell her the truth."

"Which is?"

He rubbed his face. "Some guys are chasing us, and we don't know why, and we don't know who they are, but we think it has to do with a sword and a Templar treasure in the Catskills."

Amanda sniffed and grabbed her suitcase. "That just about bloody covers it."

✠

Amanda drove as they snaked their way through the streets of Galway, her hands clenching the wheel so tightly that her fingers had turned white. Cam navigated in a hoarse voice through swollen vocal cords while Astarte peered out the back window, trying to ascertain if anyone was following. Traffic was light now that the evening rush had passed, making Astarte's job easier.

"There's nobody behind us at all," she said. "Now would be a good time to turn." She had taken the news that they were in danger seriously but matter-of-factly; her five years living with Amanda and Cam had been marked by a half-dozen similar episodes.

Cruising slowly through a residential neighborhood near the coastline, Amanda made a random turn and reversed direction in a cul-de-sac. Presumably anyone following would be approaching from the opposite direction. Nothing. "I think we're okay," Amanda said. She took a deep breath. So much for a relaxing holiday.

"What if they put a tracking device on the car?" Astarte asked. "I saw it once in a movie."

Cam nodded. "She's right." Every word seemed like an effort. "Let's ditch the car at that shopping mall up there and catch a taxi."

The cab dropped them at a nearby Travelodge where they paid cash for a room with an extra cot. "I think I fancy the Meyrick better," Amanda said, bouncing on the soft mattress.

"Yeah, but nobody's trying to throw me in the river here," Cam whispered. Cam pulled the policewoman's business card from his still-wet wallet and turned it over. "Good thing she wrote this in pencil." Using the bathroom for privacy, he dialed the number of her brother, the Galway cop, or *Garda* as the Irish called them.

"Connor McCarthy here."

Cam explained how he came to have McCarthy's number. "I've just fished myself out of the River Corrib. And I didn't jump in voluntarily."

"My sister mentioned you. Sounds like those blokes are intent on ruining your holiday."

"I think I saw one of the guys get into a pickup truck." Cam described the location and time. "Any chance you guys have security cameras?"

"We do. Let me have a look and ring you back."

While waiting, they ordered a pizza from room service, Cam only able to choke down only a few bites. "I should have ordered soup. Or maybe a beer."

"We need to figure out what's going on," Amanda said. "And then make a plan." She smiled and patted his hand. "And then have a beer."

Cam pulled a copy of Zena Halpern's book from his bag. He rasped, "I brought this because she mentions the swagger sword, and Brian seems obsessed with it. And the guys in Dublin said something about a sword." He waved the book. "Maybe there are some clues inside."

Amanda opened her tablet to the Amazon page. "Let's be smart about this." She ordered the Kindle version of the same book. "On Kindle, we can do word searches." Their accounts were linked. "Let's spend the next hour learning all we can about this sword."

"Okay," Cam said. "Here's the thing I don't understand: Why are they after me, when Brian has the sword?"

"Maybe they need you to translate it," Astarte suggested.

A little over an hour later Amanda had highlighted six or eight passages from the book. Cam had scratched a couple of pages of notes onto a legal pad. Astarte had gone in a different direction, Googling some of the references from the book and saving the pages. Amanda began. "I didn't realize how involved the Vatican was in all this."

"And I think I know why the thugs were not after Brian's sword," Cam said.

Astarte nodded. "Because they already have their own sword. From the P2 Lodge."

It was a convoluted tale, with some information clearly missing. But, after a twenty-minute discussion, Amanda thought she had a pretty good understanding of what had happened: In the 1970s, a group of right-wing leaders of Italy's business, political, civic, military and religious institutions feared that Socialism was taking over the country. Using a rogue Masonic Lodge by the name of Propaganda Due—'P2' for short—as a cover, they formed an Italian shadow government operating counter to the legal government, intent on pushing Italy back toward fascism. P2 became, in short, the *de facto* government in Italy and committed numerous crimes, including kidnapping and murder, to support its cause. The Vatican, also fearing Socialism and its hostility toward religion, became an active partner in P2, using the Vatican Bank to launder funds for P2 and also for its supporters in the Mafia. This is where Archbishop Paul Marcinkus entered the picture—a native of Chicago, he had become head of the Vatican Bank and also a senior member of P2. At some point Marcinkus and other members of P2 became aware of the Templar treasure in the Catskills, probably through secret documents kept in the Vatican library. According to Zena Halpern's book, the head of P2, Licio Gelli, distributed fifteen swagger swords to leading members of P2 and the Vatican. Two of these swords contained carvings which were clues to the location of the treasure—one of these swords was given to Marcinkus, and the other presumably to Marcinkus' close friend, banker Roberto Calvi, who went by the nickname, "God's Banker." These markings were similar, but not identical, to markings on a map used by Cam and Amanda to find buried ancient artifacts on the Catskills' Hunter Mountain five years earlier. Did the clues on the back side of the sword lead to other buried items, such as treasure? One of these swords had somehow found its way into Brian's hands. As for God's Banker, Calvi, he was found hanging from London's Blackfriars Bridge in 1982, in what most believe was a murder orchestrated by P2 in an unsuccessful attempt to cover up the Vatican Bank money-laundering. The Vatican Bank's unlawful (and immoral) activities were later exposed, with the bank suffering hundreds of millions of dollars in losses in what became know as the Vatican Banking Scandal. Later, in the mid-1990s, Marcinkus, presumably with his sword, returned to America, where he used his power and influence to avoid arrest in the Banking Scandal and also to acquire the Templar travel log describing the secret journey across the Atlantic in 1178.

This was a lot to digest. But the key takeaway for Amanda was that there were two swords. "I think Astarte is right. They have the other sword. Probably Calvi's, assuming Brian somehow ended up with Marcinkus' after he died."

"And they need us to help translate the symbols and find the treasure," Cam said.

Amanda nodded. "Right. They don't know the mountain, don't know the history. We do."

"I'm not sure the stuff is still in the Catskills," Cam said. "But you're right, I think Marcinkus is the key to this. And remember, Roberto's father worked for him at the Vatican Bank."

"And died a premature death, along with his wife."

"You think Marcinkus murdered them?"

She shrugged. "He was an accountant at the bank. Marcinkus was trying to cover up a scandal. And like I said before, what's a lowly accountant compared to a pope?"

✝

Connor McCarthy called Cam back just before ten o'clock. "I think I have something," the Garda reported. "We retrieved a partial registration on that pickup truck you saw parked in front of the drug store. It's registered in County Meath."

"That's the Boyne Valley area, right? We were just there. Any way to narrow it down further?"

"There are about 70,000 vehicles registered in that county. Farm country, so maybe a couple of thousand pickup trucks. It will take some time." He paused. "But, we did capture a picture of the driver. A woman. Not great resolution. As for her mate, we're running his face through our system, but no matches yet."

"Thanks. Appreciate the help."

"Wish I had more for you." He paused. "But my guess is, you haven't heard the last from these blokes. Because, you know, treasure."

Cam sighed. "Yeah, I know. Treasure."

✛

Cam stayed up late, surfing the internet for clues while Amanda and Astarte slept in the king bed on the far side of the hotel room. Archbishop Marcinkus seemed to be the key, the spider at the center of this web.

Cam adjusted the bag of ice from one side of his swollen and bruised neck to the other. Hopefully the Motrin would kick in. Swallowing hurt, and turning his head more than a few degrees had become almost impossible as it stiffened. The fresh memory of claw-like fingers around his throat left no doubt: It was not safe here in Ireland. Cam had been fortunate to escape from two attacks. He didn't relish a third encounter. More to the point, Amanda and Astarte were in danger.

Amanda had set an early alarm. One possibility was to take a taxi to Shannon Airport, immediately go through security (which presumably would provide a layer of protection to them), and take the first flight out of the country. From there they'd figure out how to get back to Boston. But Amanda opposed this approach, arguing that they would be in as much danger at home as in Ireland. "Once we leave, Westford will be the first place they look for us." In the end they agreed to reevaluate their choices in the morning.

He searched all things Marcinkus, pairing the Marcinkus name with other relevant search terms like 'Templars' and 'Catskills' and 'Hunter Mountain.' When he entered the name 'William Jackson,' the name of the head of the black ops team which initially found the Templar travel log in Italy and later sold it to Marcinkus, he hit pay dirt. In a book entitled *In God's Name*, which is where Cam first read speculation that Archbishop Marcinkus assassinated Pope John Paul I to cover up his role in the Vatican Banking Scandal, author David Yallop offered special thanks to *William Jackson* for the information he provided as background for the book. The Jackson name, though relatively common in English-speaking countries, stood out amidst the list of Italian names surrounding it. Cam had little doubt it was the same William Jackson. The connection corroborated the information provided in Zena Halpern's book, that Marcinkus had been working with, and eventually purchased the Templar travel log from, Jackson, the elderly black ops agent. Did Jackson know, or suspect, that Marcinkus had been behind the pope's assassination? It would explain why, though hesitant, Jackson eventually agreed to sell the travel log to Marcinkus, a man he referred to in correspondence as 'the asshole.' This particular asshole, after all, had both the means and the willingness to acquire the document through violence if necessary.

But Marcinkus died in 2006. And apparently the key to discovering the Templar treasure had died with him. Amanda believed that Cam perhaps embodied some kind of duplicate key, that his knowledge of the Templars and their history in America might be enough to finish the job left unfinished by Marcinkus. Using Amanda's terminology, Cam didn't fancy serving as someone else's key, someone else's tool. If there was a Templar treasure to be found, he just as soon find it himself.

Which, he realized, might be the only way to get out of this mess.

And he couldn't do that from this side of the Atlantic. He stood and gently shook Amanda awake. "I think we need to fly back tomorrow."

Chapter 8

Cam, Amanda and Astarte woke early, ate a quick breakfast, called a taxi, and made it from their hotel to Shannon Airport outside Galway without incident. They purchased tickets on the next flight back to the States, an early afternoon nonstop to Kennedy Airport in New York. Cam took the aisle seat, knowing that sleep would be impossible while seated upright with his sore, stiff neck. He also wanted to be in a position to study other passengers, just in case they had been followed. Not that there was much he could do in response if they had.

Amanda plopped into the middle seat, allowing Astarte to gaze out the window on the left side of the jet. "You should be able to see the sunset in the southwestern sky," Amanda said.

After takeoff, with seven hours to kill, Cam took the opportunity to reread portions of Zena Halpern's book. The story continued to fascinate him, filling in many details and much missing information regarding Templar history. The documents relied on by Ms. Halpern described how Templar Knights, in the early part of the 12th century not long after the Order had been formed, explored the hidden chambers under the Temple of Solomon in Jerusalem. Historians had long suspected the Templars had searched these chambers, but Ms. Halpern's documents provided specific details as to what they found, including ancient scrolls, maps showing the route across the Atlantic, metal devices which later turn out to be navigational tools, blocks of gold bearing the seal of King Solomon, and a human skull in an ossuary inscribed with the name, 'John' (perhaps the beheaded John the Baptist). These treasures were brought back to the Templar stronghold of Seborga, near Genoa, Italy. There the scrolls were translated by Jewish scholars employed by the Templars. These scrolls described the settlement of Onteora in what is today the Catskill Mountains, populated by religious outcasts from Old Testament times who fled the Jewish homeland rather than give up the worship of the ancient Goddess, or Earth Mother.

Cam sat back and let his mind play connect-the-dots. He and Amanda both had enjoyed Anita Diamant's classic, *The Red Tent*, in which during the time of Abraham the matriarchs resisted giving up their fertility goddesses, most prominently Asherah, in favor of the all-male Yahweh. Later, Cam knew, entire villages were slaughtered by Israelite kings insistent on religious orthodoxy. Apparently, in a footnote lost to history, some of these village residents fled, finding refuge in America before the time of Christ. Cam and Amanda had long believed that the ancient Phoenicians, also Goddess worshipers, had crossed the Atlantic to mine and trade for copper in the Great Lakes region of America; one possibility was that these Phoenicians transported their outcast Israelite neighbors across the Atlantic.

Cam shifted in his seat, turning his thoughts back to the Templars. After returning from Jerusalem to Europe in the early 1100s, the Templars methodically translated the ancient scrolls and prepared for a journey to Onteora, which they commenced some fifty years after first excavating beneath the Temple of Solomon. Knowing the Norse regularly journeyed to North America beginning in the early 11th century (they named their settlement 'Vinland'), the Templars enlisted the Norse princess Altomara, who had previously visited Onteora, as their guide. From Denmark they sailed to the west coast of Wales in the year 1178, from where they began their ocean crossing on Beltane, the pagan fertility festival falling halfway between the spring equinox and the summer solstice. Columbus would embark on a similar journey almost three hundred years later, leaving from the west coast of Ireland rather than Wales, in 1477.

Crossing the Atlantic, the Halpern book continued, the Templars "made landfall on an island of oak trees" in Mahone Bay on the southeastern coast of Nova Scotia. This was an intriguing reference to the famous Oak Island, so-called because of the non-native African oaks that soared high above the native species, seemingly beckoning sailors crossing the Atlantic. Could it be, Cam wondered, that these African oaks had been planted by earlier Phoenician voyageurs? In modern times, of course, Oak Island had become famous for the treasure rumored to be buried in its so-called Money Pit. From Oak Island, the Templars circled the tip of Nova Scotia to the Bay of Fundy, where they remarked on the monstrous tides, and crossed the bay to New Brunswick and northern Maine. Cam thought again about Columbus, about how he, too, remarked on massive, fifty-foot tides during his 1477 westward excursion from Galway. Why had this chapter in Columbus' life been so ignored by historians? Cam sensed it was relevant—crucial, even—to decoding the mystery of the Templars and their treasure.

Dinner arrived, which gave him the opportunity to discuss the Columbus journey with Amanda. "Most people don't know that Columbus sailed to Iceland in 1477. But I think he went even further, maybe even all the way to Nova Scotia."

"I can't recall even hearing about the Iceland part."

"Me neither," Astarte said.

"This comes from a letter Columbus wrote to his son." Cam read the relevant sections aloud: "*In the year 1477, in the month of February, I navigated 100 leagues beyond Thule [to an] island which is as large as England. When I was there the sea was not frozen over, and the tide was so great as to rise and fall 26 braccias.*"

Cam looked up. "A hundred leagues is about 300 miles. And a *braccia* is just under two feet. So we're talking 50-foot tides."

"Where's Thule?" Astarte asked.

Cam smiled. "It sort of moves around."

She made one of those faces that teenagers make when their parents say something aggravating.

"I'm serious," Cam said. "In Roman times, Thule was Norway. Later it was the Orkney Islands. Then Iceland. Then Greenland. Essentially, Thule was the edge of the known world at any given time."

"Well, during Columbus' time, Thule would probably have been the western coast of Greenland," Amanda said. "The Norse had abandoned Greenland by then, but the settlements were still there." She smiled. "And so, apparently, was Columbus."

"I agree. And he gives other clues. He says that when he sailed 100 leagues beyond Thule, he arrived at an island the size of England. If Thule were Iceland, and he sailed 100 leagues beyond, he'd hit Greenland. But that wouldn't make sense—Greenland is much larger than England."

"Ten or fifteen times as large," Amanda said. "You're right. It wouldn't make sense in Columbus' mind for Thule to be Iceland. For him, Thule must have been Greenland."

Their airplane was just south of Greenland now, according to the flight tracker. Cam peered out the window. The modern aircraft was essentially mirroring Columbus' journey across the North Atlantic. "That would mean Columbus sailed to Nova Scotia. It's beyond

Greenland, and it's an island about the same size as England. Nothing else fits."

"And they have the 50-foot tides in Nova Scotia, in the Bay of Fundy."

Astarte chimed in. "I've seen cool pictures. They're the largest tides in the world."

Cam nodded. Fifty-foot tides also existed at the mouth of the Hudson Bay, but that waterway would have been frozen solid in February. "So of the four data points in the description, three of them point directly to Columbus landing in Nova Scotia." He counted them on his fingers. "Thule being western Greenland. Nova Scotia being the same size as England. And the tides matching the Bay of Fundy. The only thing that is off is the 100 leagues—Nova Scotia is further away from Greenland than that."

Amanda stared past Astarte, out the window. "But you said Columbus sailed 100 leagues *beyond* Thule, beyond the edge of the known world. That's different than sailing 100 leagues *from* Thule." She shifted in her seat. "You could sail south for a few hundred miles from Greenland and still be within the bounds of the known world. It's only when you turn west, toward North America, that you are going *beyond* it. In fact, to Nova Scotia."

Cam smiled. "That's some impressive lawyering. Maybe a bit of a stretch, but definitely possible."

"I get it," Astarte said. "It's like when a quarterback throws a pass to the sidelines. The ball might travel thirty yards, but you only gain ten yards in distance. So you've moved ten yards *beyond* where you were, even though the total distance is much further."

"Great," Cam chuckled, "I'm surrounded by lawyers."

"Both of whom are smarter than you," Amanda said.

Cam was comfortable with their analysis, but he wanted to check to see how it compared to conclusions reached by other historians. He was surprised to find, though perhaps he should not have been, that most other commentators opined that Thule referred to Iceland, and that Columbus had sailed there but no further. Cam shook his head; he had seen this kind of sloppy, even close-minded, scholarship before. For example, Columbus' most famous biographer, Samuel Eliot Morison, simply threw up his hands and wrote that it would be "time and effort wasted" to try to make sense of Columbus' 1477 journey, so why bother? *Time and effort wasted?* Only if one went into the exercise with preconceived notions. All it took was an open mind, a map, and an analysis of the plain meaning of Columbus' words: He sailed *beyond* Thule, to an island the size of England, which boasted 50-foot tides. Only Nova Scotia, its Bay of Fundy boasting massive tides, fit the bill.

Cam dug deeper, eventually finding a handful of other historians who concurred with his conclusion. A book entitled *The Horizons of Christopher Columbus*, by Anne Molander, added an important layer of context to the Columbus voyage: Cam wondered why Columbus would brave the North Atlantic in the dead of winter, and Ms. Molander's research gave him his answer—the ambitious navigator wanted to take longitudinal measurements during a rare solar eclipse. European astronomers had predicted an eclipse on February 13 of that year, and Columbus knew that these measurements, and the rare opportunity to establish precise longitudinal map points, would be crucial to any future Atlantic navigational efforts. Intriguingly, Ms. Molander's research placed Columbus specifically in Clark's Harbor, less than a day's sail from Oak Island, to view the eclipse. Cam smiled: There was no doubt that Columbus kept careful track of eclipses, as evidenced by an incident in Jamaica, decades later, when the navigator cowed unruly natives by making the moon "disappear" that night at his command.

Cam rubbed his eyes and rotated his stiffening neck. This was dense stuff, parsing through archaic and incomplete writings. But the possible connection to Oak Island and its mysterious treasure was tantalizing. Could Columbus have been following an old Templar map in plotting his course to Nova Scotia? Cam would need to return to a possible Columbus connection to Templar maps and Oak Island at a later time.

For now, Cam needed to end his Columbus research detour and refocus on the 1178 Templars. He turned back to the Zena Halpern book. According to the Templar journal, while in New Brunswick and northern Maine the Templars lived for a time with the Mi'kmaq tribe, apparently renewing an old friendship. The Templar group even joined the Mi'kmaq in a battle against an enemy tribe, further cementing the alliance. Cam again paused—Prince Henry Sinclair and his crew lived with the Mi'kmaq in 1398 before continuing down the coast to southern New England, where they carved the Westford Knight and likely also built the Newport Tower. The pieces continued to fit together, the journal corroborating the legends and filling in many missing pieces of history.

The Templar group—some crossing New England by land with Native American guides, and others traveling by boat—made its way to the Catskill Mountains of New York, to the Onteora settlement, where they deposited their secret scrolls and other treasures in a remote temple high in the mountains. Of all the revelations in the Templar journals, the description of this Onteora settlement most intrigued Cam. Comprised of a matriarchal group of Goddess worshipers, these residents descended from the outcast Israelites of Old Testament times, the ones who had refused to give up the ancient Goddess. Later, Jewish refugees from the Roman destruction of Jerusalem in the first century AD joined the settlement, apparently bringing with them treasures—both religious and pecuniary—of the Jewish people. High in the mountains, this group lived in peace with the surrounding Native American tribes.

Cam and Amanda had always believed that the Templars secretly believed in the duality of the godhead—that is, that God was both male and female, and that recognition of the feminine aspect of divinity was crucial to a healthy, vibrant society. It was this heretical move away from Catholic orthodoxy which in the end caused the Church to turn on its army of fighting monks. But it was also this so-called heresy which formed the basis for the Templar alliance with the Onteora settlement. Unlike other Christians (or for that matter, other Jews or Muslims) of the day, the Templars felt comfortable within a society which venerated the ancient Goddess. More to the point, they felt comfortable entrusting their treasures—again, in the form of both monetary treasure and also religious artifacts and scrolls—to the ancient people of Onteora.

In addition to depositing their treasures in the Onteora temple, the Templars also removed certain documents from Onteora with the intention of bringing them back to Europe. It is unclear why they did so, but there were hints that they hoped to use them as leverage against—or even to blackmail—the Vatican.

Having completed their mission, the Templars traveled down the Hudson River to Long Island Sound, from where they sailed across the Atlantic back to Europe. The mission leader returned to Seborga, on the coast of Italy near Genoa, where he dictated the report of their mission. This report later became known as the Templar journals and formed the basis for Zena Halpern's book and Archbishop Marcinkus' treasure quest.

Cam looked up from his tablet to see Amanda studying him. "What?" he smiled.

"Nothing. I just like watching you when you're deep in thought. You're always so wide-eyed, like a child at Disney World."

"How do you know I wasn't looking at porn?" he mouthed, leaning back so Astarte wouldn't catch what he was saying.

"Because you have me," she said airily.

He chuckled. "Touché."

Five minutes later it was his turn to interrupt her. "I'm just reading about how Onteora was a matriarchal society. It always seems to come back to that for the Templars, doesn't it?"

"Yes. For a brawling bunch of warrior monks, they were surprisingly liberated." She paused. "In fact, I've been working on something I wanted to share with you. Just give me ten minutes. In the meantime," she smiled, "I'd fancy a Diet Coke."

"And a Sprite for me," Astarte added.

Cam stood and arched his neck. "It's not exactly a medieval quest. But I'm not above doing errands for my women-folk."

"Good," Amanda said. "In that case, find us some pretzels also."

✞

Brian staggered into the Meyrick Hotel after a late lunch, acting more drunk than he felt. In fact, he was perfectly sober, which was just one of the reasons he was in a foul mood. Who vacationed sober in Ireland? But there was a treasure to be found, and his best bet to find it—in the name of Cameron Thorne—had gone missing. Which was the other reason he was in a foul mood.

He approached the front desk, stumbling into it. A forty-something woman with half a chin more than God had given her greeted him with a professional smile. *Moira*, read her nametag. Full-figured, the way Brian liked them. He held her eyes for a second. After a lifetime of trying, and often failing, to charm the ladies, Brian had developed a keen sense of when to flirt and when instead simply to pay up. Moira crossed her arms in front of her chest and eyed him coldly, apparently amused by neither him nor his green pants. Resigned to paying up, he removed a 20 euro note from his wallet. "I was hoping you could help me. I am supposed to meet a friend, Cameron Thorne, for a drink in your bar. But he's not there." Brian shrugged. "I don't want to phone his room because I think his daughter is asleep." He put the twenty on the counter. "Could you give me his room number so I can go find him?"

The clerk flicked out her hand and snatched the bill. "As a matter of fact, Mr. Thorne checked out last night."

Brian narrowed his eyes. As he feared. "Did he leave a forwarding address?"

She glanced down. "No."

Damn. Without Thorne, there was no way to find the treasure. In fact, even with Thorne the chances weren't great. He turned and eyed the bar. "Guess I'm alone then." This would be his last night in Ireland; he would need to chase Thorne, probably back to New England. More out of habit than any real expectation of success, he offered a crooked smile. "What time you get off work?"

She had already turned away.

✠

The plane cruised at 30,000 feet, the cabin awash in an orange glow from the setting sun out the port window. The two most important people in her life seated on either side of her, Amanda's eyes flew across the screen of her tablet, her brain racing to keep up. The mysteries of the medieval Templars fascinated her: How did an obscure order of monks sworn to protect Christians on pilgrimage to the Holy Land become, in less than a generation, the most powerful entity in all of Europe? And, then, 200 years later, why did the Church turn on them, outlawing its own elite fighting force and imprisoning and executing many of its leaders? A comparable action in modern times would be the President disbanding and outlawing the Marines.

So, again, why?

Amanda and Cam had been wrestling with this mystery for the better part of a decade. As Cam had said, with the Templars, it always seemed to come back to the role of women in society—the medieval Church was about as misogynistic an institution as the world had ever seen, and the Templars, apparently, had pushed back. Fatally so.

Like Cam, Amanda believed one key to understanding the Templars was through studying their spiritual founder, Bernard de Clairvoux. He famously, and perhaps scandalously, dreamt that he drank milk from the breast of the Virgin Mary, and that this milk gave him the wisdom of God. Many historians viewed this as an attempt by Bernard to elevate the status of the Virgin Mary—and of women in general—within the medieval Church.

Whatever Bernard's true motivations, his dream and the popularity which it attracted inspired a body of artwork known as the "Lactation of Saint Bernard" paintings. Entire websites were devoted to these depictions, which usually showed the Virgin Mary holding the baby Jesus with one hand while squeezing her bare breast with the other, thereby squirting her milk into the open mouth of the waiting, genuflecting Bernard. She pulled a medieval painting up on her tablet.

The Lactation of Saint Bernard

Cam returned with the beverages and pretzels, and she showed him the image. "Remember this?"

"I'm sorry, did you want milk?" He smiled. "I thought you said Diet Coke."

"Very funny."

He sat. "I showed a similar painting to Brian at the Tower last week. Not very subtle of Bernard, was it?"

She chuckled. "No. I suppose his dream could have been that she touched his head with her fingers, or bathed him in a warm glow or something else, you know, religious. The breast milk is definitely *in your face*, no pun intended."

"I think he wanted to make it clear that the wisdom of God stemmed from something uniquely feminine, like breast milk. Just so the Church couldn't spin the message."

"Well, I think the message was spun all right. But not in the way the Church wanted it to go." She smiled. This spun message was what she wanted to share with him.

He angled his head. "How so?"

"In most of these depictions, it's clear that the Virgin Mary is, well, the Virgin Mary. Her head is covered and she's wearing white or blue, which is how she's always depicted. But I started noticing something. I started finding a bunch of depictions like this, many from medieval times." As she turned her tablet toward him, the plane lurched violently. Their drinks flew, drenching them, while Amanda clutched her tablet. Cam, who had not yet refastened his seatbelt, was thrown upward, cracking his head on the storage bin above him before bouncing into the aisle. The plane lurched for a few more seconds, then, just as suddenly as the turbulence began, the jet passed through it and resettled.

"Cam! Are you okay?" Amanda called amid the chaos and screams.

Nodding, Cam pulled himself to his feet and rubbed the top of his head. "Well, that felt good." He blinked. "Just what my neck needed."

Amanda smiled nervously as Cam stumbled back to his seat. She dabbed at her clothes with a cocktail napkin. "Perhaps someone doesn't want me to show these pictures."

"Or perhaps someone wants to make sure I'm paying full attention." He fastened his seatbelt. "Okay, show them to me now. Before it's too late."

After waiting for the captain to explain away the turbulence, Amanda turned the tablet for a second time. "So look at all these versions of the Lactation of Bernard. I've pulled up just four, but I could show you dozens."

The Lactation of Saint Bernard

Cam's eyes widened. But it was Astarte who spoke. "That's not the Virgin Mary. That's Mary Magdalene."

"Astarte's right," Cam said as Amanda nodded. "She's wearing orange and green, and her hair is down. Plus it's long and red." Artists almost universally used orange and green clothing, along with red hair, to depict Mary Magdalene, while the Virgin Mary typically was portrayed with her dark hair covered wearing white or light blue. Cam remembered Brian's crass comment about Mary being hot. Perhaps he wasn't just being a pig. "She doesn't look like she's collecting beads at Mardi Gras, but she's not exactly chaste, either."

"Okay then, so who's the baby?" Astarte asked.

Amanda eyed her. "Who do you think?"

Astarte titled her head. "It must be Mary Magdalene and Jesus' baby then."

"Right," Amanda said. "Which is what makes these images so provocative."

"Provocative is one word. Heretical is another." Cam smiled. "No wonder the plane shook. Essentially what these paintings are saying is that the wisdom of God, as given to Bernard, comes from the wife of Jesus, not his mother."

Amanda smiled. "Yes. It was one thing for Bernard to push for the veneration of the Virgin Mary. After all, everyone has a mother they loved, even the most misogynistic of the Church elders. So of course there's a place for a mother figure. But this takes things to another level. It not only says that Jesus had a wife and child, but that God's wisdom flows through her, Mary Magdalene, not just through Jesus."

"I don't know why that should be so heretical," Astarte said. "Why shouldn't wisdom come from the wife in addition to the husband?"

"It should," Cam replied. "But that's not what the medieval Church thought."

"But the Templars did," said Amanda. "They agreed with Astarte. That's what these paintings are telling us: Bernard, and the Templars who followed him, understood the importance of women, both in society and in the godhead. Balance. Duality. Not all this male primacy nonsense the Church was preaching." She shifted in her seat. "This all sets the stage for the Prince Henry Sinclair voyage and the Hooked X stuff." She explained to Astarte that the Sinclair family was long believed to be the family most closely descended from the Jesus-Mary Magdalene union. And the Hooked X, a modified runic character discovered by researcher Scott Wolter on many medieval North

American carvings, was believed to be the symbol of the family. She showed Astarte an image of the Hooked X rune.

The Hooked X Rune

Amanda took a deep breath, explaining that the upper part of the 'X,' the 'v,' represented the womb, or the female, while the lower part, the inverted 'v,' represented the phallus, or the male. The 'v' and inverted 'v' combined to represent the union of male and female and was used by medieval supporters of Mary Magdalene as a secret sign for those who believed in her marriage to Jesus. And the hook on the upper right stave of the 'X' formed a small 'v' inside the larger 'v,' representing a baby girl within the womb of Mary Magdalene, a girl believed to have been named Sarah.

"You with me?"

Astarte nodded. "I've grown up with this stuff. But I'm only now beginning to understand it all."

Amanda continued. "Here's the take-away: The Templars came to America in 1178 to find a safe haven for those who believed in the bloodline, in the Jesus-Mary Magdalene union, in the importance of women in society, before the Church quashed them."

"Which they eventually did, in 1307," Cam said. "The Church couldn't have a rich, powerful force of fighting monks questioning its teachings. And the Crusades were over, so the Vatican didn't really need the Templar army any more. So the Church and the King of France attacked. Friday the thirteenth of October, which is why Friday the thirteenth is considered unlucky. All the Templar leaders were rounded up, thrown in jail, and tortured. It took the Templars a couple of generations, until the late 1300s, to reorganize and make another trip back to America."

"Which brings us back to the 1178 trip and the Catskills treasure," Amanda replied. "The Templar treasure was never found after 1307. It had disappeared. I think the Templars saw the writing on the wall, even as early as 1178, and had already begun to hide their treasures. They weren't stupid. The Albigensian Crusade had not formally begun yet, but by the 1160s the Church had already declared that all Cathars should be imprisoned and their property confiscated." She explained to Astarte that the Cathars of southern France practiced a variant form of Christianity, one that did not recognize the moral authority of the Vatican or its priests. Later, in the early 1200s, hundreds of thousands of Christian Cathars were slaughtered by Church forces in what many historians called the world's first religious genocide.

Astarte swallowed. "Hundreds of thousands?"

Amanda nodded. "I've seen some estimates of a million."

"Just for practicing the wrong kind of Christianity?"

Amanda nodded again. "Apparently, in the eyes of the Church, it was not enough to be a good Christian. You had to be the *right kind* of Christian also."

"You mean the kind that didn't question the Pope," Astarte said.

Cam added, "And don't forget, many of the Templar leaders were from France. They probably figured, rightly so, that if it could happen to the Cathars, it could happen to them."

"Which it did, a century later," Amanda said. "They, too, were not the right kind of Christians."

"And that gets us back, again, to the 1178 trip," Cam said. "Fearing that someday the Church might turn on them, it would make sense for the Templars to go look for a safe haven. It says so right in the Templar journal—something to the effect that America would make a great place to settle, but don't tell the Pope."

"And, not to sound like a broken record, also a great place to hide their treasures," Amanda added.

Their explanation now complete, Amanda and Cam turned to Astarte. She grinned and shook her head. "Well, life in this family sure isn't boring. Let me guess: We're going to go looking for that treasure when we land."

As if in response, Cam removed his phone from his jacket pocket and sent a text, using the aircraft's in-flight cell service. After a quick exchange, he explained. "I'm going to stay over in New York for a day, visit Ruthie Sanders." He smiled. "Can't beat an eighty-year-old who knows how to text. We know she has more information, she mentioned a map in particular, stuff that wasn't in Zena Halpern's book. Clues to help us find that treasure. She made me promise I wouldn't look at the docs and map until after she died. But maybe when I tell her what's happening, she'll change her mind."

"Can't you do it by phone?"

"This is her life's work. I think in person would be more effective. And we're going to be in New York anyway."

Amanda would have preferred to join him, but someone needed to stay with Astarte, and she was fine with that. "Okay," she said. "But I don't think Astarte and I should go back to Westford just yet."

"Agreed. Head to the condo. Do some skiing." They had bought a unit at Loon Mountain in New Hampshire, hiding their ownership in a trust. Nobody else knew about it. "I'll meet you up there."

"Good. But you have to promise that you won't go looking for treasure without me."

"Without us," Astarte added.

Cam smiled. "You know I'd never search without you guys. I need your help to carry all the supplies."

Chapter 9

Ruthie Sanders didn't like to lie. But this was one of those white lies that didn't hurt anyone. Besides, she never actually told Cameron she made the soup *herself*...

Seated at her kitchen table, she picked up the phone and dialed the number of the local deli. "Hi, Menachem. Is it too late to get a delivery for today? I'm having last-minute company." Cameron had texted from the plane, so it must be important. He had been cryptic, saying only that he was working on the Templar treasure in the Catskills and wanted to talk about her map.

"For you, anything," Menachem had said. Ruthie had been married to Menachem's older brother, a pharmacist, who died suddenly of a heart attack more than thirty years ago. In her grief, and as a way to keep busy, she had joined a local group exploring the mysterious stone chambers of the Hudson Valley. Now, decades later, she knew as much about them, and other ancient New England artifacts, as anyone alive.

"Half a pound of smoked turkey and four sesame bagels." That was for her. "And a quart of matzo ball soup. Floaters, not sinkers."

"Of course," Menachem laughed.

"Oh, and some of those marzipan cookies."

"I'll send it over after the lunch crowd leaves."

Ruthie checked her watch. Barely eleven. Cameron said he'd arrive around dinner time. She needed to wash up, dress, and tidy the house before he arrived. She remembered, in her forties, visiting her aunt and uncle in Miami and laughing at how a trip to the drug store, lunch, and a game of Scrabble seemed to fill an entire day. Now the idea of driving to the deli, which she used to do without a second thought, had become a series of daunting tasks—warming up the car, navigating the traffic-clogged streets (must everyone drive those oversized SUVs?), finding a parking space, walking across the snow-covered parking lot, standing in line, securing the soup in the car so that it did not spill. She would happily tip the delivery boy.

After walking on her treadmill for a half hour and showering, Ruthie dressed and did her face. She cut up a grapefruit for lunch, saving room for the bagels as a mid-afternoon snack. She wondered about Cameron's visit. He must have found something in Ireland relating to the Templars. As she ran a wet paper towel over her kitchen table, the doorbell rang. Probably the delivery boy, arriving early. She imagined the warm bagel. "Coming," she sang. Maybe she'd even treat herself to a couple of the matzo balls.

She unbolted the door and reached for the knob. But before she could turn it, the door flew at her, crashing into her shoulder and knocking her to the floor. *What in heavens?* Dazed, she did not even see the three burly men push their way inside. One of them leaned into her face, his nose inches from hers, the rim of his cap pushing into her forehead. She blinked and recoiled, her hip throbbing from where she landed. "Nobody has to get hurt, grandma. Just do as we say."

Ruthie took a deep breath and steeled herself. *I'm not your grandma.* She knew men like this, had had nightmares about them since her days as a young child living in Poland during the Holocaust. Large men with small minds, cold hearts, and brown teeth. Why was it that evil men always seemed to have discolored teeth? It was a random thought, but a comforting one—it meant that her fear had not overwhelmed her, that her mind was functioning. Men like this could never truly defeat her, not after what she had lived through. *Play to their greed.* "I have money, in my purse," she declared, looking the intruder in the eye. She held out her wrist. "And this watch."

The man in the cap grabbed her wrist, twisting, but ignored the watch. He hauled her to her feet; she grabbed the edge of a table to steady herself. He was clearly the leader, while the other guys, younger and skittish, had closed the door and now kept watch out her front window. "We don't want your money. We want the map." His eyes were steady, and he patted what she saw was a gun tucked into his waistband. "The Templar map."

Her racing heart now fluttered. *Not the map.* She had assumed this was a random burglary, and it took a second for her brain to recalibrate, to adjust to biting into an orange and tasting tuna fish. "Who sent you?" This was a different kind of danger than she originally expected.

The man in the cap grabbed her by the nape of her neck and shoved her back toward the living room. She pretended that her hip had given way, prepared herself to stumble. But he held her up like a ragdoll. "I'm not asking again. The map."

"Yes. The map. In my bedroom. A safe."

He turned to his accomplices. "Wait here. You watch the front, you watch the back." And to Ruthie. "Come on."

She made a point of moaning, of shuffling along as she led him down the hallway toward her bedroom. The slower she moved, the faster her brain worked. She remembered Poland, being five years old, the men in black shiny boots coming in the night, her mother screaming at her father to do something, to do anything, to protect his family. And her father, his eyeglasses crooked on his face, opening the door, stepping aside, letting the men in, letting them round the family up and take them away. "How can you just … *kapitulacja?*" her mother had wailed. *Capitulate* was the English word, Ruthie later learned. But for years that word, *kapitulacja,* echoed in her head and haunted her dreams. Her father, her weak father, had done nothing. Now it was her turn. *Better to be brave and die than to be weak and live.* She took a deep breath. *But, better still was to be brave and survive.*

She pushed open the bedroom door, hesitating. *Play your part. Meek and weak.* "Sorry, I have not made the bed yet."

"Lady, I don't give a shit about your bed." He shoved her forward. "Come on."

"Okay. The safe is in there." She led him into a walk-in closet and pointed, hand shaking, to a wall of clothes hanging from a rod. "Behind those dresses."

He motioned. "Open it."

Whimpering, she lowered herself to one knee and pushed the dresses aside. Mostly obscured by the hanging clothes, she jabbed at the digital screen with a steady finger. The door opened silently. She reached inside and felt around. "Oh. I hit the wrong button. I am so sorry. Please do not hurt me." She hiccupped. "I am just so nervous."

"Try it again," he sneered.

"Can you hold back some of these clothes?" she asked.

He leaned in, one arm sweeping back her clothes, his face buried in fabric, the smell of cigarette smoke wafting off his clothes. She allowed herself a small smile. Her fingers gripped the Glock 43, specifically designed for a woman's small hand. Silently she raised the weapon and, without remorse, fired three quick shots through her gold sequined evening dress into the intruder's chest. He toppled toward her, grunting, *capitulating,* her clothes still grasped in his arms. Blood pooled on the carpet as the sound of heavy steps pounded toward her. The same sound that had haunted her nightmares for almost eighty years.

She had three shots left. That was one of the drawbacks of the Glock, only six shots. Plus the element of surprise was gone, and the intruders outnumbered her. She took a deep breath. It was in God's hands now. Reaching over the dead intruder, she closed the safe, her hand remarkably steady. She scooched to the far side of the closet and concealed herself behind another row of hanging clothes. They might get her. But they weren't getting her map.

✝

The flight landed just after three o'clock New York time. Cam retrieved his bag, helped Amanda and Astarte transfer to a shuttle back to Boston, rented a sedan, and by evening rush hour had joined a line of commuters headed for Long Island. He fought to stay alert—it was almost midnight Ireland time, and he had barely slept the night before.

He arched his head back slowly. Nothing like a trans-Atlantic flight to help with a stiff neck. In a perverse way, the discomfort was a blessing, keeping him from nodding off. The app on his phone directed him off the highway to avoid some traffic, and forty-five minutes later he turned onto Ruthie's street in a grid-like neighborhood tucked between some power lines and an office park. Immediately his foot hit the brake. Two police cars and a dark van sat in front of Ruthie's house, and police tape blocked the driveway. *Please, no.* Ramming the rental car against a snow bank beneath a streetlight, Cam leapt out and ran.

He made it as far as the front walk. "Sorry, sir," a young policewoman said, "you'll have to stay back. Crime scene."

"What happened? I'm a friend of the home owner, Ruthie Sanders."

"We're not allowed to give out any information. Active investigation."

He looked past her, saw a pair of officers profiled in the living room. "Can you tell me if she's okay?"

As she shook her head, his phone rang. Did she mean she couldn't tell him, or that Ruthie wasn't okay? He glanced at his phone. A New York number, unknown to him. Normally he would have ignored the call, but his instincts spurred him to answer. "Cameron Thorne."

"Mr. Thorne, this is Officer Barnett from the New York State Police. Do you know a Mrs. Ruthie Sanders?"

They must have seen his number on her phone from his text. He feared the worst. Swallowing, he muttered, "I'm actually standing out front."

"Please stay there. We're going to need to ask you some questions."

✠

Amanda and Astarte had landed in Boston and were driving Cam's Pathfinder up Route 93 in the evening rush hour. "Nice work, Mum, staying on the right side of the road."

"No use trying to fight the heathens," she said with a smile. Some of the past few months' sadness had wafted over her when they landed, but not nearly as bad as before their holiday. Hopefully the depression was behind her. As they crossed the border into New Hampshire, traffic thinned. "We're still more than an hour away. You want to stop for dinner?"

"How about pizza?" Astarte smiled.

"Right. It's been, what, five days? I'm surprised you don't have the shakes—"

The Bluetooth interrupted, announcing a call from Cam's cell. Amanda answered. "Hi, Honey."

"Don't tell me where you," he said tersely. "Just tell me if you've arrived at your destination yet.

"No. Why?"

"Thank goodness. Get off at the next exit."

"Why?"

"Ruthie's been murdered. I think we're all in danger."

The words hit Amanda like a rogue wave. She gripped the steering wheel, her eyes reflexively looking in the rearview window. "Murdered? By who?"

Cam explained what he had learned from the reenactment team. "She killed the first guy, by the safe. Then she got the second guy when he came to investigate. The third guy shot her, but based on the blood trail the cops think she winged him. The cops were pretty impressed. She might have taken them all, but she ran out of bullets."

Amanda wasn't sure how to respond. "Was it random?" She pulled off the exit and into a gas station parking lot.

"The cops thought so originally. But then I told them about the map in her safe. They found a bug on her phone." He lowered his voice. "So it was my text that alerted them. Amanda, my text killed her."

She steeled her voice. "No, Cameron, three thugs killed her. Not you. And at least two of them got what they deserved."

He exhaled. "What they deserved, but not what they came for. Her safe was closed when the cops arrived."

"Wow. Tough old bird. She fought them off. All for some bloody map."

Amanda guessed that the map was what Ruthie digitized and put on the cloud for Cam to access after she died. But she wasn't going to say so over the phone and put Cam in even more danger. "Where is the map now?"

"The cops have the stuff at the station. They got a locksmith to pick the safe."

"So who were the blokes?"

"Just three local wise guys. Hired by someone to do their dirty work."

"The same someone who came after you in Ireland."

"And the same someone who may be looking for us now. So, like I said, don't go to the place we talked about. These guys obviously mean business." Which meant they probably had the wherewithal to trace the ski condo back to Cam. "We have to assume our phones are hacked also, or soon will be. So turn off your traffic app and 'find me' apps and anything else with tracking."

She nodded to Astarte, who began to jab at her phone. "Cam, I have an idea." They needed to figure out a place to meet. "Remember our friends who just got engaged?" The couple shared an exercise app, the same one used by Cam and Amanda, and the man proposed by jogging in a pattern that spelled out the words, *"Marry me?"* on the app's screen display.

"Yes."

"Give me ten minutes. Love you, and be safe." She ended the call.

She pulled out of the gas station and turned into an office park, its parking lot mostly empty in the late evening. Using the lines as a guide, she drove in a careful pattern, spelling out the letters, I-N-H-O-C.

"I get it," Astarte said, "The 'In Hoc' carving in Newport."

The rock carving read in full, '*In Hoc Signo Vinces*,' a battle cry used by the medieval Templars. The carving, located in the surf not far from the Newport Tower and only visible during low tide, exhibited considerable aging. Amanda and Cam believed it may have been left by the same Templar-related explorers who built the Newport Tower.

"Hopefully Cam will figure it out also," Amanda said. Newport made for a good meeting spot, about halfway between Long Island and southern New Hampshire.

"Of course he will. Dad loves stuff like that." Astarte chewed on her lip. "And not many people know where the carving is, even if they figure out the code. Good choice, Mum."

"And if they do figure it out, I'm hoping the first two letters throw them off, make them think we are "in" someplace with the abbreviation "H-O-C.""

Astarte smiled. "Aha. Even better."

Amanda reversed course and headed back to the highway. Astarte seemed to be handling this well, but an elderly woman had been murdered, which put them in obvious danger. To keep the girl from fixating on the murder, Amanda asked Astarte about the In Hoc stone. They had brought her with them to examine the carved boulder over the summer. "Do you still have a picture on your phone?"

Astarte pulled it up.

'In Hoc Signo Vinces' Stone, Newport, RI

"What do you remember about it?"

"I liked the way lots of people all worked together to figure out the mystery. The geologist said it was a really hard rock, and parts of the carving were worn away which meant it couldn't be modern. And then one guy noticed it said 'Ding' on the back, and someone else said that's an old medieval English word for 'fight.' And then one of the Freemasons said he's seen the saying on jewelry some of the Brothers wear." She paused to think. "Oh, and there was a woman who said the letter 'V' wasn't used until after about the year 1300, so it probably wasn't any older than that."

Amanda smiled. "Good memory. And don't forget, the area where it's located is where the Templars would have landed when they arrived in Newport. And we know it was used by the Templars as a battle cry." It didn't prove the Templars brought treasure to America, but it was one of many artifacts that seemed to prove they were here.

"So do you think the Templars carved it?" Astarte asked.

"I can't say for certain, but you'd have to be blinkered to ignore the obvious connections."

✠

Cam drove north, hugging the Atlantic coast, his mind a whirlwind of conflicting emotions. He bounced between anger at Ruthie's death, pride at her stubborn bravery, guilt at having put her in danger, and exasperation that people were dying over ancient documents. But his constant feeling was one of cold fear: He had, unwittingly, once again put Amanda and Astarte in danger.

He glanced down at the speedometer, surprised to see his body had reacted to his anger and anxiety by depressing the gas pedal. He eased back ten miles per hour to 75.

Amanda's suggestion to meet in Newport, and her cleverness in communicating it to him, had been inspired. As had Ruthie's intuitive decision to digitize her map and documents and give him the password back in November. He let out an anguished sigh. Whatever story the documents told, or treasure they led to, it was not worth dying for.

He had withdrawn a thousand dollars from an ATM after leaving Ruthie's house—his pursuers knew he was on Long Island, so there was no further danger to revealing his location. But going forward he and Amanda would need to stay off the grid. He knew a Bed and

Breakfast where they could pay cash, and he had purchased three more disposable smartphones. Had he known what lay ahead, he would have bought stock in Tracfone before leaving for Ireland.

Pushing his emotions aside, he used the drive to try to figure out their next move. Part of the problem was that he had no idea who was behind the attacks on him in Ireland and on Ruthie in New York. The assailants were after information on the Templar treasure, obviously. But beyond that he had no sense of their identity, or even their motivations. Were they after wealth? Religious zealots hoping to suppress certain uncomfortable historical revelations? Collectors seeking religious relics? Cam had dealt with all three in the past, and his experience had been that each group could be ruthless—murderously so—in their own way. And what was Brian's role in all this? The police capturing the third Long Island home invader might provide a lead, but that might take days or even weeks. Based on the past 36 hours, his gut told him he didn't have that kind of time.

All of which led to one conclusion: This ended only when someone found the treasure. And since Ruthie's heroic stand meant he had the only copies of the map, that probably meant this ended only when *Cam* found the treasure.

☩

Dog tired and eager for a hot shower, Cam paid cash at the toll and began to cross the Newport Bridge just after nine o'clock. A light snow fell even as a full moon peeked from behind the clouds to illuminate the waters of Narragansett Bay. On the far shore, the In Hoc stone lay in a few feet of water (it being high tide) not far from where the Templars would have landed before building the Tower. Amanda and Astarte waited for him someplace close by. Hopefully.

He gripped the steering wheel, his eyes searching the far shoreline for any sign of them, resisting the urge to speed across the slick bridge. *Easy, you won't do anyone any good wrapped around a bridge stanchion.*

At the far side of the bridge he veered off the main road and parked in a service entrance to a Colonial-era cemetery a few blocks from the shoreline. He was certain he had not been followed, having reversed course a number of times and even once making an illegal U-turn on the interstate. But he needed to be certain about Amanda as well.

Presumably she was parked along the shoreline near the ancient artifact. Cam removed his yellow windbreaker and replaced it with a black fleece and dark baseball cap. He thought about pretending to be a local jogger out for a nighttime run, but that would limit him to a single pass through the neighborhood. He needed more certainty than that.

A few streetlights lit the densely-packed residential neighborhood, but he was able to keep to the shadows as he walked the three blocks toward the harbor. In the distance, the sound of waves gently lapping against the breakwall beckoned him. Light snow, gentle waves, soft moon. He hoped they didn't lull him into a false sense of security. Somehow their enemies, whoever they were, always seemed to be one step ahead. He had to assume that might be the case tonight.

He moved methodically, stopping a block away from the water-front to survey the surrounding streets. Idling cars, joggers, slow-moving vehicles, even utility vans—any of them could portend imminent danger. Finding nothing, he doubled back. Still nothing.

He took a deep breath. Time to move to the actual meeting spot, the road running along the shore where the In Hoc stone rested in the surf. He gripped the metal flashlight he had slid into his pocket. Thus far, their enemies had not been subtle. If they had followed Amanda, it was entirely possible they lay in wait only feet away. Cam reached the corner and crouched behind a car, scanning the neighborhood. He immediately spotted his maroon Pathfinder, breathing a sigh of relief at the sight of a pair of heads silhouetted in the front seat. At least they had made it this far. A street sign warned against overnight parking, which had the effect of limiting the number of cars to a single vehicle other than Amanda—a dark pickup truck, six or seven car lengths away. Cam squeezed the flashlight.

A spotlight went on and a door closed as an elderly woman put a small dog out on a leash in her front yard. The light illuminated and apparently startled the occupants of the pickup, a pair of amorous teenagers parking along the oceanfront. The truck engine roared to life and raced away. Cam exhaled. Turning, he scanned the area behind him one final time. Nothing. He released his grip on the flashlight. They were, by all appearances, alone.

He circled, approaching from the front so as not to startle his wife and daughter. Amanda rolled down her window and smiled. "Howdy, Sailor. Welcome ashore."

He leaned through the window and kissed her, lingering for an extra second, breathing her in, finding comfort amid the roiling emotions of the past day.

"Gross," Astarte sang from the passenger seat.

Cam winked at Amanda. Their kissing had never bothered Astarte before. But she seemed to have crossed some kind of threshold with her budding romance with Raja and was perhaps dealing with strange and new feelings in her own body.

Cam shook the thought from his head. They were a long way from normalcy, and things like Astarte's teenage love life would have to wait. He disengaged and climbed into the back seat.

"You certain you were not followed?" Amanda asked.

"As certain as I can be." They had been careful to pay cash for everything, but the rental car was in Cam's name, and he could be tracked if someone somehow gained access to the Hertz data base. Was it possible? The answer totally depended on who was stalking them, which remained a complete unknown. And his Pathfinder had been sitting in the airport parking garage for five days; someone easily could have attached a tracking device. He explained his concerns to Amanda. "So we may still not be totally off the grid."

"Well, let's get off it then. I have an idea." They picked up Cam's rental car and together drove to the outdoor parking lot next to the bus station and tourist information center. "We'll leave our vehicles here and take a Lyft to the inn. There must be hundreds of lodging spots in Newport. Even if they tracked us this far, there's little chance they can find us tonight."

Cam nodded. "Okay. But what about tomorrow?"

"We worry about tomorrow, tomorrow."

Chapter 10

Tossing next to Cam in a lumpy queen-sized bed, Amanda kicked off the covers, the regular breathing of Astarte and light snoring of Cam in sync with the lapping of waves below the slightly-open window of their waterfront cottage. She could not shake the dream. In fact, she had awakened three times now, only to have the dream repeat itself, in one form or another, every time.

She knew better than to ignore her subconscious. It was calling to her, sending a message. So rather than go back to sleep, she climbed out of bed to write down every detail she could remember while it was still fresh.

Using the light on her phone, she sat at a wobbly desk, pen in hand, and replayed the dream in her mind, dissecting and analyzing. Each of the versions of the dream had been different—disjointed and choppy, as most dreams were. But the gist remained the same and, using poetic license, she distilled the sometimes incoherent wanderings of her subconscious into a rational narrative:

She and Cam stood over the Crusader's Tomb, back in St. Nicholas Church. Nearby, Astarte and Emmy played hopscotch, using the tombstones inlaid into the floor of the church as hopscotch squares. As at the Milano Farm, Emmy insisted that every game end in the now-familiar chant: "Two, one, seven, three, Emmy!"

With an eerie creak, the lid of the Crusader's tomb rose. Vampire-like, a medieval knight wearing a Templar cloak sat up, his chain mail jingling in the still air of the church. Amanda and Cam stepped back, not out of fear but to allow the knight room to step out of his coffin. He did so stiffly, reaching for his sword. Blinking, he scanned the far wall, the wall which boasted the skull-and-crossbones above the exterior of its arched door. The figure of a large, bearded man passed through the thick wall, as if the passageway had not yet been sealed shut. The bearded man approached, his wool cloak rustling as he walked, and removed his three-cornered leather hat. He bowed, showing a bald head and aquiline nose, his skin creased and weathered. Ignoring

Amanda and Cam, he spoke to the Templar knight. "I am Columbus. At your service."

The knight bowed in turn. "It is a service for which we are willing to pay dearly, as has been agreed."

"Members of your Order have always been more than generous in our dealings," Columbus replied, his tone formal and diffident.

As Astarte and Emmy continued their game, seemingly oblivious to the scene unfolding around them, the knight pulled his sword from its scabbard—not a medieval battle sword, but rather a short-bladed weapon with a dark wooden handle, the blade encoded with a series of symbols and lines, the specifics of which were hidden from Amanda's and Cam's view. Columbus eyed the sword greedily, but the knight turned away and set the weapon aside. From inside the scabbard, the knight removed a tightly-rolled parchment scroll, undamaged despite sharing its encasement with the razor-sharp edges of the sword blade. With two hands extended and his head bowed, the Templar held the scroll out to Columbus. "Many of my Brothers have paid with their lives for this. And many more will die to protect the secrets it holds."

Columbus nodded. "I will deliver it safely. Upon my honor."

The knight studied Columbus for a count of three, a look of doubt apparent in his visage, before exhaling. Apparently resigned to the fact that he had no choice but to trust Columbus, he reached into the tomb and extracted a leather rucksack. "The charts," he said simply, presenting the bag to the navigator.

Columbus bowed and accepted the offering. "Again, more than generous."

The Templar lifted his chin. "May the Goddess bless your voyage."

"And may the Goddess bless your soul."

As the Templar returned to his tomb, Columbus turned, retraced his steps, and passed through the same stone wall through which he had entered. As he disappeared, Emmy's chant filled the church, as if in victory: "Two, one, seven, three, Emmy!"

Amanda tapped her pen. Was there anything else? She had the vague notion of someone lurking in the shadows, his face reminding her of Brian's, his eyes mismatched like Emmy's. But his role in the dream was undefined, as if her subconscious hadn't yet determined his importance in their drama.

But even without Brian, there was plenty to chew on. She eyed Cam in the blue-gray light of dawn, deep in slumber. She'd let him sleep. But when he awoke, they had some things to figure out.

✠

Cam awoke at seven to see that Amanda had already walked to the main house of the inn to scavenge a light breakfast. "I thought we should stay out of sight as much as possible," she said.

"Good idea." In addition, as much as he would have enjoyed a hot meal, he was anxious to dive into Ruthie's map and documents. After a hot shower, he had downloaded them off Ruthie's Dropbox account last night, smiling as he input the '*matzo ball soup*' password. But he and Amanda agreed they were simply too fatigued to do them justice.

"Before we tackle Ruthie's map, I had a dream."

He grinned. "Tell me your dream and I'll tell you what it means." Had it only been a week since she had said the same thing to him about his own dream, with Brian's bloody hand covering Cam's face? It felt like a lifetime ago.

"Wait," Astarte mumbled from the sofa bed as she rolled over. "I want to hear it also."

After washing up, they sat around a square butcher block table on oak chairs in an alcove of the cottage overlooking the Atlantic, the morning sun bathing their room in a warm glow, and ate croissants and fruit salad. "So, my dream," Amanda said, describing in detail an encounter in St. Nicholas Church between Columbus and the Templar knight. "The meaning is obvious: Columbus brought a scroll to North America in exchange for some maps, probably ones to help him navigate the Atlantic. What I don't know is, is it true?"

"Well," Cam said, "your subconscious thinks so. It analyzed and weighed the evidence, and this is what it came up with."

"So you think there really is a Templar-Columbus connection?"

He nodded and stood, retrieving a legal pad from his overnight bag. "Sorry to be so analytical, but I like to make lists for stuff like this. So what are all things tying Columbus to the Templars?"

They brainstormed as they ate. After ten minutes, Cam had the beginning of a list:

1. Templar flags on sails of Columbus ships.
2. Columbus in a Galway church with Templar ties.
3. Columbus marriage ties to the Sinclair family, who had historical ties to Templars and maps to America.
4. Columbus' father-in-law, himself a member of the Knights of Christ (the Portuguese chapter of the Templars), gives naval charts to Columbus as dowry.
5. Columbus from Genoa, near Templar headquarters of Seborga, where Templar journals detailing trip to North America kept.
6. Molander book detailing Columbus 1477 journey to Clark's Harbor, near Oak Island and Templar treasure.

"What about his signature?" Astarte asked. "I saw a documentary showing his signature with a Hooked X mark, like all the rune stones in North America."

Cam replied, "It's not actually his signature, it's his *mark*. That's what some people did in medieval times." He pulled up Columbus' mark, comprised of a cryptic stacking of letters and dots, on his phone.

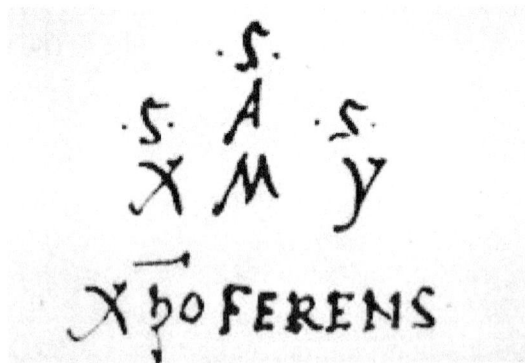

Christopher Columbus Signature

Cam pointed to the two large 'X' letters at the far left of each of the bottom two lines. "You can see the hooks on the upper right staves of the two 'X' letters. Some people think they're just serifs, or stylized pen marks. But they're not at the end of the stave, like they are with some other letters, so I think they could be intentional."

"I have something also," Amanda said. "A Genoese coin dating back to the 13th or 14th century was discovered just across the bay from Oak Island, in the town of Chester, during road construction."

Cam nodded. "Good find. I didn't know about that. If we're right that he was on Oak Island, that's a key clue."

Astarte stammered, "Um, I have another one. But I'm not sure I'm right about it."

"Go ahead, darling," Amanda said.

She swallowed. "Okay. I was working on this on the plane. For, like, forever. You know the names of Columbus' ships, right?"

Amanda shook her head. "We didn't really study him in school."

"We did. Probably too much," Cam said. "There were three— the *Nina*, the *Pinta* and the *Santa Maria*." He looked out the cottage window, over the Atlantic, half-expecting to see the three caravels approaching from the east.

"The first thing I learned is that these were not the original names," Astarte said. "Columbus changed them before his trip."

"What were they originally?" Amanda asked.

Astarte held up her hand. "I'll get to that. But first I want to explain what I was thinking." The words rushed out of her. "Dad was talking about how the Templars were Goddess worshipers, and then you started talking about the Virgin Mary, and that Bernard guy drinking her milk, and *Santa Maria* really being another name for the Virgin Mary, but then you said it wasn't really the Virgin Mary but Mary Magdalene in some of the paintings, and then Dad started talking about the Sinclairs and the bloodline and being descendants of Jesus and Mary Magdalene and the girl Sarah and the Hooked X stuff, and I remembered Columbus was related to the Sinclairs—"

She stopped to breathe. "And well, it all just came together."

Amanda smiled. "Research can be amazing that way."

"So tell us what you found," Cam said.

"Okay." Astarte shifted in the wooden chair. "Like I said, *Santa Maria* is the Virgin Mary, right? Saint Mary?"

"Sure," Cam said.

"And *Nina* means girl in Spanish. That's easy. So we have the Virgin Mary and the girl."

"I think I see where you're going," Amanda said, leaning forward.

"And *Pinta* means 'painted one' in Spanish. That one took me a while to figure out. But then I Googled it to find out what it meant in medieval times." She paused. "That was the word they used for prostitute. *La pinta*." She blushed. "Because they painted their faces, you know, with makeup."

Amanda nodded, urging her on.

"Well, then I did more research. It turns out that's what they called Mary Magdalene back then. A prostitute. *Una pinta*. Even though there's nothing in the Bible that says that."

"That was part of the medieval Church trying to denigrate women," Amanda replied.

"So," Astarte continued, patting the butcher block table, "we have the Virgin Mary, Mary Magdalene, and the girl." She took another deep breath. "Then I found the original name of the *Nina*. The ship was called the *Santa Clara* until Columbus changed it— that means Saint Clair, shortened to Sinclair. The *Santa Clara Nina*." She smiled triumphantly. "The Sinclair girl."

Cam, somewhat stunned that his little girl had done such compelling, intuitive research, simply nodded, while Amanda leaned over to give her a hug. "Bravo, darling," she said. Smiling at Cam, she said, "Never underestimate a teenager with an internet connection."

"Especially one who's been learning about the Templars since before she could read," Cam replied, chuckling.

Astarte summarized, just to make sure they both understood. "So Columbus renamed his ships after the female bloodline." She held up three fingers and counted them out:

"First, the mother of Jesus, the Virgin Mary, the *Santa Maria*.

"Second, the wife of Jesus, Mary Magdalene, the so-called prostitute, the *Pinta*.

"And third, the daughter of Jesus, the girl, Sarah, the hook inside the X, from the *Santa Clara* family, the *Nina*."

Cam scribbled a few notes and tossed the legal pad onto the table. He had quickly updated it, adding points seven through nine:

7. Hooked X in Columbus signature.
8. Medieval coin from Genoa found near Oak Island.
9. SHIP NAMES!

Cam lifted his chin. "What you found clinches it, Astarte. Sensational work."

"So what does it all mean?" Amanda asked.

"It means your dream could be, as you say, spot-on," Cam said. "I think Columbus made a deal with the Templars. They gave him maps, and he did them a favor by bringing some scroll to North America." He nodded, agreeing with himself; the assessment felt right to him. "That's the story that makes the most sense to me. Now all we need are the details." He covered Amanda's hand and smiled. "For tonight, I'd like you to dream about the Super Bowl. If you can figure out who's going to win, we can pay for that entire Ireland trip."

✠

Cam sat in the back of the car, thumbing through Ruthie's documents. He had taken a Lyft to Staples to print out Ruthie's map and documents. He had hoped the map would be simple and clear, a map with a dotted path leading to a red X marking the spot. But that's not how the secretive Templars operated. The stakes were too high, and their enemies inside the medieval Church too capable and cunning. This would take some time.

He had the Lyft driver drop him at the visitor center parking lot so he could pick up his Pathfinder and phoned Amanda. "I'm getting my car. I've been watching it for twenty minutes, and I don't see anyone eyeing it. But I'm going to take a roundabout route back to the inn." He hoped he was doing the right thing. Everything was a balancing act: They needed transportation, but were they being tracked? They needed communication, but were they being monitored? Most fundamentally of all, he wanted to honor Ruthie's memory by doing the right thing with her map, but by doing so was he putting his family in danger? "If I'm not back in, say, half hour, that means something bad has happened and you should get out of here."

"And go where?"

"At this point, to the police."

"Maybe we should go to them now."

"And say what? That some guys were following us in Ireland and we think they are still doing so here? That's not much to go on."

"What about Ruthie's death?"

"Two of those guys are dead, including the ring leader. And there's no evidence connecting that to Ireland."

"So we have to just wait until they try to kill us also?"

It was a rhetorical question, he knew, but he also understood Amanda's anxiety. He exhaled. "Look, I don't think they wanted to kill Ruthie. She fired the first shots. But okay. I'll call the cops on Long Island and give them the name of that Garda from Galway, just in case there's a connection." He hoped the gesture would placate Amanda. But as he rotated his neck, the memory of the Irish thug's strong hands around his throat, he wasn't so sure she wasn't right to be worried.

✝

Cam's words echoed in Amanda's mind. "That's the story. Now all we need are the details." She remained seated at the table by the ocean, staring at the waves crashing onto the rocks beneath the cottage window. They had chosen the private cottage both for its location along the ocean's edge and because of the seclusion it offered. Astarte was in the shower, leaving Amanda alone with her thoughts.

They had discussed most of her dream, but not the part about Astarte and Emmy playing hopscotch. Amanda recalled the words of the woman from the farmer's market, warning that Emmy's mismatched eyes were the mark of the devil. And Cam had said all they needed to figure out were the details. The obvious clichéd question popped into Amanda's head: In interpreting this dream, was the devil in the details? And if so, was the devil somehow incarnate in the person of Emmy? She shook the thought away, disappointed in herself for allowing the trauma of the past few days to make her as superstitious and small-minded as the farm stand woman.

But she couldn't shake away the image of the looming Brian-like figure in her dream, his eyes mismatched like Emmy's. Was he, rather than Emmy, the devil? Was that the message her subconscious was trying to send? She sighed and rubbed her face with her hands. It was a dream, after all. Not to be taken literally. But not to be ignored, either.

Lifting her eyes, she scanned the horizon. Three thousand miles away, just north of due east, the coast of Ireland faced her. South of that, and past the Straits of Gibraltar, Italy extended boot-like into the Mediterranean. Italy appeared as a frequent backdrop in this drama, with many of its key players located there—Marcinkus, the rogue P2 Masonic Lodge, Columbus, the medieval Templars in Seborga, the Vatican. The thing that tied everything together, the common thread, was Archbishop Marcinkus. It always seemed to come back to him. Was there more to be learned about the powerful Vatican banker?

Amanda dove in, using a Google search to learn as much as she could about Marcinkus. Her eyes widened. 1983. A young girl, the daughter of a Vatican employee, was kidnapped in Vatican City while walking home from a music lesson. She was never found. One prominent theory posited that her father stumbled upon evidence of misdeeds at the corrupt Vatican Bank, headed by Archbishop Marcinkus, and that Marcinkus ordered the girl taken as a way to keep her father quiet. Every few years a new lead in the story appeared, dominating the worldwide news cycle for a day or two before fading back to obscurity. Most recently, in September of 2017, an article appeared in the *New York Times* detailing a typewritten document, stolen from an armored Vatican cabinet and then leaked to an Italian journalist. The five-page document, entitled, "A summary of expenses sustained by Vatican City State," was authored by a cardinal and addressed to two archbishops. The document identified the kidnapped girl by name and birthdate and listed a running tab of expenses, totaling 250,000 euro (equivalent to $300,000), incurred by the Vatican for her upkeep and care, including room and board and medical expenses, most of it spent outside of Italy.

Amanda sat back. Why would the Vatican pay living expenses for a kidnapped girl? There could be only one logical answer: They were somehow responsible for the abduction. Whether they felt a moral obligation to pay her expenses, or were doing so under the threat of blackmail, didn't matter. That they were doing so at all was a clear admission of guilt.

Such a tragic story, and still unresolved. Had the girl's whole life been spent in custody, separated from home and family and country? Isolated and afraid? And all because some corrupt banker didn't want his wrists to get slapped? And then, perhaps even more damning, did the Vatican continue to keep her tucked away even decades after Marcinkus left Rome, fearing the negative publicity if its role in the kidnapping were to come out? Amanda blinked away a tear. How horrible. A life taken, wasted. For nothing.

Feeling both her outrage rising and her sorrow spreading, Amanda dove deeper into the abduction. Did Vatican leaders have no shame? She found a picture of the girl, taken shortly before the kidnapping. A pretty face, brown hair, shy smile. The face of a girl loved by her parents, a girl growing into womanhood, a young woman who would probably never have the opportunity to date or love or have children of her own.

Amanda zoomed in on the picture. *What*? She gasped.

One blue eye and one brown eye stared back at her.

✝

Cam opened the front door of the cottage to find Amanda standing at the threshold, her green eyes afire. Astarte stood a few feet behind in sweats, her hair wet from the shower. Amanda took his hand and pulled him inside. "Are you anxious to see me, or my map?" he joked.

"The map can wait, Cameron." She shoved her tablet at him. A girl's face. "Who does that remind you of?"

Mismatched eyes. "Emmy, of course." Why was Amanda so fired up?

"We call her Emmy." Amanda held his eyes. "The world knows her as Emanuela. Emanuela Orlandi." Amanda handed him the tablet. "You can read all about her here."

Eyes racing, Cam read about the decades-old kidnapping. He dropped into an arm chair. "Wow. You think that's our Emmy?"

Amanda paced the room. "It bloody well has to be. Same eyes. Same name. Same age. Both growing up in Vatican City. Not to mention Brian visiting the farm."

Cam nodded slowly. "Yeah, too much for a coincidence. Way too much." Amanda had the advantage of having had time to process this. "So what happened?"

She pushed her hair back. "Astarte, tell Dad what you think."

Astarte sat on the bed, pulling her socks on. "Maybe she got hurt during the kidnapping. She fell, or tried to escape, and hit her head."

Amanda weighed in. "If she was hurt badly, they'd have to bring her to a hospital. Which meant doctors and nurses and paperwork. Which meant the blokes that kidnapped her couldn't return her to her family because too many people could identify them."

Cam nodded again. Even the most hard-hearted Vatican official would rather not let a young girl die on his watch. And it was possible the abduction was only meant as a scare tactic, with the expectation the girl would be returned safely to her family. "So when things went sideways," he reasoned, "they had to scramble. They whisked her away, set her up in a new life in the Irish countryside, far from Rome." And, according to the accounting memo, paid her expenses.

"So Roberto is not really her brother?" Astarte asked.

Amanda replied, "Likely not. And come to think of it, there's but a slim family resemblance."

Astarte chewed her lip. "Don't we have to help her? Rescue her?" She stood suddenly. "Maybe the hopscotch chant is some kind of clue. She was really insistent we say it every time." She murmured, "Two, one, seven, three, Emmy…"

"You know, that's not a bad thought," Amanda interjected. "It could be a clue."

"If it is, it's a clue that's thousands of miles away," Cam said. "And we have our own problems right now."

Astarte blinked. "But we can't just … do nothing."

"She seems well-cared for, at least," Amanda said. "And I agree with Dad. We can't do much from here." She reached over and took Astarte's hand. "But I have a feeling that solving this Templar treasure mystery will allow us to figure out what really happened to Emmy. Then we can try to help reunite her with her family."

Astarte gently removed her hand. "Maybe it's the other way around. Maybe figuring out what really happened to Emmy can help us find the treasure."

✝

"Okay, we need to make a plan," Cam said, still shaking his head at the revelation that Emmy had been kidnapped. They sat at the table in the cottage alcove, all three chairs arranged to allow for a view of the ocean. "We can't stay here much longer."

Amanda nodded. "I agree. But we need to figure out this Emmy mystery and also Ruthie's map." She checked her watch. "It's just past nine. Let's take an hour, then pack up and hit the road."

Astarte said, "I want to research Emmy's kidnapping."

"And I'll help you with the map," Amanda said.

Cam spread some papers on the table, the morning sun bathing them in a bright light. "There's a poem also, which obviously is some kind of clue. And then some of Ruthie's notes."

"Let's ignore the notes," Amanda said, one knee on a chair as she stood and peered down, "and try to figure it out ourselves first."

"Okay. Here's the map. It's in French, and I'm pretty sure it depicts Narragansett Bay." They examined it together. The dots were smaller islands, and the spot where the horizontal and vertical lines intersected near the bottom was just east of Newport, which was located on the southern part of the larger Aquidneck Island. He had expected something to be marked in or around Newport, but there didn't appear to be anything flagged in that area. He angled his head. "Ruthie left this for me for a reason. She thought it was important."

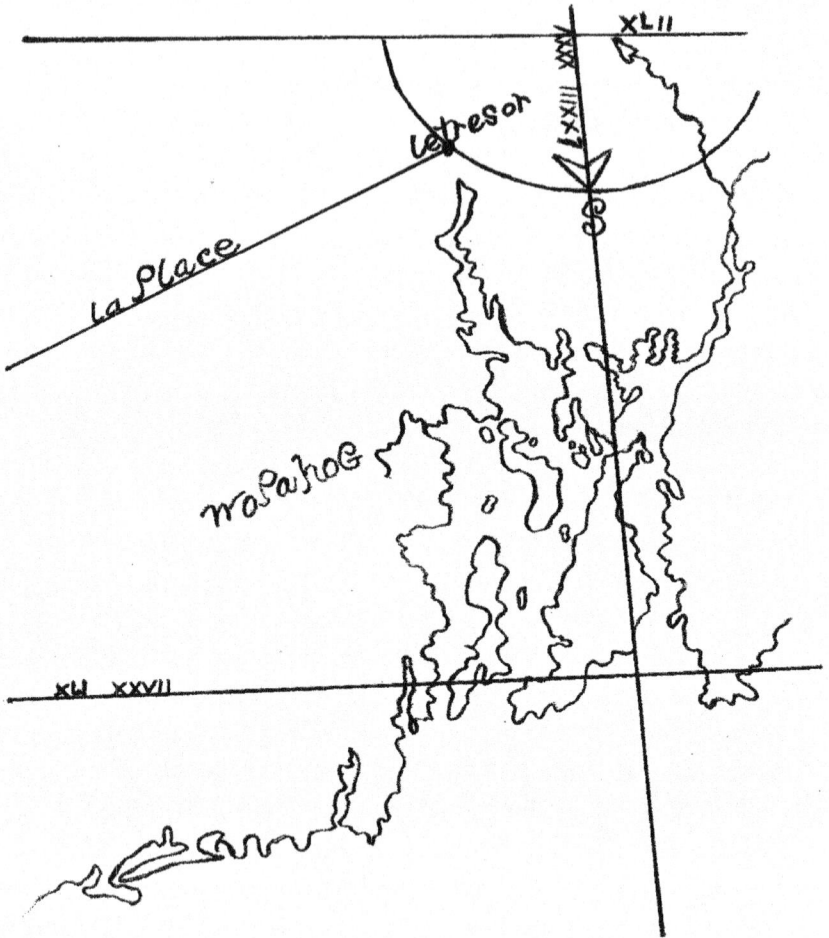

Templar Narragansett Bay Map

"This is from the Templar journal, right?" Amanda asked.

Cam shook his head. "No. Based on what Ruthie told me, the map was found with the journal, but it was a separate document. So it could have been added later." He took a deep breath. "Let's look at it piece by piece."

Amanda sat back. "To start, those straight lines look like latitude and longitude."

Cam translated the Roman numerals, beginning with the horizontal lines. "The bottom latitude line says 41 degrees, 27 minutes. So about 41.5 degrees. That's pretty accurate for Newport. And the one at the top is 42 degrees. That's the border between Rhode Island and Massachusetts. Again, accurate." His eyes flicked between Ruthie's map and the one on his phone. He pointed to the vertical line. "But the longitude is off. It says 73 and change, but it should be 71 and change."

"Not surprising," Amanda said. "It's an old French map. I'd wager they were using Paris as the prime meridian, not Greenwich."

Cam nodded. "Of course." He looked up the difference in degrees between Paris and Greenwich and did the math in his head. "That's it. It's spot on using a Paris prime meridian."

"Does that mean it's medieval?" Astarte asked.

Cam bit his lip. "Actually, not." As much as he wanted it to be, the history didn't support a medieval origin. "People didn't start using the Paris meridian until the 1600s. During medieval times most Europeans used the Canary Islands as the prime meridian."

"So this can't be medieval," Amanda said.

"Which make sense. Look at the detail of the coastline and rivers. Even if the Templars were here in medieval times, this map is too finely drawn. It's too accurate."

"Wait. There was something in Zena Halpern's book." Amanda did a search on her Kindle. "Here it is," she said excitedly. "A letter from 1657 talking about a group of Templar descendants from France crossing the Atlantic and exploring the mountains north of New Amsterdam." New Amsterdam was the Colonial name for Manhattan, meaning those mountains were the Catskills. "There was a map, written in invisible ink, at the bottom of the letter. The map makes reference to all the known markers on Hunter Mountain, all the things marked on the front blade of the swagger sword—the table rock, the white bird carving, the cave." She pointed to the map. "And it's all written in French, just like this map."

"I had forgotten about that letter," Cam said. "And to get to New Amsterdam, they would have had to go right past Newport. Maybe they drew this when they were here in the 1650s."

"Seems logical. The dates are correct, the language matches, the Paris meridian makes sense, and the level of detail seems right. Rhode Island was settled in the late 1630s, so by 1657 the coastlines were pretty well-known."

"Right. And if it was drawn later, it would have included the political boundaries, the borders between Rhode Island and Massachusetts. So, again, mid-1600s fits."

Cam turned back to the map. "Okay. So what else do we have here?" He answered his own question. "The word 'Wopahog' is probably a reference to the Wampanoag tribe." He angled his head. "But that's not right—the Wampanoag lived further north and east than that. The Narragansett Bay area was Narragansett."

"Not always," Astarte interjected, looking up at the mention of the Native American tribal names. "Before the Europeans arrived, a lot of the Narragansett land was Wampanoag."

Cam nodded. Astarte had spent her early years living on a Native American reservation in Connecticut, so she knew her Native American history, especially the New England tribes. "Interesting. I didn't know that."

"And for those who claim these ancient maps are hoaxes," Amanda added, "it's a pretty arcane detail for a hoaxster to get correct." There were always naysayers who dismissed pre-Columbian artifacts and other evidence as hoaxes, though the sheer volume of evidence was beginning to silence even the most arduous traditionalists.

Cam focused on the last two labels, on a diagonal line near the top of the map. The line terminated along the arc of a semicircle at a point marked with a thick dot. It seemed important. He pointed. "That says 'La Place.' Even I know that means the place. But what's the other word, at the dot? Is it 'Le Desor'?"

She shook her head. "That's not a word. I'm not sure the first letter is a 'D.' Maybe it's an 'O' or a 'U.'" She found a French dictionary on her tablet and tried some variations. "Damn it. I'm not finding anything, Cam."

He angled his head. "Maybe that first letter's not a capital. Not all the words on the map are capitalized."

A few seconds passed before Amanda smacked the table with an open palm. "That's it! It's a small 't' followed by an 'r.' The word is 'tresor,' Cam." She stood and grinned. "'That's the French word for treasure. That dot on the map is *the treasure place*."

Chapter 11

Energized by their discovery of the word 'treasure' on the Ruthie Sanders map, Amanda quickly packed and prepared to leave the seaside inn in Newport.

"Come on, Astarte," Amanda said as Cam loaded the car. "You can tell us what you found about Emmy in the car."

"Where are we going?" she asked with a sigh.

Amanda stopped and studied her daughter. They had been living out of suitcases, often on the run, for almost a week now. It had done wonders to shake Amanda out of her melancholy, but clearly Astarte would have chosen a different end to their holiday—tomorrow night was New Year's Eve, and Astarte no doubt was hoping to spend it with Raja. "We need to keep on the move, honey. I know you'd rather be with your friends."

Astarte took a deep breath as Cam returned for another load. "No. I get it. And it's silly for me to complain when I think about what Emmy has gone through." She began to roll her suitcase toward the door. "Wait until you hear what I learned."

Amanda and Cam lingered at the threshold of the cottage, as if the secret Astarte was about to reveal should be sheltered inside its walls.

"So," the girl began, looking down at her phone, "this information comes from the mistress of an Italian gangster named De Pedis. The mistress says the gangster was hired to kidnap Emmy to keep her father quiet because he had stumbled onto documents showing the Vatican Bank was laundering money for the Mafia. When De Pedis died in 1997, he was buried in a special basilica in the Vatican. The only other people buried there are cardinals and bishops."

"So why was this gangster buried there?" Cam asked. "I'm not tracking you."

Astarte gave him one of those frustrated teenager looks. "To keep him quiet, Dad. Or his family quiet."

Cam nodded. "I get it, sorry. The family threatened to go public unless the Vatican gave him a prestigious burial spot."

"When this went public a few years ago, the Vatican was so embarrassed, they dug up the body and moved it."

"It doesn't prove they were in on the Emmy kidnapping, but it sure is incriminating," Amanda said. "And if you're talking about making a deal with gangsters, you can bet Archbishop Marcinkus was at the center of it."

"That's what this article said," Astarte replied. "That Archbishop Marcinkus ordered the kidnapping." She smiled sheepishly. "Sorry, I should have mentioned that earlier."

It made sense, Amanda thought. As head of Vatican Bank, Marcinkus would have done almost anything to keep the bank from being linked to the Mafia. Even kidnap a girl.

"I'd happily take my chances with a jury," Cam said. "First the $300,000 in expenses to hide her, then this burial. Not exactly the actions of an innocent actor.'

Astarte stuffed her phone in her pocket. "I'll keep looking for more when we get in the car. Where'd you say we're going?"

Amanda described the treasure label on the map. "It looks like northern Rhode Island, maybe the town of Cumberland. So we're heading up there. It's about an hour away."

"I've heard of Cumberland," Astarte said, brightening. "That's where cumberlandite comes from."

"Cumberlandite?"

"It's a magnetic rock. Cumberland is the only place you can find it in the whole world. We studied it in science class. People often mistake it for a meteorite because it's magnetic and really heavy."

They walked toward the SUV, Amanda squinting in the bright sunlight, the sound of the ocean calling to her. It would have been a great day for a stroll along the Cliff Walk, but for the fact that someone might take the opportunity to toss them over the rail and onto the rocks below. She bit her lip. "Well, what's it used for?"

"They used to make cannons from it during the Revolutionary War. But now they mostly use it for jewelry. It's called the Stone of Virgo."

Amanda and Cam stopped and called out in unison. "Virgo?"

Astarte took a step back. "What?"

"Sorry." Amanda put out a hand to calm things down. "It's just that the great cathedrals of northern France, called the Notre Dame cathedrals, were built by the Templars to commemorate the constellation Virgo. In fact, they are laid out in a pattern that matches the Virgo constellation—"

Cam interjected, "The Templars loved to do stuff like that. *As above, so below,* is one of their key beliefs."

Amanda continued. "Virgo has long been associated with the ancient Goddess. So these Notre Dame cathedrals, dedicated to *Our Mother*, have long been associated with Goddess worship. Much to the chagrin of the Church."

Astarte nodded. "With the Templars, it always seems to come back to Goddess worship."

"Yes," Amanda concurred. "It does. That's the key to understanding them."

"And," Cam added, opening the hatch and tossing his bag in, "maybe the key to understanding this map. If cumberlandite is in fact the stone of the Goddess, then it's a perfect place for the Templars to use as a hiding place. Again, they loved symbolism and allegory."

Amanda said, "At a minimum, it's an intriguing coincidence."

Cam smiled. "You know I don't believe in coincidences." He stacked Amanda's and Astarte's overnight bags next to his own.

"Okay then," Amanda said. "To sum up, we have a treasure map pointing to Cumberland, which is the only place in the world with cumberlandite deposits. Cumberlandite, in turn, is the stone of Virgo, who happens to represent the ancient Goddess and is therefore venerated by the Templars. And the map itself is part of a cache of secret documents describing a medieval Templar trip to America."

They got into the vehicle, Cam driving, Astarte in the back behind him and Amanda in the passenger seat. "And don't forget the map marks the In Hoc stone," Cam added. "So whoever drew it must have known about that carving. Which not many people do."

Amanda chuckled. "This all screams *Templar*. Secret maps and hidden treasures and Goddess worship. All we need to seal the deal is find a Cistercian Abbey nearby, like we did at Newgrange."

They rode in silence for a few seconds, until Astarte leaned forward. "Um, you might want to take a look at this." She handed her phone to Amanda. "I just did a quick Google search. Turns out there *is* a Cistercian Abbey in Cumberland. Or at least there used to be."

✠

Cam drove, an oldies rock station playing in the background as his mind played connect-the-dots with the dozen or so pieces of evidence they had uncovered over the past week: No matter how he connected them, the picture that emerged centered on Cumberland. He glanced in his rearview mirror, watching Astarte tap at her phone as she read more about the Cistercian Abbey. Amanda alternately studied the traffic behind them in her side view mirror and navigated. The drive from Newport to Cumberland, though spanning the entire north-south length of Rhode Island, was only fifty miles. They should have been able to complete the trip in less than an hour in late morning traffic. But they kept to the back roads, often doubling back, concerned the Pathfinder was being followed or tracked.

They had considered dumping the vehicle, but they needed some way to get around, and most forms of transportation except walking and hitchhiking left paper trails. Even Lyfts and Ubers and taxis, which could be paid for with cash, risked firsthand accounts from drivers not likely to forget the guy with the pretty wife and exotic-looking daughter. So in the end they kept to side streets, paying cash and avoiding tollbooths.

"You know," Amanda said, "I can't help but think that the person at the center of all this is Archbishop Marcinkus."

Cam nodded. "What Astarte found out about him was pretty wild."

"I imagine that's just the tip of the iceberg."

"I wonder if Monsignor Marcotte knows anything more Marcinkus. He spent some time at the Vatican when he was younger." Stopped at a traffic light, Cam found his friend's number and dialed.

"Don't tell him where we are," Amanda said. "I don't trust anyone right now."

"Agreed." Cam made small talk for a few seconds. "I know this might be a strange question, but what do you know about Archbishop Marcinkus?"

Marcotte sucked in some air. "Enough to tell you he was bad news. What are you into, Cameron?"

"I can't tell you. At least not now. But I think it's important. Amanda's here too, you're on speaker."

The priest sighed. "Very well. I didn't know him personally, but when I was studying at the Vatican in the early eighties he was like a rock star. Larger than life. President of the Vatican Bank, but more than that. An alpha male. Big guy, nickname was the Gorilla. Did all sorts of things priests weren't supposed to do. Hung out with Mafia bosses. Corrupt. Drank and smoked. Chased women, visited prostitutes. Now, I personally don't have a problem with priests marrying, as you know. I think the Church would be a lot healthier if we did. But whoring is another story entirely. I think it was the *Times of London* that wrote in his obituary that he had a mistress and an illegitimate child. Basically, a narcissist."

Amanda sniffed. "Sounds like he should have been a politician."

"In many ways he was. He had power, he was ruthless, and he had friends loyal to him. No matter what he did, no matter how outrageous, it didn't seem to matter. Nobody could touch him. The other Vatican officials were all afraid of him. He had a way of making his enemies disappear. Like I said, he had lots of friends in organized crime."

Cam tapped his fingers on the steering wheel. This was all interesting, but it didn't bring them any closer to the treasure. "When you said he could make people disappear, do you know of any examples?"

"There was a rich baroness, I think part of the Rothschild family. Some kind of sex scandal involving Marcinkus, then, poof, she disappeared. Found frozen to death in the mountains."

"So a mobster in a clergy collar," Amanda asked.

"The word *mobster* simplifies things too much. Some people swore by him. Said he had a heart of gold, especially when it came to kids. He was also very loyal to those close to him."

Cam wondered if the Monsignor could help connect the dots. "What about the Orlandi girl kidnapping? Was Marcinkus involved?"

Marcotte exhaled. "Many people thought so, yes. But others said no way would he hurt a young girl. Apparently he worked very hard to try to secure her release. But who knows, maybe that was just for show. The abduction happened at about the same time the banking scandal hit. Maybe a coincidence, but it all seemed tied together to me at the time."

Cam thanked the priest and hung up. "So, more dirt on Marcinkus."

Amanda nodded. "But not much light shed on the treasure mystery."

Astarte had been listening to the conversation with one ear, but also jabbing at her phone with the other. "You find out more about that abbey?" Cam asked, eyeing the teenager in the rearview mirror.

"Some history." She reported that a group of Cistercian monks had relocated from Nova Scotia in the late 1800s to 500 acres in

Cumberland, where they built a sprawling stone mother house. The structure was decimated by fire in the 1950s and the brothers abandoned the property for a sister abbey in western Massachusetts. "It's now the town library. And there are walking trails all around it."

"Well that's convenient," said Amanda. "At least we won't have to break in anywhere."

"I'm curious about the Nova Scotia connection," Cam said. "Do you know where the original abbey was?"

Astarte tapped at her phone. "A town called Tracadie. Over by Guysborough Harbor."

Cam's eyes shot up. "That's where Prince Henry Sinclair and his group first landed in 1398. There's a monument to him. How close is the abbey to the harbor?" If Sinclair and the Templars were transporting treasure, it stood to reason that the later-arriving Cistercian monks might be charged with safeguarding it.

Astarte tapped again at her phone and showed him the map. "About twenty miles."

Cam slapped the steering wheel. "That's practically nothing. Way too close to be a coincidence."

Astarte grinned. "I know, Dad. And you don't believe in coincidences."

✠

Amanda sat in the passenger seat of the Pathfinder, the sun now on her right cheek, which meant they were heading roughly northeast after doubling back a few times.

"Can I send emails?" Astarte asked.

"Sure," Cam replied. "Just don't tell anyone where we are."

"Do you think that's safe?" Amanda asked. She knew Astarte wanted to reach out to Raja, especially with New Year's Eve fast approaching. But that didn't justify recklessness.

"It's one thing to bug a phone. But if whoever is chasing us has the ability to trace emails back to a certain location, then they would have tracked us already. The people chasing us are tenacious and ruthless, but I don't think they're part of the government."

Amanda chewed her lip for a second. "Fair enough. These people seem more thuggish than sophisticated."

They drove in silence for a few minutes, Amanda's mind racing, sifting through the various clues, trying to piece a series of seemingly random occurrences together into a recognizable pattern. The *le tresor* map was from the mid-1600s. She tried to place herself in the Colonial era, to think the way they thought and, more importantly, to fear the things they feared. Before she even realized the words were coming out of her mouth, they tumbled forth: "To bigotry no sanction, to persecution no assistance."

"What?" Cam replied.

"Good question," she mumbled. "Um, George Washington said it. It was in a letter he wrote to the Touro Synagogue." Touro, in Newport, was the nation's oldest synagogue. She sensed she was on to something, even though Washington spoke the words a century after the map had been drawn. "He wanted to reassure them that their religious freedom would be honored." She turned to glance at Astarte. "Did you know Rhode Island was known for its religious freedom? It was founded by Roger Williams, who was kicked out of the Bay Colony—Massachusetts—for advocating religious freedom and separation of church and state. He was lucky the bloody Puritans didn't hang him for it. Anyway," she continued, "I was just thinking about this treasure map and the political climate of the times. We're talking 1657—that's the date of the letter saying the French Templar descendants were in the Catskills. As I said, Massachusetts was in the firm grip of the Puritans. New York was almost as orthodox, even though it was ruled by the Dutch. The Templars had come here, brought their treasures here, to get away from the overbearing Church. But the Puritans were just as bad, and maybe worse."

Cam nodded. "So you think the Templar descendants may have seen Rhode Island as a safe haven?"

"Perhaps. And perhaps they decided to move their treasures here, out of New York and Massachusetts and other colonies that were turning suppressive and intolerant."

"Can you check that 1657 letter again?" Cam asked. "Didn't it say something about a hundred men?"

Amanda opened Zena Halpern's book on her Kindle. "Here it is. It talks about a voyage across the Atlantic, with 24 French noblemen and over 100 of their soldiers and servants. The letter is vague, but it shows a map of Hunter Mountain and refers to the mountains north of New Amsterdam."

"That's a large group to send across the ocean in the 1600s."

Amanda concurred. "That's what got me going on this. Why send over a hundred men to America? It must have been an important mission."

Astarte weighed in, "Like finding a treasure."

"I think more than a treasure," Amanda said. "Paying for the voyage itself would have cost a fortune. So it went beyond gold and jewels. Whatever the treasure was, it was a priceless one."

"Things like the Ark of the Covenant and the Holy Grail," Cam said.

Shrugging, Amanda replied, "Perhaps. But the Templar journals don't hint at anything so ... iconic. Instead they talk about ancient scrolls and secret documents. I think that's what we're looking for. Something the Church did *not* want them to have." She bit her lip. "I mean, why would the Church care if the Templars found the Ark of the Covenant or the Holy Grail? It would be a good thing, not something that needed to be kept hidden in some cave across the sea."

Cam nodded. "Makes sense. Finding the Ark would make them heroes. I get the sense that the Templars were afraid that what they found—and later hid—would make them, well, dead."

✠

Even with all the twists and turns, they arrived in Cumberland well before noon. Cam followed a state highway to Monastery Drive, turned onto a tree-lined access road, and parked in front of a sprawling complex consisting of a mishmash of architectural styles. "The monastery was named *Petit Clairvaux*, after Bernard," Cam said. He glanced up. "At least there are no lactation scenes decorating the façade."

"That might have actually been an improvement," Amanda said, grimacing. "It's like some collector gathered examples of architecture throughout the centuries and joined them together at the hip."

Cam studied it. "I think what happened is that the fire destroyed swaths of the abbey. But where it didn't, they preserved the walls. And where it was destroyed, they filled in the gaps over the years."

"Too bad," Amanda said. "The abbey structure itself is grand." Stone and dark wood, like a country estate. "The modern stuff is, well, less grand."

"Yeah," Cam said, "it's like hanging the Mona Lisa on the fridge next to a second-grader's art project."

"Hey," Astarte said. "I worked hard on that stuff."

A bright sun shone, and the weather was unusually warm for late December. "Feels like Ireland weather," Amanda said as they got out of the Pathfinder.

"Well, hopefully nobody's going to throw me into a river," Cam replied.

They approached an auxiliary building fronting the complex which Cam guessed used to serve as the abbey's outer entrance. They passed under a stone arch and through a heavy, ten-foot-high, dark wooden door. "Reminds me of that jail in Dublin," Astarte said.

Amanda ran a hand over the thick stone walls. "Perhaps there were things within they were trying to keep from escaping."

They entered the main library, where an informational brochure and some old photos confirmed that the complex had, indeed, been built around those parts of the abbey that had survived the 1950 fire. A friendly janitor brought them to the basement, but there was nothing to see but an unremarkable foundation. If a treasure had been hidden below the monastery, it was now lost to history.

Amanda grabbed a map of the trails surrounding the monastery complex. "There's 500 acres here. Maybe they hid something in the woods nearby."

Cam nodded. "Or it was originally in the building, and they moved it into the woods after the fire."

Amanda sniffed. "Or there was never any treasure here to begin with, and we're just chasing our tails."

Cam leaned in to Amanda as Astarte examined a photo on the wall. He patted her butt. "I've chased tail before, and it led to quite a treasure." He regretted it even before the words had left his mouth. "Sorry, that was sappy."

"You think?" She rolled her eyes, then smiled. "Besides, it wasn't treasure, it was fool's gold."

"Then I would be that fool." He kissed her quickly. It was good to have her back, sarcasm and all.

"Guys, we're in a *library*," Astarte said, rolling her eyes.

Chuckling, Cam led them outside. "Well, I say we take a look around. I've been in planes and cars for the past few days. I could use a hike."

"Are we just going to wander?" Astarte asked. "What are we looking for?"

Cam straightened. "We have one more clue. The poem. It was written in code, but Ruthie translated it. Here's the first stanza." He pulled it up on his phone, where he had saved it, and read aloud:

"Go you to where the brothers of Bernard pray,
North and west into the forest find your way,
What you think on a rise be a stone fort,
Be in truth on the landscape a stone wart."

"Wait," Amanda said. "If it rhymes in English, it must have been written in English, right?"

"Fair point," Cam replied.

"Which means it wasn't written by the Templars, or by the guys who drew the map. They all spoke French."

"Good point," Cam said. "So it must have been written later by the Cistercian monks. The caretakers."

"Then how did Ruthie end up with it?"

Cam shrugged. "I don't know. Maybe she followed the map to the abbey, then tracked down the Cistercians. They moved up to western Massachusetts after their abbey here burned down."

"But why would they give her the poem?"

Cam shrugged again. "Maybe it's one of those quests, where people prove they are worthy of succeeding by following the clues to the end. Maybe she was the first one to make it that far, so they gave her the next clue."

"Guys," Astarte said, bouncing from one leg to another. "It doesn't matter. We have the poem. And it says to go to where the brothers of Bernard pray. I assume that means Bernard de Clairvaux. And his brothers are the Cistercians." She gestured around them. "We're here. The poem says now we need to go northwest."

Amanda furrowed her brow. "Which is a different direction from where I fancied we'd look."

"Which was?"

"There's a monument here called Nine Men's Misery. It commemorates where nine Colonists were tortured and killed by Native Americans during King Philip's War in 1676. It's actually a cairn, a pile of stones, like at the old megalithic sites. In 1928, the Cistercian monks squared off the pile and added concrete along with signage to the monument. It's believed to be the oldest veterans' memorial in the States." She bit her lip. "Since the Cistercians went to the trouble of enhancing it, and since it's a cairn like the ancient burial sites, I thought it might make a good hiding spot." She looked down at the map. "But, again, it's not in the right direction."

"Interesting. But I still vote we go northwest," Cam said. "Then, if we don't find anything, we can circle around to the Nine Men's Misery memorial."

Amanda nodded. "Okay then. Northwest it is." She glanced at the trail map. "There's a trail that goes out that way. Sounds like we're looking for some kind of stone formation."

They crossed a field behind the library complex and found the path accessing the trails. The sun had dried the ground in places, but trails in shadowy areas remained spongy. Astarte, energized by the adventure, bound ahead along a path that bisected two ponds. Cam watched as, using a paper clip, she examined stray rocks along the way, concentrating on brownish-black ones with white crystals. After a few dozen unsuccessful attempts, she called out in victory. "Ta-da! Found one."

"A piece of cumberlandite?" Cam replied.

"I think so." She held up a lemon-sized dark stone, the paper clip hanging from it. "It's magnetic."

"Nice work, honey," Amanda said.

Astarte handed it to her. "It's for you."

"Hey, what about me?" Cam lamented.

"I'll look for a lump of coal for you." She grinned. "Like the naughty kids at Christmas."

She raced ahead again. She was at that age where she could be a mature young adult one minute and a goofy kid the next. Periodically checking to make sure they weren't being followed, Cam and Amanda caught up to her a half-minute later at a fork in the path. "Which way now?" Astarte asked.

Amanda glanced at the sun, getting her bearings. "To the right. The left path circles back, but this one heads basically northwest. But first let's tuck our pants into our socks. Ticks can live even through the winter and this trail gets narrow."

After a few hundred yards, Astarte stopped and pointed to her left at a cubic white-marble rock sitting atop a triangular black stone on a bed of wet leaves in a clearing in the woods. "Do you guys see that?" Each stone approximated the size of a toaster oven, with no other rocks nearby. Just the two stones, contrasting each other in color and shape, stacked together alone in the clearing.

Cumberland Stacked Stones

"That must be some kind of trail marker," Amanda declared. "Stones don't end up stacked that way by themselves."

"Agreed," Cam said. "If it's a marker, maybe it leads to the stone fort."

They continued in a northwest direction, the path fading to barely more than a thinning of the trees. Astarte, again in front, followed a curve in the trail and froze, her arm stretched out and her finger pointing. "Look at that."

A massive stone outcrop, the size of a one-car garage, rose out of the ground amidst a copse of new-growth trees atop a slope fifty yards off the trail.

Cumberland Outcrop

Cam stared. They had not seen any other outcrop in these woods, much less anything this massive. It was clearly an anomaly. Which made it an ideal marker.

"Well, that's our fort," Amanda said. "Or wart, as the poem says."

They approached. The formation was almost alien, its edges sharp and ragged like one of those Transformers kid toys. "Granite is usually smooth and rounded," Cam said. "This looks like slate. Rhode Island has a lot of it."

"Is that important?" Amanda asked.

"I don't know. But it's pretty eye-catching."

Astarte, who had again run ahead, called from the backside of the outcrop. "I found something else."

Four small stones had been carefully stacked atop a ledge running off the back of the slate outcrop to form a cairn. "Again, manmade,"

Amanda said. She shrugged. "Could be Native American, could be Wiccan, could be kids playing in the woods."

Cumberland Outcrop Cairn

"Or could be Cistercian monks marking a trail," Cam replied. "But either way, I agree. This is definitely the stone wart from the poem."

"So what next?" Amanda asked.

"I suppose I should read the next verse," Cam said. He read aloud:

"Often a wart is found on the side of a nose,
You must find where the wart's nose grows,
Follow the nose for 100 paces straight,
As would a Roman with his usual gait."

"The wart's nose?" Amanda repeated.

"I see it," called Astarte. "It's there, on the upper right. Sticking out."

Cumberland Outcrop

Cam nodded. "Cute. Instead of a wart on a nose, we have a nose on a wart."

Amanda replied, "Not bad, I suppose, for a bunch of monks sworn to silence."

"And it's pointing northwest," he said. "So 100 paces."

"Wait, Cameron," Amanda said. "What's that about the Roman? It could be important."

Astarte was ahead of them, already Googling it on her phone. "A Roman pace is a stride with both feet, not just one," she said. "It says here it's about five feet long."

"Good catch," Cam said. "We would have only made it halfway using a regular pace."

Cam began to set off in a northwest direction, counting as he went, but stopped after ten paces. "Amanda, can you wait here at the outcrop and make sure I stay on track?"

"Okay. I'll call you if you stray. But 500 feet is almost 200 yards, so I might lose sight of you."

"I'll bring Astarte with me. If you do lose sight of me, call. Then she can use the compass on her phone to set a northwest direction and track me the rest of the way."

Cam marched stiff-legged, fighting his way through the forest, intent on keeping his strides constant at two-and-a-half feet and his direction true to the nose on the outcrop. Astarte skipped along ahead, ducking around trees, anxious to find the treasure. Cam smiled. To be young and certain that just over the next rise a treasure waited to be discovered.

And then to find it.

"Look!" she called. "I think I found something!"

Cam was only up to pace number 72, but he could tell Astarte was in the general vicinity of where his 100th pace would fall. Despite her excitement, and his, he trudged along, counting his steps even as he peered ahead to see what Astarte might have found. He stopped only to send Amanda a quick text: *Come, Watson, come. The game is afoot.*

Astarte stood on a faded path which seemed to snake through the forest from the general direction of the monastery. Again she pointed, a satisfied smile on her face. "Nice pacing. But sometimes you just need to rush ahead."

Cam rolled his eyes. "Words of wisdom from a thirteen-year-old." Though in this case she was correct. He had stopped at pace 96, on a small rise above where she stood. Someone had placed a four-foot-long stone cross on the ground and haphazardly framed it with a series of curbstones and other flat rocks. A pair of stones had been stacked at the foot of the cross, headstone-like, the base stone shaped like a wheel and the upper stone triangular. Moss had grown to cover the cross, turning it bright green, adding to the eye-catching peculiarity of the manmade monument deep in the woods.

Cumberland Cross

They waited a few seconds until Amanda arrived. "Well now." She studied the monument. "The cross almost looks like a body."

Cam angled his head. The upper span of the cross was, indeed, truncated, causing it to resemble a head. And there was the hint of a curve of hips on the long span.

"What's the orientation?" Amanda asked.

Cam glanced at the sun. "East-west, with the head of the cross facing east."

She nodded. "Facing Jerusalem." As was the ancient custom of religious groups like the Templars and Cistercians. "I don't think someone burying, say, a pet would do that."

"Good point." And this felt more … ceremonial … than a normal burial site. Cam focused on the headstone. Did the wheel and triangle symbolize something? Perhaps something Masonic? He Googled 'triangle on circle' and quickly found a website showing examples of similar symbology, including an all-seeing eye inside a Masonic compass and square, the pyramid (with all-seeing eye) inside a circle on the U.S. dollar bill, and the Masonic Triangle of Enlightenment, highlighting Freemasonry's 33 degrees of enlightenment:

Imagery Featuring Triangle on Circle

The examples didn't perfectly match the headstone formation (the triangular headstone being a right triangle rather than isosceles), but it was close. The two main symbols of Freemasonry were the compass and the square, the compass being a tool to draw circles and the square a tool to make right angles. The wheel and the right triangle could be seen as physical manifestations stemming from the use of those tools. And the association with Freemasonry was consistent with the location: The Freemasons and their symbolism had long been connected to the Templars and their sister order, the Cistercians. But no. Cam shook his head. His interpretation didn't feel right. Or at least didn't feel *complete*. There was something else, something more, going on here…

Amanda interjected, seeming to read his thoughts. "The triangle is a symbol for the trinity. Father, Son, Holy Spirit. Also the three stages of womanhood—daughter, mother, grandmother. The Triple Goddess. And don't forget what Astarte figured out about Columbus using the Triple Goddess to name his ships: the Virgin Mary, Mary Magdalene and the Sinclair daughter. Based on the other clues we've found this week, that would be my guess: This is a symbol for the Triple Goddess, manifesting itself in the Jesus bloodline."

"And the circle?" Cam asked.

She shrugged. "A symbol for life itself. Which, of course, is given by women. And also a symbol for equality, because it has no divisions or sides. Think King Arthur's Round Table. So, together, the stones could signify the life-giving force of the bloodline family. Or maybe the idea that the Triple Goddess, the female, should be considered as an equal to any male deity."

Cam nodded. They had run across this theme consistently in their research on the Templars. Amanda didn't need to remind him that it was this Templar belief in the importance of women—in particular their belief that Mary Magdalene was an equal partner to her husband Jesus—which caused them to run afoul of the patriarchal medieval Church.

They stood in silence for a few seconds until Amanda shrugged again. "Or, like I said, it could just be some kids stacking rocks in the woods."

"No, I think you're right," Cam replied. "Those stones were brought out here. They've been worked and shaped. Which means someone had a plan. This was important. You don't just drag stones into the forest on a lark. And they must have had a meaning, stacked like that. Probably veneration of the Goddess, like you said."

Astarte cut right to it. "So is the treasure buried here, under the cross?"

Amanda shook her head. "I don't think so. It's too obvious. Anyone stumbling upon the cross might chance a dig. I think there's one more step to this." She turned to Cam. "Is there another verse in the poem?"

"No. That's it."

"Okay," Amanda said. "Let's think about this logically. It's safe to say that whatever clues we have, they should mean something." She looked back and forth to Cam and Astarte. "So are there any clues we haven't used yet?"

"There were some markings on the back of Brian's swagger sword that I've never seen before." He cursed himself for not taking a picture. "A cross. Then some dots. Then an X mark."

"So if this is the cross, maybe the dots indicate paces to the treasure. How many dots?"

"I didn't get a good enough look at it. A lot. More than a dozen."

Astarte asked, "Was it a regular X?"

He weighed the question. "No, actually, I think it was stylized. Sort of a Templar cross turned 45 degrees."

Astarte smiled. "I think I know what to do." She took her phone out of her pocket and explained. "When I saw this cross, something about it reminded me of the Galway Crusader's tomb, with the cross on top." She showed them the image.

Crusader's Tomb, St. Nicholas Church, Galway

Cam didn't see much of a resemblance, but sometimes he was too literal about stuff like this. He allowed Astarte to continue her explanation.

"Like Mom said, this cross sort of looks like a body, and this whole thing, with the stones set around the cross, looks like a tomb." She shrugged. "So both are tombs with crosses, both facing east. And Mom just said that all the clues are probably related."

"And?" Amanda encouraged her along.

"Well, Dad said the back of the swagger sword has a cross and an X, with some paces in between. And so does the Galway church, with the Apprentice pillar being the X, if you look at it from above as a cross-section. I bet this site is a mirror of the Galway church. A cross and an X separated by a number of paces."

"Ah," Amanda said. "I get it. Like you said, mirror layouts on both sides of the Atlantic."

"Yup." She held out her phone again. "And based on this picture, I would say the pillar is about fifty feet from the tomb, right in line with it. So I think that's where we are supposed to dig." She pointed into the woods. "Straight from the head of the cross. You can check my math, but I think it's fifty feet in that direction."

✚

Brian tramped through the woods of northern Rhode Island, hoping some overzealous hunter didn't mistake him for a deer. He had tracked Thorne to the parking lot in front of the monastery using the device he had slipped under the Pathfinder's passenger seat when Thorne had given him a ride to the Newport bus station a week earlier. Brian shook his head. Had it really only been a week since he confronted his old friend at the Tower? He flexed his hand. The cut had finally healed. But not much else in his life was in order.

As Brian expected, Thorne and his hot wife (who didn't like Brian), along with their hot daughter (who was too young to know better), had found their way to the treasure. Or at least most of the way. How they had done it didn't matter. What mattered was for Brian to get his hands on it.

Fortunately Brian had arrived in time. He had taken the first flight out of Ireland, landing at Kennedy Airport in New York just after eleven this morning. From there, while waiting in the rental car line, he had tracked Thorne to Cumberland. Halfway through Connecticut, cruising at 90, Brian had noticed Thorne's SUV leave the monastery parking lot. But thankfully he had only driven as far as a nearby hardware store, presumably to purchase digging supplies. Now, finally, nearing mid-afternoon, Brian had closed to what he hoped was within a few hundred yards.

He adjusted his Irish tweed hat and peered through the woods, a pair of binoculars around his neck and a bird-watching book stuffed into his back pocket (both purchased at a Walmart off the highway) as cover in case anyone approached. He had thrown on a long over-coat to cover his bright green pants. Thorne and family had been easy to track, three sets of footprints in the wet ground, especially once they left the trails. But Brian moved cautiously, not wanting to be made. The element of surprise was his best weapon. Other than the swagger sword itself, of course. And it wouldn't break Brian's heart if Thorne finished the heavy digging before he arrived.

✠

Cam cringed every time his shovel penetrated the semi-frozen ground, though it had nothing to do with his sore neck. This was no way to unearth an ancient treasure. This dig should be the work of trained archeologists, excavating carefully to preserve not only what lay buried but also the surrounding soil in which it was found. It was the soil, after all, which would allow the exact date of burial to be determined. But trying to get a professional archeologist to pay attention to pre-Columbian history was like trying to get a cat to belly-flop into a pool. An archeologist had once told Cam that the subject of pre-Columbian exploration of America was like pornography—many archeologists were titillated by it, but none was stupid enough to take an interest in it publicly.

Cam remained certain he was digging in the correct spot. They had paced out the fifty-foot distance Astarte had estimated and stumbled upon a sharp-edged, black and copper-colored cubic stone the size of a toaster oven. The cube sat alone like a beacon in a clearing in the woods. The stone was a miniature version of the giant slate outcrop, the nose of which had pointed to the cross to begin with. Surrounding the cubic stone, buried in leaves and a thin cover of soil, a few dozen fieldstones had been set in the ground, creating a concealed circular

area approximating the size of a hula hoop. It was a simple but inge-
nious set-up. Trees would not grow around the cubic stone—and
thus not block access to anything buried below it—due to the rock
bed preventing root growth. Cam had wrestled the cubic stone aside,
pushed away the rock bed, and begun to dig.

Amanda and Astarte had each taken a turn digging and now
stood watch a few hundred yards down the path, ready to alert him if
any hikers wandered his way. The trail map clearly stated that "collecting" was prohibited. The lawyer in him could make the technical
argument that he wasn't actually "collecting"—a term commonly
understood to refer to collectors looking for arrowheads or other so-
called "collectibles." But the truth was that he knew he wasn't supposed to be digging. Yet what choice was there? Were they supposed
to just leave the mystery unsolved and the treasure unrecovered?

He had considered purchasing a metal detecting device along
with the shovel, but he knew that without proper training the device's
chirps and beeps would be of little use. So he dug carefully, scraping and pawing lest he damage whatever had been so mysteriously
and craftily hidden. Fortunately there had yet to be a deep freeze
this winter, so the ground gave way easily to the metal shovel once
he got down beyond half a foot. He now had dug almost three feet,
standing with one foot at the bottom of the batter's box-sized hole
and the other wedged into the hole's dirt wall halfway down. How
deep should he go? At some point he would need to stop and consider the possibility that they were in the wrong location—it would
only take an error of a foot or two to miss the treasure.

Brushing his brow with the back of his sleeve, he paused and
gulped some water. The winter sun had dropped low on the horizon,
casting long shadows in the forest; they only had another hour or so
of daylight. He didn't relish the idea of staying out in the woods at
night, and the blisters on his hands and the barking from his shoulder muscles and stiff neck made it clear he could not dig indefinitely.
But how did one give up and go home when standing only a few feet
from a medieval treasure? He pictured himself digging indefinitely,
bearded and bedraggled, his remaining existence wasted in devotion
to an endless, fruitless pursuit…

The shovel thudded against something hard and hollow, perhaps
freeing him from a Sisyphus-like fate. Heart thumping, Cam dropped
the shovel and scratched dirt away with his gloved hands. Probing with

his fingers, he encountered a tattered cloth or rag. The smell of oil met his nostrils; perhaps the object had been wrapped in an oily fabric to protect it from the elements. He pushed the fabric aside and ran his hands along the flat top of some kind of box or chest. Knocking on it, he heard a faint ting. A metal box? The Catskill Mountains ancient scrolls written about in the Zena Halpern book had been hidden in clay tubes, as had been the Dead Sea Scrolls in Israel. Religious relics like the head of John the Baptist were typically secreted in stone ossuaries. And monetary treasure was, historically, buried in wooden chests. This metal casing obviously hinted at a more modern burial. Working more feverishly now, Cam scooped away the soil and pebbles, ignoring the sweat dripping in his eyes.

His right index finger slipped underneath a thin loop of some kind. Cam jabbed at it, and it lifted. *A handle.* Not wanting to break it, he returned to pushing away the dirt around the entire container, eventually revealing a rectangular outline about the size of a fishing tackle box. Odd. He had expected something larger. He stood up and took a deep breath. It would be unfair to yank it from the ground without Amanda and Astarte here to watch. He phoned Amanda. "I found a metal box. I thought you might want to be here when I pulled it out."

There was a slight pause. "That's okay, Cam, you go ahead. Astarte and I will go grab a cup of coffee and wait for you in town." He was so focused on the treasure that he almost missed the sarcasm in her voice.

✝

Jogging along the dry edge of the path, Amanda and Astarte followed the trail back to Cam. They had seen only a couple of dog walkers, both following a parallel trail which skirted the woods through an adjacent field, and a husky man in the distance with a pair of binoculars who seemed to be bird-watching.

The quiet and tranquility of the forest contrasted sharply with the turmoil in Amanda's gut. Were they truly about to uncover a medieval treasure? And unlock the secrets of the enigmatic Templars? She and Cam had devoted the better part of the last decade to their research, and had made some remarkable discoveries which changed American history. But this had the chance to surpass anything they had found so far.

Fifty yards from Cam, Amanda tapped Astarte on the hip. "Race you the rest of the way."

By way of answer the teenager bolted, catching Amanda off guard. Recovering quickly, she accelerated, stretching her strides in an attempt to overtake her athletic daughter. Amanda was a competitive gymnast as a youth, and continued to work out regularly as an adult, but as hard as she pumped and strode, she was unable to close the gap on Astarte. The girl reach Cam a couple of strides ahead of her. Gasping, Amanda said, "By race, I meant let's see who can get there slower."

Astarte grinned. "Well, that was clearly you then."

They turned to Cam, Amanda dropping to one knee next to the pit. She peered in. "I see the box. But it's not very big."

Cam chuckled. "Sorry about that. You want me to dig someplace else and try to find a larger treasure?"

"No. This'll do." She squeezed his shoulder in appreciation for his hard work. "Is it ready to come out?"

"I think so. The dirt around it is pretty loose now. Can you spread that tarp on the ground next to the hole? If the box breaks, I don't want to lose anything. If it's metal, it might have rusted."

"Which begs the question," Amanda replied. "Why bury a metal box in the ground, knowing it might rust?"

Cam considered the question. "I guess if it were modern, they'd use a plastic container. So it must go back at least fifty years."

"That would make sense if the Cistercians buried it. They arrived in the 1890s and left after the fire in 1950."

Astarte spread her arms wide in a *whatever* gesture. "Guys, can we stop talking and, you know, actually take this box out of the ground? And then maybe *look at* the treasure?"

Cam nodded. "Okay. Amanda, you take one side." They reached down and dug their fingers under the dirt beneath the box, pushing remnants of fabric aside. Moving the box gently side to side, they loosened the earth's grip on it. "Ready, lift." With a deep breath she lifted, surprised at how light the container was.

Dirt fell away as they set the box on the sky-blue tarp. The box was not as deep as she expected, more of a cash box than a tackle box. Dark green in color, with splotches of rust where moisture had penetrated the oily rags. Amanda reached over and rubbed soil away from a label on the lid, revealing the words, 'Walker-Turner Co.'

"Astarte," Amanda called, pointing at the label.

"I'm on it," Astarte replied as she poked at her phone. "It's a strong box, made in the 1930s. Worth about twenty bucks on eBay." She smiled. "We're rich."

Cam fingered a latch on the front of the box. "No key, so hopefully it's not locked. Ready?"

Amanda and Astarte nodded. He paused. "Actually, Astarte, you should open it. You figured out the clues."

She swallowed. "Okay." Dropping to her knees, the motion causing the tarp to crunch, she placed both thumbs on the front of the box and forced the lid open, revealing a thick brown cloth folded neatly to fit perfectly within the box. "It looks like a napkin."

Amanda bent her face closer and sniffed. "But it's oiled. To protect whatever is inside."

Astarte slowly removed the cloth and set it on the tarp. With a shaking hand, she unfolded it. Breathless, the three of them stared down. An old-style metal key, its teeth simple and cut at right-angles, stared back at them, stamped with the words 'Citizens Savings Bank.' Some kind of safe deposit box key.

Amanda groaned and dropped to a sitting position on the tarp. Instead of a treasure, they had unearthed another bloody mystery.

Chapter 12

The binoculars had come in handy, allowing Brian to spy on his childhood friend from a distance. And saving him from rampaging out of the woods to demand a treasure which had turned out to be no treasure at all. Just a freaking key. Whoever hid this treasure either had an incredible level of paranoia or a sick sense of humor. How many clues needed to be solved, how many breadcrumbs followed, before they finally hit pay dirt?

Daylight fading, Brian lumbered back to the parking area before Thorne and family overtook him. He dropped into the driver's seat of the rented Chevy Malibu and exhaled. What now? No doubt Thorne would figure out the key clue and follow it to some safe or storage locker. And then what? Another clue? He cracked his window, lit a cigarette, and dialed an international number on his phone. A familiar female voice answered. "I'm here," she said.

"And I'm *here*," he replied. "In Cumberland fucking Rhode Island, no closer to finding this treasure than I was a week ago."

"Tell me," she commanded.

He summarized his day. "It looked like an old key, so maybe a safe deposit box or something."

"Keep following them."

"Not that easy. He knows me. And how am I supposed to explain how I found them, much less why I'm following him?"

"Keep your distance. At some point he'll get to the end of the rainbow. Then, well, just take it, take the pot of gold."

Just take it. As if it would be that easy. Cam was no slouch, especially if he thought his wife and kid were in danger. "All right. But this is starting to get ugly. It had better all be worth it in the end."

✝

The woods had turned dark and windy. Cam glanced up. Pine trees swayed over them like emaciated ghouls, seemingly angry their secreted treasure had been taken from them. He swallowed and picked up the pace, navigating the dimly-lit trail back to the parking lot. "Let's hurry," he said to Amanda and Astarte. "It's getting late."

He had double-sealed the key inside a pair of gallon-sized Zip-loc bags and stuffed the metal box into his backpack. Alone in the oversized bags, the key seemed even more insignificant than when they had first unfolded the cloth. More to convince himself than the others, he said, "This was a cool find. We're one step closer to finding the treasure. Whoever hid it went to a lot of trouble. Which tells me it must be pretty valuable."

Proving that teenagers had an innate ability to navigate the world with their eyes cast downward, Astarte had been poking at her phone during the walk through the woods. "Until the 1980s," she reported, "Citizens Bank only had branches in Rhode Island. So we're lucky. We just need to figure out which branch has the box that fits this key."

Cam shook his head, staying left at a fork in the path. "It's not that easy. You can't just go in and try your key in every box. You need to have the correct box number."

"What if you lose it?" Amanda asked Cam.

"If you can prove you're the account holder, with cancelled checks or something, you can get around it with a court order. But we don't even know who the account holder is for this."

"Probably the monastery," Amanda said.

"Unless I shave my head into a tonsure, that's going to be hard for me to pull off. And beyond that, we don't know which Citizens branch to go to."

"It says here the bank headquarters has always been in Providence," Astarte said. "In 1991 they built a new building. But before that the headquarters was on Westminster Street."

"Is there still a branch there?" Cam asked.

"Yes."

"I spent a summer working in a bank in college. They were moving the main branch, and one of the big issues was what to do with the safe deposit boxes. About ten percent of the box owners couldn't be found. They thought about drilling the boxes, but that seemed like a good way to piss off your customers. Same thing with moving them—people would come back years later and their boxes would be gone. So in the end they just decided to keep the boxes where they were. Maybe Citizens did the same thing."

"Well," Amanda said, "that should be our first stop tomorrow morning."

"They're not open on Saturdays," Astarte said. "They close at five today."

"It's just after four o'clock," Cam said. "If we rush, we might make it. We're going against traffic."

They began to jog. Amanda said, "But even if the boxes are there, we still don't know the box number."

Cam smiled, pushing a branch aside for them to pass. "You're underestimating my charm."

Amanda rolled her eyes. "Is that what it's called?"

"Well, Mom," Astarte weighed in. "It seemed to have worked on you."

"Yeah," Cam said. "If I can find the key to your heart, no way is some old safe deposit box going to stop me."

"Ugh." Amanda scooched past Cam on the trail. "We've got no bloody chance at finding this treasure."

✠

They got lucky, the normal Friday afternoon traffic reduced by people leaving early for the holiday weekend. At 4:45, Cam pulled into a parking lot behind the 19th century Citizens Bank building perched at the point of a triangular block in downtown Providence. He parked in a spot near the entrance reserved for a Senior Vice President. "He's a banker," Cam explained. "No way is he still in the office late on New Year's weekend." He opened the door and began to get out. Smiling, he added, "But, just in case they tow us, take anything valuable with you."

Astarte held up her cell phone. "I'm a teenager. *This* is my only valuable."

They marched between marble pillars and through a revolving door, Cam carrying his briefcase and Amanda her satchel. The cream-colored, arched-ceiling lobby appeared almost church-like in its design, as if to imply that God himself was protecting the deposits. Cam approached a teller. "We would like to access our safe deposit box."

She gestured to an antique elevator. "Down one floor." She glanced at her watch. "I think someone is still down there."

Cam felt for the key in his pocket as they crossed the bank lobby. "Okay," he whispered, "let's get our story straight. Grandma's box. All she remembers is it was in the Citizens Bank on Westminster Street in Providence."

They exited the elevator to face a dour, sixty-ish woman in a dark blue business suit behind a mahogany desk. Her pencil scratched across a ledger book beneath a green banker's lamp, the smell of old books filling the heavy air. But for the fact the banker was a woman rather than a man, the calendar could have been rolled back 100 years and little would have changed. Who still used ledger books? When she didn't look up, Cam leaned in to read her name tag and cleared his throat. "Excuse me, Ms. Difonzo, we'd like to get into our safe deposit box."

She completed the series of figures on her ledger line before lifting her eyes. A thin face, her graying hair pulled back in a tight bun. Glancing at her watch, she sighed. "I'll need your room and box number."

"Room?" Cam replied. "I'm sorry, this is my grandmother's box. All she gave me was the bank location."

Ms. Difonzo spoke in a monotone, as if she had explained this a thousand times to ignorant customers before, her eyes focused on some spot behind Cam's head. "We have six rooms with boxes. Each room is named after one of the New England states—Maine, New Hampshire, Connecticut, Vermont, Massachusetts and Rhode Island." Cam bit his tongue, resisting pointing out that they knew their states. "I'll need your room and box number."

Cam forced a smile. "Yes. I just said we don't know the room number."

Nodding as if she expected such an answer, the banker opened a drawer and removed a single sheet of paper from a folder. "You'll need to get a court order. This is a summary of the procedure." She held it out toward Cam with a bony hand.

Cam let the paper dangle. The bank, and the courts, would be closed over the long weekend. How long could he and his family stay on the run? He sensed they were at a crossroads, that this mystery needed to be solved now, before their enemies had a chance to regroup. By next week it would be too late.

He put on his best smile. "Are you certain? There must be another way. The whole family is gathering this weekend, and my grandmother wants to give out some of her jewelry." He held out his hands. "Please?

How else would we have the key if it didn't belong to our family?" He pushed the old-style key across her desk.

The clerk set her jaw. "Keys are frequently misplaced. And often stolen. We have these procedures in place for a reason, to protect both the bank and its customers." She turned in her chair dismissively. "Now, if we are finished here…"

"Wait," Cam blurted. He took a deep breath, ready to take a shot in the dark. After all, a one-in-six chance was better than no chance at all. He looked to Amanda for assurance. She nodded, reading his thoughts. "Grandma always told me the family roots were in Vermont, so we'll go with th—"

"Maine," Astarte interjected. "Our box is in the Maine room."

Cam's head whipped around. *What?*

The clerk blinked, equally surprised at the girl's confident declaration. Cam tried to recover. "Yes, Maine. Like she said. Not Vermont."

"Maine," Amanda confirmed.

Ms. Difonzo exhaled and glanced again at her watch. "Very well. But we close in nine minutes. I will take you to the Maine room. But first I'll need the name associated with the account."

The name? This time Amanda jumped in. "Clairvaux," she said confidently. Whispering to Cam, she added, "What else could it be? You said that was the name of the monastery."

The clerk consulted her ledger, apparently confirming Amanda's guess by cross-referencing the key number, and snapped the ledger closed with a sigh. She stood, straightened her skirt, and pulled a ring of keys from her top desk drawer. "Once there, you will be allowed one chance to open your box. We do not allow fishing expeditions." She crinkled her nose as she said 'fishing,' as if the word itself gave off a rank odor.

They followed her down a wide hallway, Cam and Amanda exchanging a shrug while Astarte marched ahead confidently. What had Astarte figured out that they had not? She had been certain about Maine; did she also know the box number? An overweight, unsmiling uniformed armed guard had joined them, apparently protocol so nobody tried to force their way into a box. Every ten feet or so they passed a red steel door on their right labeled with the name of a New England state. The fifth door read 'Maine,' which was where they stopped. The clerk opened the door with her key and stepped aside for them to enter the vault. As Astarte brushed past Cam, she whispered, "Don't worry. I got this."

Cam blinked. *Got this?* How? He looked around. The finger-shaped vault room extended the full depth of the building's basement, the streetlights of the parking lot entering through a narrow, barred window high on the room's end wall. He was initially surprised to see a window, even a small one, in the vault room, but then recalled that the building predated electricity and therefore needed natural light. Both of the room's side walls were lined with dozens of rows of lockboxes of varying shapes and sizes. Prior to the exodus to the suburbs after World War II, almost everyone stored their valuables in boxes like these.

The clerk exhaled again. "Now, what is your box number?"

Cam stammered, "I'm not sure, as I explained…"

"Well, then, we are done here," Ms. Difonzo declared imperiously, turning on her heal.

Again, Astarte interjected. "2173," she declared, without hesitation. "Two. One. Seven. Three." She pointed. "I think it's down there."

Amanda grabbed Cam's arm. "The *chant*," she gasped. She whispered, "Two, one, seven, three, Emmy."

Astarte grinned at them. She kept her voice low. "I told you the chant might be a clue. In our heads we assumed 'Emmy' was Emmy's name. But I think it was really an abbreviation. 'M-E,' for Maine."

Cam rubbed his cheeks with his hands. It made no sense to entrust an ancient treasure to the randomness of a child's game of hopscotch. And yet, here they were. For some bizarre reason, someone had made the mentally disabled Emmy memorize the safe deposit box number. And then, even more bizarrely, she had passed the information on to Astarte.

As if confirming that Astarte had, indeed, correctly interpreted the hopscotch clue, the clerk dropped her head and burrowed her way deeper into the vault. Cam quickly followed. All that was left now was to open the safe deposit box.

✠

Amanda held her breath as Cam and the scowling bank clerk each inserted their keys in adjoining locks on box 2173. Ms. Difonzo turned her master key, and Cam followed with his, together releasing the lock with a single click. Amanda's face flushed. *Astarte was right.* Incredible as it seemed, the treasure was at their fingertips.

Smiling at Amanda and Astarte, Cam slid the brass-colored box—wide and deep but not tall, resembling the top drawer of an office desk—from its nest. The movement caused something in the box to roll, the grating noise freezing Cam as he tried to balance the item lest it shatter against the walls of its prison. Moving with exaggerated care, he set the box on a dark wooden table in the middle of the room. Nobody moved for a few seconds.

Amanda turned and eyed the irritable bank clerk. Cam had tried to be pleasant to her, only to be met with increased sullenness. Well, if there was one things Brits knew, it was how to put people in their place. She cleared her throat and allowed the full timber of her English accent to ring out. "Ms. Difonzo. We require privacy." She pronounced 'privacy' in the British fashion, with a soft 'i' sound. She lifted her chin. "Please secrete yourself to the vestibule."

The clerk's eyes narrowed. "It is bank policy that I remain in the vault."

"Rubbish. This family is a longtime client of your bank. A good banker, a *competent* banker, understands the need for discretion." Amanda folded her arms and glared at the clerk. "Or shall I go upstairs and take this matter up with your superior?"

The clerk might have joined the battle, but for the fact she no doubt wanted to end this encounter and begin her holiday as quickly as possible. "Very well," she sniffed, sullenly walking toward the hallway.

Amanda turned to the overweight guard. "And you, sir, as well. The hallway, if you please."

Finally alone, Amanda turned on her phone to videotape Cam opening the box. "Okay," she smiled. "Whenever you're ready."

The lid of the box hinged at the middle, allowing it to be folded back on itself. With a shaking hand, Cam lifted the lid. Inside, turned slightly askew, rested a dark brown tube which resembled an oversized salt shaker. Alongside it sat a gold pendant and a pocket watch.

"Zena Halpern's book talked about clay tubes containing ancient scrolls brought here by the Templars," Amanda said.

"That's what I was thinking also." They focused on the tube. "Some of the scrolls were taken from under the Temple of Solomon two thousand years ago." Cam handed Amanda the watch and the pendant. "This other stuff looks modern; we can look at it later." She placed the contents in her purse.

Amanda had thought to bring a pair of cotton gloves, and, after handing her phone to Cam, she slipped them on. Slowly she extracted the tube from the box and placed it atop her cashmere scarf.

They stared at it. "Now what?" Astarte asked.

"Normally I'd say we need a professional to open this," Cam said. "But this is not a normal situation."

Amanda nodded. "Heaven help us if we destroy a priceless artifact." She leaned closer. One end of the tube was sealed with an amber, silicone-like substance. "Looks like some kind of wax."

Cam fished his pocket knife from a back pocket. "You're the museum curator. Cut it away. But save the pieces so we can have them tested later."

"Roger that." She opened the blade. Poking and scraping, she was able to extract three large wads of wax from the tube opening. The rest of the wax crumbled and fell away. She peered in. "There's a document of some kind rolled up inside. I think it's wrapped in some kind of paper. Perhaps glassine. That's the stuff they put between frozen beef patties you buy at the supermarket; it repels oils and other moisture. It was used a lot after World War II to preserve documents."

"Try to grab it. But pull very carefully."

Good advice, but how would she know how hard to pull without ripping the ancient parchment or vellum or whatever was inside? She had another idea. Lifting the back end of the tube, she shook lightly, hoping the rolled document might simply slide out. But it did not budge, the scroll apparently having expanded tight to its cocoon walls. The light above the table was poor, so Amanda moved to the end of the room to examine the scroll under a wall sconce. As she studied it, rotating the tube slowly to determine if there was a raised corner of the glassine wrapper to safely grasp, Astarte called out. "Look! In the window!"

Amanda lifted her head in time to see a flash of green swoosh by the narrow, barred opening high on the basement wall.

She knew the truth even before Astarte voiced it. "It was that guy Brian, with the green pants," Astarte said. "I saw him. He was looking in the window."

"Shit," Cam hissed. "I was afraid of that. Did he see us?"

"I think he saw you. Mum was too close to the wall; he didn't have a good angle. And I was behind this pillar."

Cam glanced at his watch. "It's just now five. If we're lucky they won't let him in. Or at least not down the elevator."

Amanda glared at Cam. "But at some point we have to come *out*. We can't spend the weekend here." She should have pushed harder to keep Brian out of their lives.

He nodded. She studied him, knowing he was trying to formulate a plan. He had better be quick, because it wasn't likely the clerk would allow them to stay much longer. And they still didn't know what was in the clay tube.

Leaving Cam to his machinations, she gritted her teeth. The time for caution had passed. Pulling as gently as possible, she tugged at the glassine, slowly extracting the scroll from the tube. The smell of old books greeted her as fine particles of decaying animal skin or parchment or whatever had been used for paper escaped from the wrapping and wafted over her. "It sure smells old. Astarte, help me." Working quickly but carefully, they unrolled the ancient scroll. Amanda removed the wrapping and laid the scroll on the table. Eyes wide, they breathlessly stared down at thick black lines of text covering a beige-colored surface, a surface which had turned yellow in places by age. The border of the document, decorated in red with a geometric design, had frayed in places, but the entire body of the text remained intact. "The writing looks Middle-Eastern. Maybe Phoenician," Amanda said in a hushed voice, careful not to breathe on the relic.

Astarte pointed. "But the caption and the signature lines are something else, I think Hebrew."

There was no time to study it. Taking her phone from Cam, Amanda snapped a few pictures and, sensing their importance, immediately uploaded them to the cloud.

"Okay," Cam announced. "We're out of time. Roll it back up. I think we only have one choice." Amanda did so, again quickly but carefully, and slid the scroll back into the canister. Cam gently inserted Amanda's cloth glove into the opening, sealing it. To Amanda, he said, "Put the box back in the wall and call the clerk." Meanwhile, he dropped to his hands and knees and removed a metal heating vent cover from the floor. Gently he lowered the clay tube into the void. He played around for a few seconds before replacing the vent cover and wiping his hands clean on his jeans.

Amanda watched. "Good plan." She smiled. "It might even work."

"Or some rodent will feast on a priceless artifact for dinner."

She placed the safe deposit box back into the wall and turned to see Cam, back on his feet, guarding the door and instructing Astarte in a low voice. "Tell the clerk you need to use the restroom. No way will she let the security guard bring you, so she'll do it herself. Stay in the bathroom until either Mom or I come get you."

Astarte nodded. "Got it."

He took her hand. "Trust me on this, Astarte. Don't leave that bathroom no matter what."

He turned to Amanda. "That leaves the two of us and one guard."

She had no idea what he was planning for their next move, but he excelled at this type of on-the-fly planning and strategy. After years of him getting them out of tough situations, she trusted him. Not that she didn't also love to tease him. She smiled cryptically. "Let me guess. I take out the guard while you run to safety."

✠

Now alone in the bank vault with Amanda, Cam smiled at her joke. He did not expect her to take out the guard, at least not literally. But the reality was she would not be thrilled with his plan. Hell, even he wasn't thrilled with it. But Brian had somehow tracked them here to the bank, meaning he had officially moved into the enemy category. And he likely had a posse with him, waiting outside. Which didn't give Cam many options. So, thrilled or not, this was the only plan he could come up with.

"Remember that movie, *Night at the Museum*, with Ben Stiller?" Cam asked.

It took her a second, then her eyes widened. "No, Cam." She shook her head. "No."

"Sorry, I got nothing else. We can't just go marching into the parking lot. You saw what happened to Ruthie."

She exhaled. "Shit. All right. But, well, shit."

Briefcase in hand, he opened the door and spoke to the security guard. "We're all set here. But my daughter just texted us, she needs help in the bathroom."

He scowled. "What kind of help?"

Cam shrugged sheepishly. "The kind of help middle school girls need from their mothers."

Amanda cut in. "Can you escort me to the restroom?"

They exited the room and the guard locked the door. He led Cam and Amanda back to the elevator. Cam whispered to her, "Tell Difonzo I'm still in the vault. That should get her away from you."

"Then what?"

"Then ad lib. Oh, and I need your jewelry."

"All I have is my wedding ring and grandmother's brooch."

"The wedding ring is too modern looking."

She unclasped the antique amethyst and diamond cluster brooch and placed into his hand.

He hesitated, holding her eyes. It was her only family heirloom. "Are you sure?"

"Don't be silly. We're in danger, Cameron. I'd give you both my ears if I thought it would help." She reached for her purse. "Oh, and don't forget these." She extracted the pocket watch and gold pendant. "Will these help?"

Nodding, Cam kissed her quickly and exited the elevator at the main floor, while Amanda and the guard continued to the second floor. Cam ducked behind a pillar and peered through the front door. A flash of green caught his eye. Obviously waiting for Cam to exit. He took a deep breath. His plan needed one more prop.

Approaching a young, dark-haired teller, he held his hands out to his sides and smiled. "I know it is past closing time, but I've been meeting with your trust officer regarding some family business. I didn't realize the time. Is there any way I could still make a withdrawal?"

The teller smiled politely. "Of course, sir."

Fortunately he maintained his law firm accounts at Citizens. "I'd like ten thousand dollars in cash, preferably in older bills." He gave her the account number.

She blanched. A transaction of this size would take time, and the bank had officially closed ten minutes ago. "Well, yes sir. Yes, Attorney Thorne." Cam would have liked to withdraw more, but he knew anything over ten grand required extensive paperwork.

While she counted his money, he noticed a raisin-sized diamond ring in an antique setting on her left index finger. "This may sound like a really strange question," Cam said, "but do you have any interest in selling your ring?"

She covered the ring with her free hand and blushed. "It's not real. Cubic zirconium. It's only worth, like, a hundred dollars."

"I'll give you five hundred for it." He pointed his chin at the stack of money. "Cash."

"I don't know. It wouldn't seem fair."

Smiling, he leaned in. "I'm a lawyer. We don't care about fair." He chuckled. "Actually, you'd be doing me a huge favor." He shrugged, as if the details were too embarrassing to reveal. "Please."

"Well, okay."

"Thanks." He smiled. "A lot. And if you have some kind of bag you could put the money in, that would be great."

While she finished counting, he flipped open his briefcase. He had stashed half a dozen active client files in it, and he found the one he was looking for. Tucked into the file was an original property deed from the 1920s for some land in Boston. It was worthless now, the property long having changed hands and a new deed reissued by the Land Court. But it looked old, and it looked important.

Cash, pocket-watch, gold pendant, Amanda's brooch, diamond ring, deed. Plus a couple of bones from a dead mouse he had found in the heating vent and stuffed into his pocket. The makings of a treasure, or at least a modest one.

☦

Huddled together in the dark with Astarte in a janitor's closet next to the restroom, Amanda texted Cam. *We lost her. I think we are alone up here.*

As Cam expected, the clerk had scurried away, presumably back to the vault to supervise Cam, leaving Amanda and Astarte alone in the loo.

"Now what?" Astarte whispered.

"We wait until they lock up."

"And then?"

"We make ourselves comfortable. It could be a long weekend." It was actually a decent plan. It was unlikely Brian and his cronies knew that Amanda and Astarte were with Cam at the bank. And even if they did, there was no way to break into the bank to get to them. Hopefully it would be easier to figure out a way out than a way in.

"What about Dad?"

Amanda reached for her missing locket. "I'm guessing he's going to try to bluff his way past them." She shifted, trying to find a comfortable position in the cramped confines.

"Do you think the scroll is safe in the heating vent?"

"Hopefully they turn the heat down over the weekend. And it's not supposed to be that cold." She shrugged. "But obviously that's not an ideal place for it."

Astarte sighed. "Tomorrow is New Year's Eve. No offense, Mom, but this closet is not exactly Times Square."

Amanda reached out and found Astarte's face, allowing her fingers to rest against it. "I know, honey. Sometimes it's hard to live with us, to be part of our family. We don't exactly live normal lives."

"It was the same way with Uncle Jefferson. He was always going out to look for treasures, always worried about people stealing his secret documents. He used to say that normal lives were for normal people, but my destiny was different." She lowered her voice. "So, I guess, this stuff *is* normal for me."

The words tore at Amanda's heart. Uncle Jefferson was wrong: A normal childhood was exactly what Astarte should have. But first they needed to get out of this bank. Amanda forced a smiled. "If nothing else, it'll be a fun story to tell your friends when you get home. Locked in a bank, hoping the alarm doesn't go off."

"Actually, that wouldn't be such a bad thing, would it? The alarm going off? That would bring the police. And then we could just walk out."

Amanda nodded. "You know, that's a good point. Maybe we don't have to spend the weekend here." Sometimes adults made things more complicated than they needed to be.

✝

Cam had stuffed the cash in an old leather carrying bag the teller had found for him, laid the deed on top, and put the jewelry and bones into a bank envelope which he placed next to the deed. Trying to look as carefree as he could, he strolled through the bank doors, the duffel swinging at his side.

Brian stepped from the behind a van. "Hey Cam."

"Brian," he stammered, stopping midstride." He turned his body in attempt to shield the duffel. "What, um, are you doing here?"

"Same as you. Looking for the treasure." As he spoke, two large men took up positions on either side of him.

Cam nodded knowingly, as if just figuring out he had been made. "Okay. Good job. You got me to do your dirty work." He lifted the duffel. "I found the treasure. Thing is, it's not all that great. And it's not even Templar."

Brian's tongue flicked against his front teeth. He motioned his head. "Into the van."

"Okay." So far so good. He had not asked about Amanda and Astarte, so maybe Astarte was right that he hadn't seen them.

They climbed into backseat as Brian's cronies waited outside. "Let me see it," Brian said from behind the driver's seat, dropping an armrest between them.

Cam pursed his lips. From the duffel bag on his lap, he pulled out the deed, the bones, and the jewelry. One by one, he handed the objects to Brian. "I think the bones are fingers or toes of Saint Bernard. I read once that all the Cistercian monasteries got some of his bones. The deed is some property in downtown Boston." He gestured toward the bag. "And there's cash, maybe ten grand. Not sure what the jewelry is worth." He preferred not to have Brian examine the cash, lest he notice the modern dates on the bills.

Brian sniffed. "That's it, ten grand?"

"That was quite a lot of money back in the day."

"What about the Templar shit?"

"I'm guessing what happened is they took all that stuff with them when they moved to western Massachusetts in 1950, after the fire."

"So what's this?"

"A couple of monks stayed," Cam lied, "to deal with the property after the fire. Maybe one of them put his personal stuff in the safe deposit box."

Brian again clicked his tongue against his teeth, studying Cam. "Hmm."

Cam decided to go on the offensive, to refocus Brian on this treasure rather than the Templar one. "So, *old friend*, now what? You going to steal the ten grand from me?" He lifted his chin. "Just like the old days?"

But Brian would not be dissuaded. "I don't give a shit about this," Brian said, waving his hand over the duffel. "But what you said doesn't add up. Why have all these clues, the map, all the *bullshit*, if there's no treasure?"

Cam shrugged. It was not his job to help Brian figure this all out.

"Fuck me," Brian said, opening the van door. He called to the two ruffians. "Get in. Find us a hotel." He glanced at the duffel. "One that'll take cash and not ask questions."

✠

Wedged into the janitor's closet with her mother, Astarte buried her nose in the crook of her arm. She didn't like to sound whiny, but *still*. "What is that horrible smell?"

"I think it's Pine-Sol. They use it to clean the floors." Amanda gestured toward a bucket on the floor next to them. "It's coming from that."

"Is it supposed to smell like formaldehyde?" Astarte crinkled her nose. She had been hungry, but not anymore.

"It actually used to smell like pine trees. A few years ago they ran out of pine tree stumps, so they switched to a synthetic product. Anyway, I think we can get out of here soon. I just saw the lights go out from under the door."

"Good. My throat is starting to hurt. Now I know how the wasps feel when Dad sprays their nest."

Amanda slowly pushed open the closet door, the creak of old hinges filling the abandoned bank.

"Shush!" Astarte said.

Amanda shrugged. "Let's go on the offensive. If anyone asks, we were in the loo and came out to find the lights off and bank closed." She clicked on her cellphone flashlight and peered out. "Hello," she called. "Anyone here?"

Astarte grabbed her mother's shoulder and pointed at a red light glaring at them from the far end of the hallway. "I think that's a motion detector." Apparently the minor movement of the closet door had not been enough to register. "If we step out there, it's going to go off."

Amanda tilted her head. "Like you said, that's fine. We'll stick to our story." Presumably Cam had somehow lured Brian away.

"I've been thinking, maybe I was wrong. If the alarm goes off, then there'll be, like, a hundred police cars. Plus cops with guns drawn. And maybe reporters. Wouldn't it be better if we can just sneak out?"

"But that'll set off the alarm also."

"But by then we'll be out the door, not up here on the third floor."

"Okay." Amanda smiled again. "You'd make a good spy."

Amanda peered down the hallway. "The camera looks like it's angled so it covers the stairwell. Makes sense—nobody can get to this floor without coming up the stairs."

"Or down the stairs from the roof," Astarte pointed out. She smiled. "As a spy, that's what I'd do."

"Fine. Either way, you'd use the stairwell. I think we can get out of the closet without the eye seeing us." She eased the door open. Nothing. Moving slowly, and keeping to the near wall, she slid out. Still nothing. "Okay, follow me."

Astarte did so, her heart thumping. It made no sense—they were in no real danger. But it was like those childhood hide-and-seek games, where the dark unknown created a sense of suspense and even fear. Probably an instinctive reaction to an age-old terror of being hunted in the night. "Where to?"

Amanda gestured toward the elevator. "What are the chances it's still on?"

Astarte knew the elevator at school was always on. "I don't think they ever turn them off." She bit her lip. "But then why focus the motion detector on the stairwell?"

"Probably because there's another camera at the bottom, preventing anyone from getting onto the elevator from the first floor."

"So what do we do?"

Amanda smiled. "You're the spy. How do we get out?"

Astarte took a deep breath. It shouldn't be that hard. Banks were designed to keep people out, not in. "I have an idea." She led Amanda to the elevator and pushed the button, calling the car. The whir of a motor responded as the elevator ascended to them. Doors opened and Astarte stepped in. She pushed the 'B' button. "Like you said, the cameras are on the main floor, where the money is. But I bet there's nothing in the basement. Maybe in the vault itself, but not in the hallway." Even if there was a security camera, and they were eventually identified on it, they could still use the excuse they had been locked in the bank after hours.

The lift descended three floors. As the car came to a rest, the doors opened. Amanda began to step out slowly. Astarte restrained her again.

"If you go left there's a door at the end of the hallway. I remember it from when we were down here. I think it's a fire door."

"It'll be alarmed, but like you said, by then we'll be out to the parking lot." She cautiously stepped into the darkened hallway, both of them holding their breath. No alarm. Amanda smiled in the glow of the elevator light. "Once we get outside, run. And this time I won't let you beat me."

Astarte grinned. "Bring it on."

Together they scurried down the darkened hallway, the neon exit sign beckoning them to freedom. As they passed the door marked 'Maine,' Amanda slowed. "Seems a shame to leave the scroll there."

The reality was they had no choice; the vault was locked. Astarte replied, "At least you've got pictures."

Amanda lurched ahead. With two hands she shoved down on the release bar, dipped her shoulder into the door and pushed through. Immediately the cawing of an alarm assaulted their ears. They stood a half-dozen steps below parking lot grade, in a concrete stairwell. "Up the stairs and we run," Amanda yelled, her face lit by a nearby streetlight. "Only question is, which way?"

Astarte didn't have a chance to respond. A pair of hulking figures emerged at the top of the stairs, blocking their path. Between them stood a tall woman, cloaked, a hood framing her familiar face.

Astarte gasped. "Emmy!" *What is she doing here?*

The woman-child nodded, her blue mismatched eye shining in the night. Roberto appeared, standing behind her, his hand on her shoulder. She lifted her chin, threw back her hood and shook out her hair. "Henceforth you may address me as Emanuela." She lifted a black handgun from beneath her cloak and waved it menacingly. "Emmy is a little girl's name. This is adult business."

Chapter 13

Brian leaned against the motel room wall and stared at Cam, his tongue flicking around behind his teeth. Cam sat in the room's lone chair, the two thugs on either side of him. One wore a black shirt, black leather jacket and a pinky ring, like an extra from *The Sopranos*. The other wore jeans and a grey hoodie with the words 'Big Six Boxing' on the front and smelled like he was still sweating out last night's beer. As Amanda had pointed out, their adversaries in this venture—first in Ireland, now here in Providence—had the feel of organized crime. Marcinkus had been known to run in those circles, so perhaps, again, this all related back to the dead archbishop. Not that the realization gave Cam the warm fuzzies. He preferred his knee caps remain in one piece. But at least Amanda and Astarte were safe.

Though decades had passed, Cam still knew how his childhood friend's mind worked. Brian would feel some loyalty to Cam, but in the end greed would win out. Cam may be telling the truth about the treasure, or he may not be. But in Brian's mind, the only way to be certain was to test the story under duress. In other words, torture.

"Damn it, Cam," Brian said. "You gotta tell me where the rest of the treasure is."

"That's all there was, Brian. Sorry. You think I would have left some of it behind?"

Brian gestured with his chin towards Cam's satchel, which Cam had strapped over one shoulder while carrying the duffel bag out of the bank. "What's in there?"

"My insulin. A passport. Toothbrush. Phone charger."

"Don't fucking lie to me."

Cam leaned forward and unsnapped the satchel, showing its contents. "See. Junk." He sat back and raised his voice. "Look, I wanted nothing to do with this. You roped me in. I got beat up and thrown in a river and almost choked to death trying to find *your* treasure. Not to mention a sweet old woman gets murdered. Then, when I finally *find* the treasure, you complain that it's not the right one. What the hell do you want from me?"

Brian's eyes narrowed. He shifted from one foot to the other, uncertainty evident in his body language. "Fuck it. I need to take a dump." Cam guessed what he really needed was an excuse to buy some time.

Brian stepped into the bathroom before leaning his head out to address his ruffians. "Make sure he doesn't use his phone."

The door closed and Cam exhaled. He needed a plan. They were on the second floor, which meant going out the window was an option. And he had noticed an iron on the floor of the closet—he could use it as a weapon, and the cord potentially also. Plus he had his pocket knife. But the reality was he had little chance against two gangsters and the burly Brian in a physical altercation. He would need to rely on his cunning.

Brian emerged from the bathroom, interrupting Cam's thoughts. "I need to make a phone call," he said to Cam. "Go in there and close the door. Leave your phone out here."

"Did you even flush?" Cam replied.

"What are you, my fucking aunt? Just get in there."

Cam began to object, then swallowed the retort. It suddenly occurred to him that he actually wanted to spend time in the bathroom. He dropped his phone on the bureau, ducked inside, pulled his shirt collar up to cover his nose, and locked the door.

Brian hadn't even closed the toilet lid. Cam inched closer and peered down. A pile of darkened water and toilet paper filled the bowl. Using a pen from his pocket, he poked at the toilet paper wad, pushing it aside. Beneath it, resting on the bottom of the bowl, sat a pile of dark, intertwined turds. "I knew it," Cam hissed.

He closed the lid, flushed and tossed his pen into a wastebasket. When Cam's grandfather had lived with them just before dying of pancreatic cancer, Cam had learned that one of the symptoms of the illness was that bowel movements were light in color and floated in the toilet bowl due to the diseased pancreas' inability to digest fat. But Brian's dark-colored shit sank to the bottom. Which meant he probably didn't have pancreatic cancer. What a surprise: Brian had been lying to him about dying. Scumbag.

Cam mulled it over. It was one thing for Brian to turn on him today, now that Cam had found the treasure. But the cancer fabrication indicated this was a long-term play, hatched before they went to Ireland. Which in turn meant the Ireland trip was not a bucket-list item but a ruse, a way to get Cam to begin sniffing around a treasure hunt which began in the Emerald Isle.

And it also meant Brian's visit to Milano Farm was more than a coincidence. Cam thought about Roberto and Emmy and their ties to the Vatican and Archbishop Marcinkus. The pieces were beginning to fit together, the picture coming into focus. What wasn't clear was how this all ended.

✠

Standing at the bottom of the concrete stairs, Amanda made a split-second decision. She tucked her cell phone into a fissure in the bank building's concrete foundation wall, maneuvering Astarte's body in front of hers to shield the movement. Nobody else knew about the scroll, and there was no sense in forfeiting what may be their only advantage by allowing their enemies to find the image on her phone.

Their enemies. How strange to think of the harmless Emmy and the hospitable innkeeper, Roberto, in those terms. But clearly things were not as they had appeared, beginning with Emmy being anything but harmless.

Amanda stepped in front of Astarte to ascend the stairs. She had a million questions, but before she could voice them Emanuela spoke, rushing her words between the wailings of the alarm siren. "Tell us where the treasure is, and no harm will come to you."

Buy some time. The alarm will bring the police. "I don't know what you're talking about. We got locked in the bank."

"Don't lie to me. I'm not a fool." She paused for the alarm. "We knew once you found the key that you'd end up here. It was our clue, *my* clue, which allowed you to open the box."

It made sense. Emanuela and Roberto needed someone to decipher the clues and find the key. They apparently knew where the treasure was, but had not way to access it short of storming the bank vault. Amanda again played to buy some time, speaking over the alarm. "Okay. You're correct. We did find a so-called treasure. Cameron has it. Astarte and I were hiding in the bank because that bloke Brian was outside waiting for us. Waiting to steal the treasure. Which wasn't even a treasure, but just some old scroll. So we did the only thing we could to keep it safe. We put it back inside the bloody safe deposit box and handed Brian a fake treasure."

"A scroll?" Emanuela leaned forward. "What did it say?"

"I don't know. We didn't have time to examine it. It was inside a clay tube."

"That must be it," she whispered to Roberto in Italian, Amanda knowing enough of the language to understand. Emmy turned to Amanda and switched back to English. "Give me the safe deposit box key."

"Sorry, Cameron has it."

"We could easily search you, you know," Emanuela said.

"Go ahead. You won't find it."

Roberto spoke, Amanda again able to understand the Italian. Just behind him, a dark SUV sat with its engine running in the otherwise empty parking lot. "I just received a call from Brian. He has Cameron."

"Tell him to stay where he is; we will come to him." Emanuela waved her gun. "Whoever has the key, it is not going to do us any good now. We can't get into the bank." She leered at Amanda. "It's going to be a long weekend, the four of us and Brian all together." Police sirens echoed from a few blocks away. "Everyone into the vehicle."

Amanda took Astarte's hand. Brian was a greedy lecher, but at least his greed was rational. There was something feverishly frightening in Emanuela's mismatched eyes. They would have been better off in the bank closet. Amanda needed to think quickly. She played a hunch. "So, when should we expect Monsignor Marcotte to arrive?"

Emanuela's eyes narrowed. "I ... don't know what you are talking about."

Amanda set her jaw. "He's been puppeteering this from the beginning. Sending us to Ireland with Brian. Suggesting we stay at Milano Farm. What I don't get is, why?"

"Enough." Emanuela nodded to the pair of henchmen next to her and again waved her handgun. "As I said, get into the vehicle."

✝

Gabriella Difonzo stood in the doorway of a florist shop across the street, watching the scene unfold in the bank parking lot. First the SUV. Then the pompous British woman and her daughter sneaking out of the bank. *Just as I suspected.* A pair of headphones, similar to what the kids wore to listen to music, rested on Gabriella's ears, the listening device she had quickly hidden near the bank's basement door transmitting the conversation.

She had guessed wrong the first time, convinced that the pushy couple had been using their daughter as a mule to sneak the treasure out of the vault. That's why Gabriella had played along with their ruse and followed the girl to the restroom rather than stay in the vault. But she was back on the trail now. Thorne's wife had just explained that they put the contents, the *treasure* she called it, back in the safe deposit box, apparently because some guy was waiting outside in the parking lot to steal it from them. Gabriella crossed herself. Whoever he was, he had been a gift from God.

Twenty-two years she had spent working at the bank, all in anticipation of this single day. She thought back, more than two decades ago, to when her parish priest had asked her if she would be willing to serve in a job at a bank. That had been two years after Harold died in a car accident, widowing her. Not that she particularly mourned his loss; the marriage had been a mistake, a concession to her mother who longed for grandchildren. Gabriella should have listened to her heart and become a nun. *We need someone we can trust,* the priest had said. *It is not exciting, but it is God's work. And it pays well. I know your children are now off to school. But I need a firm commitment from you: You may not quit, may not even take vacation days other than when the bank itself is closed. And, of course, complete discretion is required.* She had been content helping the priest with office work and other errands. But how could she say no to such a significant and mysterious assignment?

She shifted her weight and fingered the plain silver cross that hung around her neck. Her role within the diocese had grown in importance over the years as she took on more responsibility and gained more experience. Now, in fact, the bishop himself sometimes asked for her assistance, shared with her secrets of the bishopric, entrusted her to handle delicate matters in which Church officials could not be directly involved. But her primary job remained in the bank vault. Waiting. Endlessly, mind-numbingly. Bypassing opportunities at promotion and advancement. Now, finally, the day had come. And she couldn't hear half of what was being said over the stupid alarm.

But what she could hear through the earbuds had been like angels singing. The contents of the box remained, safe in the vault.

Not that all the news had been good. The end of the parking lot conversation had been disturbing. The mention of the name *Monsignor Marcotte* had surprised Gabriella. But more than that, it had frightened her.

✝

Amanda and Astarte sat wedged into the middle seat of the SUV, between Emanuela on the driver's side next to Astarte and Roberto on Amanda's side. Amanda sighed. At least their captors had the decency not to let the two ruffians—one now driving and the other navigating—rub thighs with them.

"Where are you taking us?" Amanda asked.

Emanuela turned. "Someplace where we can talk." She, not Roberto, was clearly in charge. How odd, to see the sudden role reversal. Of course, the prior roles had only been an act. And how did Kaitlyn figure into all this?

Amanda wanted to keep her talking, to draw her out, to acquire information that might help them escape. "Will Monsignor Marcotte be there?"

Emanuela turned and glared, her former passivity replaced by a steely resolve. "This will go a lot better for you if you just shut up."

Astarte, somehow, was not cowed. "That was pretty smart, how you passed the safe deposit box clue to me." She smiled. "I couldn't get that chant out of my head."

Emanuela's face softened. "I know. Me also. It haunted my sleep." She raised an eyebrow. "And smart of you to figure out what it meant."

"Why didn't you just go open the box yourself?" Astarte asked.

The answer confirmed Amanda's suspicions. "We didn't have the key. We needed you to find it for us. The only information my father possessed was the number of the box."

Astarte pushed on. "Then why give us the hopscotch clue to find the box? Why not just take the key from us and open the box yourself?"

Roberto answered. "We did not know the bank, or the name on the account. All we knew was that the key opened a safe deposit box. We believed that, if necessary, Cameron as a lawyer would have the best chance to get past the bank security measures to access the box."

Amanda nodded. It made sense. As foreigners, probably carrying fake passports, they likely would want to avoid the U.S. judicial system. So why not let Cam do the leg work for them? "One more question," she began—

"Enough." Emanuela cut her off, straightening in her seat. "No more questions. Once we arrive at our destination, we will be the ones asking for answers."

✠

Gabriella Difonzo led the bank manager and a police officer to the back door of the bank. "This door. I was across the street buying flowers after work and I saw them come out of this door. The woman and her daughter. That's when the alarm went off."

The manager, Mr. Knotts, nodded. He was a bookish, dour man approaching retirement age who Gabriella guessed would prefer his routine at the bank to anything retirement might bring. "I'll check the security camera footage." He spoke in a funeral whisper, as if what had transpired at the bank could not be spoken about in normal tones.

Gabriella continued. "I knew they were up to something. I could *feel* it. But I am fairly certain they left the contents in the box." She was well-regarded by the bank manager, who respected her devotion and competence. She gave him the name of the key holder. "I think his wife and daughter hid in the bank at closing time while he created a distraction at the teller window."

The policeman turned to the manager. "Is anything missing?"

"I don't know yet. We will need to do a complete inventory. Complete."

"I'd like to check the vault room," Gabriella said. "That's where they were." She tapped her chin with her forefinger. "And I wonder if this might be one of those rare cases where we drill a box. If it really is the same woman on the security camera, I would think the bank is justified."

"I concur," said Mr. Knotts. "Clearly a crime has been committed."

Gabriella wished she could inspect the box alone, but the bank had certain protocols which needed to be followed. Otherwise she would have drilled box 2173 long ago, along with a dozen or so other boxes she suspected might house whatever it was the archbishop coveted. Fortunately, as clerk of the vault, it would fall on her to safeguard the box's contents pending final disposition. After twenty-plus years of untarnished service, nobody would be looking over her shoulder, or even suspect her if an item or two were to go missing. Especially with God on her side.

They began to walk back to the front door. What was in the box? Whatever it was, it was important enough to cause first the diocese and now Thorne and his family to act in an obsessively secretive manner. She was almost certain, based on a quick conversation she had with the bank teller on duty and on what Thorne's wife said in the parking lot, that Thorne had returned the contents of the box to their nest in the vault and created a fake treasure to lure away the man in the parking lot, leaving the wife and daughter hidden in the bank to retrieve the box's contents after closing hours.

Fools. The vault door had a lock for a reason. And she had the key.

✛

Brian banged on the motel bathroom door. "Come on. Get your ass out here." He handed Cam satchel. "We're going for a ride."

"Where?" Cam felt a certain level of safety here, in a semi-public place. If they made too much noise, motel security would arrive. But the unknown terrified him.

Brian sneered. "Disneyland." He turned to the two ruffians. "Make sure he doesn't make a run for it." And back to Cam. "Don't do anything stupid. We have your wife and kid."

Cam's steadied himself against the doorframe. *Shit*. He had taken solace in the fact that, at least, Amanda and Astarte were safe. Either locked inside the bank or able to somehow slip out. How could he try to make a run for it, knowing it would likely endanger his family? "You're lying. Bluffing."

Brian's gray eyes held his. "Why would I bluff? I'm already holding the winning hand."

They exited the motel room to a poorly lit parking lot, Cam feeling a bit lightheaded from lack of food. As if things weren't bad enough, he would need to eat soon or risk a diabetic episode. They piled back into the van, Cam between Brian and the thug wearing the boxing sweatshirt. Brian had clearly decided that further conversation in the motel room would be fruitless. Apparently they were on to stage two of his interrogation. Cam clenched his jaw, a wave of panic washing over him. His neck ached and his head pounded. Would they try to beat the truth out of him? And would they even believe him when he told them?

The scroll is in the heating vent, but we can't get to it until Tuesday when the bank reopens. How convenient. And how unbelievable. He imagined their possible destinations—an abandoned warehouse, a construction site, the woods. Someplace where his screams would not be heard. The ruffian to his right grinned and grunted, taking delight in Cam's angst. Cam began to sweat, whether from nerves or low blood sugar he wasn't sure. Probably both. He swallowed. He needed to do something. Soon.

"Brian, I'm feeling dizzy."

"Shit. Your diabetes."

"Yeah."

Brian spoke to the driver. "Stop at the next gas station and get a Snickers bar."

Cam had other ideas. He began to convulse, as though involuntarily. "I don't think I can wait that long."

"Fuck." Brian reached to the ground for Cam's satchel and yanked it open. Cam knew his concern had more to do with the treasure than with Cam's health. "What do I do?" he said to Cam.

"Give me the insulin pen," Cam replied, forcing his hand to shake.

Brian fumbled in the case, finally extracting the pen. Nestled inside the pen was a hypodermic needle used to deliver the insulin. Taking the pen from Brian with a quavering hand, Cam spun the dial to the maximum dosage, approximately five times a normal measure, and yanked off the cap. Spinning away from Brian, he gagged, pretending he was about to vomit. The sweatshirt-wearing ruffian to his right cringed, turning away. It was the opening Cam needed. Using a short, violent, backhanded motion, he jabbed the needle into the side of his exposed neck. The needle immediately penetrated, and Cam lifted himself in his seat, putting his weight behind the attack as his victim reached for Cam's hands in a desperate attempt to wrestle him away.

It took only a few seconds for the pen to deliver the insulin. Cam hissed as the thug gasped, blood squirting from his thick neck. "The needle won't kill you. But the insulin will. You've got twenty minutes to get an IV to raise your blood sugar." The man looked back at him with wide eyes. Cam motioned toward the van's door as the driver slowed in response to the commotion. "What are you waiting for? Go!"

The man ripped open the door and leapt from the car, one hand on his neck, his phone already in the other.

Brian didn't hesitate. With a meaty fist, he threw a roundhouse left at Cam, catching him on the side of the head. Cam had unsnapped his seatbelt before his insulin attack, and with Brian off-balance due to the punch, he took the opportunity to vault himself over the back seat and into the cargo area of the van. There, he quickly found what he was looking for: Brian's golf bag, presumably with the swagger sword still inside. Cam found the only shaft not attached to a golf club and slid it out of the bag just as Brian stood and faced him.

"Enough, Cam. Put it down."

Cam pulled the sword out and held it menacingly, crouched at three-quarter height in the back of the van. "Fuck off, Brian."

The van stopped, the black-clad driver shoving the transmission into park and racing around toward the rear of the vehicle. Cam leaned back and snapped the lock on the rear door. "What are you going to do, kill me?" Brian asked, sneering. "You don't have the balls."

The driver banged on the back window, prepared to break through. Cam only had a second or two to make his move. "And you don't have the brains to know when you're wrong." He lunged, jabbing at Brian with the sword, driving his old friend back. The sword was ceremonial, but still featured a point and sharp edges. Slashing, Cam continued the attack, catching Brian on the shoulder. It was the opening he needed. Taking advantage of the van's side door being left open when his first victim fled, Cam squeezed around the seat and jumped out. As Brian lunged to follow, Cam slammed the door on him. But the delay allowed the driver to circle the van and grab Cam's arm as he turned to run. Cam ducked and spun, swinging his fist and burying it in the thug's gut, doubling him over. For a split second Cam thought about driving the sword into the driver's back, but chose instead to play his advantage and make a run for it.

Sprinting along the busy road as car horns blared, Cam leapt the guardrail and made for the woods beyond, sword still in hand. He had no idea where he was, but he was in good shape and should be able to outrun Brian and his hired hand. A gunshot rang out, thudding into a tree not far from Cam's head. Cam's heart thumped. *That was close.* "Stop, Thorne. That was a warning shot." Something in the command, a cold calmness, told Cam to obey. He froze and turned to see Brian loping toward him, a semi-automatic rifle carried ominously at his side. Less than fifty feet away, his old friend lifted the weapon and fired nonchalantly again, this time kicking up dirt a few inches from Cam's foot. "And so was that." Brian stopped, dropped to one knee, and assumed a shooting position. "Run if you want, cowboy. But three strikes, you're out. And give me back my fucking sword."

Chapter 14

This time they bound Cam's wrists and ankles and threw him roughly into the back of the van, Brian guarding him at gunpoint while the ruffian in the black leather jacket drove. Cam managed to get into a sitting position and tried to track their progress. They crossed the river into what he knew was East Providence, but he didn't know the area well enough to make a guess as to where they were headed. He cursed. He had almost escaped. Brian would not likely be careless enough to give him a second opportunity. And the punch to the gut, not to mention the needle to his buddy's neck, would not likely engender any sympathy from the remaining thug once they reached their destination. A wave of nausea washed over Cam. He had been in fights before, but never actually tortured. His sore neck would soon be the least of his worries. He strained at his wrist ties but only succeeded in causing the plastic binds to cut into his skin.

The van pulled to a stop next to a hulking red brick building fronted by soaring Corinthian columns. Cam swallowed. Massive buildings held in noise well. Wherever they were, it was likely not good for him. He peered through some tree branches to read a sign: 'Grand Masonic Lodge of Rhode Island.' *What the hell?*

Brian opened the rear van door. "In we go."

The driver grabbed Cam's wrists and yanked him out. He shoved Cam up the concrete stairs, Cam nearly tripping a few times as his bound ankles struggled to make the climb. As they reached the top, a massive wooden door swung open to accept them. A tuxedoed man, tall and gray and gaunt, nodded gravely to them and silently spun, the motion causing his Masonic apron to billow like a sail. He carried a ceremonial sword, which he held in front of him like a knight ready to joust much as Brian had done at the Newport Tower less than two weeks earlier. Cam wondered if this sword would lead to clarity regarding some of the mysteries Brian's sword had first exposed. Or perhaps it would be used more bluntly, to extract answers from Cam.

"Follow the old geezer," Brian whispered, though perhaps not quietly enough so that their guide did not hear. He led them up a wide, dark wood staircase and stopped in front of a plain white door, where he rapped three times on a brass plate with the pommel of his sword, paused, then knocked twice more. An answering rap—four times in quick succession—greeted them, and their escort turned the knob to open the door.

Again, Cam wondered why they were here. Why a Masonic lodge, much less the Grand Lodge of the entire state? Of all the places Cam imagined the van stopping, this would have been low on the list. And of all the people he expected to see standing on the other side of the door to greet him, Monsignor Marcotte would not have been on the list at all.

"Hello Cameron." The urbane priest nodded to the thug. "You may unbind him. And please wait outside."

Freed from his constraints but not his confusion, Cam rubbed his wrists and took a deep breath. A Masonic lodge room made for an unlikely torture chamber. He scanned the soaring lodge room quickly, breathing in old leather and a hint of cigar smoke, not sure whether to be relieved to see his old friend Marcotte or angry at being deceived. And, it seemed, betrayed.

The anger won out. "What the fuck is going on?" He thought of Ruthie, dead in her condo. Of being attacked in Ireland. Of the cold fear he felt at Amanda and Astarte being in danger. He stepped forward, across the plush carpet, his voice low and strained. "You're supposed to be my friend."

"And I still am," the urbane priest cooed. "But some things are more important even than friendships."

"Bullshit. That's what people say when they want to justify their own treachery." He took another step forward. "You've been lying to me. Betraying me."

Marcotte lifted a hand, well-groomed as always in a herringbone blazer and teal tie. "Please. Calm down. I can explain."

Something about the teal tie enraged Cam. He, too, had worn a tie. A pair, actually. Plastic. One binding his ankles and another his wrists. And he, too, had worn something bound around his neck—the vice-like hands of a trained hitman, trying to squeeze the life out of him. He, at least, had survived. Unlike Ruthie. Barely able to focus through his rage, Cam lunged and grabbed the silk fabric, twisting. Using both arms, he spun the cleric around and shoved him violently against the wall next to the door. He brought his face close. "This better be good." With a second shove, he exhaled, released the cleric, and stepped back.

Marcotte blinked and rubbed the back of his head. He straightened himself. "I suppose I had that coming." He glanced at Brian, who had watched the encounter with a look of amused indifference, and closed the door to the lodge room. "Mr. Heenan, you may remain here with us."

"You're damn right I will. I'm not going anywhere."

Cam took a deep breath. It was apparent that Brian and Marcotte were working together. But that was only a small part of the picture.

His heart pounded. His outburst had allowed him to vent some of his fury. But he was by no means placated. He glanced around, taking the scene in for the first time. The 'us' in question constituted himself, Marcotte, Brian and a middle-aged man wearing a top hat along with his tuxedo. But none of this made sense. Hadn't he minutes before been held at gunpoint? And since Marcotte was working with Brian, did that mean Cam was still a captive?

Marcotte fixed his tie, walked past Cam toward the tuxedoed man, and made introductions as if at a dinner party. "This is Grand Master Ferdinand Silva."

Cam nodded curtly and turned back to the monsignor. "Why am I here?"

"Because we are at a crucial point in solving this mystery, in finding this treasure." He looked over Cam's shoulder and offered a relieved smiled. "And because I thought you would want to be reunited with your wife and daughter."

"Dad!" Astarte called, rushing toward him as he turned. Confusion washed over him again, this time accompanied more by relief than anger. Why had Marcotte brought them here? He pushed the thought away. For now, it didn't matter. All that mattered was that they were safe. *They* were his treasure, the thing that mattered most to him.

He quickly embraced them, eyes closed. "Thank goodness you're okay."

Opening his eyes, he was hit with yet another surprise: A pair of figures he knew to be Roberto and Emmy strolling up the stairs toward him. Could it be? As if adding to the mystery, Emmy's hair was down and her chin up as he had never seen her before. Astarte explained, the words rushing out like a torrent. "Emmy's not really Emmy. She's Emanuela. She didn't really have an accident. She's not really developmentally disabled. It was all an act, a cover." Astarte lowered her voice. "She's actually kind of mean."

Cam's level of confusion had almost reached the stage of paralysis. He shook his head. Emmy not disabled? He never saw that one coming. Never saw any of this coming. He turned to Marcotte. "What's going on?"

The priest smiled and again straightened his tie. "Now that we are, hopefully, done with the theatrics, I'd like to get to that. To explain everything." He bowed his head. "As I said, we need your help."

Cam took a deep breath as he eyed the priest. "Most people who want help just ask for it. Truthfully."

"Yes." The monsignor pursed his lips. "I suppose you are correct about that. But most people are not asking for help finding something that will change history." He paused. "Something that some would die for and many would kill over."

Cam was about to bring up Ruthie's murder. But Amanda spoke before he could. She, too, was angry. "Perhaps you could give specifics rather than just speaking in platitudes."

"Very well. Let's all sit down." Marcotte motioned toward a gallery of seats lining a long wall of the Lodge room, not unlike a movie theater. They sat in two clusters with a few seats between them—Cam with Amanda and Astarte, and Brian with Roberto and Emanuela. Two rival teams, preparing to do battle. Or perhaps brought together to face a common enemy.

Marcotte stood, addressing his small audience. The Masonic leader, Silva, sat in an ornate arm chair off to the side, likely wondering why a thug in bright green pants and a man who would assault an elderly priest were littering his Lodge.

"First, I want to thank Grand Master Silva for allowing us to meet here tonight. We need a safe haven, a place to plan our next move away from prying eyes." Cam doubted that was the monsignor's sole motivation. He looked up, searching for hidden cameras and microphones. The Freemasons, as a secret society, were experts at both keeping secrets and discovering them. Cam guessed that, later, this entire scene would be replayed and analyzed by experts called in to evaluate body language and voice tone to see if anyone was lying. Someone might even be watching them now on a monitor. But for now, Cam merely nodded. He wanted answers. And, not forgetting where he was fifteen minutes ago, he had a fresh understanding that being monitored was preferable to being cattle-prodded.

Marcotte continued. "The Freemasons are not involved in this mystery directly." He smiled. "But they have been the caretakers of the Cumberland Monastery lands for over fifty years, since the Cistercian monks left. And, of course, they have long been the custodians of the Newport Tower. What happens here, in Rhode Island, obviously concerns them." Marcotte smiled. "Plus, I expect we may need their assistance at some point. So my sharing this information with them is partly a gesture of respect and partly pure selfishness."

Silva, his arms crossed at his chest, inclined his head. "I am here to listen. We want, simply, what is best. And we will take necessary steps to ensure that result."

The monsignor smiled at his host. "Excellent. Moving on. As Astarte deduced, Emanuela's injury was a fake, a way for her to hide in plain sight." He took a deep breath, pausing dramatically. "What I'm guessing even Astarte has not deduced—and, Cameron, this will help explain some of my lies—is that Emanuela is Archbishop Marcinkus' daughter."

Cam's chin jolted up. *Wait, what?*

Marcotte looked toward Emanuela, who continued the narrative. She spoke matter-of-factly, tall in her chair, her accent a curious blend of Italian and Irish just as her single brown eye and single blue eye were reminders of the double-life she had been living. "At around age twelve, my mother told me the truth. Told me who my real father was. It answered a lot of questions for me—why I did not resemble my father, why he seemed to favor my brother over me, why I was so much taller than anyone in my family. And the Archbishop came to visit me. At the time, I was going through the typical adolescent struggles." She shrugged. "He was a charismatic man, a powerful man, a mysterious man. And I was at an impressionable age. He brought me gifts, treated me like a young lady. It took a while, but we became close." She paused, her eyes focused on a distant spot on the wall. "I had always had a father, but now it felt like I had a papa. He began to worry for my safety, concerned his enemies might harm me or use my existence to embarrass or blackmail him."

Roberto picked up the narrative. "I was a young priest assigned to his staff. The Archbishop came up with the idea of having Emanuela disappear. A runaway. He believed it would be safer for her to be outside of Rome, living a normal life. At his instructions, I arranged for a gangster by the name of De Pedis to whisk her away after school one day."

Amanda interrupted, turning to Emanuela, asking the question that would come to most mothers' minds. "Did your mother know?"

Emanuela nodded. "She supported the plan. Or at least did not object. She would do almost anything the Archbishop asked. But in this case she honestly believed it would be good for me to be out of Vatican City. She reported me as missing. But somehow the story exploded. The press sensationalized it. Instead of just a common teenage runaway, it became a kidnapping."

"What happened," Marcotte interjected, "was that the Vatican began getting anonymous calls—leaked to the press—demanding the release of Mehmet Ali Agca, jailed for trying to assassinate Pope John Paul II, in exchange for Emanuela's release. Other sources tied her disappearance to Marcinkus, theorizing this was a way to keep Emanuela's father, who worked at the Vatican Bank, quiet. Either way, once the press got hold of the story, the Vatican had to respond. Had to investigate."

Emanuela sniffed. "The irony was that people believed I was taken to keep my father—my stepfather, actually—quiet. The reality was that he was happy to be done with me. I was a constant reminder of my mother's infidelity. And the person blamed for my abduction, the Archbishop, was my real father. The one who really cared."

Cam turned his palms up to the sky. Marcotte had been truthful in one respect: There were many layers, many secrets, to this mystery. "So how did we get to here, to today?"

The monsignor and Emanuela looked at Roberto. He smiled, the same kind face that had welcomed them to Milano Farm less than a week earlier. "Archbishop Marcinkus was never one to pass up an opportunity for a windfall. He knew the Vatican wanted to put this scandal behind them. So he told them that the gangster, De Pedis, had contacted him and told him that Emanuela had been injured during the abduction. A head injury. Now he wanted to wash his hands of the whole mess. Marcinkus convinced the Pope that we couldn't return the girl to her mother in that condition, given the press—it would just refocus attention on the inept Swiss Guard. So he arranged for the Vatican to pay her expenses and upkeep. And he sent me with her to Ireland to serve as her chaperone."

Brian guffawed, the first contribution he had made to the conversation. "Big surprise what happened next."

Roberto glared for a second before sighing and sitting back. "Yes. We fell in love. The Archbishop arranged for a local girl, a young nun, to serve as our foil, someone for me to pretend to be married to. A cover. I believe in America you would call her a beard. Kaitlyn."

Emanuela interjected. "A spy, not a beard. Always running to Dublin to report on our activities to the bishop. The bishop was supposed to be a friend of my father's, charged with protecting us. But his idea of protection is to keep us under house arrest. With Kaitlyn's help." She raised her chin. "We could have found the treasure ourselves had we been free to travel."

Nodding, Roberto continued. "In any event, as far as the world knew, Kaitlyn and I were married, together raising Emanuela, my disabled sister." He smiled again. "With, thanks to Archbishop Marcinkus, the Vatican paying our expenses."

With a fake spitting sound, Emanuela interjected again. "They can keep their dirty money as far as I'm concerned. They are devils on earth."

The Monsignor exhaled, waving her insult away with a motion of his hand. "That brings us to today. How we got here. But not why."

"Treasure," Brian declared. "No other reason."

"Not true," Emanuela replied. "I am here for revenge."

Amanda shook her head. "We don't particularly care about treasure, and we don't care a whit about revenge. We want to know what secrets the Templars were hiding. We want answers."

"And I," Marcotte said, "am only interested in a treasure to the extent it helps me in my efforts at reforming the Church."

Brian leered. "Good. Since none of you cares about the treasure, I'll take it all myself." He sat back, clearly pleased with himself.

"What do you mean about revenge?" Cam asked Emanuela.

"Against the Church. Apparently my mother truly loved the Archbishop, and he … was fond of her. But of course there was no way for her to divorce my father and marry a priest. And Roberto and I, in the eyes of the Church, cannot marry unless he requests to be laicized, which of course would draw unwanted attention to our situation." She set her jaw. "They poisoned my childhood, now they deny me fulfillment as an adult. They are backwards, misogynistic. The monsignor wants to reform the Church. I support him in this, but I personally would not object if it were burned to the ground."

The Monsignor lowered his head and smiled indulgently at Emanuela. "I understand your anger. But let's try to channel it into something positive rather than something negative."

She bit her lip, her mismatched eyes narrowing. "Revenge is just revenge, Monsignor. It is neither positive nor negative."

✠

Astarte sat in the theater seat in the fancy Masonic Lodge, her eyes glued on Emanuela. How had she been so easily fooled? The woman had played her part expertly, adopting both the behavior and mannerisms of a young girl. But it was her vulnerability which had been most convincing. Emmy truly was a sad, confused, lonely little girl. Astarte imagined the real Emanuela, the angry adult Emanuela, must also be sad and confused and lonely in order to have pulled it off. Astarte didn't know if this revenge she spoke of would bring her any peace, but she hoped so.

The Monsignor interrupted her musings. He paced in front of them. "We all have our reasons for being here—wealth, revenge, knowledge, power. But for us to succeed, we need the contents of that safe deposit box." He turned and focused on Cam and Amanda.

Astarte wondered how forthcoming they would be.

"We don't have it," Cam said simply.

"We left it in the vault," Amanda added.

"It belongs to me," Emanuela said. "The Archbishop, my father, wanted me to have it. He gave me the box number. It is my birthright, my legacy."

Cam shrugged. "We don't even know what it is. We didn't have time to examine it."

"But we know it is a scroll," Emanuela countered.

"Yes," Amanda said. "Apparently an ancient one."

"In the interest of proving our good faith," Marcotte said, "I will tell you what I believe it is. What I am *certain* it is, based on the writings I have seen describing it. It is a *ketubah*, a marriage contract. But not just any ketubah. This is the marriage contract between, and I quote, *A Hasmonian princess, Myriam of Migdal, and Yeshua ben Josef of the Royal House of David, at Cana.*" The monsignor nodded, the room completely silent. "As I'm sure you've all ascertained, what I have just described is the contract of marriage between Jesus and Mary Magdalene."

The room remained silent. Astarte understood the stunning importance of the document. If authenticated, it completely changed the history of Christianity. More specifically, it dramatically elevated the status of women in the Church, making Mary Magdalene, rather than the Twelve Apostles, the key confidant of Jesus. It also—and this was where Monsignor Marcotte's goal of reforming the Church came into play—removed any doctrinal justification for the ban on priest marriage or prohibition on female clergy.

After a few seconds, Emanuela stood. "The scroll, the ketubah, belongs to me," she repeated, her arms across her chest.

"Nuts to that," Brian replied, turning in his seat. "It's worth a fortune."

"It does not *belong* to bloody anyone," Amanda declared. "It is a priceless piece of history, one that must be shared with the world."

"I agree it is priceless," Marcotte said, "but I'm not certain the world is ready for it. I think instead it can be used to influence the Vatican into making certain much-needed reforms. Pope Francis is receptive to these reforms, but only if he is on firm ground doctrinally. In short, he needs a game-changing revelation, like this ketubah, to justify such a radical change in policy. Otherwise the Synod of Bishops, which essentially serves as his cabinet, will never go along."

Astarte looked around. The people in the room all had different goals and agendas, but had been pulled together like those comic book characters in the movies to fight a common enemy. But those alliances were always fleeting. She doubted Monsignor Marcotte actually liked the boorish Brian. She wouldn't be surprised if the ancient document, should they recover it, got torn to shreds in some kind of epic adult tug-of-war. But first they had to retrieve it from the bank vault heating vent. And even that assumed that Cam and Amanda trusted the others in the room enough to tell them where it was hidden.

"I think we need to tap the brakes a bit," Amanda said. She focused on the monsignor. "You're assuming we will agree to cooperate with you." She made a sour face and glanced at Emanuela, Roberto and Brian. "And with them. We don't associate with murderers."

Roberto angled his head. "What are you talking about?"

"My friend Ruthie," Cam replied. "On Long Island."

"We had nothing to do with any murder. On Long Island or anywhere else," Emanuela replied.

It was a short defense, simple and to the point. To Astarte, it sounded sincere. But she had been fooled by Emanuela before.

"Tell me what happened," Marcotte said.

Cam described the attack. "Whoever did it was after the map."

The monsignor closed his eyes and squeezed the bridge of his nose between his thumb and forefinger. He bowed his head. "I was afraid something like this might happen." The priest crossed himself. "God rest her soul." He shook his head and blinked a few times, clearly distraught. "We have enemies in the Vatican. Hardliners who want to stop our reforms, who want to preserve the old ways. I have long suspected they have been watching me, intercepting my calls. I tried to be careful, but they must have begun to also track Cameron, knowing I had been in touch with him."

Emanuela interjected. "Kaitlyn," she spat. "She must have reported your visit to us."

Marcotte let out a long breath. "Either way, your friend's death is on my hands. Cameron, I am so very sorry."

Astarte noticed Cam set his jaw. "They didn't just track me. They know about the map." Cam described his encounter with the thugs both in Dublin and Galway. Apparently he believed the monsignor's claims that he had nothing to do with Ruthie's murder. "Makes sense they would be Vatican hardliners. Unless," he said, looking at Roberto, "they were your guys."

Roberto shook his head. "We don't have *guys*." He shrugged. "We just have ourselves. We followed you to Galway, and saw you get chased along the river walk. We even drove around looking for you afterwards."

That explained how their pickup truck ended up on the security camera.

"Well, if the hardliners know about the map, they probably know about the ketubah," Marcotte said. He sighed. "It has long been rumored that Marcinkus was close to finding it. They, like me, have been searching for it for decades."

Brian leaned forward. "Well, if they're going to all this trouble to kill old ladies and chase Cam, it sounds like they haven't found it yet either."

Cam leaned in. Astarte moved closer to huddle with her parents. "Do you believe them?" Cam whispered.

Amanda exhaled. "Yes. It seems unlikely they could have mobilized quickly enough from Ireland to get to Ruthie before you did."

Astarte added, "And they had no reason to attack you in Ireland. You were already doing what they wanted, following the clues."

Cam rubbed his face. "Twenty minutes ago I was ready to throw Marcotte through a wall. So I can't believe I'm saying this. But I believe them also. Everything in their story adds up; I can't find a single hole." He blinked. "But that doesn't mean I trust them." Reaching into his pocket, he withdrew the safe deposit key, stood, and handed it to Monsignor Marcotte. "A show of good faith to match yours," he announced. "I'd rather see you with the ketubah than the Vatican hardliners." Astarte hid her reaction with a fake cough. Cam hadn't mentioned, of course, that the ketubah was no longer in the box that the key opened.

Marcotte bowed his head as he accepted the key. "Thank you, Cameron. You are as generous as you are brave."

"Brave. Hah." Brian sneered. "He's still afraid his other choice is my apes start cutting off his fingers."

✝

Monsignor Marcotte had sent out for sandwiches, Brian had given Cam back his phone, and the Grand Master had shown them all to small dormitory-type rooms on the ground floor which the members apparently slept in if they over-imbibed while at the Lodge.

Cam stretched out on his cot and closed his eyes, trying to find a comfortable position for his neck. He would sort out the Marcotte lies and betrayals later; at least, it seemed, he had not been responsible for Ruthie's death and the attacks on Cam. But for now they were still in danger. The involvement of Vatican extremists in all this clearly raised the stakes. There were Catholic citizens loyal to the Church, and presumably extreme factions of the Church, in almost every corner of America. One of the few places the Church did not wield influence was here, in a Masonic Lodge. The Vatican had long opposed Freemasonry, the official position being that one could not be a Catholic in good standing and also be a Freemason. Cam had heard rumors that the

Masons, fearing the Church and other enemies, had built their older Lodges like this as virtually impenetrable fortresses, equipped to withstand an onslaught and also featuring escape tunnels leading to safe houses in the surrounding neighborhoods. Marcotte had chosen their safe haven wisely. Not that it really mattered: At some point they would need to leave the Lodge and go retrieve the scroll.

The ten-minute catnap rejuvenated Cam. By the time they recongregated, this time around a massive conference room table in the Lodge library, it was nearing eight o'clock. Marcotte sat at the head of the table, with Grand Master Silva at the foot. Astarte had insisted on joining them; she sat between Cam and Amanda on one side of the table, opposite Emanuela who was flanked by Roberto and Brian.

Cam began by thanking the Grand Master for the accommodations—the common men's room was far preferential to the rancid bathroom in Brian's motel room. But the thought of the priceless scroll sitting in the heating vent turned his stomach. What if the Vatican hardliners somehow beat them to it? Or what if a rodent dragged it away? They needed a plan, something to take his mind off of the what-ifs. He voiced his concerns, without revealing that the scroll had been moved. "By the time the weekend is over, the Vatican extremists will have figured out the scroll is in the bank vault. There's no way we can just waltz in there and take it away."

"That's why I've enlisted the assistance of the Grand Master," Marcotte said. "I agree, agents of the Vatican hardliners likely will be at the bank, waiting for one of us to try to retrieve the scroll. We should assume our faces are known to them. As Cameron said, there is no way we can just waltz in." He angled his chin toward the Grand Master. Cam noticed wrinkle lines on the monsignor's face and circles under his eyes he had never seen before; though still composed and charismatic, Marcotte was no longer a young man. "Many of the Lodge brothers are members of various trades. Plumbers, electricians, carpenters, cleaners. Perhaps our host has some ideas as to how we might access that vault room." He lifted his chin and looked to the opposite end of the table. "Ferdinand?"

Grand Master Silva was a heavyset man in his forties. He removed his hat to reveal a shaved head, contrasting with his full, dark beard. "I've made some calls." He spoke in a low voice, the way men did when they knew others would be listening attentively. "We have a brother who owns an extermination company. He has the contract for

Citizens Bank. Perhaps one or two of you could go in as a member of the crew. But that building is not due for a treatment for another couple of weeks."

"So we need to create a situation," Brian said.

Cam thought quickly. "We had a mouse die in our heating vent once. It stunk. Absolutely unbearable. I would think a bank would consider something like that an emergency, maybe even a health hazard." He played it out in his mind. "But even if we got in there, into the vault room, we need the bank clerk and her master key to get into our box."

Brian grinned. "I can pick it. You said these are old boxes?"

"Yeah."

"Those old locks are pretty basic. Banks are focused on keeping people out of the main vault, not the safe deposit boxes. Should only take me a minute or two."

Cam nodded. "The safe deposit boxes are in the basement. Exterminators would need to get down there to do their job."

"Good. Keep going, I like it," Marcotte said. "How do we get a dead mouse, or mice, or rats into the building's heating system?"

"It's not hard," Brian said. "You just pop open the cover of a return vent, drop some bait in, stick a few rats in, and then close the cover. The rats will eat the poison and die someplace in the ductwork. I knew a guy who did it once to torment his ex-girlfriend."

Cam shook his head. It was just the type of thing Brian would know how to do. "And where do you get the rats to begin with?"

"Shit, you've gotten soft, Cam. Go find a dumpster in an alley. You can't *not* find a rat."

✛

Amanda was pleased to have some alone time while the Grand Master gave Astarte and Cam a tour of the Lodge. She had been dying to translate the ketubah. Which was a great sign, she realized. It had been months since she felt, well, *passionate* about something. Her malaise was, it seemed, finally behind her. She would need to tell Cam. She smiled to herself. And to thank him in, well, a *passionate* way.

After bolting the door of her dormitory room, she sat at a small desk and used a laptop the Grand Master lent her to download a picture of the scroll she had saved on the cloud. She studied the text, trying to find a similar script online, but without luck. "I'm going at this ass-backwards," she declared. "We're pretty sure it's a bloody ketubah." She quickly learned that Jewish marriage contracts during the time of Christ were written in Aramaic, the common language of the time, so that the parties to the contract could read and understand it. She found an example of ancient Aramaic. *Bingo*. The scroll text matched.

Next, she found a translation of an ancient ketubah and wrote it out. She compared the ancient ketubah script to the scroll they had found. With a few exceptions, the text matched—she guessed the exceptions were things like names and dates and locations. Using an Aramaic translator she found online, she translated the twenty or so words that did not correspond. It required a bit of guesswork—the Aramaic word for *spouse* was also the word for *cloud*—but after an hour-and-a-half of work, she was able to scribble a rough translation of the ketubah onto a sheet of yellow legal paper, leaving out some of the more mundane economic details:

"On Yom Revi'i, the twelfth day of Adar in the year 3786 since the creation of the world, here in the city of Cana, Jeshua, son of Joseph and of Mary, said to this virgin, the Hasmonian princess Mary of Migdal, daughter of Syrus and of Eucharia: 'Be thou my friend and wife in covenant according to the law of Moses and Israel, and I will work for thee, honor, support, and maintain thee in accordance with the custom of Jewish husbands. And I will set aside for thee 400 silver coins, in lieu of thy virginity, which belongs to thee according to the law of Moses, and live with thee in conjugal relations according to universal custom.' And this virgin consented and became his wife. The dowry that she brought from her father's house amounts to 200 silver coins. And thus said the bridegroom, 'All my property, even the mantle on my shoulders, shall be mortgaged for the security of this contract and of the dowry.' The bridegroom has taken upon himself the responsibility for all the obligations of this ketubah, as is customary with other ketubahs made for the daughters of Israel in accordance with the institution of our sages—may their memory be for a blessing! It is not to be regarded as an illusory obligation or as a mere form of document, and everything is valid and established."

Beneath this paragraph, two witnesses, their names written out in Hebrew, had signed.

Amanda sat back. Her head spun. Was she really looking at the marriage contract between Jesus and Mary Magdalene? Much of the language was rote, but there were a few details that caught her eye. The first was the obvious reference to Cana, the wedding referenced in the New Testament at which Jesus miraculously caused wine to appear. No wonder the Virgin Mary had been so distressed at the thought of running out of wine—she had, apparently, been cohosting the event. Next, the language of the original ketubah (and other ketubahs Amanda found) referred to the bride simply as 'my wife.' In this ketubah, Jesus referred to Mary Magdalene more elaborately as 'my friend and my wife in covenant,' which connoted a much more co-equal relationship. Monsignor Marcotte would surely appreciate that, as did Amanda. Third, the bride price of 400 silver coins was double that recited in the sample ketubah. With a quick internet search, Amanda learned that a "premium" price of 400 silver coins was customarily paid for brides with royal blood. Finally, the ketubah specifically and repeatedly referred to Mary Magdalene as a virgin, contrary to longstanding Catholic tradition identifying her as *La Pinta*, the prostitute.

Amanda deleted the search memory and turned off the laptop. Folding the sheet of legal paper into a small yellow rectangle, she slipped it into her bra and rushed from the room.

She needed to find Cam. And he needed to find that ketubah.

✟

Later that night, approaching midnight, Brian and Roberto drove back into Providence to place the rats and poison in the bank's ductwork. They had enhanced the plan and intended to put a few dead rats into the vents along with live ones, just in case the live ones didn't take the bait. The inclusion of the already-dead rats would also accelerate the spread of the stench. Cam was happy not to be included. He, like most people, was repulsed by rats. And it gave him a chance to pull Monsignor Marcotte aside for a private conversation in a small office near the entrance to the main Lodge room.

Energized by Amanda's translation of the ketubah, but equally fearful of its ramifications, Cam grabbed a wooden box off a shelf as he entered. "You know what this is?"

Marcotte offered a tired smile. "It looks like the case I used to keep my baseball cards in when I was a kid."

"It's a voting box. Every Freemason is given two marbles, one white and one black. When a new member is being voted on, they line up and secretly drop one of their marbles into this box. At the end, when they open the lid on the box, if there is even a single black marble, the candidate is rejected."

Marcotte nodded. "Blackballed." He rubbed his eyes. "It's getting late, Cameron. We should get some sleep. What's your point?"

"Brian Heenan is my point. There's a reason the Freemasons don't want reprobates in their organization. It's the same reason people like you and I shouldn't associate with the Brian Heenans of the world."

"And that reason is?"

Cam was surprised Marcotte was being so obtuse. He had always, at least until today, thought his friend had a strong moral compass. "Morality. Ethics. Scruples. Decency. Call it what you want." Not to mention safety. People like Brian had a habit of leaving their coconspirators dead in a ditch.

Marcotte linked his fingers and held them under his chin as if in prayer. "I don't disagree with you. But there's an expression I've come to appreciate in the winter of my life. I believe it is from Bulgaria. It goes like this: *In times of great danger, you are permitted to walk with the devil across the bridge.*" He smiled. "This is one of those times. We—and by that I mean society—are in great danger. Brian is the devil who can help us across the bridge."

"How so?"

"I needed the sword to find the ketubah, and Brian had it. The clues engraved on the back side were, I believed, a crucial piece to this puzzle." He looked to Cam for confirmation.

"Yes. We would not have known where to dig in Cumberland without it."

"So, as I said, I needed Brian's sword. And he wants to profit from our find. So I made a deal." He leaned forward. "A *necessary* deal." He lowered his eyes. "And, yes, I lied to you as part of it. I needed you. And you would never have agreed to spend time with him if you hadn't thought he was dying, right?"

Cam shrugged. "I don't know. Maybe. But you could have asked."

Marcotte shook his head. "No. The stakes are too high. I could leave nothing to chance." He reached out and covered Cam's hand with his own. "Even if it meant jeopardizing our friendship."

Cam remained silent, still not ready to forgive the priest. And still not totally trusting him. If the stakes were truly that high, what was preventing him from lying again?

The monsignor continued. "We needed your cooperation, your help. We weren't even certain you would commit to chasing the treasure; we had Emmy tell Astarte about Brian visiting the farm with his sword to intrigue you, to keep you focused on the quest." He leaned forward. "But I didn't lie to you when I said I think Brian Heenan is a reformed man. At his core, I sense goodness."

Cam rolled his eyes. "Goodness? That's what you call it? I call it greed." He leaned forward in his chair. "Look, I get that you sometimes need to make a deal with the devil. But don't delude yourself into thinking you're dealing with someone *good*."

Marcotte turned his hands up to the ceiling. "Perhaps. But I maintain that your old friend may, in the end, surprise you." He smiled. "And now he's putting dead rats in the bank's heating ducts—a perfect job for our new friend, the devil, don't you think?"

Cam ignored the question. "And how do the wise Bulgarians suggest you get rid of the devil once you've let him into your life?"

"Money. That's what Brian says he wants. If it comes to that, I have plenty to give. But perhaps a payoff won't be necessary."

Cam shook his head. No. The priest was being blind. Cam knew Brian. Getting rid of him would not be easy, payoff or not.

Chapter 15

As was her custom, Gabriella Difonzo arrived at the bank fifteen minutes early for her appointment, this one with a locksmith. She stood by the rear door as a light snow fell, taking shelter from a cold wind in the stairwell. Out of the corner of her eye a passing car headlight reflected off something shiny. A phone, tucked into a crevice in the concrete. She pocketed it just as Mr. Knotts ambled across the parking lot toward her.

Ten minutes later, the locksmith pulled up in a beige pickup truck. She strode out to meet him. It was the Saturday morning of a holiday weekend, but contracts like these, where the bank would pass the cost of the locksmith on to the box holder, were like a license to print money. No doubt the locksmith would charge triple his normal fee. Even so, it had been impossible to get someone to come out the night before, despite Gabriella's best efforts. She had barely slept, wondering what historical relic could possibly have been secreted in the safe deposit box. From the looks of things, Mr. Knotts had not slept either. But his concern centered on what might have been *removed* from the box, whereas Gabriella was focused on what had been left behind.

She led the locksmith, a heavy-set man with pants too long and a droopy walrus-like mustache, through the back door, down the hall, and into the vault room. Mr. Knotts sat at the center table reading the business section of the newspaper. Gabriella pointed. "Number 2173."

The locksmith peered at the lock and grunted. Turning, he waddled out of the room, presumably to retrieve the necessary tools. Mr. Knotts lowered his newspaper and sniffed. "What is that horrid smell?" he asked.

Gabriella had a bit of a cold, but she noticed it also. "It's worse in here than in the hallway."

"It smells like a dead animal."

"I didn't notice it yesterday."

Mr. Knotts stood. "I'm going upstairs to check the rest of the bank."

He returned five minutes later, just as the locksmith did. The locksmith strung an extension cord to the wall and put on a pair of dirty goggles in preparation for drilling the box. Mr. Knotts barely paid attention. "The smell has permeated the entire bank." His round face glistened with sweat. "I am going to call an exterminator. If we wait until Tuesday, it could be unbearable."

Gabriella ignored him. She stood behind the reticent locksmith, watching the metal drill bore slowly penetrating the outer case of the box. "Careful," she yelled over the sound of the drill. "Don't damage what might be inside."

He grunted in acknowledgment, metal shards flying from the box and settling on his beard. With a final screech, the bit burst through. He withdrew the drill and removed his goggles. Instead of opening the box, he removed the extension cord and began to coil it. "That can wait," Gabriella snapped. "Please remove the box and place it on the table."

He grunted again, complying with her request. As he hoisted it out, he shook it. "Feels empty."

Now he finally talks? Gabriella wished she could box his ears like the nuns used to do to recalcitrant students. "*Gently*, or you'll be paying for any damage," she hissed. "Set it down and leave the room."

As the door to the vault clicked close, she lifted the lid of the box with a shaking hand. Mr. Knotts leaned in, the coffee on his breath unpleasant even over the pungency of the dead rodents. But neither stench was as offensive as the light reflecting off the inside of an empty safe deposit box.

✝

Monsignor Marcotte walked into the basement kitchen of the Grand Lodge as Cam, Amanda and Astarte picked at a late breakfast. Cam peeled a banana. He needed to stay sharp. This whole game was a tightrope walk, with irrational personalities like Brian and Emanuela and even the monsignor playing the parts of wind gusts. And it wasn't just himself, but also Amanda and Astarte, at risk.

The priest smiled. "We got lucky. The call just came in from the bank. They need an exterminator ASAP."

"Looks like you finally chose Brian for a job he's well-suited for," Amanda remarked.

"Touché," Marcotte replied.

"So when do we leave?" Cam asked.

"Five minutes. We need to get you and Brian into uniforms and teach you how to use the gear. It'll just be you two, plus the owner."

Cam pictured them in the vault room, Brian picking the lock while Cam fished the clay tube from the heating vent. "Wouldn't it be better to have more men? We don't want the bank manager, or whoever it is, looking over our shoulders."

The monsignor nodded. "Good point. I'll make a call." He began to leave, but turned. "Oh. One more thing you should know. I just got word that a delegation from Rome landed in Boston this morning. Vatican hardliners, here unofficially. Limos are taking them to Providence as we speak."

It was the opening Cam was looking for. At some point he needed an explanation for why the safe deposit box would be empty. "Sounds like they're on to us. Hopefully they won't get to the bank before we do."

Marcotte nodded again "It's a risk. And I agree, the arrival of a delegation indicates things are escalating."

"Delegation?" Amanda asked. "Is that some kind of euphemism?"

Marcotte pursed his lips. "Fair point. Perhaps a better term would be *team of operatives*. We will need to be careful."

✝

Gabriella sat at her kitchen table with a cup of tea and an uneaten biscuit. She had been replaying the past eighteen hours in her mind, beginning when Cameron Thorne and his family had arrived with a key to box 2173. If Thorne had left the bank with the box contents, as it now appeared, why had his wife and daughter remained behind? It didn't make any sense. Yet the box was empty, its mysterious and presumably invaluable contents gone. She shifted in her seat, the corner of a hard object in her slacks pushing against her thigh. *The cell phone.* She pulled it from her pocket and tried to turn it on. Password protected. *Damn.* Another dead end.

Her phone rang, an old rotary attached to the wall. She really needed to update the place—it had barely changed since her own mother grew up here after World War II. Now that she was no longer needed at the bank, perhaps she'd finally have time for a hobby or even some travel. Or perhaps the bishop would have another assignment for her...

She lifted the receiver. "Hello."

"Ms. Difonzo, I hope you are well." The bishop himself calling. She stood taller. "Things have taken an urgent turn. Can you come down to the Diocese offices?"

She was out the door in five minutes, stopping halfway down the front stairs to retrieve the cell phone, which she sensed might be an important clue. The diocese offices were located in a drab, three-story, brick building made even more bland due to being adjacent to the soaring, Victorian-era, Cathedral of Saints Peter and Paul. Gabriella glanced over her shoulder for another look: Her mother had once told her that the cathedral was so majestic that naming it after a single apostle—either Peter or Paul—simply would not have sufficed. The receptionist brought her to an empty conference room overlooking the highway. Just on the other side of the highway, looming large in the distant, stood Citizens Bank. Somewhere deep inside, box 2173 sat empty. "Please wait," the receptionist said. "The bishop will be with you shortly."

Five minutes later the rotund bishop, attired in his black robe and cape with red piping, approached. Behind him followed a parade of three men, all of them wearing clerical garb, skull caps and large crosses. The fourth, a strikingly handsome man with light blue eyes and jet-black hair, wore a dark suit with a maroon tie. All the clerics, including the bishop, seemed to defer to the square-shouldered man in the suit.

"These gentlemen are from Vatican City," the bishop said by way of introductions. She noticed he didn't say they were from the Vatican itself. "They are here regarding your assignment." For a moment she thought she might be in trouble. But the bishop smiled kindly, even as he breathed heavily from the exertion of the walk down the hallway. "Please tell them about Mr. Thorne's visit."

Gabriella summarized as best she could. She wanted to look at the blue-eyed man, his eyes like magnets to hers, but she found she could not make her mouth form coherent sentences when she did so. Instead she focused on a spot on the wall above his head, promising herself she could have a long stare when she finished speaking. "When we drilled the box this morning," she concluded, "it was empty." She pulled the phone from her purse. "But I did find this just outside the rear door."

The bishop took it. "You have done well." He nodded to a subordinate. "Try to get into this phone. Top priority." He turned to the blue-eyed man in the suit, giving her an excuse to do the same. "Major Pfyffer. All is not lost. We believe we have located Thorne. Which means, God willing, the scroll will soon be ours. I will pray."

He spoke, his accent cultured and smooth. "Pray if you must, Your Excellency. But I believe God prefers it when men serve him by taking action, rather than waiting for the Almighty to intercede on our behalf." He stood, the simple movement displaying both grace and power. "With Thorne located, I expect that soon we will put an end, *finally*, to this nonsense."

✚

Brian and Cam had been dropped off at single family Colonial not far from Brown University in downtown Providence. A large white work van sat in the driveway, the words 'Abad Brothers Pest Control' emblazoned on the side in royal blue. A tall, thin man with olive skin wearing dark blue coveralls stood in the van, arranging equipment.

"Come on, Thorne," Brian said. "Time for our training."

Brian didn't completely trust his childhood friend, and he didn't trust the Monsignor either. For that matter, he didn't trust Roberto and Emanuela. They, like the rats he had stuffed into the bank's heating vents last night, would do what was best for themselves. Just as he would do what was best for himself.

Abad stepped out of the van to greet them. Brian guessed he wasn't happy about this assignment, about potentially jeopardizing a lucrative account. But the Grand Master had asked for a favor, so he, unlike everyone else in this adventure, was not doing what was best for himself. Poor sap.

The van interior was immaculate, equipment stacked neatly and canisters of chemicals clearly marked. Abad pointed to a couple of pairs of coveralls, which Cam and Brian, slipped into. "You'll also need to wear these respirator masks," he said in what sounded to Brian like a Turkish accent. Brian was glad for that—he'd rather not have his face on any bank security camera footage. "Gloves also, of course. Rodents carry all sorts of viruses dangerous to humans." He then lifted a box of plastic bags. "When you find a dead animal, slip it into the bag, seal it, and then double-bag it."

"How do we find the dead rodents if we're wearing respirators?" Cam asked. "Don't we need to, you know, sniff them out?"

Abad shook his head. "I will tell you where to look. I know the rats like I know my wife's face."

Brian swallowed a guffaw. No doubt Abad's wife would appreciate the comparison. In any event, he planned to ignore Abad's instructions once they got inside the bank. He had had his fill of rats last night. He was there to get into the safe deposit box, grab the damn scroll, and get the hell out. If Cam wanted to make things look good by digging around for dead rodents, well, that was his business.

✛

Cam and Brian rode silently in the second row of Abad's van, coveralls on and respirators in their laps. Another couple of workers were apparently meeting them at the bank. Cam had no interest in sharing a laugh with his old friend, reflecting on how far they'd come in thirty years. Mostly because he no longer considered his old friend a friend. But also because, in many way, they had not come very far at all. Already by the end of middle school Brian was known as an expert shoplifter. That he was on his way to pick the lock in a bank vault should not have been so surprising.

A few inches of snow had accumulated on the streets. Traffic was light in the city due to the snow and the holiday weekend as they descended the hill past Brown University and crossed the river. Workers were busy readying the river for the WaterFire New Year's display, in which floating braziers illuminated the city's rivers, drawing revelers to enjoy music amid the flickering firelight. He glanced at his watch. Not yet noon. The extermination should take less than an hour. If all went well, maybe they could even check out the festivities before returning tonight to Westford. Not that anything had seemed to go well lately.

Cam broke the silence. "Just so you know, I'm not leaving you alone in the vault room. I'm going to be there when you pick that lock." He knew the box was empty, but needed to play it as if he treasured its contents.

Brian answered after a long stare. "We both know you can't beat me. Not at shit like this."

They pulled into the bank parking lot, reconnoitered with the other workers, grabbed supplies, put on their masks, and were let into the bank by a frowning, bookish bank manager standing by the back door.

"Thank goodness you're here," he said, a handkerchief over his nose. "The smell is getting worse."

"Wait here," Abad said to his team. To the manager, he said, "Give me a quick tour of the bank, especially the ground floor. Take me to the rooms where the smell is the strongest."

Cam eyed the parking lot through the same door Amanda and Astarte had used to escape. He was surprised not to see signs of surveillance by the Vatican hardliners. Was it possible they were so far behind in following the clues and/or following Cam that they hadn't made it to the bank yet? Doubtful. Perhaps they had already come and gone, having found the scroll. Or perhaps they were just good at hiding. Cam exhaled. Not that it mattered. He had one chance to retrieve the scroll; he'd worry about the Vatican extremists later.

Abad returned ten minutes later. "Work in pairs, room by room. Each room has a name." He nodded toward Cam and Brian. "Start in New Hampshire, then go to Maine. Focus on the heating vents by the windows." He touched his nose. "That is where they are."

The manager had opened all the vault room doors. As instructed, Cam and Brian began in the New Hampshire room. Cam dropped to a knee and removed a heating vent cover. "What are you doing?" Brian asked, his respirator giving him a Darth Vader-like rasp.

"Looking for dead rats," Cam replied.

Brian eye's narrowed behind his mask. "You do know that we're not *real* exterminators, right?"

"Yeah, but I still want to make it look good. This is how Abad makes a living. We can't just leave the rats in the ducts."

Brian dropped into a wooden chair. "What a fucking Boy Scout."

Cam bit back a retort. He reached deeper, cringing as pain shot through his neck. Pushing the pain away, he felt around. His gloved hand rubbed against a carcass. He instantly recoiled before forcing his arm back into the vent. Grabbing the rodent by the tail, he extracted it and double-bagged it as instructed. In a second vent, he found and bagged a second rat. "Okay. Let's go to the next room."

Brian stood. "Halleluiah."

✝

Franz Pfyffer von Altishofen sat straight-backed in the passenger seat of the Land Rover the bishop had secured for them. He stared through a pair of high-powered binoculars toward the rear entrance of the Citizen's Bank building. His paternal grandfather, after whom he had been named, had been the eleventh member of the Pfyffer line to serve as Commander of the Pontifical Swiss Guard, the body-guards of the Pope. Franz hoped, and expected, to be the twelfth. But that would require a change in leadership at the Holy See, a pope willing to turn the Church back to its traditional roots. Back to the orthodoxy of the Middle Ages, when men such as Franz pledged fidelity to monastic orders like the Knights Templar and defended the Church with their lives. The Swiss Guardsmen shared the Templar cross with their forebears, as well as their willingness to die for their religion. But today's Vatican leaders, soft and undisciplined and even in some cases heretical, were not worthy of that loyalty. Franz longed to wear the scalloped cross on his chest, to continue the family legacy of service. But only when the Vatican ship had righted itself.

Known as Major Pfyffer to his men, and originally trained in his native Switzerland, he did not formally serve in any nation's military. Yet he had fought alongside Americans, Germans, Israelis and even Russians. He was a soldier for hire, willing to fight for any cause so long as Jesus was on his side. Sometimes the battle lines were blurry and he had to make a judgment call as to whether the battle was a just one. Not this time.

Unfortunately, they had waiting too long to call him in. Yes, he was expensive. But only because being fully equipped, prepared and trained required a large outlay of resources. He himself did not profit from his services, at least not in the pecuniary sense—one could not do the Lord's work with greed in one's heart. At least not do it well. He shook his head. An old woman was dead, and the map still not recovered. *Amateurs*. In this case, dead amateurs. Like the dead rodents in the bank.

Lowering the binoculars, he sniffed. The whole dead rodent thing, well, smelled bad to him. The bank clerk, Difonzo, had said there were no foul aromas at closing time last night. European rats, at least, did not decompose so quickly. Especially at the same time that a priceless, ancient scroll had gone missing.

✠

Cam and Brian, clad in exterminator's suits, entered the bank vault's Maine room. This time, while Cam again went for the heating vent at the far end of the room, Brian searched for box 2173. "Fuck me," Brian cursed from only a few feet away. Cam looked up. "I think it's been drilled." He slammed his hand against the wall of boxes.

"How can you tell?" Cam asked, dropping to his knees, trying to appear nonchalant.

"Because of the goddamn hole where the lock used to be." He tugged at the box. "The other lock, the master lock, is still holding."

"Can you pick it?"

Brian tossed his mask aside. "Why bother?"

"I don't know." He needed Brian to be distracted. "Maybe that's an old drill hole. Maybe they left stuff in there."

"And maybe there's a fucking Tooth Fairy."

But Cam knew Brian couldn't walk away, no matter how unlikely it was that the scroll remained in box. Using a toothpick-like tool, Brian wiggled and prodded. Meanwhile, Cam reached into the heating vent and felt for the clay tube. Instead his hand bounced against another rat. *Shit.* Quickly he bagged it and set it onto the floor next to the two dead rats from the other room. Reaching back in, his fingers found … nothing. Had the Vatican hardliners retrieved the canister before him? Or had the rat pushed the tube deeper into the ductwork, the cylinder-shaped vessel perhaps rolling away? He stretched, his mask flush against the opening of the heating vent as his entire arm probed the void. *There.* His fingertip felt something. Straining another inch, ignoring the pain in his neck, he flicked at the object, hoping to spin it back toward him. A rolling noise echoed in the metallic cavity, the sound like a lullaby to Cam's ears. He closed his fingers around the tube.

Brian called out. "I'm in." Cam, his arm still in the vent, turned his head. Brian yanked the safe deposit box out and dropped it on a table, making a loud clang. "You said you want to watch? Then get your ass over here. Watch me open a fucking empty box."

Cam extracted the tube, shielding it with his body. He could feel Brian's eyes on his back. "Be right there. Found another rat." Not wanting to risk Brian seeing him put something into his pocket, Cam reopened the storage bag closest to him and dropped the tube in with the dead rat—the ten-inch cylinder, turned diagonal, barely fit. Standing, Cam stacked the three bags on the floor, placing the bag with the clay tube on the bottom. He removed his mask and joined Brian at the table.

Unceremoniously, Brian yanked open the lid. An empty box stared back at them. Cam bit back a smile, glad to have the mask shielding his face. Brian threw the box against the wall beneath the window, the impact gashing into the drywall. Following his throw, he kicked the box, sending it careening into a chair, toppling it. He then reached down, grabbed a bagged rat, and flung it, Frisbee-like, across the room. It hit the far wall with a thud. He began to stretch for the second bag.

Cam stepped in front of him. "What are you, three years old? You going to punch a wall also?"

"Fuck off, Thorne."

Brian reached around Cam for the second bag. Cam had no choice. He couldn't risk Brian lifting the second bag and noticing the tube in the bag beneath it. He swatted Brian's hand away and dropped his hands to his side, guessing how Brian would react but also knowing the blow would be worth it. He braced for the assault. Not that it helped much. From one knee, Brian threw a vicious uppercut, burying his fist into Cam's gut. Cam collapsed, his last willful movement aiming his body so that he landed in a way to shield the dead rat and scroll. Writhing, he fought for air as his world darkened. He had almost drowned once, the panic at not being able to breathe the worst feeling he had ever had. This wasn't far behind. His body screamed for oxygen.

Brian stood over him. Vaguely Cam heard the words. "No, not a wall."

Brian stormed out, kicking the door to the Maine room as he left, his curses echoing back into the vault from the hallway even through Cam's haze. After a few seconds, Cam pulled himself to his feet, staggered across the room and closed the door, latching it. Still gasping, but working as quickly as he could, he removed the clay tube from the bag alongside the rat. With an unsteady hand he unzipped his coveralls and slid the canister into the deep side pocket of the cargo pants he wore underneath.

Hunched over, he exhaled and patted the tube. It was hardly a fitting location for an ancient scroll that would be considered a priceless relic by both Christians and Jews. But it was better than being stuck in a bag with a dead rat.

✠

Brian didn't even wait for Abad and his team to finish in the bank. The last Cam saw of him was his green leg disappearing into the back of a taxi. *Good riddance.*

Abad asked Cam about it as they exited the bank parking lot in the van. "So you did not find what you were looking for?"

Cam, again riding in the second row of seats, shook his head. "Dollar short, day late."

The exterminator breathed what Cam interpreted as a sigh of relief. Had they stolen something from the bank, Abad would be an obvious suspect. But no harm, no foul. Actually, that was not entirely true. Cam felt for the clay tube. In this case, the harm had yet to be discovered.

"I'll bring you back to the Grand Lodge," he said, turning onto the highway ramp.

"Thanks."

Cam was tempted to text Amanda, but they had agreed on communication silence just to be safe. No sense doing something stupid now, only minutes from completing his mission and—

An SUV stopped short in front of them, slamming its brakes. Abad did the same. *Shit.* Cam immediately sensed danger. From the left, a yellow Land Rover swerved closer, pinching Abad against the ramp's Jersey barrier. And from behind, a tow truck rammed Abad's bumper, the front seat air bags pinning Abad to his seat. Cam's heart raced, his eyes searching for an escape route as he felt for the clay tube in his pocket. Cam reached for the door handle. But even before the van stopped shaking, three masked men carrying semi-automatic rifles had poured from the Land Rover and surrounded the vehicle.

Cam's door flew open. A strong hand snatched the front of his coveralls and twisted, an assault weapon raised ominously in the other. "Come with us." Bright blue eyes peered through the black ski mask. No raised voice, no anger. Just the German-accented voice of a man used to giving orders. And used to having those orders followed.

✛

Cam's captors didn't even bother to tie him up. Instead they placed him in the middle seat of the second row of the Land Rover, sandwiched between two masked operatives carrying semi-automatic rifles. The men, when they spoke, conversed in German. Disciplined and efficient. Probably military. Only the driver seemed to be American, darting down snowy side streets in what turned out to be only a three-minute drive. A sign in front of a low brick building told Cam they had arrived at the Providence Diocese offices.

"Get out," the leader said in accented English from the passenger seat. "And, Mr. Thorne, please, nothing stupid. You are not Tom Cruise. This is not the movies." He held up his gun. "And we do not miss."

Cam slid out the door. He thought about trying to somehow lose the clay tube, perhaps by tossing it down a sewer grate as they passed. But to what end? He was only of use to them because they believed he may be in possession of the scroll. Without it he had nothing. And did he really want to destroy an invaluable historic artifact?

They hustled Cam inside and down a staircase to a windowless storage room in the basement. The team leader removed his mask to reveal a handsome face and conservative haircut. Tall, solid build. Late thirties, probably. In most people's eyes a businessman or banker. But here, in this setting, clearly in command. Cam sensed his skills went beyond just special ops; this was a man skilled at fixing problems of all kinds. As if reading Cam's thoughts, he said, "My name is Pfyffer." He smiled. "It is my real name, which I feel comfortable using because I am, well, beyond the reach of law enforcement. We have a mutual problem, you and I. There is unfinished business from your visit to the bank."

Cam stared back. He was out of cards, out of moves. He began to reach into his coveralls. A hand flew out and snatched his wrist, twisting Cam's arm behind his back. A spasm of pain shot up Cam's shoulder. "Relax," he reacted. "I'm just getting something from my pocket."

Pfyffer nodded to his underling. "Slowly."

Cam again reached into his coveralls, this time extracting the clay tube. "This was in the safe deposit box. I hid it in a heating vent and retrieved it this morning."

"Yes. We know." The operative reached for the canister before seemingly changing his mind and retracting his hand. "It is best if you hold onto it, Mr. Thorne." To his underling, he said, "Please tell the bishop the artifact is ready for examination." Turning back to Cam, Pfyffer said, "Out of respect for your efforts in retrieving the scroll, we would like you to be present when it is tested. You may be asked to testify, to attest that the artifact never left your sight between the time you retrieved it from the bank and it was examined."

Cam blinked. That was smart of them, assuming they wanted to establish the authenticity of the scroll. Many people would be disinclined to trust a group of Vatican hardliners, no matter what the artifact and/or no matter what the test results. His testimony would be crucial to establish chain of custody and provenance. Which was probably why he was still alive. He caught himself—his assumption was flawed. Why would a group of Vatican hardliners want to *authenticate* the ketubah? The whole point of this, the reason the hardliners had mobilized, was to prevent the ketubah from seeing the light of day. There must be another angle to this, something Cam had not considered...

The arrival of a middle-aged woman with long black hair and a skunk-like white streak running down one side interrupted his musings. "This is Professor Cilesia," Pfyffer announced, his weapon hidden from view. "From Brown University. She is here to examine the scroll." Thin and tall, she wore black leggings, black boots and a heavy white cable-net sweater. Everything about her was black and white, including a black bag she wheeled behind her. Cam hoped her analysis would mirror her attire—the scroll was either authentic or not. He was tired of all the gray in his world.

She nodded at Cam as she opened her case. The operative sat near the door, his eyes on Cam. "This will be a preliminary examination, obviously," she said. A conversational tone, apparently unaware that her host carried an assault weapon. Not warm, but professional. "But usually I can tell pretty quickly if something is ancient just by looking at the medium. Is it vellum or parchment— that is, animal skin? Or is it made from wood pulp, which we call paper? If so, is it something modern with a water mark? If it's old, we can carbon-date it to determine how old. We can even do DNA testing if it's vellum to determine what kind of animal skin it is." She set her microscope on a work bench. "We can also test the ink if necessary. Certain chemicals were added to ink in modern times. Eventually we get a firm answer. The science doesn't lie."

The science doesn't lie. Very black and white, befitting her appearance. How many times had Cam heard that in his legal career, only to learn that the science had, in fact, been flawed? But for now, he'd defer to her analysis. Not that he had any choice.

Working deliberately but carefully, she removed the scroll from the tube with gloved hands and unrolled it on a black cloth she had laid on the table. "Hmm." Using a magnifying glass and moving methodically in a grid pattern, she slowly examined the document.

Cam's impatience got the best of him. "Well?"

The professor ignored the query, continuing with her examination, seemingly oblivious to the historical ramifications of her conclusions. Cam considered the possibilities. Writing on paper wasn't developed in Europe until the eleventh century, so if the scroll was made from paper it could not date to the time of Jesus. During Jesus' time they would have used animal skin.

"Interesting," she said, peering closer, apparently focusing on an area where the writing surface had yellowed.

"What?" Cam asked, without receiving a reply.

She removed a device from her bag that looked like an x-ray reader, plugged it in and held the document up to it. It showed that the writing surface was somewhat translucent, but Cam didn't know what that meant. Next she attached a digital camera to a microscope and took a few dozen pictures of the document.

Finally, after working in silence for another ten minutes, she nodded to Cam. "The medium is paper. Wood pulp. I'm guessing after 1880, before which most papers were made with rags."

Cam blinked. "So it's modern?" *How could that be?* "But it's so yellowed."

"Counterintuitively, the older rag paper doesn't discolor as much as the later wood paper due to acid in the wood pulp."

Not that it mattered. Paper, no matter what kind, did not exist in the 1st century. "Are you sure?"

"I'm sure that it's paper not parchment, if that's what you're asking."

"So it's not ancient."

She shook her head. "No. Definitely not."

Pfyffer stood, his head angled. Apparently he was as surprised as Cam was. "To be clear, the document is not ancient?"

She pushed back her hair. "No. Not ancient. I am certain."

"Can you test the ink?" Cam asked as the team leader moved to the corner to make a call.

"No need. Paper is paper. You can see the weave lines." She pointed them out to him under the magnifying glass. "And parchment is much smoother, like an old glove. Plus it has an animal smell." She let him touch the rough surface of the paper and confirm the absence of any animal smell.

Grudgingly, he nodded. It seemed impossible to argue with her findings.

She rolled up the scroll, reinserted it in the tube, and looked over to Pfyffer. The operative nodded, and she began to pack up her equipment. Cam's mind raced, searching for an explanation. He had been certain that the scroll was ancient. Otherwise what was all this about?

Cam tried not to sound whiny. "But it's written in ancient script. Aramaic."

She shrugged. "That may be. But the paper is post-Civil War. If I had to make an educated guess, I'd date it to around 1900. I'll send over a written report in the next day or so with a firmer date."

The team leader ended his call and thanked the professor as she exited the room. "You are free to go as well, Mr. Thorne. Apparently this has all been much ado about nothing. But we will keep the scroll." He smiled. "It may be modern, but its content is nonetheless *disturbing* to my clients."

"That's it? I can really just go?"

The team leader stepped aside. "Yes. However," he said with emphasis, raising an index finger, "we expect you to do the right thing. As I said, you may be asked to testify as to the chain of custody of the scroll, if word of its discovery somehow becomes public." He smiled. "That is why I was careful to never let it out of your sight."

Cam exhaled. So that was the angle he hadn't seen. Allowing Cam to maintain control of the artifact the entire time removed any possibility the Vatican hardliners had switched the scroll and replaced it with a modern forgery. Cam knew the scroll examined by the professor was the same one he pulled from the heating vent. And he was certain nobody else besides Amanda and Astarte knew it had been hidden there, removing any possibility of an earlier switch. In other words, the lawyer in him had no choice but to conclude the ketubah was not ancient.

"So, as I said, you can attest to the scroll's chain of custody, its provenance. Regarding its authenticity, Professor Cilesia is a leader in her field, beyond reproach. And her conclusions were clear: The scroll is not ancient, and therefore cannot be authentic." His blue eyes held Cam's. "Presumably you don't dispute these findings?"

Cam had no reason to. He would need to confirm that the professor was not affiliated with the Vatican, but otherwise he had no reason to question her conclusions. He had been trained to analyze and weigh evidence, and in this case it was overwhelming. "No."

"Good then. It is rare in my line of work where things end peacefully." He reached into his pocket and tossed Amanda's phone to him. "We no longer have any need to hack this." Motioning to the door, he continued. "I strongly suggest you put this all behind you and enjoy New Year's Eve with your family." He touched the weapon holstered at his hip, his eyes turning cold. "And Mr. Thorne. Please don't make me regret choosing the word 'suggest' over something less open to misinterpretation."

Chapter 16

Emanuela paced in front of an oversized window in the ornate lobby outside the Masonic Lodge room, watching traffic zoom by on the highway in the distance. They were a long way from the Irish countryside. Finally. But it had not been a successful journey.

Had her father sat in a similar location, here in Rhode Island, trying to find the ancient ketubah? She knew he had spent the latter years of his life, after leaving the Vatican, here in the States, chasing the mystery hinted at by the clues on the swagger sword. And then came the stroke, leaving both his powerful body and sharp mind enfeebled. In 2006, he had managed to drag himself to Ireland for one final visit; he had been a dutiful father, visiting yearly while stationed in Rome, sneaking in and out of the farm so as to not arouse suspicion. But this final journey had so weakened him that he had done little other than sleep and rant, a far cry from past visits when they spent their days golfing on the 6-hole course Roberto had shaved into the rolling farmland, the archbishop sharing stories of life in the Vatican and lamenting the backward, narrow-minded thinking of the Catholic clergy. The one thing he had passed on during this final visit was the clue which she in turn had passed on to Astarte: *2173ME*.

"You must not forget this," he had insisted, grabbing her hand. "Promise me."

"I promise, father. 2173ME. But what does it mean?"

The archbishop had shaken his head, his eyes afire. He would die within the month. "I do not know. Only that it is key to finding the ancient marriage contract. Your legacy."

Only when Marcotte arrived at the farm, a decade later, did the pieces begin to fit together. Apparently the swagger sword and the 2173ME clue and the map Thorne somehow acquired were pieces to the same puzzle, a puzzle that could only be unraveled when *all* the pieces were assembled together. And even then, the puzzle could only be deciphered by someone with the requisite expertise in the Templars and medieval history. Her father had been close—he knew for certain the scroll existed, and he had collected many of the clues (in one case that she knew about, he literally beat the information from an elderly

231

monk, breaking his ribs and fracturing his skull). But he had died never having found the elusive relic.

She cursed in Italian, under her breath. "*Merda.*" Now, here in Rhode Island, they had assembled all the pieces and correctly interpreted them, thanks to the knowledge of Thorne and his wife and even the girl, Astarte. But still the ancient scroll eluded Emanuela as it had her father.

"Do you believe him?" she asked Roberto, in Italian. Other than in bed, they rarely spoke their native language. But the lie that had become their life was over; by flying here, they had already blown their cover. Finally. They should have broken away years ago.

Seated in a high back chair in the corner, Roberto nodded. He had just received a text from Brian, telling them that the safe deposit box was empty. "No reason for him to lie about something that is so easy to verify."

She sniffed. "This is Brian. He does not need a reason to lie. You do not think he took the scroll and ran?"

"If so, why bother sending us the text? And to what end? Marcotte has already offered him a fortune for it."

Emanuela turned to pace in front of another window, this one looking out over the river. "Maybe someone offered him two fortunes."

Roberto chewed his lip, the way he did when thinking. How many decades had Emanuela spent isolated in that farmhouse, watching Roberto chew his lip? And to what end? For the millionth time, she wished the teenage version of herself hadn't fallen for his easy smile and twinkling dark eyes. Not that he was a bad guy, or even would have made a bad husband. And, despite it all, she still loved him. But no man was worth the sacrifices she had made. She had almost thrown up her hands and walked out a year ago, tired of waiting for a legacy from her dead father which seemed to grow more illusory with every passing year.

"I have had enough," she had announced. "I want to leave. I *must* leave."

Roberto's sad eyes had widened and pooled. "You are leaving me?"

"I do not want to leave you, Roberto. I want to leave *with* you."

He had spread his arms. "But this is our life." Unlike her, he enjoyed the simple life they had at the farm. Of course, he did not have to pretend to be mentally disabled, did not suffer the sneers and insults of the local women convinced that her mismatched eyes were the mark of the devil, did not have to look the other way when the sanctimonious Kaitlyn sniffed around their bedsheets. "God has a plan for us, to wait here until a path to the scroll is revealed. And it is what your father wanted. What he made us *promise*."

"That's horseshit, Roberto. It's been decades. If God had a plan, it's changed. And my father is long dead. I cannot live this life, this *lie*, any longer."

Then the mysterious American priest had arrived at the farm, promising that the illusory legacy was, indeed, within reach. Perhaps God did have a plan. So she had stayed.

"Two fortunes?" Roberto answered, bringing her back to the present. "No, I think not. A man like Brian, he would not know how to fence a religious relic. It is not like you can just post it on eBay."

"You say *a man like Brian*. He is nothing if not resourceful. Somehow he acquired my father's swagger sword."

Roberto shrugged. "Yes. A petty thief, like Brian, can be resourceful." Not to mention lucky, as he was when the archbishop's dim-witted maid sold Emanuela's father's belongings, her inheritance, at a yard sale after his death. "But fencing a religious relic requires connections that I think lie outside of Brian's world."

"Okay, let's assume you are correct. Let's assume the safe deposit box was empty. What next?" They had almost surely blown their cover by flying to America; Kaitlyn no doubt had run straight to the bishop in Dublin. There was no turning back now, no possibility of living in anonymity on the Irish farm. Which, in fact, was fine. But of the many possible paths going forward, which should they take?

"We are close, I can feel it," he said. "And Marcotte agrees."

"We *were* close," she replied. "It looks to me like the black-booted tyrants from the Vatican beat us to that safe deposit box. Now we are not even in the game."

Roberto stood and reached for her hand. "You ask, what next?" He gave her his best bedroom smile. "I will consider this question. But you know I do my best thinking when naked."

She exhaled. Her life's quest—her legacy—was in jeopardy, slipping away. And her would-be husband, her partner, her ally, was thinking about getting laid. She swallowed her anger. She had read once that everything in life was about sex. Except sex itself. That was about power. She exercised her power now. "No, Roberto. Not now. I need you to think with your *other* head this time. If you come up with a plan, a good plan, I promise you there will be plenty of time for us to get naked."

✛

Amanda and Astarte sat in the Masonic library, nerves on edge, killing time until Cam returned. Emanuela and Roberto were nowhere to be found, which was fine with Amanda—she had no interest in making small talk with people with hatred in their hearts, no matter how justified it might be.

Together they thumbed through illustrated tomes displaying richly-drawn scenes from Masonic lore, most published in the 1800s. "These are worth, like, more than our house," Amanda said, one eye on the door. She tried not to show her alarm, but Cam should have been back an hour ago. And Monsignor Marcotte had heard nothing from the exterminator.

Astarte's phone dinged, signaling a text. "It's Dad," she said. "He's on his way, be here in ten."

Amanda closed her eyes in relief. "Good."

"And he says we should pack up."

Amanda hadn't expected that. "Why?"

Astarte shrugged. "He says he'll explain everything when he gets here."

They packed quickly and, with the monsignor, met Cam at the Lodge's front door. He smiled ruefully. "I don't imagine Brian is here."

Marcotte angled his head. "Isn't he with you?"

Cam exhaled. "We need to talk."

Seated again around the table in the library, Cam summarized his morning. "So, beside Brian throwing a temper tantrum and running off in a huff, Vatican operatives abducting me at gunpoint, and the scroll turning out to be modern, things went just as planned."

Amanda covered his hand with hers. She was just relieved he was okay. She said, "Other than that, Mrs. Lincoln, how did you enjoy the play?"

Cam smiled. "I'm impressed. An American history joke."

Monsignor Marcotte rubbed his cheeks with his hands. "You're certain the scroll never left your sight?" he asked humorlessly.

Cam nodded.

"And you trust this professor from Brown?"

"I Googled her in the taxi over here. She's an expert in her field. Her bio even mentions she's a practicing Buddhist. So I don't think she's in bed with Vatican hardliners. And she let me touch the scroll—it was fibrous like paper, not animal skin."

Marcotte's shoulders slumped. "How could the scroll be modern?"

Cam shifted. "I've been thinking about that. Here's what I think happened. The Cistercians arrived in Cumberland in the 1890s. Well, what are monks famous for doing?"

Astarte raised her hand as if the question came from her teacher. "I read about them. They pray. And they copy old documents."

"Right," Cam replied, "especially important religious texts. So this ketubah is probably a copy of an older document. The dates work—the professor said the paper was from around 1900. And the copy would be important documentation if anything ever happened to the original."

"But a copy isn't going to be enough to convince people," the monsignor said. "We're talking about rewriting the history of Christianity. That requires an original document."

"Well," Amanda said, "if this is a copy, where is the original?"

"If the monks were copying, they needed to have the original," Astarte said.

"Not necessarily," Cam said. "This could be a copy of a copy of a copy—"

Amanda cut in. "I don't think so. Think about all the clues, about the effort made to hide and preserve the ketubah here in America. I think the original is here. I can *feel* it."

"Maybe there's another clue," Astarte said. "Maybe we missed something."

Marcotte asked, "Could that be why Brian left? Does he have another clue?"

Cam shook his head. "No. The Brian that left the bank today was on his way to get drunk or kick a cat or something. He was like a three-year-old who just dropped his ice cream."

"And he has no reason to come back here," Amanda said. "He took the ten grand with him. When I was packing up I checked his room and found the duffel bag." She shrugged. "I wanted my grandmother's brooch back."

They sat in silence for a few seconds. "Hold on," Cam said. "Wasn't there something else in the safe deposit box with the scroll? A gold pendant? And also a pocket watch?"

"Yes," Amanda hissed. She stood. "And they're still in that duffel bag."

Amanda leading, they raced down a back staircase to the lodging rooms in the basement. She pulled the duffel bag from underneath Brian's bed, reached in, and retrieved the oversized pendant and pocket watch. She ignored the cubic zirconium ring Cam had purchased from the bank teller.

"Do you think they're clues?" Astarte asked.

"Maybe," Amanda replied. She opened the bronze cover of the watch. The watch face was decorated with a simple Christian cross. The hands had stopped at exactly noon or midnight.

"The hands look like an arrow," Astarte said.

Amanda nodded. "Good point. What are the odds it stopped precisely at twelve o'clock on its own?"

"But pointing at what?" Cam asked.

"Remember the moss-covered cross in the woods behind the monastery?" Astarte asked. "Does that match the cross on the watch?" They both had the shape of a modern cross, resembling a lower-case 't' rather than a plus sign. "Assuming so, the arrow is pointing in the direction of the head of the cross."

"That's where we dug and found the safe deposit box," Cam said. "Due east."

"Perhaps there's something else," Amanda said. She fingered the plum-sized pendant and examined it closely. "I think it's a locket." Finding the latch, she flipped it open. Inside sat a small, almond-sized stone nestled atop a folded piece of yellowing paper. She handed the stone to Astarte and began to unfold the paper.

"That paper looks like the scroll," Cam said. "Same discoloration."

Even unfolded, the paper was no larger than a notecard. Black lines of script, written in a flowing, cursive hand, filled the space. Amanda read aloud:

"Nine brave men did meet their fate,
Their sacrifice monks did commemorate.
They joined Jesus their Lord in heavenly rest,
Yet still guard the scroll of your earthly quest."

"Not exactly Shakespeare," Amanda said, "but it works." She took a breath, the excitement rising inside her. "The nine brave men meeting their fate refers to the Nine Men's Misery memorial. That's where we need to look. They *guard the scroll.*"

"That's it," Cam said. "It has to be." He help up an image on his phone of the trail map of the land behind the Cumberland library. "And look. The Nine Men's Misery memorial is due east, precisely, from the moss-covered cross." He glanced at Astarte. "You were right, the hands on the pocket watch point right to the hiding spot, to the memorial."

Monsignor Marcotte, who had been silent until now, spoke. "So there was one more clue, after the safe deposit box? But why?"

"It's a *cairn*, a pile of stones," Amanda said, her voice raised. "The Nine Men's Misery memorial is a cairn. An ancient sacred site, just like at Newgrange." She moved around the small room excitedly, quickly pulling up and displaying a picture of the rectangular rock pile on her phone. "Here it is, the cairn."

Nine Men's Misery Memorial, Cumberland, RI

Amanda continued. "The Cistercians wouldn't want to leave a religious treasure in some sterile bank vault. The marriage contract of Jesus and Mary Magdalene deserved some kind of sacred shrine, someplace peaceful and out in nature."

Marcotte nodded. "I agree. The Cistercians worshiped the old Irish pagan sites like Newgrange. Cairns were sacred to them."

"And," Cam said, "they added concrete to the stone pile to secure it, to make sure nobody moved the stones or disturbed the scroll."

Astarte held up the small rock Amanda had handed her. "That's probably why the stone was inside the pendant also, to drive the point home that we need to look at a stone pile."

Amanda grinned. "So what are we waiting for? Let's go find that ketubah."

"What about Emanuela and Roberto?" Marcotte asked. "Shouldn't we tell them?"

Amanda's patience had worn thin with the sanctimonious priest. For some reason it was okay to lie to Cam, but Marcotte continued to remain loyal to Emanuela and Roberto? "Not a chance, Monsignor. You're lucky we're even letting you come."

☩

Emanuela crouched in the hallway outside the room Brian was using as a bedroom. Roberto had heard people running down the back stairs and had followed, texting her to join him ASAP. He pointed toward the room. "They're all inside," he whispered. "The ketubah at the bank was only a copy. They think the real ketubah is still on the monastery grounds. All we have to do is follow them, then grab it." He smiled. "You promised that if I came up with a good plan, we could get naked for a long time."

She slapped him playfully on the shoulder. He had done well. Very well. They were back in the game, and Roberto would have his unclothed reward. More importantly, once the ketubah was released to the press, the Church would have no choice but to back off its ridiculous ban on priest marriage. Then she and Roberto could finally live as a normal married couple. And she could even reveal her true parentage, claim her true legacy as the daughter of Archbishop Paul Casimir Marcinkus.

But most of all, she would have the satisfaction of watching the misogynists in the Vatican squirm and writhe as their precious, sacred dogma was exposed as being nothing more than self-serving and hypocritical constraints designed to perpetuate the rule of a corrupt clergy. She smiled. Maybe she'd even return to Rome and take an apartment inside Vatican City, parading around, hand in hand with Roberto, lifting a middle finger to senior Vatican officials as they crossed paths in the park.

✝

Monsignor Marcotte threw his belongings in his overnight bag and hurried down the wide stairs of the Masonic Lodge. He had some important decisions to make, and almost no time to make them. In his younger days he would have prayed for guidance. But there was no time now, and in any event he no longer believed God responded to the pleas of man. The Persians had a proverb he particularly appreciated: *Pray to God, but tie your camels tight.*

In his case, he had tied his camels tight for the past couple of weeks. But now he had no choice but to let some of them wander. Thorne and Amanda, especially—they had picked up the scent of the ketubah again, and the best thing he could do would be to release the reins and let them track it as they saw fit. Brian had become unleashed and, to continue to torture the metaphor, was probably lost in the desert. As for Emanuela and Roberto, he had no choice but to leave them tethered, in reserve for future use, since Amanda had made it clear they were not welcome to join this particular excursion.

This excursion. Marcotte shook his head—that made it sound too leisurely, like a field trip. He needed a better word, something more epic. *Quest?* No, that was too much like something from a fairy tale. Perhaps *mission*? He pictured Tom Cruise jumping from a helicopter, dodging gunfire as he plunged. Thorne had proven himself to be resourceful, but he was not *that* good. Still, *mission* seemed to fit…

Marcotte blinked his train of thought away. *Focus.* He knew what his mind was doing. Thinking about camels and Tom Cruise was a defense mechanism, a way to avoid confronting the real demon that haunted him: Would his fate be to come within inches of recovering the ancient ketubah, to almost hold in his hands a document that would change the history of Christianity, only to have it slip away?

So much was at stake, so many lives potentially affected. He picked up the pace, an old man taking the stairs two at a time. Time was running out. He was so close, after so many years. But close was not enough. History cared not a whit for ancient secrets *almost* revealed.

✝

Emanuela and Roberto slipped out of a side door of the Grand Lodge. She was fairly certain they had not been seen. "You have the car keys, right?" she asked.

"Yes. And my wallet and our passports." He zipped his jacket. "But that's all I had time to grab."

She nodded. "Nothing else is important."

Their rental car was parked half a block away, on the street. A light snow continued to fall. A handsome man, his dark suit and maroon tie visible under his overcoat, sat on a bench near the entrance to the Lodge, feeding a few pigeons at his feet. He glanced up and smiled, blue eyes twinkling. "Good day," he said, his accent German.

Roberto smiled back. "Morning."

Emanuela frowned. Why was a man wearing a business suit on the weekend? And, even assuming he had some business to attend to over the holiday, why then was he sitting outside feeding pigeons in the snow? She took Roberto's arm, pulling him along, and shook the thought away. They needed to get to their car and be ready to follow Thorne and family when they left the Lodge.

✠

Franz Pfyffer let out a long breath and slid his hand though his dress shirt to finger the plain gold cross hanging there. He sank back into the park bench, ignoring the pigeons fluttering at his feet. There was no doubt the woman he had just greeted was Emanuela Orlandi, just as his latest missive from Rome had indicated. The eyes, of course, gave it away. And the computer projections of what the abducted girl would look like as a middle-aged woman matched almost perfectly. But he never gave the kill order, no matter how justified, without reflection and prayer. He closed his eyes, seeking guidance.

First he pushed aside his anger. She had, along with the priest, Roberto, not only played the Vatican, but embarrassed it. Her disappearance—and the Vatican's failure to find her—had become a scandal in Rome at a time when the Church was already weakened. On a personal level, many blamed lax training among the Swiss Guard—commanded by his grandfather—for the abduction. It had taken a full generation to rehabilitate the family name. But none of his personal desire for revenge mattered. What mattered was what God wanted. Here Franz found clarity. It was one thing to oppose the Vatican, to disagree with its policies as Monsignor Marcotte was doing. Or even to find those policies abhorrent, as Thorne and his wife did. But it was another to try to embarrass and damage the Holy See, to actually do it harm, as, according to what his team had learned, Emanuela and her priest lover seemed intent on doing. Those in opposition needed to be dealt with. Those intent on doing harm needed to be eliminated.

Standing, Franz watched as Emanuela and Roberto stepped into a blue sedan half a block away. There was an expression he heard once from a lawyer that applied here: Emanuela Orlandi was, as the daughter of Marcinkus, *the fruit of a poisonous tree*. The archbishop had been a Godless man, whoring and gangstering and profiteering while claiming to be doing God's work. Franz's grandfather had abhorred him, cursed him for the shame he brought upon the Holy See. It was no surprise that the product of Marcinkus' seed had turned rancid as well.

A member of Franz's team sat at a table by the window of a coffee shop across the street. Franz sent a quick text. "Proceed with elimination." He was certain his man would know what to do, would know to make sure no bystanders were walking by when he pushed the detonator. Just as he was certain God would do nothing to interfere with the elimination of fruit from a poisonous tree.

Franz stood and began walking in the other direction, the pigeons following. He had barely cleared the park when the explosion thundered. His body, trained in combat, did not even flinch, even as the pigeons cawed and took flight. Franz crossed himself. *God save their souls.*

Chapter 17

Cam glanced over at Amanda as he drove the Pathfinder north out of Providence through a light snow, this time taking a direct route to Cumberland. He had noticed that she made a point of grabbing the front seat ahead of Monsignor Marcotte, a subtle but telling message to him that, while they were allowing him to join them, he was no longer in charge. The clergyman sat quietly in the back seat behind Cam, staring out the window while Astarte texted friends on her phone. Cam glanced back as his wipers squeaked—he had always thought of the monsignor as dapper and in control. Today he just looked tired and even a bit confused, like he had just awoken from a nap. Not that Cam felt sorry for him. He had taken advantage of their friendship, lying to Cam, foisting Brian on him, even putting his family in danger. And for what? For a priceless scroll that could shake the foundation of modern society? Cam chuckled to himself. Given the stakes, he couldn't really blame the monsignor for telling a few lies and betraying a few friendships...

Amanda interrupted his thoughts. "Assuming we interpreted the poem correctly, the scroll is buried in the cairn. How are we supposed to get it out?"

"Maybe there's a loose rock with a void behind it."

She scowled. "Sounds too obvious. One thing we've learned is there's always a twist with the Templars."

Cam smiled. "Well, good thing we brought Astarte along. She has that devious kind of mind."

"You know, you just can't take a document like this and drop it into the lap of the world," Marcotte said abruptly from the back seat.

"Why not?" Amanda retorted. "First you have it tested and authenticated, then hold a bloody press conference and announce what you've found."

The monsignor shifted in his seat. "Because it's too ... sudden. Like, out of the blue, being told you were adopted. People need time to get used to things like this."

"What you mean," Amanda replied, "is that the Church needs time to somehow spin the message. Or to undermine the find." She narrowed her eyes. "Or even steal it back."

Marcotte shook his head. "You forget, I'm not on their side. But the Church does a lot of good in the world. I don't want to see Catholicism destroyed. I want to see it *reformed*."

Amanda shook her head. "Sorry, Father. That's just not realistic. The Church will always default to obfuscation and denials. It's in their nature. *You* won't see reform until *they* get hit between the eyes with it."

✝

Cam pulled into the snow-covered parking lot of what used to be the Cistercian monastery and was now the Cumberland public library. He circled around back on the access road, Amanda noticing that the four-wheel-drive vehicle easily navigated the few inches of snow. The library itself was closed for the holiday, but the trails through the woods behind it attracted a handful of dog-walkers and joggers out for some New Year's Eve Day exercise. Amanda smiled ruefully. None of them had any idea what was hidden in the woods nearby. Hopefully the area by the Nine Men's Misery memorial, located on a remote trail, would be unpopulated.

Cam grabbed the shovel from the cargo area, along with a flashlight and tarp. Amanda frowned. "You sure that won't draw too much attention to us?"

"Good point." He folded the shovel in half and handed it to Astarte; his backpack was filled with the tarp. He smiled. "Astarte, you can carry this with the dynamite."

"Can't, Dad. My pack is full. I've also got the blowtorch."

Marcotte watched the exchange, slack-jawed. "Are you two serious?"

Amanda touched his arm, feeling bad for insisting he stay in the car. But she still didn't trust him. "Just ignore them."

"You sure you don't want my help?" Marcotte asked.

Amanda shook her head. "Nothing personal, but your help always seems to involve nasty blokes with ugly intentions." Cam had told her about Marcotte's comment that it was okay to let the devil help you cross the bridge in times of danger. "We'll chance our way across this bridge ourselves, thanks."

✙

Driving the same van he had used to transport Thorne the night before, Brian used the tracking device still attached to Thorne's Pathfinder to follow his childhood friend back to the Cumberland monastery. Brian's temper tantrum at the bank had served its intended purpose, making Thorne and the monsignor believe Brian had taken his ball and gone home. But even the three-year-old Brian would not have just walked away from a treasure. And the ten grand from the duffel bag barely covered his expenses.

For the second time in two days Brian threw on an overcoat to cover his green pants, slid his semi-automatic rifle into a deep pocket, grabbed the binoculars, and followed Thorne and family into the woods. They took a different trail this time, heading north from the parking area rather than northwest. He glanced up at a trail marker: 'Nine Men's Misery Trail.' Brian didn't know who the nine men were, but he was well-acquainted with misery and comfortable in its presence.

He loped along, keeping his distance, a half-smile on his face.

✙

The snow-covered trail ran through the winter woods, the trees forming a canopy of white above them. Cam watched Astarte. Unlike yesterday, when she skipped ahead, today she seemed subdued, as if tiring from this adventure. Or perhaps unnerved—in the past twenty-four hours, the dark shadow of looming danger had engulfed them. Cam and Amanda had tried to shield Astarte from it, but she was no idiot.

A quarter-mile in, the Nine Men's Misery monument slowly came into focus on a short spur off the main trail, the grey-white stones, camouflaged by snow, barely visible atop a knoll.

"I almost walked by the bloody thing," Amanda exclaimed, stopping only when Cam turned to point to it out. It seemed to float in and out of view from behind the tree branches as if an apparition.

"Some people say it's haunted," Astarte said, reading from her phone. "They say the ghosts sometimes hide the monument from visitors they feel are unfriendly. Some medical students dug up the bones in the late 1700s because they thought there was a giant buried here."

Amanda shivered. "Well, the ghosts will likely not fancy us digging into the cairn."

Cam smiled. "And yet they didn't hide it from us."

Cam's inclination was immediately to examine the cairn, but Amanda drew his attention to the setting. "This is a beautiful spot. Up on a hill, with a stream running below. And you can hear the birds singing, even in the winter." She closed her eyes and lifter her face to the snow. "I can see why they chose it." She squeezed Cam's arm. "We're in the right spot. I can feel it."

Astarte nodded. "I agree with Mum. This feels right."

They all walked around the industrial freezer-sized cairn, examining it. As they had read, the monks had added concrete to the cobblestones originally marking the gravesite, stabilizing the memorial and preventing any attempts at further disturbance. In front of the cairn the monks had erected a concrete site marker with a faded metal sign mounted on its face. Captioned, "Nine Men's Misery," it read:

> *ON THIS SPOT WHERE*
> *THEY WERE SLAIN BY*
> *THE INDIANS*
> *WERE BURIED THE NINE SOLDIERS*
> *CAPTURED IN PIERCE'S FIGHT*
> *MARCH 26, 1676*

"Wow," Cam said. "I know that's not considered old by European standards, but 1676 is getting back there in American history."

Amanda smiled. "In Britain we teach the 17th century as part of *modern* European history."

Astarte brought them back to the present. "Um, guys, the ancient scroll?" She had circled the cairn, pushing the snow off with her sleeve. "I don't see how we get inside."

Cam dropped to his knees in the snow and felt underneath the cairn, searching for a void or opening. Using the folding shovel, he next probed even deeper. Exhaling, he stood and brushed himself off. "I couldn't find any openings either."

Amanda had also circled the pile, pushing and twisting the stones in hopes one might move or trigger an opening mechanism like in an action movie. "I struck out also."

Cam clapped his hands together to fight off the cold. "We can't have come all this way only to fail now. There must be a way in." He turned to Amanda. "Can you read the poem again?"

She had taken a photo with her phone and read aloud:

"Nine brave men did meet their fate,
Their sacrifice monks did commemorate.
They joined Jesus their Lord in heavenly rest,
Yet still guard the scroll of your earthly quest."

She shrugged. "It tells us where the scroll is hidden, but not how to get in."

"Wait," Astarte said. "There was something else in the locket." She pulled a small stone from her pocket. "This was sitting on top of the poem. Maybe it was meant to do more than just point us to a stone pile."

"You think it's some kind of key?" Cam asked, peering at the almond-sized dark rock. It was smooth-faced, an unlikely candidate for a key. But maybe…

Astarte squinted, studying it. "I wonder," she mused. She moved toward the front of the monument, where the concrete pedestal-shaped pillar stood. She brushed away the snow, turning to make sure Cam and Amanda were watching. Cam understood immediately what she was doing. The magnetic piece of cumberlandite would adhere to the metal sign.

But before Astarte could touch the stone to the sign, Amanda burst her bubble. "I see what you're doing, honey, but it's not going to work. The metal has a green patina. So it's likely copper. Not magnetic." She touched Astarte's arm. "Nice try, though."

Astarte's shoulders slumped briefly, then she seemed to regather herself. She shook her head, as if not accepting the laws of nature. She held the stone up against the sign and released it. Rather than thudding to the ground, it snapped against the metal, drawn to it just as she expected. Just, apparently as the Cistercian monks had planned almost a hundred years ago.

"Wait, what?" Amanda said. She tapped the sign, scratched it with her fingernail. "It's copper. I'm certain."

Cam stepped forward. "I wonder." He removed his utility knife from his back pocket and snapped open the screwdriver. Ignoring the cold, he threw off his right glove and set to work removing the four screws holding the sign in place. They had been set deep, and the decades of weathering had encrusted them, but eventually he wrestled them out. Cam pulled the sign loose and turned it over.

"There," Astarte said triumphantly. A metal plate the size of a playing card had been attached to the back of the thin copper sign. "They put that metal there to make the sign magnetic. I was sure this would work. It's the final clue. Why else would the monks have put the stone in the pendant with the poem?" She pointed to the void revealed by the removal of the sign, a rectangular hole the size of a paperback book. "This is the right spot. It has to be."

Cam set the sign atop the pedestal and took a deep breath. This felt right, felt like the end of the road. They had followed clues, deciphered riddles, parsed poems. Not to mention dodged bullets and outsmarted enemies. Now, here in the serenity of the woods, their journey was ending.

He quickly brought Amanda and Astarte together into an embrace. "Love you both so much," he breathed.

Amanda squeezed his arm. "Love you too, honey. But will love you even more if you find that scroll."

Astarte grinned. "And I suppose I can tolerate you. If you find the scroll, that is."

He rolled his eyes. "Why am I always the sappy one?"

He brushed aside some cobwebs and turned on his cell phone flashlight. The void angled back and then down, widening where it turned downward. But the dogleg shape made it impossible to see the bottom of the niche. "Smart," Cam said. "I can't see the bottom. If they ever needed to replace the sign, the scroll would remain hidden."

Amanda bit her lip. "Assuming the scroll really is in there."

He stood on his tiptoes and leaned in, burying his arm to the shoulder. But still he couldn't reach the bottom. "Damn," he breathed.

Amanda smiled. "Maybe they had longer arms back then."

"Can I see?" Astarte asked. Cam stepped aside as she peered into the void. "I have an idea." She withdrew a makeup compact from her purse and snapped off the mirrored top. Next she popped a piece of chewing gum into her mouth. "I read this once in a Nancy Drew book," she explained. She chewed vigorously for a few seconds, stuck the gum to the back of the mirror, and handed it to Cam. "Stick the mirror on the back wall of the hole, where it angles."

Cam nodded. "Got it."

He did so, then shined his light onto the hole. By moving his head side to side and forward and back, he could see the entire void reflected in the mirror. "There. In the left front corner." He felt a flutter of excitement. "I think I see a canister."

Amanda looked in over his shoulder. "I see it also."

"That must be it." He removed his jacket. "Now that I know exactly where it is, I can reach for it better." Opening the longest blade on his utility knife, he reached deep into the hole again, aiming for the tube. With a flick of his wrist he scraped his target. Stretching even further, the stone cutting into his armpit, he held the knife with the tip of his fingers and flicked at the canister again, this time causing it to roll toward the middle of the void. Another flick brought it even closer. "Okay," he breathed. "I'm getting there. It's in the middle at least." He knelt down, untied his boot and pulled the shoelace through. Making a slipknot, he leaned deep in again, swinging the lace at the tube and finally looping underneath it. Slowly he tightened the knot and then lifted, holding his breath, concentrating on not scraping the canister against the side of the void and dislodging it, his mind oddly reverting back to the old Operation game he played as a child. At the halfway point he planted his feet firmly on the ground and reached his left hand into the hole. Slowly he felt for the tube, cupping his fingers underneath. *Got it.* With a flourish he swung his arm out of the hole and, exhaling, handed his prize to Amanda. "Ancient scroll in a tube, take two," he said.

"Better let me open this one," she said. "You were bad luck last time."

A tinny clank echoed from inside the pedestal, interrupting them. "Speaking of bad luck," Astarte said, "I think that was my mirror falling."

"That's not bad luck for us," Cam said, smiling. "That's bad luck for the Vatican hardliners or Brian or whoever else comes looking for the scroll. All they're going to find at the bottom of that void is your broken mirror."

Amanda had spread her scarf on top of the cairn and laid the canister atop it. She took Cam's knife and pried out the beeswax from the top of the tube. She peered in, then sniffed. With her phone she shone a light in, confirming the contents. "A scroll. And it smells like animal skin. Parchment." She grinned. "I'm not going to open it out here, but I think we hit the jackpot."

✣

Astarte jogged ahead on the snow-covered trail, her half-empty backpack bouncing on her back. She was anxious to get back to the parking lot and, finally, head back to Westford. She checked her phone. Not even three o'clock. If they hurried, she'd still have time to take a quick shower and meet her friends at Papa Gino's for dinner. Then there was a party that Raja knew about. After everything she had been through, her parents just *had* to let her go, even if only for a few hours. Not that they'd let her stay until midnight. She'd need to figure out some way to convince Raja to kiss her before then, and also to remember not to eat any garlic bread at dinner. Maybe some joke about it being midnight in Ireland, where she just was, and people must be kissing over there already...

A gloved hand covered her mouth and jerked her head sideways. Before she even knew what was happening, she had been yanked off the trail and behind a tree. Panic washed over her. She began to kick and fight and try to scream. The arm twisted her neck further, threatening to snap it. "Enough of that. And don't say a word." A man's voice, his acrid breath close to her ear. *Brian.* She sensed his presence even though she could not see him. "Listen carefully. You *will* be coming with me. The only question is whether I kill your parents or not. Your choice." He pressed his full body into hers, the shovel in her backpack digging into her spine. "Come quietly and nobody gets hurt. Or make a scene and I start shooting."

Panic turned to cold fear. This was an evil man. She did not doubt that he would kill if necessary. Her mouth still covered, she mumbled, "Okay," and nodded. Westford and her friends and pizza suddenly seemed far, far away.

"Good. Smart girl. Stay smart and nobody gets hurt. All I want is the scroll."

Swinging her away from the main trail, he led her through thick brush and down a steep slope before ducking behind a thicket of trees. She had to force her legs to move, as if she were wading through deep snow. They watched as Cam and Amanda ambled past, oblivious to the fresh tracks leading into the woods. "Come on," he said, his glove tightening over her mouth as if he could sense her desperate desire to call out. They cut through the woods, in a direction that Astarte could see would lead them back to the parking lot in a more direct path than the winding one Cam and Amanda were taking. In less than a minute they burst through the underbrush and stepped over a guardrail to the parking lot bordering the woods. To their right, a hundred yards away, Cam and Amanda would soon be joining them in the parking lot at the main trail entrance point. Brian pushed her in that direction, toward a lone gray van parking haphazardly across two spaces near some kind of maintenance garage. A few other cars were also parked in the lot, but their occupants apparently were off in the woods, oblivious to the drama unfolding nearby. At the van, Brian stopped and leaned against the side of the vehicle. Drawing her backward into his body, he looped his left arm around her neck and with his right drew a long gun from his overcoat. It looked like the same kind of gun, a semi-automatic rifle, those shooters used when they attacked schools. She fought, unsuccessfully, to take her eyes off it, knowing how lethal the weapon could be. "Now we wait," he growled, his breath again on her face. "Remember, do nothing stupid and nobody gets hurt."

She wanted to believe him, yet knew better. People intending no harm didn't carry attack rifles. But she also knew there was nothing she could do about it. His left arm was like a vice around her neck. And the gun made an escape impossible even if she somehow broke free.

Ten seconds passed, Astarte and her captor frozen in time against the side of his van. First Amanda, then Cam, exited the trail to the parking lot. They froze without taking a second step. "Astarte," Amanda yelped, covering her mouth. Cam merely stared, his mouth open.

"Stay there, Thorne," Brian said calmly. "Don't try to be a hero. You know how I hate heroes."

"What do you want?" he asked, swallowing.

"Simple trade. The scroll for the girl. A treasure for a treasure."

Cam raised his chin. "You expect us to trust you?"

"Really, Cameron?" Brian said, his voice rising. If Astarte hadn't known better, she would have thought his feelings had been hurt. He cleared his throat. "You really think I would kill her just for the fun of it?" His body seemed to sag a bit behind her. She glanced over at the garage building only a car length away. There, by the propane tank, that door was ajar. If she could break away, get through the door. His hand was gloved, but if she bit hard enough…

Amanda cut off Astarte's strategizing. She strode forward, the clay tube held out in front of her like a baton. "Deal, Brian. Here it is. Just don't hurt her."

Brian raised the gun. "Stop right there." He swallowed, close to Astarte's ear. "How do I know that's the real tube?"

Amanda angled the tube so that the open top faced him. "You can see the scroll inside. And if you let me get closer, you can smell the parchment." She shrugged. "Besides, who carries around an extra clay tube?"

Astarte thought about the movies, thought about doing something heroic like telling them to keep the tube, to not worry about her. But the truth was she wanted them to do anything they could to get her away from Brian. She murmured through the glove. "That's it. That's the right one."

"Okay," he said after a few seconds of consideration. "Put it down, roll it toward me, and then back up." Amanda did as instructed, though the tube got caught on some slush halfway. When she had retreated, Brian pushed Astarte forward, his body still against hers, the gun still raised. "Bend over slowly and pick it up," he commanded, removing his left hand from her mouth and using it to grab the straps of her backpack. She did as told, clutching the tube as he yanked her by her pack with him back to the van. "Now. Give it to me."

Behind her ear she could hear him breathing in, sniffing the parchment. He grunted in approval, skooched himself and Astarte over a few feet, and slid open the rear door of the van. Astarte couldn't see behind her, but she felt his body turn and imagined him reaching back to place the clay tube on the back seat. Closing the van door, he pulled Astarte back against him once again. Fumbling with her straps, he breathed into her ear. "You're almost safe. Listen carefully. I'm going to count to three. At three, run away as fast as you can." His voice again seemed to crack. "And tell your dad that, for once in my life, I tried to do the right thing."

✝

Franz Pfyffer sat on a tree branch at the edge of the parking lot, an HK417 battle rifle slung over his shoulder, watching Thorne and his wife trade the clay tube—apparently the real scroll actually did exist, as Franz suspected—for their daughter. *Good.* There was no reason for the little lamb to be hurt.

But the ancient scroll was becoming more than a nuisance. His gut had told him this wasn't over, that Thorne had not given up on finding his treasure. So Franz had freed him, then tracked him. A simple plan to end a mission which had been fraught with a series of unfortunate developments. He peered through his scope. The propane storage tank by the maintenance garage was the first lucky break his team had caught. Or, just as likely, a piece of divine intervention. As the ugly American with the green pants, Heenan, pushed the girl away and turned back to his van, Franz steadied his weapon. At one point Franz feared Heenan had spotted him when the sun broke through the clouds and reflected off his binocular lens. But apparently he was so caught up in the moment that the incident had not registered. *Amateur.* Small details mattered.

The girl ran. Franz waited until she reached the edge of the woods, steadied his breathing as she and her parents raced away from Heenan and his assault rifle. This would soon be over. *All clear,* a voice in his head announced. With a steady hand Franz fired a pair of shots at the propane storage tank. The first 51-millimeter round easily penetrated the metal shell, rupturing it. The second ricocheted off an adjacent steel support beam, creating the intended spark. The highly flammable propane gas erupted immediately, the ball of flame visible to Franz microseconds before the sound of the explosion echoed back to him. The flames roared out to engulf the nearby van, the American's body frozen in place, his face silhouetted in the front seat, one green-panted leg still extended out the front door. Within a few seconds the van's gas tank itself conflagrated, the second explosion punctuating the first.

Like a gymnast, Franz swung himself from his branch to a lower one, then soundlessly dropped to the snow-covered ground. *Job done.* The clay tube might survive a fire, but not an explosion. And, of course, the ancient scroll was no match for either one. Just as people like Thorne and Monsignor Marcotte and Brian Heenan and Emanuela Orlandi were no match for those who did God's work here on earth.

Chapter 18

Cam had set the alarm early, glad he had limited himself to a single glass of wine to celebrate New Year's Eve. He was looking forward to a brisk winter jog before heading to New Hampshire for a family ski day. It was a New Year's Day tradition for them—getting a few runs in on the groomed trails before the rest of the world rolled out of bed. And, after everything that had just happened, he felt they needed normalcy more than anything else. But first he pulled Venus to him, content to let his mind wander for a few minutes, reliving the previous day's adventure as the dog licked his hand.

After circling around to leave the woods from the far side of the parking lot, thereby avoiding being questioned by the Cumberland police, Cam, Amanda and Astarte had returned to Westford in time for Astarte to invite a few friends over for pizza. She was understandably shaken by the day's events, and Cam and Amanda wanted to keep her close by, so hosting seemed like a good compromise. After dinner, Astarte and her friends had taken advantage of the temperate weather and headed out to the lake for ice skating and a bonfire. Raja and a few others had joined them, Astarte intent on trying to teach him to skate, though Amanda commented that it seemed he clung to her for support more than perhaps was necessary. Cam was happy for her, proud of the mature young woman she had grown into. And admiring of her resiliency. From hostage to pizza party, barely missing a beat. He had read once that some people survived calamity, while others, like Astarte, seemed to grow from it, as if strengthened by the heat of its fire.

Not that the weekend could be called a success. They had been so close to saving the ancient scroll, so close to forcing the Western world to rethink the role of women in society. And then, in the flash of a fire ball, it was gone. As was Brian. Cam had not mourned the loss of the man Brian had become, but he did grieve for his boyhood friend, for the youth whose innocence had been jerked away far too young. Astarte had repeated Brian's final words, about telling Cam that he had finally tried to do the right thing. It hadn't really made sense to Cam. Brian had stolen a priceless artifact from his childhood best friend while taking that friend's daughter hostage at gunpoint. *The right thing?* Perhaps in Brian's dark world the act of not killing an innocent girl qualified as a noble, selfless act.

Gone, too, were Emanuela and Roberto, apparently at the hands of the Vatican extremists. Marcotte had called with the news last night. "I don't think you're in any danger," the priest had said. "Major Pfyffer had a clear shot at you in the parking lot if he wanted to take it. But now that the ketubah has been destroyed, the danger is over in their mind." Cam felt a pang of sadness for Emanuela and Roberto; she would never have her revenge, and, more importantly, they would never have the chance to find happiness together. What a waste.

Cam swung his legs out of bed, washed up, and ate an apple and frozen waffle. After stretching and kissing a sleeping Amanda goodbye, he bundled up and put Venus on a leash. A cold wind greeted him in the gray morning light, taking his breath away but also clearing his head. Astarte had said something else about Brian, that he had told her to run away as quickly as she could. Why? Did he know what was about to happen and wanted her far from the explosion? That made no sense—how could he have known? Monsignor Marcotte had filled in some of the blanks: Major Pfyffer and his team had captured Marcotte from Cam's car in the parking lot and forced him into revealing that Cam and Amanda were in the process of retrieving the ancient scroll. Pfyffer had, in turn, taken the opportunity to eliminate both Brian and the scroll with a pair of shots, thereby successfully completing his mission.

Cam shook his head. None of that explained how Brian may have foreseen the propane explosion or why he told Astarte to run. Perhaps Marcotte was holding information back, as he was wont to do. But something still didn't add up. Cam feared that at this point it never would.

✠

Cam showered quickly before sending Venus in to wake Astarte. "Lick her face until she gets out of bed, girl." Giggles cascaded down the stairs from her room a few seconds later.

"I'm making sandwiches," Cam announced. There was no reason to spend fifty bucks on lunch in addition to the pricey lift tickets. They hadn't had time to go to the supermarket since returning, so he pulled out jars of peanut butter and jelly and found frozen wheat bread in the freezer, which he put in the toaster. Astarte had left her backpack hanging on a peg by the front door yesterday afternoon, so Cam grabbed it, pulled the folding shovel out, and brought the pack into the kitchen. While the bread toasted, he knelt in front of the refrigerator and slid a couple of cans of seltzer water into the main pocket, the first can tinging against something at the bottom of the pack. Still crouched, Cam reached around the can, his hand closing on a cold cylinder of some kind.

He froze. *No. Way.*

A few seconds passed, Cam's arm still in the backpack as if tethered there. It was as if he couldn't withdraw it until his brain had made sense of it all. He blinked as Amanda wandered into the kitchen, her hair wet from the shower. "Um," he gulped, "so I don't think we're going skiing."

✛

Amanda stared at the ancient scroll, unfolded on her kitchen table like the Sunday newspaper. She covered her mouth, afraid even to breathe on it. "Bloody amazing. It's the real deal, Cam."

"Well," he smiled from across the table, "I think we'll need to get it tested."

"I know. But it's parchment, and it matches the later copy the monks made. Or the monks' copy matches this, I should say. If it's not the actual ketubah, it's an ancient production."

Cam nodded. "And why would anyone in ancient times fabricate a marriage contract between Jesus and Mary Magdalene?"

"Only reason I can think of is they had a death wish." She sighed. "Something like this could get you burned at the stake pretty quick."

Astarte stood nearby, sipping her coffee, not wanting to get too close with the liquid. "It's the real one. I can feel it."

"If so," Amanda said, "it's bloody well-traveled." She summarized. "From what we know, ancient Israelites brought it to the Catskills after the Roman destruction of Jerusalem, then the Templars retrieved it in 1178 and brought it back to Seborga, near Genoa, only to have Columbus turn around and return it to Nova Scotia in 1477. There the Cistercians safeguarded it and eventually brought it to Cumberland."

"And now us," Astarte said, grinning.

The room silent for a few seconds until Cam spoke. "I still can't believe Brian put it there. In the backpack. He really did do the right thing after all."

They had replayed the scene in their minds, all of them remembering a slight delay with Brian fumbling with Astarte's backpack after seemingly placing the clay tube in the back of the van. They agreed he must have performed a slight of hand, sliding the tube up his sleeve and then dropping it into her pack.

"But I didn't feel anything," Astarte said.

"I'm guessing you were pretty scared," Cam replied. "And the pack was loose. Not surprising you didn't notice."

"The question, of course, is why?" Amanda said.

"I think he must have known what was going to happen. That's why he told Astarte to run. Maybe he saw the sniper in the tree. Maybe he even parked next to the propane tank on purpose."

Amanda nodded. "Could be. That parking lot was empty, and there really was no reason to be over near the garage building."

"That's *how*. But we still don't know *why*." Cam shook his head. "Marcotte kept insisting he was changed, reformed. But to let himself be blown up?" He held up his hands. "I don't know."

"It does seem a bit out of character."

"A bit?"

"Well, maybe more than a bit." Amanda smiled. "How about *totally?*"

"Marcotte kept telling me he had changed," Cam repeated.

"So are we going to tell the monsignor?" Astarte asked.

"I think we have to," Cam replied.

"Agreed," Amanda said. "But the scroll's ours. We found it. We get to choose the narrative."

Cam pulled his phone from his pocket. Smiling, he angled his head. "It's barely seven o'clock. Too early to call?"

Amanda shook her head. "He's a priest. If he's hungover, it's his own fault." She grinned, holding his eyes. Cupping her hand aside her mouth as if telling a secret, she pointed at the scroll on the table between them and stage-whispered, "Plus, you know, it's the bloody *Jesus marriage contract.*"

✟

Monsignor Marcotte was at their front door within a half hour, dapper as usual in a blue blazer and pressed slacks. Cam greeted him. All they had told the priest was that they had made an urgent discovery they wanted to share with him. In the meantime, they had photographed the scroll.

Wordlessly, Cam began to usher the prelate toward the kitchen.

"Wait," Marcotte said. "Before you show me your surprise, I have something for you." From beneath his blazer he pulled the swagger sword. The wooden handle had been burnt off in the fire, and the metal darkened, but the carvings were still visible on the blade. He handed it to Cam. "It was in its case, partially protected. Pretty much the only thing to survive the fire. When I drove down with Brian's aunt to retrieve his effects, the police gave it to me. I'd like you to have it." He paused. "I think *Brian* would have liked you to have it."

Cam smiled sadly, his eyes misting as he studied the sword. It would make quite a keepsake. Much more so than Marcotte currently realized. "Thank you," he said simply.

"Now," the priest said, continuing toward the kitchen. "What did you drag me out of bed to see?"

Cam gestured at the scroll. "It was in Astarte's backpack. Somehow Brian slipped it in there before the explosion."

Marcotte staggered, steadying himself against the kitchen counter. "My God," he whispered. "I thought it was gone forever." He shuffled closer, his hands crossed on his chest. "Is it the real thing?"

"I think so," Amanda said. "In fact, based on everything we know, I'm almost certain."

The monsignor reached out with a shaky hand. "May I touch it?"

"Not the written areas," Amanda replied. "But the corner should be okay. It's smooth, like glove leather. Like old parchment."

He stared, reverently, for a few seconds. Then he turned suddenly and engulfed Cam in a hug. "Thank you, my friend. Thank you for trusting me."

Cam smiled at Amanda over the priest's shoulder. "You're welcome. But I can't say I *always* trusted you."

Stepping back, Marcotte nodded. "Yes, but the old saying is true. *To believe with certainty, we must begin with doubting.*" Smiling, he continued. "And now, I think it is safe to say, you believe me when I say that Brian is reformed?" He frowned. "Or, *was* reformed?"

"How could I doubt it? He did an incredibly selfless thing. But I'm still not certain why."

"May we sit?" the priest asked. "Apparently the past few days have taken a toll on this old body."

Cam and Astarte and Marcotte moved to the living room while Amanda stood at the kitchen table and carefully slid the scroll into an oversized Ziploc bag and sealed it closed.

The priest answered Cam's question. "It took Brian a long time, but eventually he came to grips with his experience as a youth. With being abused." Marcotte fixed his eyes on Astarte. "With being *sexually abused*. When it comes to abuse, it is important to not hide behind euphemisms." He paused. "Slowly Brian's anger turned to acceptance, and his acceptance to resolve. He wanted to redress the wrong. Unlike Emanuela, he did not want revenge, did not want to kill the Church. He wanted change. In this, he and I saw eye-to-eye. The Church is sick, but it is curable." He motioned toward the ketubah in the next room. "And the marriage scroll was the perfect medicine."

"You know," Amanda said as she reentered the room, "Emanuela was wrong. When back at the Masonic Lodge she said that revenge was neither positive nor negative. It's totally negative, totally destructive."

Marcotte lifted his chin. "Yes. And Brian came to understand that. Again, he wanted reform, not revenge."

"But Brian was such a … lout," Amanda said, throwing up her hands as. "I'm having trouble reconciling the man you're describing with the man we knew. All he ever talked about was getting rich from the treasure."

Marcotte nodded. "That was part of our plan, a role we needed him to play. To win Emanuela's trust, we needed someone she felt she could understand and control. And no man is more understandable, more controllable, than a greedy one. Simply feed him money, and he will do your bidding." He turned to Cam. "And, as I told you, we feared you would not agree to let him back into your life. But I *needed* him. Needed his sword. So we made up the cancer lie." He sat back. "Brian was by no means perfect. In fact, *lout* is a fair description of him. But some of what you saw the past week was an act."

Cam leaned forward. "So that was the plan all along? For Brian to let himself get killed?"

"Not at all." The priest held a long blink. "With this sacrifice, Brian surprises even me. He must have been faced with a terrible choice: Allow the scroll to be destroyed, or himself perish. And think about what he accomplished. Not only did he save the scroll, but he freed us from the Vatican hardliners. They believe the scroll was incinerated; in their mind, they watched it burn. Brian must have played out the possibilities in his mind and understood we were out-gunned, realized that his grand sacrifice was the only way for us to win, the only way for us to walk away with the ketubah." Marcotte bowed his head. "I am humbled at what he has done."

Cam chewed his lip, his eyes drifting out over the frozen lake. A memory washed over him: He and Brian and friends playing pond hockey on a cold, sunny day. Brian scored the game-winning goal and celebrated by diving headfirst into the snowbank ringing the rink. Extracting himself, he brushed the snow off his face and put his arm around Cam's shoulder. "Who has more fun than us, huh buddy?" he asked. "I'll tell you who: Nobody!"

Cam blinked away a tear. His friend had been in pain for a long time. And Cam had not been there for him. But at least, in the end, with the help of Monsignor Marcotte, he had found some peace. For Cam, that decided it. The Catholic Church may be an imperfect institution. But as long as men like Monsignor Marcotte were in positions of authority, it was worth saving.

Cam saw the path ahead, knowing intuitively that Amanda would see it the same way. They would make public the ancient ketubah, share it with the world. The marriage contract was drawn as a commemoration of love, of joy, of honor. It should be used accordingly, as a tool to build and enhance and improve. Not a weapon of destruction. Amanda was correct: Nothing positive came from revenge. Monsignor Marcotte would have his reforms. But Emanuela, even in death, would not have her vengeance.

The End

Dear Reader

I love to get reader feedback, both to help me continue to write in a way and about things that you (hopefully) enjoy and also to improve on the things you don't. Please feel free to reach out to me at dsbrody@comcast.net, and/or also to leave a review at Amazon or Goodreads.

If you enjoyed *The Swagger Sword*, you may want to read the other books featuring Cameron and Amanda in my **"Templars in America"** series, all of which have been Kindle Top 10 Bestsellers in their categories:

Cabal of the Westford Knight
Templars at the Newport Tower (2009)
https://www.amazon.com/dp/B00GWTZYLS

Set in Boston and Newport, RI, inspired by artifacts evidencing that Scottish explorers and Templar Knights traveled to New England in 1398.

Thief on the Cross
Templar Secrets in America (2011)
https://www.amazon.com/dp/B006OQIXCG

Set in the Catskill Mountains of New York, sparked by an ancient Templar codex calling into question fundamental teachings of the Catholic Church.

Powdered Gold
Templars and the American Ark of the Covenant (2013)
https://www.amazon.com/dp/B00GWTYJ5K

Set in Arizona, exploring the secrets and mysteries of both the Ark of the Covenant and a manna-like powdered substance.

The Oath of Nimrod
Giants, MK-Ultra and the Smithsonian Coverup (2014)
https://www.amazon.com/dp/B00NW13QTG

Set in Massachusetts and Washington, DC, triggered by the mystery of hundreds of giant human skeletons found buried across North America.

The Isaac Question
Templars and the Secret of the Old Testament (2015)
https://www.amazon.com/dp/B016E3X2QK

Set in Massachusetts and Scotland, focusing on ancient stone chambers, the mysterious Druids and a stunning reinterpretation of the Biblical Isaac story.

Echoes of Atlantis
Crones, Templars and the Lost Continent (2016)
https://www.amazon.com/dp/B01MXJ0BNX

Set in New England, focusing on artifacts and other evidence indicating that the lost colony of Atlantis, featuring an advanced civilization, did exist 12,000 years ago.

The Cult of Venus
Templars and the Ancient Goddess (2017)
https://www.amazon.com/dp/B0767Q4N1S

Set in New England, triggered by the discovery of a medieval journal revealing that the Knights Templar came to America before Columbus because they were secretly worshiping the ancient Goddess.

Available at Amazon and as Kindle eBooks

Author's Note

I have always been fascinated by Christopher Columbus. He was too smart and too savvy and too sophisticated to believe he had actually made landfall in Asia. His writings and logs indicate he possessed ancient maps and charts, and he was an astute student of ancient voyages, both real and legendary. So what were his real motivations? And what was up with the Templar crosses on his sails? Could these crosses, I wondered, be a clue as to where he obtained the ancient maps and charts?

Likewise, I have long felt that the Vatican Banking Scandal of the late 1970s and early 1980s was one of the most compelling and elaborate power plays of my lifetime. Think about it: Senior Vatican officials allied themselves with the Mafia and a group of fascists, under the umbrella of a rogue Freemasonic lodge, in an effort to bring down the Italian government. If I came up with this as a plot for one of my novels, many readers would roll their eyes in disbelief. Yet that is precisely what happened. And it may have been much worse, with senior Vatican officials rumored to be involved with crimes ranging from murder to the kidnapping of children to even the assassination of the pope. That the Vatican lost hundreds of millions of dollars in the scandal was, because of the magnitude of the other crimes, only a footnote to the story.

A mysterious map of Narragansett Bay, written in French and believed to date to the 1600s, provided an opportunity for me to link Columbus to the Vatican Banking Scandal. This story, of course, is the result of that effort. The map is part of the same cache of documents relied on by researcher Zena Halpern in writing her 2017 book, *The Templar Mission to Oak Island and Beyond*. I have taken the liberty of redrawing the map to remove some of the extraneous markings and make it easier for readers to examine, without materially changing any details or features. For readers and/or researchers interested in studying the un-redrawn version, it is reproduced below (I have been unable to determine what the dots marked "un," "deux" and "trois" in the Newport area, and the horizontal lines labeled "vingt" and "trente," are intended to represent):

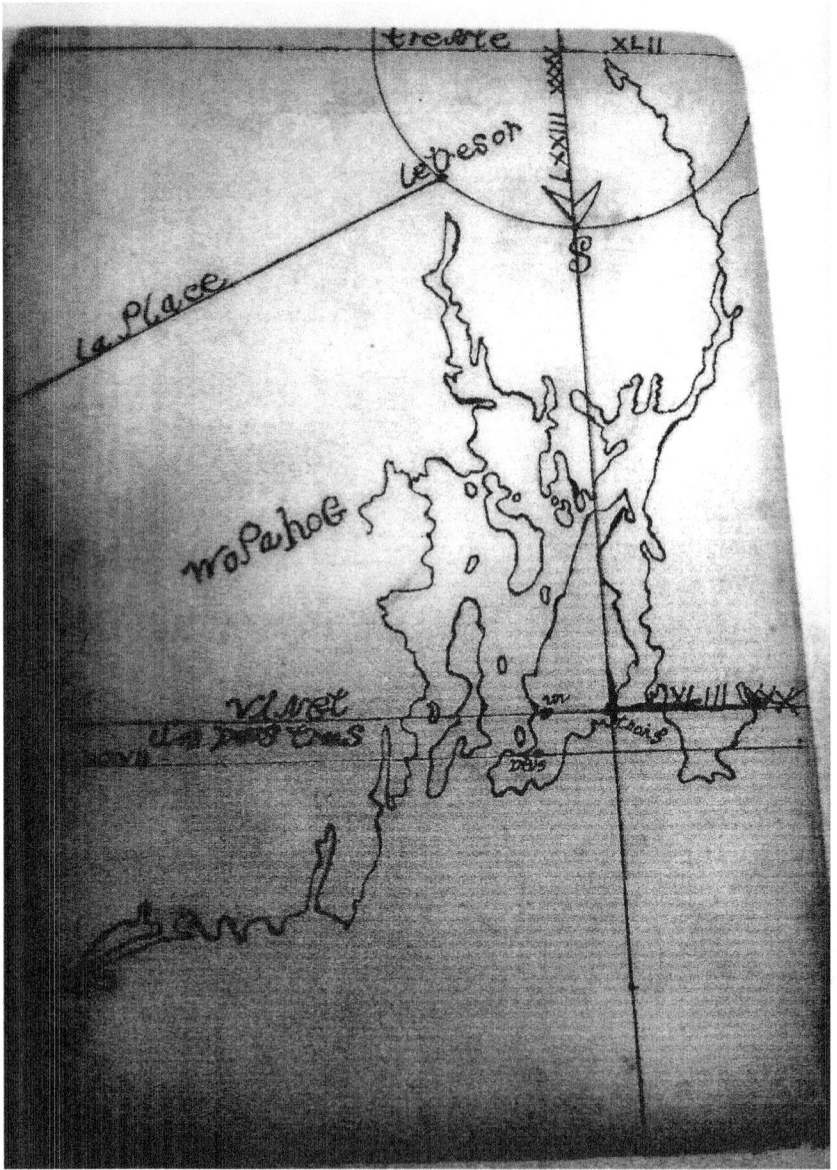

Is the map authentic? It appears to be, though I cannot say for certain, just as I cannot say the 1178 journal itself is. Look for upcoming books by researchers Scott Wolter and Donald Ruh, which should shed more light on this purported 1178 Templar journey to the Catskills.

As is the case with all the books in this series, if an artifact, site or object of art is pictured, it is real (except as specifically noted here). And if I claim it is of a certain age or of a certain provenance or features certain characteristics, that information is correct. Likewise, the historical and literary references are accurate. How I use these objects and references to weave a story is, of course, where the fiction takes root. For inquisitive readers, perhaps curious about some of the specific historical assertions made and evidence presented in this novel, more information is available here (in order of appearance in the story):

* The swagger sword pictured in the book is real. The markings do, indeed, mirror markings on a map leading to buried artifacts on Hunter Mountain. The swagger sword, and others like it, were (as stated) given to leaders of the P2 Masonic Lodge, including Archbishop Marcinkus. The markings on the back side of the sword blade, however, are fictional.

* The Newport Tower winter solstice alignment is real, as shown in the images. A large and eclectic group gathers every year on the winter solstice at 8:30 AM to view the phenomenon.

* As alluded to above, the Zena Halpern book, *The Templar Mission to Oak Island and Beyond* (2017), is a real book. It describes the 1178 Templar journey to the Catskills in detail. According to this book, and as stated in this story, one of the items retrieved by the Templars in the Catskills and brought back to Seborga, Italy was "an agreement of union between one Hasmonian princess, Myriam of Migdal, and Yeshua ben Yoseph of the royal House of David, at Cana," which agreement bore the seal of King Herod. See page 221. Ms. Halpern had planned to write a follow-up book, which would have analyzed the Narragansett Bay map, but unfortunately she passed away in May of 2018 before completing the work.

* For support for the assertion that the Guinevere character is a member of the Gunn clan, see Kerry Ross Boren and Lisa Lee Boren, *Following the Ark of the Covenant: The Treasure of God* (Cedar Fort 2000), at page 60.

* The Ruthie Sanders character is fictional.

* The Upton Chamber, located in Upton, MA, is an actual stone chamber which features a corbelled roof. Luminescence testing on soil behind the chamber entrance wall indicates the cave was built prior to the early 1600s, conclusively establishing that it is not a Colonial structure. The chamber is open to the public; more information, and location, can be found here: https://www.uptonma.gov/historical-commission/pages/heritage-park

* Newgrange and other surrounding megalithic sites were, as claimed, owned by the Cistercians during medieval times as part of their Mellifont Abbey holdings. https://en.wikipedia.org/wiki/Newgrange . Many historians believe the Newport Tower was modeled after the Mellifont Abbey lavabo. See Steven Sora, *The Lost Colony of the Templars* (Destiny Books 2004) at page 89. See also Carl Christian Rafn, *Supplement to the Antiquitates Amercanae* (1841), reprinted here: http://www.jasoncolavito.com/the-newport-tower.html . See also https://atlantisrisingmagazine.com/article/the-newport-tower-mystery .

* The Archbishop Paul Marcinkus character is a real historical figure. The following sources support the assertions made in this story:

— that he was a possible accomplice in the murder of Pope John Paul I: David A. Yallop, *In God's Name* (Bantam Books 1984).

— that he was closely associated with key members of the rogue Masonic Lodge, P2, and members of organized crime in Italy: ibid.

— that he was the head of the Vatican Bank and ensnarled in the Vatican Banking Scandal: ibid.

— that he may have been involved in the murder of banker Roberto Calvi (found hanging from London's Blackfriars Bridge), a leading figure in the Vatican Banking Scandal: ibid.

— that he may have been involved in the 1983 kidnapping of Emanuela Orlandi generally, and specifically that he may have ordered gangster Enrico de Pedis to commit the crime: https://www.nytimes.com/2008/06/25/world/europe/25italy.html.

— that accounting documents show that the Vatican paid $300,000 for the living expenses of the kidnapped girl, Emanuela Orlandi: https://www.nytimes.com/2017/09/19/world/europe/emanuela-orlandi-vatican-vatileaks.html .

— that his obituary made reference to a mistress and child: https://www.excatholicsforchrist.com/articles.php?PageURL=Marcinkus.htm . See also Philip Willan, *The Vatican at War* (iUniverse 2013) at page 168.

— that in his later years he purchased the cache of documents and maps describing the 1178 Templar expedition to the Catskills, and at one point owned one of the P2 swagger swords: *The Templar Mission to Oak Island and Beyond*, at pages 269-272.

* As of the date of publication of this book, Emanuela Orlandi remains missing, some 35 years after her kidnapping. The assertion that Archbishop Marcinkus is her father is purely fiction.

* The summary of Plutarch's writings recounting the ancient Carthaginian journey to a land that some historians interpret as being New England is accurate, as is Barry Fell's analysis of same. See Barry Fell, *Saga America* (Times Books 1980), at page 64 and following.

* The description of Galway's St. Nicholas Church and its architectural and ornamental features is accurate. The church does incorporate parts of an older, medieval Templar church, there is a skull and crossbones carved above an older church entrance, and there is a Crusader's tomb and so-called Apprentice Pillar (shaped like a

Templar cross), all as described in the story. See generally, Jim Higgins and Susanne Heringklee, *Monuments of St. Nicholas' Collegiate Church, Galway* (Rock Crow's Press). I also relied on excerpts from an as-yet unpublished guide book authored by Mr. Conor Riordan of Galway, entitled *Galway Legend, Mystery and Dark History.* Mr. Riordan offers tours of Galway, including St. Nicholas' Church. See this web site: https://www.galwayprivatetours.com .

* Christopher Columbus was, indeed, in Galway in 1477. As I have described, he wrote about "people from Cathay" washing ashore. He prayed at St. Nicholas' Church. And he wrote about a voyage in which he sailed "one hundred leagues beyond Thule." For a thorough analysis of this journey "beyond Thule," see David Sarfaty, *Columbus Rediscovered* (Dorrance Publishing 2010), at pages 142-145. For the assertion that he made this journey in order to view a solar eclipse from the southern coast of Nova Scotia, thereby acquiring vital data regarding longitudinal measurements, see Anne Molander, *The Horizons of Christopher Columbus* (Lulu Press 2012), at page 11. A stone monument stands in Galway commemorating Columbus discovering "sure signs of land beyond the Atlantic" in 1477. My assertion that he met with Templar representatives while in Galway is speculative.

* Bernard of Clairvaux (later Saint Bernard) was indeed the spiritual leader of the Templars, having written their original charter. A body of artwork depicting "The Lactation of Saint Bernard" can readily be found on the internet. Many of these works appear to depict Mary Magdalene rather than the Virgin Mary.

* For more information on the Hooked X rune and its significance and meaning, see Scott F. Wolter, *The Hooked X* (North Star Press 2009).

*An outcrop along the shoreline in Newport, RI with the carving, "In Hoc Signo Vinces," does indeed exist, as pictured. This slogan is translated as, "Under This Banner We Are Victorious," and was a Christian and later Templar battle cry. Some historians believe it was carved by the builders of the nearby Newport Tower. Its location is not publicized due to fear of vandalism.

* For information on the Columbus familial relationship with the Sinclair clan, see question 2, here: http://www.clansinclairsc.org/600thcelebrat.htm .

* For information on the coin from Genoa found near Oak Island, see here: http://www.adventuresofnicky.com/blog/361_the-knights-templar-and-oak-island.html?refresh .

* Astarte's analysis of the names of Columbus' three ships is not fictional. He did indeed rename them all before his journey. "La Pinta" was a term used to describe a prostitute in medieval times, and the *Santa Clara* was the original name of *La Nina*. A discussion can be found here: http://worldmythtory.blogspot.com/2012/10/columbus.html

* Cumberlandite is the state stone of Rhode Island, is magnetic, and can only be found in that state. It is known as the Stone of Virgo: http://www.francesjane.com/cumberlandite.html

* The information about the Cistercians first building a monastery in Tracadie, Nova Scotia (near Guysborough Harbor), later relocating to Cumberland, RI, and eventually settling in western Massachusetts after a major fire in Cumberland, is accurate. See: https://www.spencerabbey.org/our-history/the-foundation-of-petit-clairvaux-1825-1857/

* The Nine Men's Misery monument, as pictured, is located off a trail on preservation land behind the original Cumberland monastery, which today houses the Cumberland Public Library. The moss-covered stone cross and other stone "trail markers" shown in the book are real. To the best of my knowledge, however, there is no treasure of any kind buried on these lands or within the monument.

* The translation of the ketubah used in this book is based on the ancient form of actual Jewish marriage contracts (though I did shorten the text a bit by removing extraneous references).

* The Franz Pfyffer von Altishofen character is fictional, though 11 members of the Pfyffer family have served as captains of the Pontifical Swiss Guard: https://en.wikipedia.org/wiki/Pfyffer

The question remains: Did Jesus and Mary Magdalene marry and have children? I don't know. In many ways, it doesn't matter. What matters is that, over the centuries, powerful and influential groups of people have believed the legendary union to be a reality. These beliefs, in turn, have motivated their behavior. And it is, of course, behavior that changes history. So, real or not, the marriage has become an integral part of our history.

This kind of stuff keeps me up at night. Hopefully it has brought some enjoyment and intellectual stimulation to you as well. Thanks for reading.

David S. Brody, August, 2018
Westford, Massachusetts

Photo Credits

Images used in this book are the property of the author, in the public domain, and/or provided courtesy of the following individuals (images listed in order of appearance in the story):

* Swagger Sword Blade, courtesy Zena Halpern

* Newport Tower Winter Solstice Starburst, courtesy Richard Lynch

* Mellifont Abbey Lavabo, credit Tony Mulraney

* Newgrange Burial Mound, credit "Tjp finn" and Wikipedia

* The Hooked X Rune, courtesy Scott F. Wolter

Acknowledgements

Readers may not realize that the finished version of a novel is often the fifth or sixth draft of the story, each draft becoming iteratively improved (hopefully) over the prior version. Those tasked with reading these early versions, armed only with red pens and caffeine, perform an invaluable task. I offer heartfelt thanks to Kimberly Scott, Benjamin Brody, Jeff Brody, Cat Skinner, Tracy Lee Carroll and Patrick Shekleton.

Fellow researchers who assisted and guided me in my research include Michael and Mary Yannetti, Patrick Shekleton, Zena Halpern, Richard Lynch and Alessandra Nadudvari. The inclusion of their names in this paragraph list does not necessarily indicate these experts agree with my research conclusions, but it does mean they were invaluable to me in my efforts to write this book.

Lastly, to my wife, Kim: This is my eleventh novel, and I still remember nervously handing over to you the first draft of my first book. You shepherded that novel to a successful completion, and you have skillfully done so almost a dozen times since. As I have commented before, it is no easy thing to criticize a spouse's creative work. Thanks for knowing when to crack the whip and when instead to crack open the rum.

Printed in Great Britain
by Amazon